3

Come to the Lighthouse

Part of The Golden Age Chronicles

To my mother,

My #1 supporter

Chapter One

There have been stories circulating the coast of New England for decades - centuries even. Stories of creatures from the sea meddling with passing sailors. Myths of treasure and sinking ships that never made the papers. These were the stories that I grew up on. As a little girl, I would stay up late reading the legends found in antique books at the thrift store, researching the mysteries of the giant squid and other creatures never found alive, wishing to meet those few souls who belonged to a different time.

It was no surprise that at twenty years old, I decided to move to New England. I didn't feel like I was doing anything worthwhile in the Midwest. I had tried for years to find contentment but concluded that I wasn't going to find it by living in my parents' home and following their dreams.

That's when the panic started to set in my mind at the thought of what I was doing. Not even a day had passed since I arrived in Boston, coming from a town that was now several states away and no one had heard of. I was to live there off the coast of Massachusetts, hours away from home, as the city's lighthouse keeper. Everyone knows the life of a lighthouse keeper is both deadly and lonely (and pays very little), but I was willing to put up with those kinds of things.

I had spent more than a year researching the lives of lighthouse keepers. Their strenuous job meant that the statistics of suicide and insanity skyrocketed. Of course, there were many hardships that the keepers who came before me had to deal with that I never would. Many parts of the lighthouse were automated, and it was easier to get supplies nowadays. I would have my own boat to go into town, which meant starvation wasn't going to be a worry unless it was of my own doing. There really wouldn't be a whole lot required of me until storms headed their way into the harbor, threatening to take over ships. I would have to sound the fog signal, keep the light flashing every 10 seconds, and make sure the fresnel lens stayed intact.

I had little training, if any, but the job listing had been up for months with no takers. How unequipped I was; the isolation wouldn't bother me as much as the thought of failing. I had wanted something like this for so long. I didn't want to set myself up for heartache. And that's what it would be. After all, it had been drilled into me my whole life that my only purpose was to get married and raise a family. As much as I wanted to please my parents, I wasn't cut out for domestic life. Then again, how was I supposed to help aid ships if I couldn't even hold a baby properly without feeling out of place? How ironic it would be if I ended up having more instinct seafaring than with babies.

It's not that I minded the thought of having someone at my side. But to find someone that didn't make me feel like a trapped bird? Well, that was a different story. I knew what many men were like. They wanted a trophy wife, someone to do their laundry and warm their bed at night. I wanted an equal. I didn't want someone to complete me. I felt perfectly whole by myself.

As it were, leaving my family was more difficult than I could've imagined. We were a tight-knit bunch and did practically everything together, but I left them for an adventure while they stayed in a place that was only known for its cornfields.

It's funny how they never tell you in the books how hard it is to leave those you love. Not really. It makes me wonder what kind of people wrote all those stories as if one love outweighs another. Maybe that's how it looked, that I loved the sea more than anything else in this world. That I would give myself to her. But I would. That's the scary thing. What kind of person did that make me?

I was roused out of my thoughts as I headed to the ferry that would take me to Little Brewster Island, where the lighthouse was situated. The current light keeper was scheduled to meet me there and walk me through everything.

The hired movers began driving the truck that contained all of my things onto the ferry (though putting vehicles on ships always seemed like a strange practice to me). The keeper, Thomas, had hollowed cheeks and gray hair down to about his chin, with a wiry mustache and stormy eyes. He was

11

quiet and weary - nothing outstanding about him or out of the ordinary.

He looked at me, or studied more like, to see who would be taking up his work, his mantle. He had questioning eyes, but he seemed to keep his thoughts close to his chest....

"Ms. Fellows?"

I nodded, extending my hand. "Yes sir. And you're Thomas?"

He took my hand, shaking it. "Aye. You're quite young."

"I'm very capable, I assure you." He remained silent, walking forward.

After we disposed of the formalities, I followed him onto his boat, christened Mermaid's Lagoon. He'd be passing it on to me. I wondered if he thought me worthy.

Thomas would be training me for one week. What a short amount of time to learn such a daunting job, one that would consume my life.

I watched in awe as we came up to Little Brewster Island's shore. Thomas had told me that the lighthouse on one of the neighboring islands fell out of commission due to a recent storm, causing the foundation to crumble.

"If ya were to see tha thing, it looks like somethin' rammed right into it."

That was peculiar. I made a mental note to search the news about it and see if I could pull up pictures. I'm not sure why I hadn't seen it pop up before.

Thomas gave me a little tour of the lighthouse and the small keeper's quarters next to it. I was thrilled when I saw it, feeling quite pleased with how my new home looked. The house had a red base and white painted bricks that gave it a cottage-like feel. The lighthouse was beautiful in its own right, made up of white and black bricks. Inside the house, I noticed that the kitchen was quite small, which suited me fine, as I wasn't the best cook.

In the dining area, there was a little wooden table set with chairs that reminded me of the ones Van Gogh painted in his bedroom. Yellow wildflowers stood in a glass bottle on top of the windowsill, probably picked along the shoreline outside. Beside the kitchen was a cozy living room with an old chestnut velvet sofa, along with bookshelves built into the wall. I felt giddy and wondered what books Thomas had filled these shelves with. I followed the keeper upstairs to see the bedroom, and I was glad I had brought all of my sheets and pillows.

It was dusty and outdated on the second floor, and I could tell it wasn't very insulated. No matter. I had brought plenty of chunky knit sweaters and socks with me. But I knew with summer approaching, I would have a rough time. I didn't take to the heat well and would probably live in linen for many months.

When we came back down, we saw the ferry approaching. We opened all of the doors and allowed the cool breeze to waft in while we began hauling the belongings into the cottage.

Chapter Two

The first boxes to come out of the truck were, of course, my books. I picked up one of them, an expensive hardcover copy of Rebecca, a gift from Jason, my childhood friend. He was one of the few that helped me pack up to move here. I had an inkling he volunteered so he could see me off and get one last hug in, but I didn't mind. We had danced around a mutual crush for years, and it was him that I would miss the most outside of my family. I was around him practically every week, and he was always there when I needed him. There was a part of me hoping that moving would stir him to act, to speak out on these feelings that neither one of us wanted to address. But instead, there were just more sideways glances and brushing hands. He promised to keep in touch, so I would have to be content with that.

I then headed inside the house ready to unpack. The movers dropped box after box at my feet, and I was ripping them all open, antsy to organize. Only two men were accompanying me to move things out of the truck. Nick and Andrew. They both seemed to be in their mid-twenties, with enough muscle to get the job done.

Looking back at my books, I decided to start with Hornblower. The stories retold Horatio Nelson's life with his loyal friend William Bush. I traced my fingers along the navy and gold etched spines, illustrations of rope circling the letters. I put them on the shelf that was the easiest to reach from, knowing how often I would go back to them. I put all of my Daphne du Maurier novels next to them, envisioning Jamaica Inn for the thousandth time, with smugglers sneaking in and out. I spent another hour that way, pulling books out and daydreaming about the contents inside.

Finally, furniture started coming in, my jewelry cabinet headed straight to the bedroom, and my elevated globe went next to the library in the living room. Soon enough, it was starting to look like I lived here all along. My antique paintings fit right in, their contents being mostly windjammers, lighthouses, and rocky shores. I had pirate cameos, Italian mirrors, and frames from over two hundred years ago.

As I moved about and organized my things, Thomas seemed to watch with a nod or raised eyebrow from time to time. I was anxious to talk to him, to get his opinions and guidance and, hopefully, some stories. I had music playing from my phone - songs of Celtic tales and sea shanties, and the occasional alternative story. I danced around the rooms, not caring if the movers were watching as I pretended to be an Irish lass seeing off the local sailors.

Eventually, everything was inside and we sat around to let the breeze cool us off.

Thomas walked over to my espresso machine.

"How do ya even work this dang thing?" I laughed to myself, walking over to the kitchen.

"It's simple once you do it a few times. Let me show you."

He stepped aside, watching in befuddlement. I just got a hmph in reply. He still acted as though it was above his level of comprehension, which it might have been when one used the same coffee pot for over 25 years.

I asked him what kind of coffee he liked. His reply was anything dark with a splash of milk. That I could do. I started to brew a dark smooth roast, and then decided I would foam up his milk to make it that much more amazing. He may not like me taking extra liberties with his coffee, but I was hoping he would like it. I took great joy in making coffee for people. Maybe it was because I wasn't the best cook, and this was the one thing I knew I could do well. I had learned throughout my short years in this world that coffee was a kind of love language. If you make someone a good cup, they will most likely hold you in higher regard.

Once I was done, I readied the table with everyone's preferred hot drink. Soon enough, we were all gathered around Thomas, as he told of his very first day on the island and the anxieties and excitements that came with it. We were all enamored with him. Staying like that for a while, I relished the calming sound of the waves and breeze, birds flying by, and the lovely smell of freshly brewed coffee.

We went back to Mermaid's Lagoon to get some food for the night. I recommended Yvonne's for dinner. It was in Downtown Crossing complete with a library lounge and hanging portraits. When we walked to our table we were graced with marble floors, decadent crystal chandeliers, and gold accents everywhere we turned. It blew me away with its old-world elegance and charm. Thomas turned to walk away, but I sprinted in front of him.

"You aren't going to dine with us?" He shifted on his feet, looking uncomfortable.

"I reckoned you wouldn't want an old man like me dining with you and your workers."

"Nonsense! I am very grateful for you, and I know the guys would love to hear more of your stories." He seemed to mull it over in his mind for a bit, before looking at me.

"Aye, suppose they do. I'll stay."

I beamed at him, ready to show him I was appreciative. Our waiter came by to get our orders, and I wasn't surprised in the slightest that Thomas decided to start with some hot buttered rum. It was an easygoing night, everyone got along, and conversation flowed easily. Nick and Andrew may have not felt the pull to the sea as Thomas and I did, but they made good company.

It turns out I had museums to visit, curiosity shops to explore, and a plethora of cafés and the like to fill my free time. The world felt like my oyster, my own adventure to ravage and take full advantage of. It was such an exhilarating feeling. It felt like some sort of high you could ride the waves on, one that I never wanted to crash from. Disturbed from my thoughts, I felt my phone buzz, and when I looked down I saw a message from Jason.

I smiled, relieved he was keeping to his promise.

'How's the move going? Settled in yet?'

I sent a quick reply.

'Things are good. Dinner with the movers and Thomas, the keeper to train me. Will talk more later.'

A response was sent in less than a minute.

'I'm intrigued. Eager to know more about your new surroundings.'

I put my phone back down, as it was my time to order my food. I went for some pub grub and a steak ale pie, while everyone else got an assortment of burgers and fried fish. The music playing in Yvonne's was eclectic, to say the least. There were a couple of folk songs I recognized, along with a few violin-based instrumentals. I could easily see this being my go-to place. Once our meals came, we all ate in contentment. It had been a long but fulfilling day. Things were getting done and no one had a breakdown, which was all I could ask for.

Afterward, we all walked around the streets for a bit, enjoying how alive the city became. I could hear distinct singing somewhere to my right and smell all kinds of scents wafting in and out of the air around me. A couple was laughing to my left, and a family was walking ahead of me, somewhat like my own. They were hugging and talking about their day with each other. As much as I loved being alone, moments like these made my heart fill up, being reminded how small I am in this world.

Eventually, we made it back to our little island for the night. I immediately went to my room, wanting a bit of time to myself. It was my first night away from home. It made me think of the previous night, sharing a bed with my sister Cyra while my parents were in the other room along with my brother. We all stayed up to talk and laugh and ended up looking at old family photos. There was one of me and my grandma, my first time being on a beach. I had a huge toothy grin on my face; you could tell I was having the time of my life. My grandma looked so young and graceful, happy to be by my side and experiencing that moment with me. There was another of me and my friend, hand in hand, running towards the water. You could see my brother diving in the distance. It's one of those photos that you know you'll remember forever and have in your house on a mantel wherever you go.

We turned the TV on next, not quite ready to end the night. Finding a channel that was playing old movies, Treasure Island filled the screen. I knew the story by heart, and so did my dad. We were the only ones who enjoyed the film, but for once the rest of the family didn't mind indulging us. We laughed at the pirates and their language and secretly admired Jim Hawkins. I'd been obsessed with pirates from an early age, perhaps since I watched Peter Pan for the first time.

Many kids wanted to be Wendy, Peter, or one of the lost boys always getting into mischief. But I wanted to be on Captain Hook's crew. I was told it was unladylike and wrong to want that. But it was all just pretend. What difference did it make?

Once the lights were turned off and the room grew quiet, my sister and I looked at each other under the covers.

She whispered, "So. Do you think Jason will make a move?"

She was always one to get right to the point. I rolled my eyes, even though she probably couldn't see me very well.

"I don't know. We've liked each other for a while. But I don't know if he'd make me happy."

"You always talk like dating him would be forever. You know you don't have to marry him."

I sighed. "I don't take relationships lightly, Cy. You know that. I don't want to put the time in and end up getting hurt in the process."

"Getting hurt is just a part of life. Anyway, he's a nice guy. He's practically family." I had heard as much from my mother for years.

"I don't know. I need to know he's ready."

She huffed at me and then seemed to be done with talking. I knew what my family wanted. They wanted to see me taken care of. They wanted the same future for me that my mother had.

Except I had already surpassed her as far as independence went. I didn't want to keep dwelling on it, as there was little point. It was a conversation now in the past. I turned over, hoping sleep would take me before I had a chance to think of any other situations.

The next morning felt sort of hazy in my mind. I wished I had the awe and imagination of a child while keeping the freedom I've come to acquire as an adult. I hated that feeling of dread that came with change. I didn't remember feeling that when I was younger. It was a scary thing to face, as inevitable as it was. Because as scary as change is, it would be infinitely scarier to never change at all.

Waking up had been another reminder of what I left. I thought of the goodbyes that were given. I didn't want to forget my sister's reaction when we watched movies together and the look on her face when the two main characters finally kissed. I didn't want to forget the mornings when my mom and I were up before everyone else, grabbing breakfast and talking about everything under the sun. I didn't want to forget the way my animals snuggled with me in the afternoons, or my dad's blank stares when he was trying to figure someone out. Or even late-night chats with my brother while we were driving around town. These were the things that would start to fade in my mind. A few tears were escaping, and my face getting all red and puffy.

I wished I could have it all. But that's not what the world is all about. We are all greedy creatures, trying to pick and choose what will mean the most to us. Part of me wanted to go back and see them again, screaming to let me stay home. But this was my new home. I had to count on the fact that calling it 'home' would get easier every day.

Chapter Three

Making my way downstairs, I spotted Thomas outside near the docks. I had not even changed yet, but I was already making my way out to sit next to him. He kept his eyes towards the water world, maybe lost in thought. I wondered if he could read my mind after he finally spoke up.

"Yer gonna do jus' fine."

He was a very strange man. I wondered if my first opinion of him was miscalculated. He may be more interesting than most.

"Ya know how to swim?" I nodded again. He looked towards the ocean.

"Read maps?" I continued to nod.

"Ya know, yer gonna be the only one in these blasted states that even have this as a full-time job." I chuckled.

"I did my research. Do you not like America?" He huffed.

"Does anyone? 'S built on piracy and lies."

I shrugged. Every American knew as much. But foreigners were particularly against everything that made America, America.

"Where are you from, Thomas?"

"Was born 'n Ireland. Spent ma childhood 'n northern Scotland, moved here when I was about yer age. Been here ever since." A man of culture, who had probably seen his fair share of tragedy in the world.

"What made you decide to move here?" He sighed, his shoulders sloping. His eyes seemed to be somewhere else.

"Hard to make a living at tha time. I was a man of the sea, with no place to call ma own. I was out of work. America was promising jobs for everyone. It seemed like the only choice." He gestured behind us, back towards the lighthouse. "This lighthouse was first built in 1716, which makes it the oldest one in America. It's been burnt on many occasions, destroyed by the British at least twice, and was eventually reconstructed in 1783. It wasn't the height it is today until 1856." So much bad luck, it seemed. But I was honored to be a part of its ongoing history.

Thomas continued, "The storms surrounding the island were always known as treacherous, as the very first keepers had drowned trying to get back. The city council decided that it was best that someone remained on the island, even after several ships near the coastline started to go missing. You know what that entails if you see any vessels start to head towards the harbor."

My mind whirled with what could've happened to these ships. Where did they go? What was preventing them from sending out distress signals?

We fell into silence again. I was pondering on his life if he regretted coming here. He didn't seem to have any family. After a while he got up, probably to go try and work the espresso machine, which I had an inkling he wouldn't be able to figure out, so I got up to follow. I kept my right hand close to my necklace, feeling the grooves in the gold starfish. It was the last thing my family gave me, the beads looking like sparkling candy.

The sight in the kitchen was no surprise. Thomas was fiddling with the espresso machine, exasperated. I smiled to myself and went over to help him. He simply grumbled and went to sit at the table. As I made coffee for the both of us and sat our mugs down, he put his hands on his knees, clearly ready to get down to business talk.

"We'll start nice 'n easy today. I'll show you how to turn tha light on at night, how to sound tha fog signal, and what to do if a ship needs assistance."

"Sounds easy enough."

"Aye. Too bad I can't mock up a storm for ye. That's when tha real fun starts."

"Will we have time to sail today?"

He seemed to mull it over in his brain.

"We'll see. I haven't been out there as much as I was even a year ago; strange things 'ave been happenin' 'n these waters."

He sounded ridiculous, but I found myself to be intrigued nonetheless.

"What do you mean?" He made a show of staring out the window towards the sea, the wind beating on the glass as he did so.

"Ships be goin' missin'. Sure ya heard. Never was fast enough. Every time I go out there when I see the signals, they always be gone. No trace of 'em."

It was a peculiar thing. It reminded me of old sailor's tales, stories of giant sea creatures that could swallow ships whole.

"What could cause something like that?" He shook his head.

"By the gods if I know. We've had whole search parties out when it first began, but no trace. After a while, we all become too scared to go out."

I wondered if it were a situation like the Bermuda Triangle. But it was such an odd thing for this shoreline to experience. There had always been terrible storms, but I had rarely heard of something like this in a modern-day example.

"Of course, it used to happen on a much lower scale." He said as an afterthought.

"And you say it's only during bad storms?"

"Naturally, miss."

We let the subject go for the time being. After finishing our coffee and changing into more suitable clothes, we went to climb the lighthouse, which stood at 89 feet. Thomas took great care in showing me the routine he had kept for most of his life. He had nimble, bony fingers that were well-calloused, and although this structure was not his, he seemed to have a certain pride in explaining everything to me. I watched with close attention as he showed me how to work the computers and lights. I was relieved to find my tasks to be easier than expected. Thomas informed me that the next day he would be an observer, watching me perform these same actions on my own. We descended back down, and I found with some surprise that my phone read that the time was only noon.

"Perhaps ya can see why this job has fallen outta demand."

His statement made me wonder what he did with the rest of his time. We decided to go on the boat and explore the area. Thomas took me to the closest island adjacent to Little Brewster - the one with the destroyed lighthouse. It was such a sorry sight. Only half of it remained, quite literally crumbled to pieces.

Thomas told me that thankfully no one was there when it happened, but it was an odd occurrence, to say the least. Lighthouses were built to withstand storms and waves. So what made this one so vulnerable? It was a mystery that kept scratching at the back of my thoughts. Not only was it strange, but it was a fear of mine that the lighthouse I would be taking care of would face the same fate. Thomas seemed to notice my thoughts and spoke out.

"Happens once 'n a lifetime, dear."

With that, we went on. The rest of the sailing went pretty well, and I felt a peace wash over me being on the water. It was a strange thing, the type of high humans can experience when some form of nature captivates them. I am always humbled when staring at the ocean. Being in some vast space that is full of mysteries I couldn't touch, an entrancing sparkle as the waves shift from place to place. Creatures threatening to come to greet you at any moment. There was so much power where we sat. It was hard not to romanticize such a force.

We sat in place for a few minutes. Thomas had a questioning look in his eyes. I could start to tell then when he had something to say.

"What is it that made ya want this life?"

It was a valid question. I felt as though we'd start an interview at any moment. I pondered on it for a minute, wanting to have a solid answer. I wasn't in any despairing need the way Thomas was when he started this job. I was a stranger to this way of work.

Despite my love affair with the sea, I was new to this way of employment.

"It represents everything I've ever longed for. Freedom. Adventure. Peace. I look out at the horizon as we're doing now, and I've never felt such a sense of belonging in all my life."

He smiled a genuine smile, and I noticed a slight twinkle in his eyes. It was as if we had some sort of understanding with each other, escaping to the ocean for different reasons, but loving her all the same.

"Bless yer heart, lass. Reckon the sea needs you as much as you need her. I can see it for meself."

He was studying me again. I wondered what he meant. Every sailor had a rather vivid imagination and superstitious spirit. The wind around us grew stronger, and I shivered from the breath it left on my skin. We made our way back to Little Brewster, satisfied by our little exploration. It was a glimpse of what was to come.

Chapter Four

For lunch, we made an assortment of sandwiches with fresh ham, thick slices of cheddar, arugula, spinach, and a light dressing made of lemon and vinegar. I decided to go through a little extra effort by smashing potatoes flat, seasoning them to fry, and topping them with pesto. Thomas seemed to generally be a man of few words, but it was a comfortable silence I welcomed, content just to have this companionship for a short while. To my surprise, he stood up abruptly to start scraping plates and washing them. He hummed to himself what seemed to be a sea shanty I had heard only once or twice.

So far I realized that though this may be a great adventure in the undertaking, it was not without its slow graceful moments. I was thankful for it. I felt myself to be an anomaly of a person, yearning for both routine and spontaneity, thrill and tranquility.

I was brought back to reality by another text from Jason.

'How did the goodbyes go by the way?'

My heart felt gutted for a second all over again from the mention of my family leaving. I didn't want to think about it again and emotionally exhaust myself, despite him probably just wanting to be inquisitive.

'Hard to get through, there were tears all around.'

I waited for a reply.

'I know it hurts. I hope it gets a little easier. Are you on your little island?'

I decided to send him a picture of my view at the moment, the window in the kitchen overlooking the docks.

'That's quite a view! Does it feel like home yet?'

I smiled with pride.

'Strangely, it does. Like it was mine all along.'

I thought of all the exploring I did with my brother Hunter and Jason as kids. We would spend hours in the woods behind Jason's house looking for little treasures or making small houses out of fallen logs. He would love to scout this place. I eventually slipped my phone into my pocket to draw my attention back to Thomas. He was done with the dishes and drying his hands.

"Has there ever been a ship around here that has needed help from you?"

He nodded. "Aye. Happened once around a year after I took the job. Had to propel the Lagoon a couple of miles out. A fishing boat had crashed into one of the

31

bigger rocks 'n was quickly sinking in the storm. But when I got closer, there was no one there." I felt a chill go down my spine.

"No survivors?"

He was deep in thought, transporting himself back in time most likely.

"I stayed, waiting for a sign. I dove a few times, trying to find if some unlucky soul was drownin', but no luck. It was like no one was ever there."

Strange occurrences were a hard thing to swallow. Something out of the ordinary always seemed like it was more myth than reality. I couldn't help but feel like there were things Thomas wasn't telling me. I reckoned it was just because he hadn't known me for long. The longer we stood there, the darker the skies became, the wind pounding on the door.

"Storm likely to be comin' in. Best we stay in rest of the day."

With that Thomas went to sit in the living room, resigning himself to a book he had in his satchel. I sat on the loveseat next to him, checking my phone again. Another message from Jason, asking if he could call me.

"Thomas? What kind of Wi-Fi do we get out here?" He huffed to himself.

"Surprised ya didn't ask sooner. We connect to a satellite. Give it here."

I handed my phone to him, and he started to type things into my settings. He handed it back to me, and I thanked him. I told him I was going to spend some time upstairs and set off. I lit some candles around the room and reveled in the patter of rain on my windows. It was becoming quite a lovely day to spend in my little cottage.

Then I accepted the invite for a video chat from Jason. He was in his pajamas lounging in bed, with messy hair that was sticking up in every direction. Something about seeing his face again was filling me with chaotic anxiety. He beamed at me.

"Hey there. How's it going up there in Boston?"

"It's a rainy day here. Thomas the keeper has been showing me some of his daily tasks. What have you been up to?"

"This Thomas sounds interesting. Oh nothing much, work is annoying me."

Jason was a man who was in constant annoyance when it came to his occupation. He took on all of the odd jobs in town that had something to do with cosmetics and the renovation of a home. He jumped from thing to thing. I had an inkling it was caused by his bipolar disorder and ADHD, which, thankfully, he took meds for.

"No surprise to me."

He gave me a smile that looked akin to bashful, and I dreaded whatever it was he was about to say.

"You look beautiful today, Adira."

I loved it when women complimented me. I felt pride and a connection building every time it was done. But hearing it from Jason was a different thing altogether.

"Thank you, you look... handsome."

I hated how the sentence sounded to my ears. It felt terribly forced and awkward. Why did I have to be this way? Was something wrong with me? But instead of laughing at me, he just continued to smile bashfully.

I didn't know what to think of this. I had relationships before, albeit quick high school romances, but I knew how they worked. So why did simply talking to Jason feel different? I couldn't even put my finger on what it was I was feeling. My intuitive senses seemed to be trying to tell me something, but what it was I could not decipher.

"So how are you going to spend your time in your new place? Sounds like your job won't take you that long." I shrugged.

"Doing what I always do. Read. Explore the city. And the surrounding islands."

"There's more than one?"

"Yep! Even a decommissioned lighthouse on the neighboring island crumbled to pieces."

"Woah. Well, I hope you keep exploring to a minimum." I wore a puzzled look.

"Why?"

He didn't keep his eyes on me, but rather around his room.

"Well, it'd be dangerous to be out by yourself. Especially out in the city. I'm sure there's tons of men who'd be looking your way." This oddly struck me. I was curious about his reply.

"You think I can't handle a couple of roaming eyes by myself?" He seemed to be fidgeting more with each passing second.

"Of course not, I just think it would be hard to resist. I almost feel jealous I won't be with you." This conversation was taking a direction I wasn't sure I wanted right now.

"Jason, you know we're just friends, right?" He got very quiet. I was feeling guilty, despite needing to say what I had. I wanted to know how far his interest went.

"I just... I'm scared." Now he was confusing me.

"We're both in different directions in life. You know that. I've just started a new job, in a new city. I can't help but feel like you could've said something sooner."

"I do, but I'm hoping you feel the same way I do despite it all. That you might...." I hated it when people beat around the bush.

He continued, "Is it too soon? Too soon to say those three words?"

I couldn't believe what I was hearing. To go from never addressing these feelings, to him wanting to throw those words around had me struggling to keep up.

"I think you need to seriously consider why you chose to wait all this time to talk to me. I need to go." During his protest, I ended the chat.

I sat there in utter shock. I couldn't process my feelings. Too many things had happened that day. I had been waiting for this moment, but I worried about what it might mean. Everything was just building up inside, and I let out a strangled sound. I started to cry uncontrollably, in a state of confusion and overwhelming change.

It was a moment of complete loathing for everything around me that can only be understood by those who go under mental torment every day of their life. I wouldn't call my case severe, but anxiety and depression had made a home in me, and I would forever be burdened by it. It made itself known under taxing situations, yelling at me to go retreat.

I wished at that moment I had my mother to go talk to and confide in. But she was gone, and the only other soul here was an equally emotionally constipated man who was at least three times my age. Thomas spoke in riddles, and I was too exhausted to work on a puzzle. So instead I lay in bed, doing breathing exercises. I would have to learn to rely only on myself. I blew out my candles and decided it was time for tea.

If Thomas saw my tear-stained cheeks while I walked down the stairs and to the kitchen, he made no vocal note of it. I found my Earl Grey tea bags and put the kettle on. I crossed my arms and let out a long sigh. I suddenly felt like a middle-aged mother, tired of her kids' shenanigans, begging for a moment of solace. I knew I was dramatic and found most people insufferable, but it was days like these that made me remember just how little tolerance I truly have.

I got out the milk and tea as the water came to a boil and fished out one of my mugs from the cupboard. It was an old beer mug with the Cutty Sark on it. I made my tea and went to sit back beside Thomas. He looked up then.

"Shall I make us a fire, dear?"

Although it was practically summer, the breeze was constant and the air was always cool. A fire sounded like just the thing to raise my spirits. I wordlessly nodded, and he got up to pick a few logs out of a brass bucket by the fireplace.

The next few hours were spent reading and refilling mugs of tea as the storm raged on. At some point Thomas fell asleep with his book still open, so I brought out some blankets and draped one over his sleeping form. I took another for myself and cocooned myself in it, feeling a coziness settle around me as I welcomed sleep.

Chapter Five

Thomas was up bright and early, and, to my surprise, I smelt coffee. Did he finally figure out how to work the espresso machine? I turned around to look in the kitchen and, sure enough, there he was, looking quite smug that he managed on his own. I smiled at his accomplishment and graciously accepted a mug. He even remembered how much milk I took, and I thanked him for it. We sat at the table together, both not ready for food just yet. Before I would start practicing the duties of the lighthouse, that was the day I would be shown how to aid ships should they need me to come out at sea.

I dressed myself in an oversized striped shirt with a black cotton jumpsuit, easy to move around in. I slipped on my combat boots and met Thomas back downstairs. The weather was already warming up, and I put my hair up in a knot. I nearly fell over jumping into Mermaid's Lagoon, excited to start more training. Thomas sailed us out a good few miles from our island to show me a realistic distance that ships would be at during a storm where we could still see them. Then he sat for a moment in thought, probably conjuring up what he wanted to say.

"Depending 'n how bad 'tis, ya may need ta swim out. Sometimes, they'll need guiding back ta safety or to abandon ship. All depends on circumstances."

I nodded, expecting as much. Then he gestured with his head to the water. I looked up at him, confused.

"Go on then." Did he really want me to jump in now?

"You could've told me to dress differently if you were going to make me swim."

He laughed heartily.

"Ya think you'll have time for that, lass? Yer tellin' me if a boat needs yer help yer gonna change 'nta a purty suit first?"

I started to blush, feeling stupid. Very well. I went to the ledge of the boat and made to dive. I soon felt the ocean embrace me, and I was invigorated by the cooler temperature of the water. I swam as far as I could, knowing Thomas would expect as much. I pushed myself as far as I could go, and then I went up for air, swimming a little further still. At last, I let my arms rest for a second, floating a good several feet from the boat. Thomas looked satisfied.

"Let's hope ya can do tha same when storms be ragin'!"

I could hear him chuckle to himself while he ushered me to come back. I swam with ease, and he helped to hoist me back onto the boat. He handed me a towel, which I gratefully took and wrapped around myself. Thankfully, despite the breeze, the sun was out. Once we made our way back onto Little Brewster, I went to change. While in my room, I looked at my phone, checking for notifications. I noticed there were none from Jason. I couldn't tell if he was trying to give me space after my abrupt end to the call last night, or maybe avoiding me from hurt feelings. Or maybe he was just busy? It was going to eat away at me, as he did nothing to warrant my weird response. I continued to make my way through the messages and decided a quick video chat with the family might be nice. I plopped on my bed, with a fresh linen top on and old Ralph Lauren jeans, feeling quite refreshed after getting to swim.

I was greeted by my mom smiling on the screen, clearly happy to see that I called. I beamed back at her, as she pointed the camera to our golden retriever who was just happy to be included. My heart ached to be with them and cuddling my dog.

"Everyone misses you, Adira! Tell us how things are going!"

"I miss you guys too! I expect frequent pictures and calls from everyone! Things are good here. I started my training and, as menial as the tasks are, I think I'll be happy here. Thomas is still strange but made me coffee, so I can't complain. How are things there?"

They all laughed at the mention of the aloof keeper.

"Things are good here. Same as always. So...." It was never good for my mother to end something with so.

"What?" I said it with caution. Just one word could make me feel like a little kid again getting caught in trouble.

"Have you heard anything from Jason?" Of course, that's where the conversation was heading. I should've known.

"Uh yeah. A bit. He called me last night."

Surprise lit up her features, albeit a fake surprise. She clearly had an inkling about this phone call already.

"Interesting. He's been acting a little strange...."

"What is it, Mom? What's the problem?" I did not like the feeling of my stomach flaring at the moment.

"Well, your brother had him over last night, probably after your call. I've never seen the boy look so miserable. Wonder why."

Why indeed. This was something I wasn't sure if I wanted to talk about right now. But I also knew my mother would bug me relentlessly if I didn't say it now.

"Oh. He actually tried to tell me he loved me. So, that was fun!" That's when her mouth fell open, and I heard a chuckle from my father.

"But, you're not even dating!"

I nodded, a tight expression on my face that probably resembled one of those cats they make memes out of. She started to shake her head.

"As you can imagine, I did not take it well. I hung up on him." It was her turn to do a nervous chuckle.

"That's... alarming."

A big understatement. I had a sort of love for Jason too, but it was too soon to tell what kind it was. There was a curiosity in me, and I knew I felt attracted to him. We had a lot of good memories together, and anytime we were in the same room, I could hardly think about anything else but him. He was soft, gentle, and had a knack for science. I would watch him take apart computers and anything else he could get his hands on for hours.

All I could do was stare at them, waiting for more words to come out. Mom told me not to worry, to tell him he should take things slow. Told me it was in my hands. All very obvious statements that did not make me feel any better. I started to feel that fleeting panic again and tried to change the subject. But as I was well acquainted with, nothing interesting ever happened where I previously lived. One of the exact reasons I left.

"Well I would love to chat more about how emotionally stunted Jason is, but I have to make lunch now. Love you!"

We said our goodbyes, and I found myself relieved to be done with the conversation. I loved my family, but I did not like talking about Jason. My feelings for him were a strange thing I was yet to make sense of, and, until I did, it felt like going in circles trying to talk about it.

I went back downstairs to see Thomas napping in the recliner. I went into the kitchen, eager to make something. I decided on some cheesy garlic pasta. As the water was boiling, I also cut up some cherry tomatoes and zucchini. I went with the bow tie pasta that I always imagined the Eleventh Doctor inventing sometime in the past, and threw it in. I put on some French instrumental café music and waited.

Once the pasta was finished I made a dish for the both of us and called Thomas in. He was grateful I cooked, and we sat listening to the music. The following routine commenced with him washing the dishes. We were eventually done with the domestics, and he had me lead the way back to the lighthouse. There were more living arrangements within the lighthouse that Thomas was using at the moment but would be left to me in less than a week.

It was another thing to call my own and decorate how I saw fit. I was endlessly excited about the possible nights spent within the structure, and I knew I would need to fill it with some books and snacks.

He watched as I performed the tasks he had shown to me just the day before, with a nod or a criticism every now and then. Everything was in wonderful shape despite the age of the building and the wear and tear of being out at sea.

"Will I ever hear much from the council or Lighthouse Association?" He shrugged.

"Probably not. They let ya do yer thing unless upgrades or improvements need to be done."

I nodded, satisfied with the answer. I always enjoyed jobs where I was the sole employee. We stood outside on the balcony of the lighthouse for a long time. Eventually, he spoke up.

"I saw a mermaid once."

What do you say when someone says that? I wanted to say he was drunk, or it was dark out and he didn't know what he saw.

"...Oh?"

"Had a tail that shone brighter than the moon. Most beautiful thing I ever saw." I was still at a loss for words.

"Where?" He looked down, peering towards the rocks by the shore.

"Was after a horrible storm, one of the worst in my years. She was grasping onto the rocks there. Had silky long dark hair. She was hurt, or exhausted, couldn't tell. I had just come out of the lighthouse, and for a minute, we just looked at each other. Then fear must've taken over, 'n next minute with a whip of her tail she was gone."

I felt entranced by his words, and I wanted to believe him. I believed all creatures were real in theory, but realistically it's hard to tell if any of it was true.

"When I was a little girl, all I wanted to be was a mermaid. I dreamed of having a tail and getting to swim with dolphins. Soon after I dreamt of pirates.

Mermaids have always held a place in my heart." He looked at me, almost with an inquiring look.

"Y'know, I've always believed the sea chooses some of us to be of service to her. We don't see it that way, because our love for her is so great, it doesn't feel like such a horrible thing. I've been serving her most of my life, 'n she's let me in on a few secrets. I think she has something greater 'n store for you."

He stopped, tilting his head slightly. Whatever else he had in mind to say he must've thought better of. I was left feeling a strange heaviness in my chest and an overwhelming curiosity. I looked at the sun glittering over the water, and, as my eyes searched for Thomas, he was gone. For the rest of the afternoon, I was left alone with my thoughts.

I went to walk over to the rocks Thomas mentioned, where he saw his mysterious visitor. I made my way down to climb them, one of the most secluded parts of the island. I knew they used to provide tours of the lighthouse, and this was an area they kept visitors away from, treacherous as it was. There were barnacles and little clam shells all about, and I could even see a starfish or two submerged in the water. During low tide, I would have to come back out. But as the tide came farther in, I knew my time exploring now was limited. I wasn't sure what I was looking for. A sign to tell me what Thomas said was true? Even if it were, there would be no trace. My attention was brought to the sky in the distance, as lightning danced across the horizon. Surely storms so frequent weren't normal.

I eventually made my way back to my little cottage, and I had it in my mind to try to convince Thomas to go into the city for dinner, and, hopefully, let me operate the Lagoon. I then wondered if that's why Thomas had named his boat that. There were still so many mysteries about the keeper I wished I knew. I doubted I would uncover much more with just a few days of being on the same island together. I tried to push it out of my head to go get dressed for a night in the city.

Chapter Six

On the Mermaid's Lagoon, I decided to send a short text to Jason. I felt bad that I had caused him grief when he was just trying to articulate his emotions.

'Hey! Are you doing okay?'

I didn't know what else to say from that. I still didn't know what I wanted from him. Every time I was around him I felt cornered into a decision I wasn't prepared for. I slipped my phone into my bag as the city came more into focus.

Thomas took care to tie us to one of the many docks and the smell of Boston wafted around me. Some mixture of tobacco, pollution, and cedar wood? It excited me nonetheless. I asked Thomas what he frequented when he went into the city.

"Aye. Let's go to tha Burren. Best Irish pub here."

Pub grub sounded like just the thing, so I happily started to follow Thomas as he made his way through the bustling streets. Upon arrival, I noticed its black exterior with bright red shiny doors. There was a sign advertising live music, and I was antsy to get in and take in the surroundings. I ushered a grumbly Thomas inside to take our seats. He went to sit at the bar, but I tugged on his sleeve to direct him toward a booth.

I still had several months before I was legally allowed to drink. After our orders were taken, I appreciated the atmosphere for a few minutes. The live music was an eclectic mix of Irish Americana, very fitting. People were laughing and some were dancing around sloppily, but despite all of the action, it was a very cozy place to be. I could tell why Thomas liked it. I felt my phone buzz and immediately knew who it was.

'Hey. I'm alright. How are you? I'm sorry I said what I said. I understand if you don't want to talk anymore.'

I let out a deep sigh.

'I never said that. I'm glad you're doing well. And no need to apologize, it just took me by surprise.'

He read it, and I watched the typing bubble in anticipation.

'Would you call me when you have the chance?'

And there was my anxiety, making its ugly head known once again.

'Sure.'

I should just stop picking up my phone at this point. I needed time to think. Our drinks came, one ale and one water with lemon. Thomas snuck me a sip of his

48

ale, which I found to my surprise I enjoyed. We laughed for a bit as we people-watched, and then we were talking about our lighthouse. It was ours. Thomas would always hold a piece of it. He would forever be a part of its history, and I was grateful that I came into his company even if for a short while.

We talked of his departure. It was creeping up on us, like thunder in the distance. I was in conflict if I craved more of his stories or more of my independence. It did not surprise me that I got along better with this older man than with most of the people my age. I was usually the odd duck in any setting. I wasn't a pretender. That made me an outcast. I knew what I liked, and I was proud of it. I often felt resentful that others couldn't come to the same conclusion. But Thomas understood. Eventually, our food came. We both got shepherd's pie. It was without a doubt the best I ever had. The crust was buttery and flaky, and the vegetables were not too mushy.

After our trip to the pub, Thomas had a place he wanted to introduce me to that he promised I would fall in love with. And in love I was. I gazed upon Brattle Book Shop with unbridled glee. Thomas told me this was one of the oldest bookstores in America, and I wanted to jump up and down.

"When I saw yer book collection, I knew you'd like this place as much as I do."

I grinned, affirming his assumption. We both went in separate directions, eager to peruse the carts and carts of antique books. About fifteen minutes into browsing, I found an old folio edition of North and

South by Elizabeth Gaskell. I could hardly believe my luck, and I clutched it tightly to my chest. I saw Thomas trying to argue the price of a book with one of the employees, and I chuckled to myself from the amusement of it.

An hour later we had brown paper bags full of books. We were both elated. I thanked Thomas for showing me such a gem, and he curtly nodded, somewhat embarrassed by the gratitude. We made our way back to the fishing boat, and Jason popped up in my mind again. For supposedly liking this boy most of my life, he sure made my head run in circles.

Once back on our little island, I said good night to Thomas and made it back up to my bedroom. My heart started racing again. Would he want to video-chat again? No. I would just say no. I decided to end my misery by opening my window to hear the waves, climb under my covers, and call him myself.

I heard the most faked husky 'hey' I have probably ever heard. Surely no one sounds like that naturally. Especially him. Jason had always had a very soft voice, but not in a gravelly morning voice kind of way. More in the high-pitched sense. It never bothered me, but I found myself overanalyzing it now. Yet it was amusing, thinking he was possibly trying to win my affection with such a weird small thing as changing his voice.

I greeted him back and silence ensued. He asked me how I was for the second time that day. At least he wasn't altering his voice this time. I told him about my dinner and asked about his, and then we finally started to breach the subject that prompted this call in the first place.

"Adira, you know how I feel about you... and you should know that I used to pretend we'd be out on dates together. When you, me, and your brother would go out walking around town, grabbing coffee together, I would tell myself we were dating." I didn't say a word, waiting for him to continue.

"I waited and waited for you. You're the only girl I've ever felt comfortable around. The only one that brings me peace. I want to know if you want to take our relationship further. Do you feel the same way I do?"

I knew this was coming. I knew the moment he asked to call this was where it was headed. But still, I felt myself slipping away from rational thinking, and a manic monster seemed to replace my brain. I felt jolted. What was I to say??

"I... yes. Sure. Why not?"

Was that me? Did I just say that? I surprised myself with my response. I thought I was repulsed by the idea of long-distance relationships. I thought I was heading in the direction of leaving this in the past. But no. The manic heathen that I am decided to tell this boy I wanted to date him. This all sounded so very high school. I could practically see him smiling to himself.

"Really?" Yep. He was smiling. And sounding emotional.

"Yeah...." I couldn't take it back. Not really. It was already said.

"I'll try not to say those words right now, even though I'm thinking them!" Gosh, was he even trying?

Despite everything we ended up talking for around half an hour. He seemed to want to go over his finances with me and what he wanted in the future as if we were already planning on tying the knot. His seriousness rubbed off on me, and I indulged him in the conversation. After we hung up and I realized what I had done, I felt severely exhausted. I couldn't tell if I wanted my mother more or for sleep to take me. My body was shaking from pent-up stress. I ended up just laying in bed, waiting for my brain to get the hint and go to sleep.

The next few days were spent preparing for Thomas to leave. There was little left to be trained on. We went over the history of the island and the lighthouse, all the strange occurrences Thomas had seen, and what to expect as far as cosmetics were concerned for the lighthouse. At night we would talk about mythology and local folklore. Thomas gave me a list of paintings to watch out for in the Boston Art Museum. I didn't question him. Instead, I promised they would be sought out. We frequently went out in the city, looking for supplies to keep me well-stocked and restaurants to remember for later.

I tried to take note of the people in Boston. These would be the closest neighbors I'd have. There were many types of locals I had come across. There were the pretentious Harvard students, who thought they owned the city. There were business owners, who were always in a rush and always on the verge of spilling the contents of their to-go cups.

And then there was the glue of the city that kept everyone together. The families sharing one-bedroom apartments, and the employees who stuck with the same job for years despite hating the tasks they were given. The singles who fancied themselves independent and were convinced they'd find their other half at the right time.

Despite the people-watching I had commenced with Thomas almost every evening, I was no closer to befriending anyone. I wasn't disappointed but content to know I'd be okay whether I had kindred spirits here or not. I had countless books at my disposal, and sailing would be my new favorite way to pass the time.

Before I knew it, the morning had come when I would have to say goodbye. It was a bittersweet parting. Thomas would be retiring back to Scotland. Despite growing old and living a life full of hard work, he was going to miss his routine. But he would still live by the sea. He told me he could never part from it. It was something I understood well. I wished him good luck, and he grasped my hands tightly, saying I would need it more than him. Such curious things that came out of his mouth. I was always on the verge of asking him more questions, and every time the moment would slip away before I could. He had only one suitcase full of belongings, bestowing most of his possessions to me. He wished to start a new chapter of his life. There was but one thing he left me that interested me more than everything else. A book of Sailor's Tales. It was an old weathered copy, nothing special. Just a printed canvas binding with the spine starting to fray. But it was wonderful for me. My feelings were growing for this man I barely knew, this strange keeper who had seen things only described in legends.

It was just a week. Thomas wouldn't dare call me a friend under such circumstances, but I could see a look of pride in his eyes when bidding me farewell. That was enough for me. I watched as he took off in the taxi in the middle of Boston, the fog swarming all around. I made my way back to the harbor to officially become the new lighthouse keeper.

I decided on my way back to Little Brewster to make a stop at the neighboring island. I had been eager to explore the destroyed lighthouse for myself. I anchored close to the shoreline and trudged up to the crumbled bricks. I could immediately feel an eerie quality in the air around me. I felt a shiver escape me as I continued exploring. I climbed past the rubble to make my way into what was left of the lighthouse. I sat towards one of the edges, sifting through the damage. Curiosity overtook me, and I was on my hands and knees looking at what happened to this light. Something gold caught my eye, and I snatched it.

It was a ring, and one that looked like it didn't belong. It was not from some boutique or Claire's store. This was real gold. There were intricate carvings on the sides and front, and the middle had what was either a midsized garnet or ruby. I imagined a great Spanish king wearing a ring like this. It was very odd to find it here, where there was nothing but piles and piles of bricks. I rubbed some of the dirt off and slipped it on one of my fingers.

Getting up, I looked at what was left of the structure. It did look as though something ran into it. But what? And what would've happened to it? My first thought was a boat, but surely no sailor would let their boat come anywhere close to these islands. They would've kept out at sea and waited until the storms passed to head into the harbor. It took years and years of wear and tear to take out a lighthouse built from stone, and, from what I understood, this lighthouse was built much later than the one on Little Brewster.

Finding the strange ring only confused me more. I thought of recent events. The stories of missing ships. Disappearing out of nowhere. Could it be that one of the missing ships had run aground, straight towards the light? Lighthouses may have been built for raging storms and waves, but they wouldn't be quite so strong under solid mass.

It still made no sense. The boat would've been seen by Thomas surely, or found. He would've told me when I asked about the damage. Or, at least, I thought he would. With no way to contact the former keeper, I just had to trust he told me the truth. That there were no freak accidents that caused the demise of this lighthouse. But I doubted. And the longer I stood on this island, the more dread that filled me.

Chapter Seven

When I got back to my new home, I decided to break the news to my mother that I was no longer single. I video-chatted her, telling her what had transpired. She laughed at me, at how unpleasant I was being about finally dating Jason.

"Adira Becker has a nice ring to it I think!"

She seemed pleased as punch, whereas I wanted to run in whatever direction that stayed away from the topic of marriage.

"I intend to keep Fellows in my name as long as I can, Mother. Besides, I'm in the pros and cons phase of this relationship." She rolled her eyes, continuing to giggle with my sister. I did not feel quite as amused as she did.

"What's there to know about Jason? You two have been around each other since you were about ten!"

"That may be true, and as good of a friend as he's been to me, that does not automatically mean we will work out as a couple. I want to go with the flow."

My sister decided to chime in just then.

"That's code for no commitment." You could then hear the faint sound of my dad's bellowing laugh.

"Whatever you want to call it, Jason still lives several hours from me. I'm not sure how long this can really last." Mom shook her head at me.

"Then why did you say yes?" Ah. The question I had yet to answer.

"Because I worry I will never know otherwise. I don't want to continue, always wondering if Jason was the one."

That seemed to shut them up, seemingly satisfied. We went on to talk about my brother Hunter needing to find a new job, Cyra finally getting to drive a car, and other small changes.

Once I was done catching up, I decided to rearrange some of the decor left in the lighthouse. A lot of it was outdated, probably untouched by Thomas out of disinterest. However, I was a woman who took great care of my surroundings. I believed a home was an extension of yourself. I trashed a lot and took some paintings I had yet to hang up into different rooms. I also had a plethora of candles, so I took several variations up to the lighthouse. I lit one that smelled of pine and a hint of eucalyptus, hoping it would help relieve the place of its dingy smell.

In the basement of the cottage, I found an old divers helmet made of brass and copper, in great condition. I spent a good chunk of the day adding a light inside of it so that I could repurpose it for one of the living room end tables. It turned out beautifully, and I felt proud of my efforts. Sifting through the rest of the basement, junk would be a chore for another day.

The next morning I dressed in a smocked linen dress and fashioned tiny braids in my hair. I wanted to go into Boston and find a pawn shop to ask about the ring I had found. I went to Longfellows for coffee and pastries located in Cambridge and kept walking until I found something akin to an antique or curiosity shop. I found one eventually that seemed to be in good shape and chanced a peek inside. From floor to ceiling, there were chipped frames, ticking clocks, and an occasional stuffed deer. It was good to know that nearly every antique owner was just as eccentric as the other. I walked up to the desk, watching the woman behind it fill out a crossword puzzle. She wore tortoiseshell glasses and had a glass of iced tea next to her on the counter.

I cleared my throat to get her attention. She looked up at me, clearly uninterested.

"Hello! I don't want to interrupt what you're doing, but I was hoping you could give me a little more information about a piece of jewelry."

I took the ring off my finger, handing it to her. This did not capture much more attention from her than my words, but she held up her hand, telling me she'd be a moment. She retreated to a room in the back of the shop, hidden only by a red velvet curtain with tassels dragging at the floor. As she took her time, I wandered around her shop, looking at all of the strange things she had for sale.

"Where did you get this?" I jumped from where I was standing, and I whipped myself around to see the lady invading my personal space, with a searching look in her eyes.

"It's, uh, a family heirloom." She scoffed at me.

"Don't bother lying. This is no heirloom. This is a piece of jewelry that's been missing for several hundreds of years."

I tried to wrap my head around the possibility. Could it be by sheer chance that the ocean washed up a rare piece on an island next to such a widely populated city? It all seemed so hard to believe. She beckoned me to follow her back to the desk, where she pulled up an old painting where the man was wearing the exact ring I now had possession of.

She continued to stare at me with suspicion.

"Do you know who this is?"

"Should I?" I knew of a lot of historical figures, but remembering what they all looked like was another thing.

"This painting was done after the War of the Spanish Succession. Who you see in this portrait is the King of Spain. A Bourbon. King Philip. This ring he wore on many occasions is made of 18-karat gold and ruby. It was believed to be lost on a Spanish doubloon, nothing more than sunken treasure...."

And here I was, with said ring in perfect condition. Another rarity if this ring was at the bottom of the ocean for hundreds of years. Her suspicion was valid. I wish I could explain it myself.

"And here you are, with a ring that would be hard to price coming from my shop. This piece is easily worth millions."

My eyes went wide, and I felt a sort of giddiness that few can feel in their lifetime. I was now in possession of a nearly priceless item.

"One might ask what a girl is doing with a rare highly-searched-for so-called family heirloom. Some heirloom all right." She looked like she wanted to jump me and, seeing the ring on the counter, I quickly snatched it and placed it back around my finger. I backed towards the front door, looking to make a quick exit.

"Well, I'd love to sit and talk prices, but I'm really in a time crunch and have found out what I needed to know. Goodbye!"

Then I practically bolted out of there. I took a brisk walk around the block, wanting to put a bit of distance between me and that shop. I felt like holding onto this historic ring rather than telling my story to some private collector and having doubts about its authenticity. It felt hard to believe in my head if it was real.

I walked back to the Lagoon, content to be done in the city for the day. I looked at the weather forecast, and there were expected storms heading our way. I hurried back home, excited to man the lighthouse by myself again. By the time I tied the boat and walked on land, there was a drizzle. I hurried up the lighthouse, sounding the fog horn and firing up the light and lens. Thomas told me to keep an eye out for anything in the distance during these storms, seeing as that's when the ships had been disappearing.

There had not been any significant sightings the week before, so I was antsy to see something. I didn't want anything to go wrong, but there was a certain thrill in the idea of having to go investigate something out in those waters. I watched from the very top of the light as the rain started to fall faster and the droplets heavier.

I thanked god I had thought to put a kettle in there with some water the day before as I made myself a London Fog. The storm continued to get worse, and I took it all to mean it was still the beginning of summer, where the seasons were changing and the weather was most certainly always bad, just as it was in the winter. As I watched lightning dance in the distance, there was fog surrounding the island. It was so thick you could probably scoop some with your hands. The wind was pushing the water every which way, creating waves that wanted to swallow the island. Fear crept into the back of my mind, begging to be let in.

The lightning seemed to almost be attracted to this lighthouse, creeping closer and closer until it flashed the whole room with its illuminance. My London Fog grew cold while I watched the progression of events. As lightning seemed to swarm about, that's when I saw it. If I had blinked twice I might've missed it.

Out there was a blip. A ship came into view once I grabbed my telescope, trying to zoom in the best I could. But the type of ship it was had me worried. It was an old-fashioned Brigantine, and I feared it may not hold up. I sounded the fog horn again, hoping to alert whomever it was of what it was heading towards. Still, it swayed on, threatening to tip over with the waves pushing and pulling about. It dawned on me I'd have to go help. It was only my second night and I was doing something most modern keepers only did once or twice in their lifetime.

I grabbed some supplies, making my way down the spiraling stairs and out the door. I ran towards Mermaid's Lagoon, untying her as quickly as I could and getting her out into the open. I looked out for the ship, and, with terror, noticed it was nowhere. My heart was beating rapidly, and I snatched my telescope again, looking out. I scoured the area where I had seen it, and still, there was nothing. But there! It seemed to flicker in and out of sight. I tried moving the boat out in their direction as fast as the engine could go in those conditions. I kept my eyes on the figure, watching as it seemed to vanish in and out, like a flame.

But the closer I got, the harder it was to see the ship. Eventually, the flickering had stopped, and the ship was gone. I continued out anyway, hoping to find some evidence of what had just happened. When I got to the area in which it would've been, there were still no signs of what I had seen. No loose cargo, no people, and no boat.

I was not only soaking wet, but delirious. Everyone was somewhat aware of this occurrence, and still nothing could be done. I was hired to hopefully add some explanation, and so far all I had done was believe bogus stories and feel completely helpless.

Once back in my cottage with the light going, I wrote down what had happened. Sometimes you need everything displayed right in front of you to make sense of it. I thought of all of the possible scenarios. I thought that maybe I had just not gotten there in time. I made plans to go out during the next storm, hopefully before anything happened. I wanted to see with my own eyes, right in front of the phenomenon, what was happening.

Within the comfort of my bed, I told my mother what I saw that night. She told me it was probably nothing, that whatever ship was out there was just going further out to sea. I wanted to believe her. Then she berated me for going out and trying to help. As if she didn't know every job out there involves risk! When I worked customer service jobs, robberies happened right in front of me. Sometimes we had to handle things with blood. Some places had risks of shootings. My job was no different. Part of the gig was making sure people were okay.

In some cases, I would be the only one to see these souls at sea in danger. I was not afraid of such things. The longer you spend within the world, the more numb you feel at the wicked inner workings.

Soon after my talk with Mom, I had a message from Jason.

'Were you not going to tell me about tonight??'

I had regrettably not thought to text him. This was something you'd probably tell your boyfriend.

'I'm sorry! I probably would've. It's been a crazy few hours. I'm still getting over the adrenaline rush.'

'Are you okay? Did you get hurt at all?'

'I'm fine! Just a storm and a ship, Jason. It wasn't a life or death situation this time.'

'What do you mean this time?'

Was everyone back home this fearful of my job?

'I will have to go out there anytime I think a ship needs assistance.'

I had thought everyone had known this about being a lighthouse keeper, despite me being one of the last few full-time keepers.

'It just worries me, Addi. I don't like that you're all out there alone.'

'Addi? You haven't called me that before. And you knew this job would be isolating. I don't mind!'

'I wish I were there with you. I'd feel better knowing you had someone there to protect you.'

I tried not to get irritated when Jason got all macho, thinking I was only safe when a man was present. But it left me feeling incapable when I knew I was not.

'You can't protect me against nature. And sorry to say, I think I know more than you in this area!'

'Ah yes, you spare no time reminding me how much smarter you are than me! Just wishing I could see you more, that's all.'

I couldn't deny how nice it would be to have someone around, despite taking pride in managing fine by myself.

'Me too. Try and get some sleep!'

'Is that your way of telling me to stop bothering you?'

'Maybe. I'll talk to you later.'

Then I rolled over, wrapped the blankets around me like a burrito, and let sleep take over.

Chapter Eight

The first thing I did when waking up was check the weather. Unfortunately, the skies were clear. I grumbled to myself and reluctantly got out of bed. Coffee was the second priority of the morning, which was a first for me. Normally it would be the last thought when going to sleep and the only thing on my mind upon waking up.

Nevertheless, after said coffee was made, I dug out some Age of Sail books from under the side table in the living room. I flipped through the classifications of common sailor ships through the Golden Age, looking to compare what I had seen the night before. I stopped at the section for brigs of many kinds, staring at the various illustrations of Brigantines. It was exactly what I had seen the day before. Why would a brigantine replica from the 1700s chance sailing out during a storm, late at night?

I tried researching what historic ships would be making their rounds to Boston during the summer, but all of them were either frigates or sloops. The idea of a private collector coming by was even less likely. I threw the book and my laptop to the side out of frustration. Checking my phone I saw another text from Jason. A link to another bookshop in Boston.

'Thought you might like to check this place out.'

It was one of those bookshops that were piled high from floor to ceiling with books. You never came to find something with purpose. These places specialized in finding specimens of books that were near extinct. A bibliophile's haven. I was brimming with excitement. I thanked him and told him how I'd be rushing over today.

It was the perfect distraction for what would be a boring night with no ships to chase after. Once I figured out the confusing directions, I stumbled in and was hit with utter silence. I looked to my left, seeing the owner looking straight at me as if I just interrupted a funeral. The smell of his cigarette hit me in the face, and we were stuck in a staring match. I managed to make my way past the man with a frown stuck on his face, trying to make myself scarce. I found some old editions of Jules Verne novels, and I took my time looking at the illustrations and smelling the pages. Eventually, I moved on to admire the owner's vast collection of antique globes. What always baffled me was that these booksellers had some strange method to the madness. They knew where every single copy was and could probably pull a novel out of thin air.

After some time of drooling over elaborate spines and notes on introduction pages, I heard the shop doorbell ding and feet shuffling. I could hear someone coming closer, nearly right to the section I was looking at. I felt slightly annoyed that whoever came in here decided to peruse this exact spot of the store. The next thing I knew I was jumping where I stood out of fear of this other customer touching my shoulder. I whipped my head around and saw none other than Jason Becker. He was laughing at me, and I was still too stunned to speak. Then he wrapped his arms around me and we were both laughing.

"Why are you here?! When and how?"

I heard more chuckling into the side of my neck.

"I'm great, Adira, thanks for asking. Of course, I had to come visit my girl. I missed you too much!"

I stepped back a smidge to look at him. I was taking in the fact that he was here and it was just the two of us. We walked out so close to each other that we were hip to hip, and I felt positively giddy about it. Being around Jason in person made it easier to remember why I liked him. I took him to the pub Thomas took me to, wanting to associate this place with my favorite people. We sat across from each other, and he attempted to play with my hair. I knew he wasn't a fan of my longer hair. He liked it short and framing my face. It would only be a matter of time before he was begging me to cut it. But I was becoming a fan of having it long and wispy, starting to lighten up from being in the sun.

"I can only stay for a few days, 'cause of work. But I wanted to surprise you."

"I'm happy, I really am. I'm glad you came! I can't wait to show you around."

He paid for my meal, being a true gentleman through the whole endeavor. It felt nice to be doted on and admired. When we were younger, I always assumed the boy in front of me would never go for someone like me. I felt myself to be too strange, too thick and curvy for his liking, too this and that. I never stopped making reasons why he wouldn't give me a chance. Years later, there I was, having lunch with him. Dating him. We were awkward with one another, trying to find a new normal in our updated relationship status.

We eventually made it back to Mermaid's Lagoon, and Jason went to the wheel immediately. I found myself growing weary of the obvious.

"Hope you don't mean to stay by the wheel, dear." He gave me a turning nod of the head, almost dismissive.

"C'mon. Let me drive you! You don't have to do it all while I'm around."

I laughed nervously.

"Have you ever driven a boat, Jason?"

"Well, no. But my family rented one on the lake every summer back home. It can't be that difficult." One eyebrow slowly raised. I'd be damned if I let this man start acting like he knew everything.

"You don't even know how to get to the lighthouse, move over."

But apparently, I was not clear enough, because Jason powered up my boat and tried to speed to god-

knows-where. I let out a yelp at the rush of
acceleration, following a long string of grumbles. I
was not in the least pleased with this game.

"Jason!! Stop right now!!"

He merely laughed and continued to drive with no
direction. Despite being able to see the lighthouse in
the distance, he used everything in front of him with
a lack of knowledge. As funny as this would be to
anyone else going in circles, this was my boat and I
felt a strange attachment to her. I pounced on my
boyfriend, forcing him to stop. He said nothing as he
moved, still in his playful mood. I rolled my eyes and
took over the wheel, anxious to get him away and
onto the island.

Upon arrival, Jason seemed genuinely delighted at
my living situation. I experienced that new joy all
over again, living vicariously through a fresh set of
eyes. He ran like a child all over the island, with
wonder and mirth. I simply smiled, loving to show off
what was now mine. We traveled up the lighthouse to
the balcony at the top. There we watched clouds pass
by over the water. There was not much conversation
between us, as Jason snapped shots of the scene
before him. It was a companionable silence I enjoyed.

I showed him my cottage with pride, boasting over
the built-in bookshelves and old windowsills. I had
dried flowers hanging all around and seashell
specimens laid out on various surfaces. I made us a
pot of Earl Grey, and we went to relax on the couch.

"You don't know the sense of peace you bring to my life, Adira. I think it's exactly what I've been needing." I smiled, happy for the compliment.

"I'm glad to be of service. So, what do you think of my humble abode?"

"It suits you. I wish you could've found something back home that suited you more, but then you wouldn't be you."

I knew he wasn't fond of me moving somewhere new by myself. He'd probably never be okay with the fact.

"Well, now you have a reason to explore and take a vacation now and then! I'll show you some culture, Mr. Becker."

He turned to look at me, and I wanted to hide under the intense gaze.

"Would you like it if I came more often? I don't want to overwhelm you, but I feel better when I'm around you."

Did I want him around more? I hadn't considered the idea.

"I mean, sure. As long as your job and college are okay with it, I wouldn't mind." He looked away, and I saw his jaw tensing.

"You don't sound happy about it, Addi." I never seemed to say the right thing to appease him, even though I shouldn't have to. All I could do was nudge him as if the whole conversation was a joke of some sort.

More time went by and we had started a fire at some point, content to watch the flames dance. I played with the ring on my finger I had found, and Jason was watching.

"Where did you get that?"

"I found it here. It's amazing the kind of things that will wash ashore." He grazed it with his fingertips as if it would break if he tried anything else.

"It's beautiful. Guess I'll know what styles to look for in the future."

I tried desperately not to feel too weird about hints towards a future with him, or any other premature notions. But it chewed at me, making me progressively more uncomfortable.

"You don't have to say anything. I know you don't take things like that lightly. It makes it all the more fun chasing you for your affection."

Did he take this all as a game? Was I just a challenge for him? It was a curious thing to say. Every time I felt a flutter in my heart for him or finally felt content with where we were heading, he would say something I ended up overanalyzing.

The rest of the night was spent with me trying to make more casual conversation, steering away from topics that may turn over with too much emotion. I wondered if I was ready for a relationship. What kind of man did I really want? Jason was a great guy (my family made sure to remind me of that at any given moment), but my head wanted to sabotage every moment we had together. I had not even thought about kissing him since we had gotten together. I had thought about it plenty while growing up, and now that he was right here it had not crossed my mind. Surely that wasn't normal. I wish my feelings for him were as clear to me as my feelings for the sea. I never had doubt when it came to that kind of love. It grew all the time, and every new thing I learned about her had me set aflame with intrigue and awe.

Chapter Nine

One of the following evenings that came was met with gray stormy skies, which had me set in anticipation. Jason was on the couch looking at news articles, and I had in mind to get supplies ready before the rain started. I got everything set up in the Lagoon and started to braid my hair and find my leather boots. Jason was unaware of what I was doing, and I intended to keep it that way. Soon enough I heard droplets fall onto the cottage and knew it was time to head out. I wanted to make progress where the keepers before me couldn't.

As I stepped into the boat I heard the front door to the cottage open.

"What are you doing?!" I was not going to let my overprotective boyfriend stop me from doing what needed to be done.

"Just doing my job. Go back inside, Jason."

He shook his head, walking closer to me.

"And what could need doing when storms are approaching? Shouldn't you be in the lighthouse?"

"The lighthouse is on and ready. I need to be out in the water." He went to grab my wrist, beckoning me to go with him.

"No, Adira. It's too dangerous."

I could feel my anger flaring, and I didn't want to fight right now.

"I don't care. You need to let me handle this." He grabbed me more forcefully, tugging.

"It's not right! What reason could you possibly have to go out there right now?" I snatched my arm away from him, baring my teeth in the process.

"Ships are disappearing weekly! It's been going on for decades! I want to know why!"

"You can't figure it out, Adira! What makes you think you'll be the one to solve the mystery?"

I couldn't believe what I was hearing. He had no right to be telling me how to do my job, to march into my house and loom over me every second of the day. I growled, angry that I brought him here. I ran back into the boat, starting the engine while I heard him yelling my name. I had already wasted time, as thunder made its presence known. I drove as far out as I could while still seeing the lighthouse in the distance. It would be guiding me tonight.

I stood still for a while, getting soaked to the bone. I continued to observe the storm's progression. This was about the time I saw the ship last. Sure enough, about fifty feet from where I was drifting, was a ship coming into view. Not the same ship, but one of the same era it seemed. I could only stare as the vessel rocked from side to side, fighting against the waves and rage of the skies. I took my telescope out and noticed the men on the ship trying to get control. They were up on the rigging and masts, swaying in the wind. I was struck with terror, afraid they'd fall into the water. I inched my boat closer, ready to dive in after the sailors. But to my horror, the ship started to fade in and out of reality.

There was nothing I could do. There were no visual tricks or blind spots. The ship had simply vanished. I wished I had the forethought to climb onboard when it was within my grasp. I cursed at myself, angry I hadn't done more. I was trying to wrap my head around the idea that what was happening here could not be explained. This was a phenomenon.

I made my way back to the cottage defeated. I had not made as much progress as I was hoping for. I slammed the front door when entering, completely ignoring Jason. I headed straight for my bedroom, wanting to write down what just happened. I was too late. I wasted time, I didn't take the jump, and I'd have to be patient in the meantime waiting for my next opportunity.

I watched the storm's progression through my window. We would have clear weather for a while after this, and there was little I hated more than waiting. I debated going downstairs to make food, but I was still mad at Jason. He would probably try and critique my cooking anyway. During my sulking, I heard a knock on my door. I guessed it was time to face him despite my thoughts. While opening the door there was no time for me to think before Jason's lips crashed onto mine, and I was standing as rigid as a lamppost. I continued to feel shocked, not moving my lips. When he tried to pull away, his glasses got stuck in my hair, and he had to carefully unwrap my hair from the frames.

"You're not so good at this. Guess we'll have to practice more!"

I was still freaking out.

"What made you think that was a good idea??" I couldn't tell if he was trying to look smug or trying a strange bashful front.

"I thought it might calm you down."

"Sorry, but shutting me up with a kiss isn't my idea of calm." I shut him back out, not liking where this was going. I needed to think of how to handle this. This relationship was morphing into something I didn't like. I paced back and forth, coming to a halting decision. I went back downstairs, standing in front of him.

"This can't keep happening, Jason. You can't keep trying to make decisions for me, trying to stop me from doing things. This ends now."

He was shaking his head, looking confused.

"I think it would be best if you head home tomorrow."

His face remained the same, unnerving.

"I understand, Addi. I'll give you some space." It was my turn to shake my head.

"No. No, I think maybe this was a mistake." Even then it was hard to be firm with him. Despite what he'd evoked in me, I hated the thought of hurting him.

"You don't want to be with me...."

He sounded like a kicked puppy, and I couldn't stand it.

"I just think maybe you need time to grow. Away from me."

I didn't want to look at him after that. I wasn't sure if what I said was sinking in yet, but I didn't stay to find out. I went back upstairs and to my bed. I didn't want to pay any mind to what was gnawing at the back of my thoughts: never finding my person. It wasn't something I used to want. Maybe it still wasn't. But it's human nature to want companionship. The hard part is not settling. I didn't want to think of Jason as settling, but maybe he and I weren't compatible.

Instead, I thought about adventure. Seafaring was the only thing I was sure I wanted. It brought me insurmountable peace. There were other things that mattered, but it didn't help what I already knew about myself. I scared people away. They either left or treated me like a bird in a cage. And I hated both. Maybe the latter was worse. I wished, not for the first time, that I belonged to a different time. A time when sailing away from your problems was a lot more normal than it is today. That's what I dreamed of.

People I'd never met, places I'd never been, and a time that was no longer there.

The following morning was silent. Jason and I endured the boat ride to Boston, not sure how to part ways. He was still a friend of the family, whether we were dating or not.

"I hope I'll see you again, Adira."

"Take care of yourself, Jason." Then he was gone.

Chapter Ten

It'd been a week since Jason had left. I'd had my parents calling me telling me how miserable he was, how he'd been telling them all about his love for me, and how badly he wanted to talk to me. All guilt trips. I'd be lying if I said it wasn't at least a little effective. I still wasn't sure if I made the right decision. It had only been two weeks since we had dated. My family, after learning both sides, made it clear they were not happy with me. I felt stupid about the whole fiasco. I had more free time than I cared for and was waiting for a distraction. I didn't want to think about my feelings. I had no one to tell who would understand, and I wished Thomas was still around. An outsider looking in, who knew of my inner person. Who I am in essence.

I'd stayed up on the lighthouse balcony for most of the afternoon, watching the clouds. There was a fifty percent chance there'd be rain tonight, and I hoped it would pan out. I sat with the book Thomas gave me, about halfway through. There was little I didn't already know about sailors' tales, but I appreciated the personal experiences. One sailor claimed he had met members of the Brethren of the Coast and been invited to join them. He had declined and was one of the few who refused and lived. He had saved several from dying, earning much respect from the pirates he had encountered. There were many more stories worthy of a book entirely of its own, with creatures that only exist in mythology. I hoped to have stories of my own one day. There was so much I had left to do there. I wanted to keep a catalog of the shell specimens I found, I wanted to find places to take my siblings when they wanted to come visit, and I wanted to swim in the ocean at night and play up the tale that lighthouse keepers were crazy.

It was around six in the evening when the rain presented itself. I still had no desire to go inside, instead enjoying my hair getting wet and feeling cooler against the summer heat. The clouds engulfed the lighthouse, growing darker with each passing minute. I knew many people who were fearful of storms. But it was a strange comfort to me. Back home these would be the days where I would read endlessly, with constant cups of tea at my side, falling asleep to the pitter-patter against my windows. Thunder could be heard in the distance, which meant lightning would probably soon follow.

The sky was howling, and I found it hard to keep my footing with the wind threatening to whisk me off. I felt myself being pulled into this show of light and anguish. I could not tear myself away from where I swayed. The storm continued to get worse, and I started to worry that I was going to fly away from the sheer force of the wind. My fingers started to prune, and lightning seemed to be attracted to the lighthouse, getting closer and closer. Did this happen last time? I couldn't remember. I tried to get back inside the safety of the lighthouse, but as I went for the door handle, panic set in when it didn't budge. I was stuck out here. I could hardly see now, as the skies were a dark angry gray, and I was holding onto the railing of the balcony for life.

I saw a different type of light somewhere far out. It was a golden hue, flickering. Was this part of another ship? I tried desperately to keep my hair out of my face, leaning over the edge to try and see more of this strange light. As I did, I could feel myself losing my footing.

I screeched as I toppled over onto the other side of the railing, trying to grab at anything I could. I felt my arm burning as I just barely grabbed one of the metal column parts of the balcony. I was dangling like a rag doll, and the waves crashing against the lighthouse and island almost touched my shoes. There was no time to think about how this felt like a freak storm. The wind was begging me to let go, and I knew I couldn't hold on much longer. I looked around me, seeing things on the ground rise and fly around my swaying form, and I briefly wondered if these were hurricane-like conditions. I could hardly tell what was happening.

Despite my best efforts, my fingers were slipping, and the waves were spraying my legs. I swore I could hear ship bells somewhere, and, before I could fall, I felt myself being thrown back toward the ocean. There was no time to react, as I was being hurled into the crashing sea with nothing to grab onto, and the last thing I saw was lightning striking the top of the lighthouse and a clear wave of shock emitting from the building.

I was still trying to shake the sleep from myself as my eyes stung, not feeling anything other than grogginess. I tried sitting up, before realizing I couldn't. I was curled in on myself, with no room to move. Then the sleepiness was gone, replaced with alertness. Where was I? I thought I was in my bed, sleeping. I tried to thrash my limbs around and finally saw where I was. I was in what looked like a fishing net. With each passing second I became more confused. I still didn't know how I got there. I tried to look outside the net the best I could, and my eyes widened. I was being hauled up by an old galleon. Looking up I saw men facing down toward me, yelling. I tried again to claw and tear my way out, but I ended up just swinging back and forth. I heard laughing above and wondered if this was some weird new human trafficking scheme. Why in the world would they come to the lighthouse and get me? Then I realized. The unusual lightning storm the night before and glimpses of the lighthouse letting out shock waves crossed my mind. I got knocked out, hitting the waves with the force I had. I could feel it then, the groggy headache.

I was almost on these people's deck and noticed their clothes. They were all dressed like, for lack of a better word, pirates. Was this some crazy acting show you could pay half a hundred to see on an authentic pirate ship replica? I looked for tourists, anyone who dressed with a modern fashion sense, but there were none. I was left to their mercy, with absolutely nowhere to go. Wherever my lighthouse was, it could not be seen from this fishing net.

I could hear one of the sailors say, "This ain't no runaway, lads."

What was going on?? Another said, "Don't untie 'em yet, cap'n ain' out yet!" There was grumbling all around the deck, and I couldn't believe the authenticity of these outfits. It was amazing. I could hardly wait to speak to who was in charge, to see what I just got myself into. It would be soon, as I heard another door open, and heavy loud footsteps were coming closer to the heap that was me, a fish out of water it seemed.

A deep voice bellowed, "Let me see what we got!" Men were grasping at the ends of the net, cutting knots and reaching for me. I swatted their hands away, fine to stand up by myself. As soon as I did so there were collective gasps let out all around me. I was looking at what seemed to be the captain, right in the eyes.

In the same dark and slurring voice, he said, "It's a woman."

Chapter Eleven

"Should we throw her overboard?" A voice came somewhere to my left. I scoffed. There was more muffling going on around me. None of them were happy that I was on their ship.

The captain spoke again. "No no, I want to know what she's about."

I looked at him then, properly taking in his appearance. He was a man of average height, with messy dark hair a little past his shoulders and facial hair that suited him. His eyes were colored the same, reminding me of dark chocolate. His skin was tanned from years of sailing, and I could tell he was toned despite all the layers of clothes. He wore an old weathered leather hat and lots of jewelry. He struck me as a chaotic individual, but he was clearly attractive.

His crew, on the other hand, had seen far better days. If their clothes weren't torn, they were grimy, and some were missing parts of their body, from a tooth to a limb or an eye. If these were actors of some sort playing a role, they were using past injuries to their advantage. I wasn't sure how likely that was now.

I saw what appeared to be the captain's first mate lean closer to his superior and say under his breath, "The men won't be happy with a woman on board for long sir. You know what they say." The captain huffed.

"They weren't grumbling when we ran into Bonny now, were they?"

Was he referring to Anne Bonny? Surely not. I wasn't sure what to think. I needed to know what was going on.

One of the hands exclaimed, "She ain't even got all her clothes on!" I shot him a glare. I was wearing a smocked dress with leather boots and soaked to the bone. Before anything else could happen, I noticed the captain looking at me with recognition. He strode up to me and grabbed my hand. I tried lurching back, but he held on with force.

"Where did you get this?"

My ring. The one I found in the ruins of the other lighthouse.

"What does it matter?" That apparently wasn't the right answer. He was clearly annoyed, throwing my hand out of his grasp and marching back to his first mate.

"Put the lass in the brig."

I tried kicking the men who tried to snatch me and flailing my limbs like a madman. The last thing I wanted was to be in a brig. I was hungry, impatient, and sore. I tried running across the deck, but two men quickly brought my hands behind my back, tying them together with rope. I stuck my jaw out at them, as that was about all I could do. They took me down below past the crew's quarters. Before I knew it, I was locked in the brig with absolutely nothing to pass the time with. One of them had shaggy dirty blonde hair and a face full of freckles, and the other was completely bald with a wiry thick beard speckled in gray. They looked at each other, considering talking to me, but must have thought better of it. I was soon alone and left to ponder.

I didn't want to think about what could be the alternative to these strange events. I knew some loopholes technically allowed for time travel, within a few hours or so. But to go back several years? Centuries even? I wondered if Thomas ever experienced anything like this and if my family tried texting me. I didn't have my phone on me, and I hoped it wasn't at the bottom of the ocean. I wasn't sure how I hadn't managed to lose my ring, being tossed about in the water for who knows how long.

I heard footsteps and in came the captain after about an hour of being in there. He smiled a toothy grin, where I could see glints of gold and silver. He bowed dramatically, and I had a hard time staying mad.

"John Sterling, at your service." I raised an eyebrow, amused at his fake name.

"That doesn't sound much like a pirate to me." He laughed, a deep gravelly laugh.

"You think we're all born pirates, love?" He sounded like he was British but picked up a bit of everything from the Caribbean. It was fascinating.

"You don't have to act, okay? I just want to know what I'm doing here."

He looked at me, confused.

"You tell me. One bloody storm nearly ruined my ship, and the next morning we see ya floating out there like the dead."

"But what are you doing here? Who are you with?" He swayed from side to side a bit, never looking away.

"What's it look like? We don't look like a bunch of bad eggs for not!" His roundabout way of speaking was starting to grate on me.

"Could you please stop speaking in tongues? Just cut it out, I'm too tired for this." He tilted his head at me, confused. Clearly, we were not understanding one another.

"You are one strange creature. What's your name?"

"Adira Fellows. And don't call me a creature. We're not in the dark ages."

"'Dira. What a lovely name! I'm not sure what you're on about, dove, but if I don't figure out what to do with you my crew might just throw you over the side themselves."

"There's an A in there. Adira, not Dira. I don't know what the alternative is here, Captain, but getting thrown overboard is starting to look appealing." He looked me over once more like I was not making any sense.

"Let's get you some food, then maybe we can understand each other, so-so?" I tried speaking to him more, but he dashed out.

He came back in with a bowl of hard tack which seemed to have been cooked with brown sugar. It looked soft, and I didn't see any weevils, so I counted my blessings and took the meal. He unlocked my confinement and made a move to sit across from me.

"Whatever you are about to say, please just do so with truthfulness," I uttered in between mouthfuls.

"How did you end up here? We may be pirates, but some of us are gentlemen. Couldn't just leave ya out there."

"I'm a lighthouse keeper and ended up on the balcony during a bad storm. I lost my footing and must've hit my head pretty hard when falling. I don't know much more than that."

He looked at me, apparently just as non-trusting of me as I was of him.

"We're quite a way from the nearest lighthouse. 'M afraid we can't be backtracking, love."

"Where are you headed? I should be able to make passage back to the next harbor."

"We won't be making stops for some time. Frankly, 'm not sure I want to tell you where we're headed." As much as I understood his hesitation, I was starting to feel fear of not knowing when I'd get back home. I was completely out of control, and I did not want to become well-acquainted with the feeling.

"Are you really pirates? You're not messing with me?"

"In the flesh. We're no tradesmen if that's what yer on about." I shook my head.

"And what's the date?"

"Seventh of June, darlin'."

"Yes, but what year?"

He laughed in my face. "Good God must still be nursing that head trauma. It's 1720."

As soon as the words were said I felt something drop in me. I wanted to keep doubting the reality that I had found myself in, but it was increasingly clear I couldn't. They did mean Anne Bonny. I had somehow wound up in the most notorious pirate age in history.

Chapter Twelve

I was left staring intently at nothing in particular, and John most definitely questioned which one of us was more insane. He reached out to put a hand on my shoulder, trying to ground me. Despite the gesture coming from a stranger, it did help a little. I needed to articulate how to tell this man from a different time that I somehow belonged to the future.

"This is going to sound crazy, but I'm not from around here... or anywhere in this time." It was a loaded statement, yet he didn't look the least bit confused.

"So you traveled in time?" Instead of disbelief, he was simply waiting for an answer.

"I, I must've. I shouldn't be here. This is three hundred years in my past." He started to pace, looking at the floor as he stroked the stubble on his chin.

"So it may be. But we do not know how you came to be here." I became exasperated not for the first time that day by his carefree attitude.

"Are you not baffled? This is... I don't even know how this is possible! And you're just accepting it!" He turned his head towards me again, tilting to one side.

"Stranger things have happened. Surely you've heard. Sea monsters, lockers for dead sailors, water that can make you young again. What's one more to the pile?"

Of course, I'd heard. Or rather read. Everyone knew the myth of the Kraken, nymphs, and sirens. They were all stories.

"All legends, nothing could ever be proven. They are put into stories to start conspiracies and scare children." He laughed again, throwing his head back dramatically.

"And why would these creatures want every ordinary man and their mummies knowing they exist? They torment men of the sea, no one else."

A childish part of me wanted to believe him. After all, Thomas swore that the mermaid he saw was real. That she was the most exquisite thing he had ever seen. But now was not the time to get sidetracked. I wanted to know what was next. So I waited.

"I wouldn't believe you if you weren't so strange. And the ring you're wearing." Of course. Perhaps he heard of the wreck.

"What do you know about my ring?"

"Well, it's not yours, firstly. The king of Spain wore this. I'd know because I'm the one who sunk his ship. Unfortunately for us, he lived. I can assume how you managed to get this." So the story from the antiquer was right.

"It had wound up on an island close to my lighthouse, and that's when I started to suspect something weird was going on. Things wash up all the time, but this was inside a demolished lighthouse."

His face visibly paled, clearly lost in a memory and trying to solve a puzzle.

"I... I assumed his ship had sunk soon after we raided it. I saw it fading in front of me. I thought it was Davy Jones."

"Was it storming? Lots of lightning?"

We stood still, slowly piecing together what had happened.

"Yes. We had come back later, trying to find more coin, but only found bits and pieces left of what was. We didn't think much of it...."

That was what destroyed that lighthouse. It didn't stand a chance against a massive ship colliding with it at full speed. That confirmed my suspicions.

"I think I know what happened. Sort of. My lighthouse, something about it is messing with the voltage and electric charge of the lightning. It's creating its own phenomenon, and anything that's around it is getting wrapped up in the process."

"I'm not following all that, but if the lighthouse is the cause, it'll likely happen again. There's only one problem with that." I saw multiple problems but was more anxious that this one had nothing to do with statistics.

"We can't be waiting around for another storm to hit. Pirates are wanted all around these waters." I was starting to worry now.

"What are you saying?"

"I'm saying that we have to leave. And 'm not sure we'll be coming back this way for a while." This was not happening.

"How long?" He looked uncomfortable.

"Could be six months or so, love."

I was trying hard not to enter into a full-blown panic attack. How could I stay here for that long? How was I going to function? I had no antidepressants, no coffee, no phone, no family. I was shocked into silence. While I was trying to process this piece of information, the same man who had locked me up came into view. The captain turned to him, annoyed and waiting for him to speak.

"Navy's here, Cap'n," he spoke breathlessly.

I was confused for a moment, knowing that our navy didn't form until around 1775. I had forgotten that the British had a close watch on the colonies during this time of history and likely got a little too curious about pirates who weren't already employed by the king.

"You have to make a decision, lass. You can either swim to the harbor and hope a respectable tavern takes you on, or you can learn the ways of my crew."

Chapter Thirteen

I didn't know what to say to that. On the one hand, my inner child was screaming at me to accept the offer of piracy and carry on the rest of my days in the Golden Age. But there was the other side of me that thought of my family. That thought of all of the finer things that came with living in modern times. How could I choose? I was still so indecisive, craving second opinions to tell me what to do. It felt like a degradation of my character, a reminder of how incapable I was. The captain was getting bored of my lack of an answer. Meanwhile, I had a fleeting wonder if I had ever read about him in any of my history books. There were so many pirates that were probably left out of papers or those that did get included but, as time went on, their stories were no longer published.

I tried to take a logical look at my options, but the creeping excitement in the back of my mind was winning over. What if this was my chance at real adventure? An opportunity for a break from life, living as a nomad of sorts, for a time. Besides, he didn't say he'd never come back. If I could connect with him, or with enough of the crew, I could probably convince them to come back sooner. The more I mulled it over, the more resolved I was. Yes. I would stay on this ship and learn to seafare.

After I gave John an answer, he ordered one of his hands to go get me better clothes. Thankfully I had curves that would probably help keep oversized clothing on my frame, however, I was a lot shorter than most of the men. The captain left me to dress in his cabin where I could have some privacy, and I tried not to dwell on what I was getting myself into. I was grateful I had my leather boots. I put on a ruffled cotton shirt, tucking it into tan breeches. I rolled up the pant legs and slipped my boots on. I used a maroon sash to wrap and tie around my waist to keep the shirt from pulling out and to cinch myself in. I kept my jewelry on and examined myself in a gold ornate mirror. I smiled, pleased with the final look. I headed out, searching for John or someone else to tell me what to do.

They were all scurrying around the deck as the helmsman set to sail. Eventually one of the men came to greet me. He had more facial hair than his captain, but his hair and eyes were just as dark. He looked to be more Hispanic and like he hadn't slept in two days. He attempted a half smile.

"Name's Marco. I'm the captain's quartermaster."

"I'm Adira. Nice to meet you." He seemed stunned that I had just made a pleasantry directed at him.

"Yes, well, the captain would like to introduce you to the crew, if you could come with me." I said nothing more and followed him closely. He took me to the forecastle, where I went to stand next to the captain, Marco opting to stand on the other side. John looked me over, clearly elated with my new attire.

"Attention!"

He cleared his throat once, which seemed to have the desired effect on everyone on deck. They turned to look up at us, taking me in.

"I know you're all wondering about this morning's entertainment, and I have some exciting news. Adira Fellows has decided to join us in our efforts!" There were a few nods and even fewer claps. It was a rather awkward show in response. They knew before I did that their captain was not done with his speech.

"If I see one of you try to treat her like one of yer whores, you'll be answering to me. Got it?" That gained multiple grumbles of acknowledgment, lest a harsher sentence be construed. Once that was out of the way, John continued in his carefree state.

"Now let's get a move on before we're all bits of a dog's breakfast!"

His talk seemed to be over as he began whispering to Marco, the latter nodding his head several times. I stayed standing where I was, unsure of what I was supposed to do from there. After John was finished talking to Marco, he sauntered back towards me.

"We have to assign you a role, but 'm afraid there's little left for you. You could always be a powder monkey."

"Are you serious? You want me working alongside a bunch of 12-year-olds? There's nothing better for me to do?"

He pursed his lips, clearly pleased with my predicament.

"Unless you want to be sweeping the decks or scraping off barnacles. Although...."

"Yes?"

I was pleasantly surprised at John's playful demeanor. I expected a captain with a harsh attitude, someone who would've had no issue with their crew treating me like a prostitute.

"Our navigator isn't exactly made for the role. He's had trouble pointing us in the right direction. If you're saying you're from the future, surely they've made advancements?"

"Of course. Technology has gone a long way, but without any of the devices we're left with basic knowledge. I've been trained in navigation. I could still help."

He was nodding, still thinking it over.

"All right then, I'll have you act as assistant navigator. This is all such a rush, innit? Let me introduce you to Finn, our navigation man."

We walked side by side, coming down from the forecastle to the second stern gallery. I realized early on that this was a three-decker, which was pretty big for a pirate ship. I wondered where they managed to steal this and how many guns it had. Upon entering the gallery I saw a man hunched over charts facing the windows, too engrossed in what he was doing to notice (or care) that we came in.

"You ever look up from those charts, Finn?"

I saw what I assumed to be a mug of coffee swaying next to him on the table, every once in a while dripping a little onto the papers.

"Not if you want me to get us to our next stop, Johnny." I had yet to hear anyone call the captain that.

"Don't get used to the nickname love, only two people on this ship are allowed to call me that and live to see another day."

Finn finally turned around to face us, with a fond smirk. He had dark orange hair, a Roman nose, a tired but kind face, and soft blue eyes.

"Me 'n the captain go way back. But I assume the two of you aren't here to talk about the past?" John stepped forward.

"Dira here will be aiding you in navigation for the foreseeable future, or until I find something else for her to do." I scoffed, and Finn seemed to be taking my presence in for the first time. He trusted his captain, to not be immediately arguing or refusing to work with me. He eventually gave a half nod.

"All right then." Before I could respond, John made for the door, leaving me and Finn alone.

Chapter Fourteen

Luckily he got right to the chase. "Are you knowledgeable in navigating?" I nodded.

"As much as I can be. I was taught by a lighthouse keeper."

He signaled for me to come over to the desk, where charts of all kinds were sprawled out. He pointed to an astronomy chart with star locations. He took his finger to one on the left-hand corner.

"This is where we are now."

Then he moved to a navigational chart. I like to compare them to geographical maps, showing depths, ridges, islands, and shallows. I was relieved to see it was a coastal chart, which was one of the biggest scales you could acquire. He took a parallel ruler from a steel cup and started to draw a line. Once he was finished he checked the line for safety, continuing with measuring and marking the heading. Then he transferred the leg to the compass, repeating the process. It appeared as though the course was headed deeper into the North Atlantic, towards Spain. It wasn't all that surprising; the Spanish were known for having all kinds of ships full of gold. Cargo and merchant ships were always passing by those waters.

Finn looked at me expectedly, for reasons I could not conjure. Maybe he was searching for my opinion or words of acknowledgment. The type of voyage we'd be going on was roughly five thousand nautical miles, and, in this day and age, that could take up to two months, depending on multiple factors. I voiced all of this to Finn, to which he said, "Aye. But you forget there will be plenty of opportunities on the way to replenish. It's been a while since we struck gold. We need a temporary fix. Finding overloaded merchant ships near Spain is our best bet. Which I'm sure you know."

I appreciated that Finn did not undermine me or my abilities but treated me as an equal. It was a feeling that was unfortunately hard to come by even in my time. Thinking of Finn's reply made me curious to know their next move, once their greed was quenched a little.

"What took you all to Boston?"

I tried an innocent approach, hoping to glean some information.

"Supplies, mostly. We were in the Carolinas for a while, crossing off leads and recruiting a few hands. We can't stay in one place too long, or some gentlemen think it wise to arrange a jury for one lad or another. Johnny is hoping to stick closer to the Caribbean. It's more of a safe haven." This wasn't good news for me. If they were hoping to stay away from New England permanently, that meant I'd have to risk going onto the mainland anyway. I could not stay here forever. I needed to talk to John again. He noticed my uneasiness and gave me something to do.

"Why don't you go out and find the captain? Show him the directed course." I nodded silently, rolling up the chart and making for the door. I walked out and realized the sun was quickly disappearing. I forgot how long the day had been. I scanned the deck, but John was nowhere in sight. I went to his cabin and knocked on the door. I heard heavy footsteps, and the door opened abruptly. He stared down at me, amused.

"Has no one ever told you not to come to the captain's cabin uninvited?"

I rolled my eyes.

"Can I come in?" His expression turned playful.

"What's the occasion?" I wanted to laugh, but I was too eager to ask him about Boston.

"Finn asked me to go over the charted course with you."

He leaned on the doorway, and I was forced to admit to myself just how dangerously charming he was.

"Is that all?" I wasn't sure what it would mean for me to doubt his past words, but I couldn't afford the certainty of asking.

"I need to ask you something."

He had a knowing glare in his eyes, and I hated that he seemed to already know everything I was about to say. Was he a good people reader or was I just always that obvious? He gestured for me to come through, moving to the side with a smirk playing on his lips. This was my second time being here, but seeing it in candlelight felt completely different. Everything took on a beautiful otherworldly glow, and I couldn't help but admire his collection of books and paintings. His bed was surprisingly bare for a showy captain, but he had a velvet armchair in the corner that somehow made up for it. He beckoned me to sit in it, with him sprawling on his bed. Surely he didn't act like this with the rest of his crew. Nevertheless, I obliged, passing the chart to him. He kept it at his side, clearly wanting to hear what I had to say first.

"Finn and I were looking at the course for Spain, and I was noticing how much time this would inevitably take. I just need your word that I'll be back in Boston in half a year or less." He simply stared at me, making me squirm.

"Didn't I already give you my word, love?"

"All you told me was how long this voyage of yours would be. No promise of coming back here was given." He looked as if not a care in the world bothered him, which made me jealous. I wish I could be that carefree.

"Ah. You seem to me like a soul meant for the wonders at sea. But, if you wish to return after our fun in Spain, then who am I to stop you?"

I still felt like everything he said was not to be trusted.

"So you'll provide me passage?"

"You have my word, darling." So then. It was settled. My shoulders loosened a touch after the words were said aloud. Despite everything, I wanted to trust this man. I wanted to have my grand adventure with a promise of home. Anyone else would do the same. These were the things I'd keep reminding myself of at night.

He smiled to himself, probably thinking I had more to say. He then spread out the chart, analyzing the course he would be directing in the morning. He nodded, seeming to like what he saw.

"Was this your work?"

"This was all Finn. I just stated what he already knew."

"You'll be directing soon enough."

He seemed sure of it, and maybe so. Maybe I'd be a world-renowned pirate by the time this year had gone and passed. But then again, I couldn't stick out too much, afraid of changing anything. I hoped I hadn't altered too much already with the little time I'd been here. I just had to be cautious and look for any changes as soon as I came back. I didn't know if I'd even go back at the right time. I could see my past self, or end up several years in the future. Was it a gamble I wanted to take? I didn't know enough about the science behind what had happened. All of that would have to wait, and I hated anything to do with needing patience.

Eventually, I had to force myself out of my thoughts as the room grew silent again. John was humming some tune to himself and getting a bottle of rum from a cabinet. He took a swig and handed it to me. I let myself take one sip, hoping it wasn't laced with anything weird.

"Don't worry. You'll get more of the exotics later."

Whatever that meant. I merely shrugged. It occurred to me I had nowhere to sleep at the moment, and I was always someone who went to bed early.

"One more question: what will be my sleeping arrangements?"

He took a minute to process, and then the look on his face told me I wouldn't like his answer.

"To tell you the truth, love, I don't really trust my men to be sleeping in the same space as you. Think ya might just have to stay in my cabin."

"Where will you sleep?" He scoffed.

"I'm no puritan. We can share a bed and not get all hanky panky. Unless you want to of course." Oh god. I didn't even want to acknowledge that statement.

"Yeah, well, just stick to your side of the bed then."

"It's all my bed, in case you haven't noticed." So much banter, this one.

"Just know I'll have a knife on me at all times, Captain. So, can I have some sleepwear or will I be that much more uncomfortable tonight?"

He leaned off his bed, closer to me, holding my eyes with his.

"Dira, do I make you uncomfortable?" All intentions of replying came to a halt as my cheeks burned.

"I don't trust you." That seemed to allure him even more, and he almost looked like he didn't believe me.

"You don't have to." He stood up, striding his way to the other side of his cabin and opening a drawer.

Continuing to mutter, "You certainly ask for a lot."

He threw a piece of clothing at me, and I caught it clumsily. I held it up, to see it was like a longer version of my shirt. A ruffled linen shirt with long sleeves. I then silently prayed my bra would last half a year without any proper care.

John then turned around. "Well then, don't take too long."

I refused to be shy around this man, so I undressed as quickly as possible. I stared at his back intensely, lest he should be caught peeping. Thankfully, he remained a true gentleman, which was another pleasant surprise. Once the nightshirt was on, I took a glance in the mirror, noting with slight unease that the shirt only reached slightly above my knees. I knew how this century viewed a woman's body, and no man except her husband should be seeing her in this state. However, I had to remind myself I was not a woman of this century, and that in my time this would be considered a summer dress. So I cleared my throat, and John promptly turned to look at me. He was already dressed in a similar shirt, with loose pants. The trousers would've been too big for me, which he clearly saw.

He blew out all the candles, with only moonlight filling the room through the windows. He quickly jumped in bed, patting the space next to him. I thought of how strange every turn of events was since they got me out of the water, and that they probably had barely just gotten started. I made my way closer to the bed, avoiding John's gaze as I got under the covers. As awkward as I felt, I couldn't deny how quickly I was reminded of my tired state. Being in a new place, using the entirety of my social battery, and overthinking had left me not caring that John was there. Before I could help myself my eyelids were drooping, sleep taking me in minutes.

Chapter Fifteen

I felt disoriented. I was in a sleepy haze, trying to figure out where I was. There were too many bright lights around me to notice what was happening. Slowly things came into focus, and what I saw left me wanting to hit somebody. Still in my sleep shirt, I was put in a chair, in what appeared to be a dining room or maybe an interrogation room. I couldn't really tell. What looked like the whole crew had surrounded me, with John and his stupid smug face standing directly across from me. He, fortunately, must've had the chance to get in his proper clothes. The little twat.

"Should I even ask what's going on?"

Someone out of the crowd spoke, "You have to agree with the code!"

I looked around for anyone to give a bit of clarification. I finally landed eyes with Finn, glaring at him.

He finally relented. "Every person recruited into piracy has to read and agree to the code. Formally known as the pirate code." I didn't think it was real. I immediately perked up, eager to get to be a part of such a tradition.

"So, this was made by the Brethren of the Coast?" The same man who spoke earlier and had put me in the brig, Boone, spoke again.

"Course. Who else? Captain's one of the members." I couldn't believe it. I was in the presence of a member of the Brethren. I wanted to jump up and down. This is the type of group I would spend hours in my childhood researching. As I looked at John, he rolled his eyes, becoming impatient.

He put his hands out to quiet the chatter. "All right, all right. Let's let Marco do the honors, shall we?" Everyone sat down, and Marco was left standing.

"Articles of the Code state each member shall receive a portion of goods stolen. Punishment for betraying your crew or the Brethren shall be marooning. Fighting amongst members must be settled by dueling or contest, the nature of which shall be ratified by your captain. No drinking, gambling, or staying up past curfew except when given leave by the captain. Lastly, after serving a given amount of time, any member can announce their intention to retire and be given an appropriate share of the present spoils and dropped off at a port of their choosing." The last rule particularly had me relieved. If John wanted to stay up to code, he had to allow me to retire. Even if it was less than a year.

Marco started again, "I hereby request Adira Fellows to swear by the code, and live by the code." All heads turned to me in anticipation.

"I swear." As I made a pact with the articles, there was newfound respect in the eyes of what was now my crew. I became one of their own.

As we all sat round the table, someone whom I assumed to be the cook came by with several goblets dripping with a liquid that looked like melted honey. Boone pushed one my way, while many others egged me on to take a big gulp. The more I looked at the contents, the more wary I became.

"What's in this drink?"

Marco smiled for the first time that day. "Rum... and gunpowder."

I couldn't help the exasperated smile I wore, because, of course, it was that. In my many historical pirate books from back home, one of them mentioned that mixing gunpowder with rum for smugglers was a sort of rite of passage. It signified sealing your allegiance with someone. I knew drinking this would be a vital step in earning the trust of everyone here. I braced myself, taking a deep breath in and smiling at the buggers all around me.

I threw my head back, the goblet along with it, taking a long hard swig. It burned my throat immediately going down, and I found myself fighting back coughing. Everyone cheered me on, and I took a few more gulps, forcing myself to down the liquid. It made my eyes water and my chest hurt, but it was done. Everyone downed their goblets in solidarity, and a couple of the men started singing God knows what afterward.

I went back to John's cabin, wanting to be by myself for whatever amount of time was allotted to me. I thought about Jason for the first time since the incident and found myself wishing I could tell him about today's events. What would he think of me now? Would he cower in the presence of these people? Would he beg me to not go parading with them for half a year? Or would he look at me in awe? I thought of my sister. How excited she'd be for me, knowing one of my biggest dreams as a child became a reality. My parents would be frightened and tell me to stay far away from them. And, of course, there was Thomas. He would remain a mystery to me, and I thought for sure that he already knew, in a way.

John entered abruptly, striding in and forcing me to give my thoughts a rest. He was changing as he walked, so I averted my eyes to my fingers, playing with the threads of the blanket. When I felt the bed dip I glanced his way. His breath smelled of alcohol as he turned to me, uttering on.

"You seem perfectly well adjusted to the ways of piracy, Ms. Fellows."

So it would seem. "Your kind is rather glorified in my time, Mr. Sterling." He raised his eyebrows, pleased with this new information.

"Oh, do tell."

"You already know how common folk find the life of smugglers fascinating. But in my time, it's a romanticism of days past. Of recognizing your complete freedom and independence. Those two things will appeal to people until the end of time." He turned his body towards me, intent on learning more.

"Surely what we do is not much different from rebels in the future?" I wasn't sure what to tell him. The golden days of his life now would soon fade away, and the world would continue to grow more dark and constrictive.

"In a way perhaps. But never with such style, such presence, and the ability to travel anywhere, anytime. Your kind is unique in that way."

This seemed to leave him in deep thought, and I suppose it would be a little worrying, finding out your way of life would soon lose its vastness and opportunity.

"I suppose we must not dwell on what will one day come to be. People like us, we must focus on the now, on the adventure right in front of us."

They were wise words, and I would not expect them to come from a crude thief. But that was the assumption I made on first arriving, and books will never be completely accurate to real life.

"You're very right about that. And I'm sure you are about to tell me to do just so." He lolled his head, tiredness setting in.

"Yes, well, let us have our fun, Dira. You will have your boring little life back before you know it."

He was right. And the strange reassurance comforted me, even if it was not his intention. With our eyes on the ceiling, both of us full of rum, we fell to sleep.

Chapter Sixteen

The feeling of sunlight on my eyes awakened me, or at least allowed me to squint. Someone was standing in the doorway, and once I noticed their stout frame I knew it was Boone. I grumbled at him, mad that he was letting the light in. But a second later I realized he saw me and John in the same bed. In his bed. Suddenly I was inclined to hide under the covers. Instead, I lay there gaping at him, waiting for Boone to state his intentions.

"Cap'n. You awake?"

The man in question was sleeping like a rock. So naturally I kicked him in the shin - and I immediately regretted it.

His eyes flew open, and, as fast as lightning he was on top of me, a knife pressed to my throat. He was breathing heavily, and I stayed completely still, afraid that in his sleepy haze, he wouldn't know who I was. The steel was close to piercing my skin. But as recognition fled into his face, draining him of aggression, the air felt a lot heavier. He still had one arm pinning my wrist down to the bed, and once I knew my life wasn't being threatened, I was acutely aware that I had a man on top of me. I could feel the heat rising on my face, which of course John noticed, having not taken his eyes off of me. He gave me a wicked smile.

"Good morning, love."

My brain was malfunctioning, despite knowing that Boone was just there, witnessing this turn of events. I finally got my senses back to scoff and push him off me. That left him leaning on the bed, suddenly realizing who else was in the room. But to my dismay, he was not fazed.

"What is it, Boone? How many times do I have to tell you not to barge in here in the mornings? Or anytime, for that matter."

The man seemed to remember why he was there and stood a little straighter.

"There's, uh, a bit of a situation you may want to sort out, Cap'n."

John cursed as he got out of bed, as even I knew Boone was going to be vague until John went out there to get things in order. He clumsily got himself dressed, opting to keep his sleep clothes on under the rest of his garments. Before leaving the room he winked at me, as I stayed in the bed gaping.

After taking a moment to process the never-ending madness that was happening, I got dressed and left the cabin. The first thing I noticed was Finn talking to the helmsman, giving him directions to follow. Then, as I looked a little more to the right, I saw the captain standing with Boone and two other men. My curiosity got the better of me, and I crept a little closer to listen in on their conversation.

"Some of us just think you're getting a bit soft, Captain. There's no reason you should've invited that doll on board."

"Listen, lads. She could become very useful in future operations. Having a woman on board makes it much easier to fool our opponents." They continued to look at each other, not convinced.

"Yes, but what will she do when we have to take over a ship? Sit there and look pretty?" John huffed at them.

"Course not! Come come, do you have no faith in me?" They both were giving him looks of doubt, which told me all I needed to know.

I backed away before they could see me eavesdropping. I hoped that what John had said was not all there was to my situation, that he didn't just invite me on as a pawn. But then again, what other reason was there? It left me feeling used, nothing more than an object. I tried reminding myself that this was nothing more than an adventure, a means to an end. I would be gone in less than a year and of no consequence to them, and vice versa.

I put those thoughts to the side to go join Finn near the wheel, seeing if there was anything on the agenda for me that day. Finn wasn't much of a smiler, and he was not a man of pleasantries. But in his presence was a comfortable silence, with the wind flying through our hair.

"Johnny wants you to have some training under your belt. I suspect that's what you'll be doing today. We have our course mapped out, so no navigation will be needed at the moment."

"I'm sure it's something to do with putting on a show."

Finn turned to me, confused.

"What do you mean by that?" I shrugged.

"Just thinking that the only reason the captain would've thought to bring me into his crew would be to have me work my feminine magic on your foes."

He thought about that for a moment, both of us turning to face the sea and holding onto the railing.

"Perhaps. But you underestimate him. You wouldn't know this, and he certainly doesn't tell this to any of the hands, but Johnny's a good man. He saw a lass that got put into a difficult situation and knew that there could be mutual benefit."

"So, you don't think I'm crazy either? For claiming to travel through time?" He chuckled.

"I think there are many strange things in this world that we do not understand and may never make sense of. This could very well be one of them."

An hour later, amongst the hustle and bustle of every man committed to the inner workings of their vessel, Marco and John stood facing me. Turns out John had already thought about what I would need to be doing while raiding a ship, which was to be right alongside the rest of his crew. That involved knowing the nitty gritty details of being a scoundrel and learning how to be fluid with my motions. Marco was the one to speak first.

"Your first task will be successfully climbing the rigging. You need to do so fast and efficiently. It's a crucial step in getting your sea legs."

He then demonstrated, climbing up the rope like a monkey. After jumping back onto the deck, he gestured for me to mimic the action.

I could already feel the nausea eating at me as soon as I stepped onto the ledge, holding onto the roping with both hands. I was shaky and stiff, and somewhat embarrassed that two experienced sailors were watching me with such intensity. I tried to focus only on the rigging, forgetting everything else. Slowly I lifted one foot ahead of the other, moving my body like clockwork. I was making my way to the mizzenmast topsail, knowing that once I completed my task I would move to the main topsail.

Before I knew it I had it down almost to a science. Albeit I was a little slow despite the two hours of practice, and I was irritated at myself for it. Marco tried reassuring me that most of the men on the ship had been doing this for years and that it was only natural that it would take me a while. But it was no comfort to me. I knew there was more to it than that. I had always been someone who took a minute too long to react, and I was worried that in the moment it would cost me my life. I wasn't fit to be a sailor. It was a sore fact, and dwelling on it made me want to sit in isolation away from prying eyes.

But being amongst pirates left little time to focus too much on emotions. I couldn't tell if John was happy with my progress or not, and I cursed myself for caring about what he thought. It should be of no consequence to me. I told myself it mattered because he could still strand me somewhere, with no way to get home.

Eventually, it was time for lunch, and I learned there was no real designated place to eat. There was a type of freedom on this ship that spoke highly of its captain. Of course, there was still order, but it was clear that trust ran deep here. It was easy to get wrapped up in the contentment of this life. The food wasn't bad; most of it was still fresh from Boston. We ate meat and bread with watered-down rum. I wasn't too sure how much I could drink before it affected my system, which sat at the back of my mind. I ate beside Finn, as his companionable silence suited me. We both leaned on the railing of the deck, our plates in our hands.

John was talking to the helmsman, and he patted the man on the back. I was fascinated with him and his history. I wanted to learn more about him, more about how he ran his ship. He caught me looking, but what's dreadfully horrible about that man is he likes to stare back. His head tilted low, with his dark eyes piercing mine. Under his eyes was almost just as dark, and I couldn't tell if it was old makeup or lack of proper sleep. I eventually looked away, too cowardly to rise to the challenge the captain gave.

The next order of business for the day would be how to use a gun. I found that this may be the most daunting. I was strictly against killing, always had been. I didn't know if I'd be much use to anyone in this department, but to say it aloud in front of John seemed like a mistake. I tried to keep my mouth shut as Marco taught me how to hold a pistol, but it was clear that my hands were shaking. He came back around to face me.

"Adira, you need to realize we don't like firing at people. We do it when we must. This way of life means you kill or get killed. Do you understand that?"

Of course, I knew what Marco was saying.

"You need to understand that I will only be shooting in defense. I refuse to kill. Is that going to be a problem?"

He looked at John, the two of them having a silent conversation.

"You got a lot of nerve."

Thankfully Marco left it at that, as he was the type of man who found it exhausting to argue with people.

We carried on with the rest of the practice and found that my aim was pretty horrible regardless of what my intentions were with a gun. At first, Marco thought I was missing on purpose, but soon found out the truth of the matter. The three of us agreed I was a lost cause in this area. Keeping to schedule, the swords were brought out next.

Chapter Seventeen

The day had gone by long and hard. I practiced swashbuckling, acting, climbing, swinging, and several other activities. I was thoroughly exhausted. My muscles were aching, and I longed for a bath. To my dismay, I was told the crew was only allowed to draw a bath once a week, and there was no privacy out at sea. I would have to be hosed down on the deck, while everyone else waited their turn. It was something I was willing to put off for now.

As nighttime came I got ready for bed. John walked in just a second after I got dressed. I climbed under the covers without a word, feeling melancholy.

"You're becoming quite comfortable sleeping in my bed."

I rolled my eyes at him, not in the mood for his antics.

"Oh sod off, would you?"

He raised his eyebrows at me.

There was no real reason to be frustrated, but I could not shake off a growing sadness within me. I turned myself away from him, huffing as I did so. He said nothing as he blew the candles out. In reality, he was being very patient with me, as he was the captain and I was a new addition to the crew. I had no right to talk to him the way I did, but, for whatever reason, he endured it.

I laid still for several hours and had still not fallen asleep. Eventually, I gave up and tried to get up with as little noise as possible. I padded lightly to the door, grabbing a scarf as I went out. I wrapped it around myself and was thankful to be the only one on deck aside from the watchman for the night. He was up in the crow's nest, which left the whole deck to me. I sat down, cross-legged, looking up at the stars.

I knew the reason for my agitation. I missed home. There was no longer the safety of the lighthouse, of knowing my family was waiting for me if it all became too much. One always talks of the life of an adventurer, but we never mind the things they leave behind. It was setting in that it would be six months before I saw my world. Before knowing what comfort felt like again. What was I thinking of leaving home? I had fallen in love with a rose-tinted way of life. I could not stop the few tears that escaped.

I heard light footsteps before someone had come to lean beside me. It had to be John. I tried my best to let the wind dry my tears instead of adding to them. I was not sure why he was near me right now. Did he not realize I wished to be alone?

"It's home you miss." Was it that obvious?

"How did you know?" We both continued stargazing.

"Happens to all of us, love. Can't be helped." I thought about that for a moment.

"This is different. This isn't my world."

"Do you want it to be?" I looked at him then, not sure where this was going.

"What do you mean?"

"You don't strike me as someone who's lost or finds herself stuck. You seem... fascinated. You could've easily declined my offer of piracy and taken the chance of getting back on your own. But you didn't." He was right. A moment of silence stretched on.

"Why are you helping me?"

He looked away, and if it was a different man I would call it bashfulness. But John was not bashful. I don't think there was a moment in his life that led him to be bashful.

"I saw myself in you. You and I? We're two birds of a feather."

I was too indecisive to be like John Sterling. Too slow, too harsh. I waited for him to continue.

"I know what you long for."

And there were his eyes, directed back at me. I was starting to worry that he knew exactly what I was thinking, at all times.

"And what do I long for?"

In the back of my mind, there was a red light going off. Telling me that this conversation was heading into dangerous territory. But something was pulling me in, and I could not look away.

"For this. I have a feeling that you, my dear, did not fit in your world. You crave what I have."

He leaned in close, his face next to mine. He reached his hand out, directing my attention to the star's reflection in the ocean. It sparkled and shone.

"You want this. You want the wind in your hair, the sea mist all around you. You don't want others telling you how to live."

Everything he said was true. I knew it from the bottom of my soul. And I was scared to know what it meant.

"We're strangers still, but I wish you could tell me what to do."

"You're afraid. Let it go, darling."

"Did you come out here to get me to go back to bed?" He smirked.

"I have more... effective methods if that were so." I shouldn't have asked. I couldn't help the reluctant twitch of my mouth that came.

"I'm sure you have a plethora of women waiting for you somewhere."

"And I'm sure you have some respectable gentleman waiting for you back home, hm?" I decided against entertaining that question.

I eventually followed the captain back to his cabin, and sleep came more easily. When I woke up the following morning, I was pleased to be the first one awake. Both times so far I had been rudely awakened on this ship, and this was a welcome change of pace. I wasn't sure what time it was, but it appeared to be a little gray outside. My attention turned to the sleeping person beside me, and I saw just how much younger John looked while he slept.

He wasn't an old man by any means but seemed to be in his late thirties, possibly early forties. In slumber, I could imagine how he might've looked as a young man when he was my age. It struck me then just how appalled my mother would be knowing I was sleeping next to a man almost twice my age. The thought made me want to laugh, knowing she'd be talking about Jason right about then and how at least he was closer to my age. It felt weird to be thinking about Jason at all. It was probably a good thing that I had broken up with him when I did. I still didn't know if I'd be able to make it back to my time.

It was something that had been plaguing me since I got hoisted up onto this ship. I had to trust John and reevaluate in half a year. Speaking of the devil, he started to stir. I would not hear the end of it if he caught me staring, so I slowly went to sit up and stretch. I heard a sort of growl and caught another urge to laugh.

"I hate mornings. I'd like to skip them altogether." I chuckled then.

"But then there would be no need for coffee." I watched him from the corner of my eye as he got up.

"We will always need coffee, my dear."

As I fetched coffee for Finn and me, I couldn't help but sigh in contentment feeling the sea breeze fill up my lungs. We had been sailing away from Boston the moment I agreed to join the crew. Land could no longer be seen, just the deep blue stretching on for miles in every direction. It was an equally invigorating and terrifying sight.

Finn and I spent the whole day filing records and charts, trying to organize the clutter that the captain had a habit of creating. It made sense he had Finn and Marco with him, as they could pick up the damage that John left in his path. I listened to Finn as he told me stories of John Sterling and all of the crazy scenarios he wound up in. But the more I learned about this man, the more I wondered what sort of pirate he was. He did not seem attracted to vengeance the way most were. There were things Finn wouldn't tell me, either because I was still new to this ship or because John simply didn't want anyone to know.

I hated not knowing things. Perhaps the project of understanding these men would be just as rewarding as all of the treasure and seafaring.

Chapter Eighteen

It had been three weeks since I stepped foot in a different time. I had lived more in those weeks than I had in twenty years. The skills I'd learned, the people I'd met, and the things I'd seen were awe-inspiring. Maybe not to the average person. But to me it was everything. I had started to master prioritizing my thoughts, and, after hours and hours of aggravation, I had come to grow familiar with life at sea.

I thanked my lucky stars I was not one to get seasick. I had guessed that with the speed we were sailing, we had passed St John's. Everyone was still in good spirits, as we had enough fresh amenities for another week. Several members of the crew and I had started to form a type of banter with one another, and I was pleased they accepted my presence.

Of course, there was another thing I had grown a little too comfortable with. Nothing had happened between John and I. Because he was my captain, and I was just passing my time. Not to mention he was insufferable. But sometimes I'd wake up and have my arm draped over his chest, and I would feel a comfort like no other. I knew what it was. I just felt safe with a man next to me. It was the security I was feeling.

But sometimes I wondered if John viewed it that way. Sometimes I would tell stories to the men, and he'd be standing or leaning on something with a look of something akin to longing. There was another occurrence, after one of our daily sword fights, where he told me well done. He gazed at me with pride.

There were many things about the man that had me wanting to pull my hair out. He was a ruthless flirt. Any woman who breathed seemed to be susceptible to his ways, and, even worse, he knew it. It didn't matter if they stuck around; he liked winning the game. He came by it honestly. And then there was his attitude. The fishmonger went about his life without thinking of the consequences, without a thought of anxiety in his head. It was maddening.

What I needed was another woman on board. I wanted another sensible person to talk to and to have at my side. But as I had little say in who the captain invited, I settled for Finn. He quickly became my confidante, as his disposition was comforting to me. We would spend hours in the gallery, and one day I told him about Jason.

"He does not know how to woo a woman." I laughed, his thick Scottish accent making the sentence that much better.

"No, he doesn't. But I find myself still plagued with thoughts of him." I was searching for advice, and he knew it.

"Why you wasted your time on him I'll never know, but perhaps it's too late."

"Too late for what?"

"What I mean to say is maybe you're already in love with him." Everyone back home seemed to think so.

"Oh, God. There wasn't enough time for that!"

"Yes, but you say you knew him most of your life. You can love someone and not be committed to them yet." He continued.

"Mind you, if that's what's happening here, let it be known I think he's a fool."

I laughed, wondering not for the first time what Finn would do if he ever met Jason. All of these thoughts about Jason made me wonder if I was just lonely. I was always a hopeless romantic, but only recently had I started to want romance in my life. I loved watching other people fall in love, content to dream myself up as some grand adventuress.

Eventually, our conversations moved to the weather, as it was always a constant worry. That morning we had a reason for it, as we woke up to a sky that was angry crimson. Our talking thus far was in an effort to avoid dread. The saying "red sky at night sailors delight, red sky in the morning sailors take warning" has stuck with me since I was a child. It was an ancient rhyme that I remembered seeing a variation of in the Bible. Every mariner had heard it one way or another, so we all knew what kind of trouble we were in. I was never scared of the idea of storms until that day when the difference was that we would all be swept up in them. A storm could quickly turn into a life-or-death situation out at sea.

"Batten down the hatches!"

John bellowed out to the hands, with a following order to put on the storm sails to prevent us from having to furl the sails. This was a tricky bet, as messing with the sails meant less time to try and outrun the storm. The ship was light in cargo, which put us at a bigger disadvantage, both of these meaning we would end up having to turn into whatever storm approached us and sail at an angle. The helmsman, Rayner, was a strong man who did not take his job lightly, and his stony features gave away no fear for the task at hand.

The fact was that more pirates died from the sea itself than from any man. The only thing we had going for us was that we were sailing further into the middle of the North Atlantic. What everyone feared the most was a hurricane. Unfortunately, this was the season for it. We watched as the clouds darkened with each passing hour, like sitting ducks. I briefly wondered if it would be storming back in Boston if something would travel through time again. I wasn't sure how quickly storms progressed in these circumstances.

No one had eaten thus far, with too much to prepare for and get done. John had me check the crow's nest to see how far out I could see the darkness. I took my telescope and made my way up. I moved about the roping with ease now, but that did nothing to calm my nerves. Already feeling the wind pick up, I looked out into the distance. To my dismay, thunder could be heard, but I kept hoping we were still too far north to be considered in danger.

But the heat was intense. There was nothing to deny there. There seemed to be clouds for miles, as I suspected. I told the captain of the news, and he let his head hang upwards to the sky. It was a look more of an annoyance than true worry. Even in dire situations, John doesn't feign worry. I noticed the men on the masts sway as the wind blew against them. Marco was spent worrying enough for both himself and John as he pestered the crew to move quickly with their activities. There was no point in reassurances, as only time would tell what the ocean had in store for us. The ship creaked with every wave then.

An hour later the wind had picked up significantly. The only sounds to be heard were a mixture of howling and thunder. John and Marco continued delegating, and soon we were all made to bring out any rope we could find. I asked John if he'd ever been in a hurricane before.

"Aye. The first one was when I was under someone else's crew, starting to make a name for myself. A lot of men died that day, getting flown overboard. The captain was careless." He knew what I was thinking. That I had thought him to be just as careless. Wasn't he?

"There's no sense in being serious all the time, but that doesn't mean I'm senseless." Guilt came to the surface, and I scolded myself for assuming.

"I didn't assume anything. I still don't trust you, John." I regretted the words as soon as I said them. He looked at me with a hurt expression. It was only there for a moment, replaced with a mask. He came closer.

"And what don't you trust about me?"

I wasn't sure what game we were playing.

"Why does Finn hide stuff about you? What do you not want me to know?" He scoffed.

"You think you need to know everything about me just because you're on this ship?"

"I think you're hiding something. Or maybe you aren't who you say you are."

It took me a while to trust anyone, even if I had every reason to believe in them. Finn had told me from the beginning he was a good man. They had all but proved they were pirates. But I couldn't help but think there was a more sinister reason they took me on. It was a horrible thing to accuse John of, but he should be used to it. He started pacing around me.

Eventually, he stopped in front of me again, pulling his sleeve up. I saw a canvas of scars. Thrashes, brandings, and grazes. I didn't know why he was showing me this. I wanted to look away, not think about the pain he must've been in or how he got all of these scars. Then he moved to pull at his shirt, showing me his chest and shoulder. It was scattered with bullet wounds and gashes. I looked at his face, his stony expression.

"Believe me, you don't want to hear every story. I'm a pirate, Adira. This isn't some fairytale."

He left me standing there, feeling ashamed.

Chapter Nineteen

The storm sails were secured, and it was then decided that part of the crew should go down to stay with the cargo. We were trying everything we could to have the outcome be in our favor. It was probably sometime after three in the afternoon, but it was hard to tell with how dark it was around us. Everyone was almost certain we were in for a hurricane, which was just my luck. I went around trying to be useful, tying everyone down with rope.

Those of us with more gumption decided to hold our own rope, which ended up being Marco, John, Finn, and me. We debated tying Rayner to the wheel but opted against it since he would need a full range of motion. As time passed, the wind started to sound like a train that never ended up passing you. Rayner continued to sail with the storm, his hands gripping the wheel so hard his knuckles were white.

Despite the size of the ship, we were being tossed from side to side. It felt like we were on a roller coaster, but crashing down was not as thrilling. Water continued to dump onto the decks, and if it got any worse we would have to bring men out from the cargo to get buckets out and start dispersing. There was no screaming like I thought there'd be, but plenty of loud grumbles and yelling. The waves continued to get higher and higher around us, and there was very little control we had over the vessel.

As we dropped from another towering wave, water came surging down on us and filling our lungs. I was disoriented, trying to cough it back out and fight my blurry vision. The men with buckets finally came running out, but amongst the chaos, I realized with horror that Rayner wasn't at the helm. I could hear Marco somewhere close to me yelling his name. He couldn't be seen amidst the spraying mist and threatening waves. I could no longer cling to my rope and do nothing. I let myself free and leaped to action, while I could make out John calling for me.

I raced across the helm and to the front of the ship, trying to search out Rayner. John continued to yell at me, beckoning me back to the mast. The ground started to tip, and I tried to grab at whatever I could, which ended up being the wheel. The galleon immediately started falling to the side into the water, and, with my heart racing, I tried climbing the wheel the other way around. Once the wave made its way back down, the ship finally started to stand upright, and if I didn't feel like I was having a heart attack I probably would've laughed in triumph.

I continued trying to steer us at an angle, as I assumed Rayner had gone overboard and I could do nothing for him. He would be mourned for later when the rest of the crew was out of danger. I jerked my arms too hard, and the ship started screaming in protest. I heard yells towards the left side of the ship, seeing Paul, the cooper on deck, being flung overboard. Marco and Finn were staggering across the boat, grabbing ropes and throwing them into the sea. John's pleas could be heard again, and I chanced a glance behind me to see him scrambling up to where I stood. He leaped the last bit of distance, his arms flying to my waist and yanking me away from the wheel.

"What are you doing?!" It came out like a growl.

"What does it look like??"

We were staring daggers at one another, with his back against the wheel and both arms still holding me in place.

"Go back to your post. Now!"

I jerked at his grasp, staggering back to the mast. As I tied myself back, a little tighter than necessary, I could feel Finn's eyes on me. But the one wonderful thing about being in a dire situation is not having to address people's concerns during the occasion. John steered the wheel the way he does everything else. In a nonconventional way that ends up working.

Soon enough we were successfully sailing at an angle with the storm and could finally entertain the possibility of living. It was almost fun to sway this way and that and to ride with the waves once you didn't see people flying about.

Eventually, we started to reach the outskirts of the storm and began untying the men to start assessing any immediate damage. John kept his eyes ahead, any trace of annoyance or playfulness gone. I went to check if the anchor was still held up because if that dropped we were all as good as dead. As I was securing the anchor, I saw something flash by in the water underneath me. At first, I thought it was a reflection of something, but then I saw it again a little further out. I kept an eye out, but nothing more was to be seen.

Shaking off the weird occurrence, I climbed back up on board. We all waited out the rest of the storm with silence, antsy to be back in calm waters. It was a quick and violent thing, happening so fast you barely knew what was going on. Once the worst had passed, reality set in. We lost Rayner. Others too. I didn't even know their names. There were over a hundred souls on board, and it was tricky to remember everyone when I didn't work with them all.

But they were a part of the crew. We were a team. And lives were lost. I had never been in an event where death became involved. There's no way to prepare for that. No books to read to make yourself okay with it. It left us all sobered, and, for me, it was a traumatic event that wouldn't be the last. Everyone here was familiar with it, but I had to digest it.

We wasted no time getting a ceremony of sorts ready. This was a life of fast progression; you had to say goodbyes all the time. John got out Marco's prayer book, and we all stood together at the end of the day. The sun was just starting to set as John began his speech. I tried offering relief to those who needed it with words of encouragement. But it does little when you've been in misery and danger for however brief the time.

We had been able to carry on in the midst of a storm. That could not be denied. It was what we had to focus on instead of the loss. There was a prominent sense of fatigue all around as everyone settled down with the last and only meal for the day. It was the same we had been having: cured and salted meat. Today the cook decided to put a little lemon juice from a vial into our watered-down rum to fight off scurvy. It added a punch, but a welcome one after what happened.

After downing the rest of the rum, I decided to go find Finn and ask him about The Look he gave me during the storm. I found him in the gallery, trying to recover whatever charts and maps he could. Some of them were sopping wet and would have to be dried in the sun the next day. He heard me come in; I could tell from the way his shoulders raised a fraction. As always, he said nothing upon my entrance.

"So...." I'd have to try and drag it out of him.

"Yes?" He continued his work, not looking up. Typical Finn behavior, I was coming to find.

"What was that look about?" He glanced my way for a second, which was the best I was going to get with him.

"What look?"

"Oh, y'know. The one you were giving me when the captain chewed me out." He rolled his eyes.

"Johnny did not chew you out, Adira. And I'm surprised ye worried about me eyes when we were in the middle of a freak storm." Avoiding the question, I see.

"Yes, well, I'm a multitasker. So I ask again, what were you thinking?" He turned to fully look at me then.

"Do you have to know our feelings at all times now? Every one of us?" Ah. John must've talked to him.

"No. Just the ones directed at me."

"I'm sure you'll find out soon enough, lass."

So he wasn't going to tell me. I let out a sigh and left him to his work. It was almost time to turn in for the night. John was still at the wheel, so I decided to go ahead and change into my sleepwear for the night.

I went to light all the candles in the captain's cabin, letting in that soft glow I had started to become accustomed to. I heard the door open and shut and turned to look at John. He was tired and worn out. He looked as if at any moment he would breathe fire like a dragon. I wondered if I should even ask what I did wrong today. I wasn't sure why I wasn't allowed to try and help in a crisis like I tried to do. He stood in front of the bed, facing away from me.

"John-"

"Get out."

"What?"

"I said get out." This wasn't about needing to change. Did he need time to himself?

"I don't-"

"Get the hell out!" Up until now, I didn't think John would raise his voice at me without being in a dangerous situation. I was stunned and tried mustering up the feeling in my legs to walk out. I didn't know what to say. I wanted to ask him why, but I didn't know what it was he was thinking. I didn't want more of his anger to be directed towards me.

I walked out, wanting to cry. I hated how vulnerable I was to people's emotions, that even then one flip of a switch and I was at someone's mercy. I tried pacing back and forth on the deck, but I was beat. I needed sleep. I thought about sleeping close to Finn but knew he probably wouldn't have much to say. It would be awkward silence that night.

I would have to sleep downstairs and choose a hammock from one of the dead. It was a morbid thought that I didn't want to ruminate on, and walking in made me burn with shame. Who knew what the crew was thinking right then? I treaded silently with my head down, like a kicked puppy. I was so confused. That's all I could think about. Was I being too pushy? Too demanding? Maybe John and Finn were right.

I didn't need to know everything. I was trying to pry on lives that had been through hell. Why would they want to tell me about their past? They had harder lives there than anyone in the modern world. It was a culture shock. Something I should've respected. But instead, I was trying to force connections, force them to like me so that I could get my way. I was wrong about it. In the morning I would need to apologize, to swear to do better. Until then I had to lay in a hammock while all of the men stared at me and whispered rumors.

Chapter Twenty

I got next to no sleep, feeling groggy and sore. I thought about my actions the whole night long. Although I did manage to be down there all night without being attacked or touched, which either meant the men had come to respect me or John had been over-cautious. I didn't think about that long before getting up, as I was in a state of restlessness.

I first went to help wash things with the cook, Darien. There were a lot of things that we had forgotten to tie down the day before, which resulted in a lot of spillage and chaos. Darien complained the whole time about how this dropped our food supply by about fourteen percent and asked if I knew that the captain still owed him from their last loot. Of course, I didn't know, which resulted in a thirty-minute conversation about how he thought the ship should be run. After everything was a little more organized, I made my exit, not wanting to give him any reason for me to be his next gossiping chip.

There was still time to kill, so I went to check out the gun ports and see how the hands and powder monkeys were faring. That's when I learned that the real reason pirates looked so cool with all of their earrings was just so they could hang wax from them, to stop themselves from going deaf after firing the cannons (or as an insurance policy to have a proper burial). I found that more amusing than I probably should've and didn't end up helping them with any of their duties. I finally decided to head upstairs.

Upon being met with a sunny and clear sky, I saw John talking to Finn. I wanted to get this anxiety out of the way, so I walked over right at the end of their conversation, and both turned toward me. John would still not look me in the eyes. But he did speak to me, which was better than nothing.

"I've chosen Finn to be our new helmsman. He seems to be the right fit for it." Finn said nothing, simply observing the captain and me. John continued.

"Which makes you our only navigator."

It didn't worry me too much, as I knew Finn would be there to help if I needed it. I merely nodded, wanting to ask him something else.

"Can I... may we speak in private, Captain?"

He looked towards the ocean, maybe silently asking for its advice.

"Very well, Ms. Fellows." He headed towards the gallery instead of his cabin, and I tried not to think anything of it.

As I shut the door behind me, an uncomfortable tension filled the room. He finally looked at me, still with tired eyes. I had to apologize.

"I'm sorry, John. For my foolishness. My world is different from yours, this you know. But perhaps I didn't try to understand what that meant for me."

He stayed silent, which only made my worry grow.

"Everyone back home talks freely of their life, of all of their shortcomings and tragedy. I forget it's different here." I just wanted him to understand.

"That's not what bothers me. Anyone in their right mind would be weary of us. I knew it would be hard for you to let go. To stay here, without precaution." I felt a weight lift off my chest, and I could finally breathe. But then....

"Then what have I done? Did I break any of our agreements?" He shook his head.

"You put my crew in danger. And what's more, you put yourself in danger. You had no idea what you were doing. I can't have that happen again. Honestly darling, you're lucky you aren't swimming with the fishes right about now."

I tried to stifle my anger that threatened to spread, hoping this wouldn't be another man trying to tell me how to live.

"I only did what you would've done."

He shook his head.

"Difference here is I've been on these waters longer than I've been on land. I know how to steer a ship. Even when I don't know what I'm doing, I know the technicalities."

He started to pace, his mind buzzing.

"Also, truth is, dearie, you don't know much at all about me. Nothing more than the stories going around my crew."

I knew then that the first thing I'd be doing when I got back home was looking John up. I wanted to be the one with all the information, should I ever be in this situation again.

"Perhaps you're right. But what will you have me do when we're fighting other men and trying to take over a ship?"

"No no, I know what you can do. We've trained you well, but this wasn't something we prepared you for. I believe you are easily worth five men. It's the circumstances none of us can control. You have not dealt with the likes of nature that we have. You have not seen what those waters contain."

Any trace of anger that was in me went away like a puff of smoke. There was something John Sterling feared more than man. Something out there he knew he would not be able to come away from. I thought back to the glint that caught my eye during the storm. He didn't wish to control me, or even keep me from all harm. He wanted me to realize there were things no one could come back from. And I could respect that. But I was curious.

"What's out there, John?"

"I wasn't joking that first day you came on my ship. Most myths you hear or read are there for a reason. People don't just pull that stuff out of thin air."

I made a move to sit down, contemplating our conversation. I was relieved that John wasn't mad, but scared. It was a vulnerability he would never say out loud.

"You make the world sound like such a foreign place, Captain."

He sat down across from me.

"You have no idea, love. But in time, perhaps." I still had something to get across to him.

"I'm not some fragile being, I want to make that clear."

"I know, darling. Inexperienced, yes. But there's something about you...."

"Let me guess, not like other women?"

"Aye."

I wasn't sure if we were about to start flirting or if he was trying to tell me I was weird. Before finding out, I made the excuse of needing to dry the maps in the sun and made a brisk walk back up to the deck. I set up a table a couple of feet away from Finn, in case I got bored and wanted to bother him.

He looked natural at the wheel, with an easily stoic stature. With matters resolved and being back en route, things started to look up. I started to hear thuds below my feet and voices raising. I looked around me and noticed the lack of crew members above deck. John had retreated to his cabin, which left only about three men up there. No one was doing their job, which meant I didn't have to either.

I walked away from my table cautiously, making my way back downstairs. What I saw was truly a sight to behold. Everyone was dancing around a shantyman, in this case, Harry, one of the hands. They were all stomping their feet and cheering each other on. I recognized the tune as 'Hanging Johnny,' which was ironic considering the name of their captain. Their laughter and joy were infectious, and I found myself jigging right along with them as we all took turns drinking. There was a pride to be taken in being alive for another day, making a perfect excuse to celebrate. It was one of the things I admired about this age of piracy.

They lived with a ferocious spirit and carried on every day as if it were their last. After all, why should we deprive ourselves? Why should we go on with false pretenses? I realized that in a way, I looked up to these people. I wanted to carry on living the way they had. It made me think how joyous it would be to live out the rest of my days like this - as a pirate. So I sang loud, not caring who heard it or how horrible it sounded. Because I was not alone!

There was acceptance there. We were all filthy and strange-looking, but we were happy. Being there as I was, there wasn't time to worry and fret forever. Everything pointed forward. I wondered then if pirates were ever the enemy. They gave better lives to soldiers and stole mostly from the rich and corrupted. As I danced I tried to imprint this memory in my mind forever.

Triumph after disaster.

I came out staggering onto the deck as the moon hung high in the sky, with a full belly and a warm heart. My worries over the future were pushed to the back of my mind. I twirled absentmindedly for some time while the stars made their presence known. Things felt very grand and splendid after Harry had passed around his stash of whiskey. I was in that sort of bliss that one comes into knowing you are not being judged. And the alcohol helped too.

I walked over to one of the open barrels that someone had forgotten to close with fresh water. I noticed the moon's reflection calling at me, beckoning me to stretch my hand out. It could not be ignored, and, as my hand submerged in the water, I felt peace. There was a connection forming that could hardly be explained, only felt. As I relished in the calm, John came within my field of vision, leaning on another barrel.

"You're not contaminating the drinking water, are you love?"

My head lazily turned to him, as I was always on the cuff between irritation and amusement with him.

"Now where would be the fun in that?"

I finally retracted my hand from the barrel, putting its lid back where it belonged. John looked at me peculiarly.

"Your skin seems to shine in the water doesn't it?"

I looked at my arm, and, sure enough, I had a healthy glow, almost glistening.

"Can't say the same about yours, Captain."

His curiosity was hidden then with a new bout of playfulness. He wasn't quite so laid back as usual. I suspected he was still processing Rayner's death, along with my own actions.

"Still catch you staring, Dira dear."

I blamed the alcohol for leaning closer, our noses almost touching. I could smell the rum from his lips, with a musk of salt air and sandalwood.

"Do you know what I think?" I had entranced him, and I relished in the fact.

"Hmm?" The shadow of a smile could not be helped.

"I think you are a better man than you let people believe." He had started to twitch his hand, I noticed.

"I'm a rotten scoundrel, darling."

"I believe you are drawn to doing good. You crave it. You want to be admired."

His hand had started to gravitate towards my neck, close to my face. It was like we were in the same orbit. He traced the corner of my jaw, absentmindedly, his fingertips barely touching my skin. I wanted to be closer still, and, as we both moved to close the small space that was left, a splash in the water below caught our attention. We jumped and the moment was gone as we each fled to the railing to see what we had just heard.

Chapter Twenty-One

As we peered over into the ocean, there it was again. The silvery substance started to take form as it came up to the surface. I looked at John, unsure if I was seeing things that weren't there. But from what I could tell, he only seemed annoyed that our conversation had been interrupted.

"It appears we have company."

A head emerged from the water with silky black hair and skin that glistened, pearl-like. I thought about the way my skin shimmered just moments before and wondered if this was a regular occurrence in these times or if I should chalk it all up to being tipsy.

Just moments later, two more heads came up, all of them similar to the other. John was looking at them much the same way I looked at him. With amusement and annoyance.

"What can I help you ladies with?" The captain asked, dripping with sarcasm.

They didn't answer, instead peering at me with a look of wonder. It made my skin crawl and the hairs on the back of my neck stand up. They turned their heads to the side in unison, like a confused animal. But that's when I noticed I was doing the same. We stood in a trance like that for some time, completely forgetting the captain next to me.

One of them, with eyes that shone like the stars in the sky, raised her hand out to me - an invitation. John made his presence known again, clearly not understanding their intentions.

"And what do you want with her?"

As she opened her mouth and uttered one word, her voice was slow and melodic, smooth and ethereal.

"Come."

Something in me wanted to obey her, to get rid of these clothes and follow them, down to the depths of the sea. Before anything else could happen, John took the initiative to respond.

"Sorry mates, no can do m'afraid." They shot daggers at him, and I wanted to laugh seeing someone else besides me be the one to do it.

"We do not require your presence."

Once the words were said, we heard footsteps from below coming up. Probably one of the watch guards for the night. They didn't want an audience, as once they heard the man they splashed back into the water, scurrying deeper and deeper before their silver tails could no longer be seen. I turned around, annoyed at the meeting cut short, to see Boone as clueless as ever. He waved at the captain and me, while I sighed and turned back around.

"Wonder what all that was about." Yes, so did I.

"So those were... mermaids?"

"In the flesh. Or uh, scales."

My first official sighting! So Thomas was right.

"How often do you see them?" I had so many questions.

"Every now and then. Horrible gossips, they are."

I couldn't believe he was being so relaxed about it, as if it was the norm.

"What do you know about them?"

"Well, there are different kinds, o'course. Some are more nasty than others. But 'round here they usually just like to mess around and tell tales. Similar to us, I s'pose."

I contemplated that, curious to know what they did with their time. What did they like to eat? Were there mermen? Could they talk to other sea creatures? As if reading my mind, the captain relented.

"They don't tell you too much about themselves. They like being mysterious and all."

I suppose I would too if I was as sought after as they were. Then I remembered how late it was, and I'd be feeling it the next day if I prolonged sleep too much longer. I made my way to the stairs when the captain called out.

"Are they treating you well down there? You can come keep my bed warm if not."

I stopped in my tracks, smirking to myself. I knew then that the crew probably wouldn't harm me if I spent more nights with them. I wanted to tell him otherwise, just to have a proper bed and a warm body to sleep next to. But then I thought of my shipmates and the fact that if I continued to sleep in the captain's quarters, they would think John was showing me special favor.

"As appealing as that sounds, I think we have a sort of understanding," I told him.

If I didn't know any better I could've sworn I saw disappointment on his face before he drew up one corner of his mouth.

"'Spose you can hold your own, then."

I gave him one last smile before we went our separate ways.

The next morning I woke up with a severe wave of nausea and a pounding headache. Everything felt too bright and my mouth was as dry as cotton. I saw

John coming down the stairs and standing next to me, looking down with fake pity.

"Finally decided to wake up, did we?"

I felt like throwing up.

"Shut up, would you?"

And right then and there, it all came flooding back. I had thought about kissing John Sterling. I was this close to actually doing it. I groaned, feeling very foolish. I had dreamt of mermaids last night after my encounter, completely forgetting that I had made an idiot of myself. But John didn't say anything about it, which hopefully meant he was just as loopy as I had been (he often was), and, despite being irritated with me, probably encouraged the behavior. I decided I didn't like being drunk. I liked the burning sensation of rum and appreciated the newfound necessity of it, but the feeling that followed after too many guzzles was not something I felt like repeating. I was brought up to believe drunkenness was a sin, and, after last night, perhaps I still believed such thoughts.

John, on the other hand, was almost always drunk on something. Or maybe that was just his personality. He walked about, grabbing certain things and stashing them in one of his belts. I lay there worried that any sudden movements would be the end of me. But then there was that wonderful substance brought right under my nose, my savior.

"Drink up, love."

I downed the coffee with vigor, no doubt getting some all over my chin and nightshirt. I left the mug on the nightstand and waited. John stared at me with that stupefied grin on his face that was insufferable to look at. I threw the covers off of me and stood up slowly. No time could be spared afterward when all of a sudden, I heard that same grating voice.

"CAPTAIN!"

There were about five seconds to spare before Boone came tumbling down, much like the last time weeks before. I squinted at him, having a hard time not wanting to murder the blurry blob.

"For God's sake! What?!"

He was panting, and I decided I wanted to be sitting down for this.

"We have another problem!"

We all watched in anticipation as the captain looked through his telescope and we waited for confirmation. He then retracted the device, putting it in a pocket on his person.

"Don't worry lads! We'll sort this out!"

Marco looked at him skeptically before voicing his concerns.

"John. We don't have time to sort this out. We're being followed!"

Marco was speaking for all of us.

"Yes yes, I can see that, thank you. But I have a plan."

The crew was silent, waiting for our captain to divulge this so-called plan. Seeing as how no one was speaking yet, Finn spoke out.

"Go on then!"

Being put on the spot, John paced back and forth. We all watched, and I took note of someone in the back (probably Darien) passing a flask to the person next to him wordlessly. Then they proceeded to pass it back and forth, taking swigs silently as we waited for direction.

The captain turned back around with an aha moment etched across his face.

"We'll take over their ship."

Darien decided to speak up.

"How're we supposed to do that?"

Then Marco moved to step in before any more meaningless statements could be said.

"We could easily take down a sloop of war. They wouldn't stand a chance. But there's a slight problem. The moment we do so we'll be biding our time. Once those men don't report when they're supposed to, the Navy will just send out another ship."

He had a point. I looked at Finn as he put in his two cents.

"Therein lies another problem. Once that's done they'll likely send out two ships as a precaution. And a galleon has no chance in outrunning more agile vessels."

Each passing moment that went by left John more fidgety and deep in thought. Boone spoke up next.

"So what yer sayin' is, we're doomed either way?"

Marco shrugged, and Finn nodded. The captain chose then to elaborate.

"We all knew when we stole this ship it wouldn't be forever. We're not trying to be like Blackbeard. We're trying to stay hidden. So here's what we do. We'll trap them in the line of fire. Once they realize we won't be giving in, they'll surrender pretty quickly. They know how many guns a Spanish galleon has. Then we steal their ship, giving us the speed we need to outrun whomever the Navy sends out next. They won't be able to follow us for long I suspect, considering where we're heading."

It was settled then. We would fire at the sloop until they surrendered and use the galleon as a distraction for the next group the Navy sent out. Any men we found would be given the option to join the crew, and the rest would be marooned on a small island close to Spain.

We were all given orders to prepare for an attack, and many were made to play the waiting game on deck. We needed to be ready for anything. I could hear the master gunner and the powder monkeys yelling and running around beneath my feet, along with Marco telling everyone to grab their weapons. John came up next to me, gesturing to follow him to his cabin. As we entered, he opened a trunk by his desk, revealing various shining swords.

"Go on, then. Take your pick!"

I felt like a kid in a candy store, being told I could get whatever I wanted. As I assessed each one, I noticed John standing in front of his mirror, putting on his tricorn hat and picking up a small glass pot. I observed him for a while as he reached for a small brush and opened the lid of the pot. Ah, kohl.

There was something alluring about a man putting on makeup. I normally wasn't attracted to it at all in my time, but the way John was smudging it around his eyes and putting on more jewelry was strangely captivating. I had been caught staring, as I could see the glint of his gold teeth as he smirked.

"Would you like some, Ms. Fellows?"

I wordlessly came up to him as he passed me the pot. I wore eyeliner nearly every day back home, as I enjoyed the intensity it brought to my eyes.

"Do you apply this every day?"

"When I remember to. It helps protect the eyes from the sun. But I confess I think it adds to my charm."

"More like scares people away." His eyes twinkled.

"That too."

As I tried applying it like any other eyeliner, John seemed dissatisfied. He took the product from my hands and held out one hand under my chin to steady my face. He used the other to smoke out the kohl under my eyes and had me look up to apply some in my waterline. He reached a point he seemed happy with and turned back around to the mirror.

I looked absolutely wicked. But with my finally tanned skin and sun-kissed hair, I could not look away from my new persona. I felt like a whole different person. And there was John behind me, looking at me through the mirror.

"I think you're ready now, love."

We went out after choosing my cutlass and prepared to live up to our legacy. Whether I liked it or not, I was turning into him, a bonafide pirate.

Chapter Twenty-Two

As the sloop approached us, they started to raise flags. I was in charge of keeping an eye on their actions with a telescope, so I signaled John to come by. I silently thanked Thomas for teaching me flag signals for this exact moment. I watched through the glass as they rose an L.

"They want us to stop." The captain chuckled.

"I thought as much. Boone! Tell them we require assistance!"

Boone raised the Victor flag, setting our trap in motion. I watched as they responded with a P - a confirmation of sorts. John looked smug already as they continued our way. This seemed too good to be true, but I was just as anxious to see the plan in action.

As they were within range, both ships were at a standstill. Each was just as curious as to who would make the first move. The captain decided we should initiate, so Boone flew up a W, signaling we needed medical assistance. As John and I watched through our telescopes, we saw the lieutenant talking to his captain. They were skeptical. We watched them put up a one-flag signal. They were asking if it was urgent or common. Boone replied urgent, and we drew our glasses up again. They were still hesitant. We had not raised our Jolly Roger for obvious reasons and knew what their next question would be.

Right on time, we heard the master gunner yell fire, and a cannon to the right of our ship fired toward the sloop, puncturing the lower whale. Cries of victory could be heard from the powder monkeys, and we watched with concealed glee as the naval officers scurried around their deck. The next words uttered by our captain filled my body with a fresh wave of adrenaline.

"NOW!"

Everyone surrounding me threw their grappling guns toward the sloop and hooked on. Once the line was secured we pulled with all our might. The captain was behind us, encouraging us. The goal was to get the sloop as close as possible to ours.

"Heave, men!"

Once the distance wouldn't leave anyone dead trying to pass from ship to ship, we all clambered over onto enemy grounds. Thankfully the officers were resigned to their outcome. It was over before it had even begun. Some of them even looked happy to see us, perhaps looking forward to resigning as servants of the Navy. John swaggered onto the deck, already having spotted their captain. He strutted over to him, feigning patience. The captain drew out his sword, handing it to him with a face full of disgust.

"Bloody pirate."

John winked. "One of the best, mate."

Boone went to tie the captain's hands, as John faced the officers.

"Alright, lads. Here's how this is going to go. You can either join our crew of misfits or get dropped off at the nearest foreign island. The choice is yours."

Two distinct groups were made, as Finn and I watched the officers make their decision. The majority of them joined our ranks with little hesitation, which had John beaming like a fool. The rest we sent to the brig, along with their captain, where they would be getting reduced rations. The ex-officers were happy to show us where their provisions were as we brought all of our valuables from the galleon onto the sloop.

The transition was fairly quick, and I was amazed at how easy it was. We were extremely lucky that the Navy sent out a smaller vessel based on a hunch. There was little profit to be made, but the crisis was averted. Finn took to the new wheel and we immediately set course. There was no time to lose. As the galleon started to get smaller from a distance, the hands got to work. They immediately started the repairs on the lower whale, singing as they did so. Darien was released from his duties as the cook, as John took one look at the former Navy's cook and saw much more potential. Darien seemed to be relieved by this thankfully, and under Marco's direction helped the other hands in giving the exterior of the ship a paint job.

As dusk approached, most of the labor had been followed through. I was fascinated with the new charts to add to our previous collection and had started a filing process I was quite proud of. Little pleased me more than a renewed method of organization. My main job from here would be to follow the stars, and it just got a lot easier. They had in possession a planisphere, which had been in use for two hundred years at this point. It was easier than deciphering the constellations with only the aid of your mind and made me feel like a proper astronomer without all the extra work.

It looked like John would be taking a renewed interest in having me next to him during the night, as the down-size of our ship meant cramped sleeping quarters for the men. There were also new men on our crew that the captain would have to test for loyalty down the road. He had told me as much while I was hauling out all of our constellation charts. I accepted my fate fairly easily, already used to sleeping with him, however wrong that sounded.

"Will you miss me once you're all alone again in your lighthouse?"

He had said it in jest I'm sure, but it had reminded me that I would be alone again. I found I would miss the company I had there. Even if it involved putting up with John's antics.

"I'll miss the freedom to be whatever I desire. But I could do without you, Captain."

He grinned at me, and I felt my heart swell up. I couldn't recall feeling that before with something so small. Once I realized my reaction, fear followed. To become attached to him, of all men, would be wrong. For so many reasons.

We had both gone to what would be the new captain's quarters and started putting everything in its own place. John was humming a tune to himself while I listened in silence. My previous thoughts had spooked me into an awkward tension around him again. I had found some pieces of silk that were probably used to repair clothing after a battle, kept for the captain and anyone of importance on board. I decided it would look fascinating braided into my hair and started with small strands to create a gypsy-like style. John had a couple of rings in his hair that probably hadn't been taken out for some time. It suited him, and I found myself envious.

As I finished with my hair, I saw John staring with that smug look of his. I felt antsy under his gaze, wanting to hide away to stop the heat rising to my face.

"What now, John?" He tilted his head.

"Jus' thinking that I can't see you as anything other than a pirate."

His words thrilled me, and I felt pride for myself in a way I hadn't known. We stood there for a while longer, as a mischievous smile graced my lips that could not be helped. It felt so out of character for my personality, but the more time I spent with John, the more my personality seemed to evolve into something else entirely. It was in me all along I believe, but that strange part of my soul that had been kept under lock and key had then thrown caution to the wind, coming out to play as it desired.

John took one of the gold rings out of his hair, and then wordlessly secured it into one of my small braids. I felt like I could hardly breathe as he looked at me.

"Now that's better."

His voice sounded lower than usual, and I could only watch as he reached a hand up to my face, tickling my skin as he just barely held his fingers towards my jaw. I absentmindedly parted my lips, seemingly a natural reaction for him being this close. His face seemed to mimic mine, both of us waiting to see if something would happen. That's when I started having second thoughts. Oh, how I wish I hadn't. I closed my eyes, almost pained to say no. I turned my head, and the captain was left to stare at me, his eyes searching for an answer.

"What's stopping you?"

I waited for my heart rate to lower a fraction, trying to regain the air in my lungs. I took a good look at him; his whole demeanor seemed to be on edge and his pupils were dilated. I decided then and there that I very much liked that look on him. He was trying to figure me out while playing it off as nonchalance.

"So you do have someone waiting for you back home."

But it wasn't that simple.

"I did." He was trying to work out how to respond.

"I find that holding yourself back from what you want isn't good for us commandeers."

"What is it you want from me, Captain?"

Of course, his words distracted me and started to steer the conversation in another direction. I was not surprised.

"Well, what's on the table?"

He could be so infuriating.

"You're just a bad idea. And continuing to sleep in your bed won't help anything." I could tell he was becoming impatient.

"I think you need to ask yourself what you want."

He strode over to his sea chest, pulling out a blanket.

"As for the bed, you're welcome to it."

There was no difference in his tone. He spoke in his usual carefree manner. Which irritated me greatly. I wanted to know what was inside his head, without thinking of my own. That's how I liked to operate. I refused to think about my emotions until they were overflowing and begging to be let out, resulting in a grand meltdown. I wanted to say something, to at least explain myself.

"I can't be with one man and move on to the next like that, the way you can with women. Okay? I was with someone, back in my time. I'm still trying to get over him."

While I talked he laid out the blanket on the floor next to the bed, and he started to search for any spare materials to make it more plush.

"If he wasn't right for you, then why are you still mourning? I say good riddance."

"Because he's been around forever. I'm scared to let him go. Besides, no one should have to be a rebound." He looked up at me, confused.

"What's that then?" Oh, right. That word probably didn't mean what it did in my time quite yet.

"I mean no one should have to feel like a replacement. I don't want some fleeting relationship, John. That's not me."

He seemed to find enough for his makeshift bed to finally settle down.

"You're getting ahead of yourself, darling."

Everything he was saying was true. So why wasn't it enough?

"What if I'm messing everything up? What if you're supposed to meet some distinguished lady and have six kids?"

Something I said must've upset him because, as I looked over at him, he was a tad panicked.

"M'not sure what you're on about, but that definitely doesn't sound like me. Do you need some rum? I think I need some rum."

I had run my mouth again and got caught up in my what-ifs. I didn't even know if John was trying to get with me. I was jumping to conclusions and worrying about something he may have not even thought about. I had tried to classify what was going on, which couldn't be done. I wasn't even going to be there long enough to worry. Whatever it was that was happening between John and me was not something that could be put in a box. And I was making a fool of myself.

He handed me a bottle, and I accepted it gratefully. He still looked miffed, and I had only myself to blame.

"I don't think I've ever met someone who worries as much as you."

I was relieved he was trying to make fun of the situation. That was one area in life where we did not relate.

"Quite the charmer, you are."

He put his hand on his chest, pleased with himself.

"I do have my moments."

"I'm sorry, John. You were right."

He had already gotten under the covers on the floor.

"Don't mention it, love."

Then I was left to think how he had paid attention to what I had said about the sleeping arrangements. Whether it was out of respect or to avoid any more confrontation, there were some miracles to be had. I would miss the warmth, but I reasoned this was for the best. Something was brewing between the two of us. I wasn't sure what it was yet, but I needed everything to slow down.

Chapter Twenty-Three

Eventually, I had gotten over my panic, and I did everything else. I hoped in time I would learn from these men and throw my worries out the porthole. One of these days I would not let my anxiety consume me. I realized it did not matter what group of people I surrounded myself with, there would always be a select few who would have to handle the blows of my mental turmoil. It was worse when I didn't have my meds. Finn was trying to teach me new things to focus on when I felt out of control. I was endlessly thankful for his patience and wondered often where he got it from. It had been a few days since we took over the sloop, and we were heading for Horta to drop off the remaining officers and their captain, who still insisted on not joining us. I had a loosely based guess we had passed the Kane Fracture Zone, but couldn't be entirely sure.

Between Finn and I, we were able to stay on top of our course, with the help of the planisphere. I also had multiple changes of clothes, after altering some naval uniforms. Things were running in order, and it was a nice change of pace to get to know new faces amongst the familiar. John had seemingly backed off from his endless flirting and snark, probably assuming I wanted nothing to do with him based on how I reacted that night. There was no sense for me to ruminate on how I handled things; what was done was done. I had decided not to worry about what happened between John and me. Things would work themselves out, and, if they didn't, I would be gone in about three months anyway.

Marco had informed us that when we eventually got to Spain, we would have to take time to careen the ship before making our way back to Boston. I had never participated in such a task and imagined it was a lot more work than it was in my time. We would be looking for a safe harbor away from prying eyes, which meant we may have to stop before marooning the officers on Horta. Boone then decided to tell me about the threat of shipworms, a saltwater clam that made its home on floating wood. Once they dug into the hulls of ships, they transformed them into something like a honeycomb, making them very vulnerable to stress from wind or water. So in short, they were bad news.

Darien then told me not to worry, because this was supposedly an excuse to party. Finn chimed in, saying that one party in the Carolinas had lasted for months on end. I was curious to see a pirate party in action and found myself for the first time feeling excited to clean something for what lay ahead. Until then I took up the side job of being a seamstress, helping to repair my shipmates' clothes. I had insisted that they get sprayed down with seawater before being handed to me, for I refused to work with smelly garments. Fortunately, they obliged, and I had my work cut out for me that day. I wasn't the most skilled with sewing but knew how to patch up holes and stitch seams more precisely than most men.

I decided to do my duties on the deck, all of the clothes lying in a wooden bucket by my feet so I could feel the sun on my face and socialize. As I worked with my hands, I focused on the sounds all around me. Every time someone walked by, I could hear the jingling and rustling of fabric. They were pleasing sounds to me, and I valued every one of their self-expressions. I thought of the style of the 21st century and how disappointing it was compared to the time I found myself in. Why didn't people want to wear works of art anymore? Pieces made with love, mementos adorning you and reminding you of all the things you care about. It was endearing.

At some point in the afternoon, Boone had spotted something way out in the distance, a mere blip in our field of vision. Seeing anything out there other than endless blue thrilled everyone on board, and we were all curious to figure out what it was. The wind was in our favor for once, and within thirty minutes we were able to make out a ship. Finn wanted to know if he was supposed to stay on course or steer clear from the oncoming obstacle, but John refused to answer until he could make out what ship we were dealing with. I was made to get an alternate route ready should we have to abort, so I had charts laid out all around the gallery, trying to work quickly. I wish I had a sextant, but they wouldn't be invented until closer to the end of this century.

Thankfully I was put out of my process quickly, as Marco came barging in, urging me out on the deck again. Coming out, I saw John looking out of his telescope, wordlessly handing it to me. I looked at the ship, and it was easily identifiable as a merchant vessel. The captain had concluded the same thing, and the three of us waited to make out more details. Cargo ships were weighed down significantly, which gave us the edge on time.

It was a Spanish ship, and I was inclined to think it was part of the West Indies Treasure Fleet. They were made up of a convoy system of transatlantic sea routes. Finding them in this location would make perfect sense if this were the case. I told John of my suspicions, which filled him with fervor. There was no question as to what would happen next. We immediately prepared for the siege. After we got a little closer, Boone raised our Jolly Roger flag and we got the cannons ready for action. We weren't so concerned about the damage this time around, as the plan involved sinking the ship once it'd been plundered.

Marco was in charge of getting a team together to cross onto the vessel, which consisted of most of the former officers, for a chance to prove themselves. It would be interesting to see their performance. Finn sailed us on by with a smile on his face. This was what pirates lived for. It was the highlight of the journey. I decided to help with some of the men in the cargo hold to make more room for our pillages. It would be just short of an hour before I would get to witness our first ransack.

Chapter Twenty-Four

The Spanish were a prideful bunch. It took three hits before they surrendered, which suited us just fine. One of the impacts sat low, meaning the vessel wouldn't last long if it didn't get repairs right away. Darien and I delegated where everything went as the men came back and forth from ship to ship. The first thing to come on board was a variety of spices, sugar, and tobacco. I had never heard of some of the spices before, and I began opening up bags to smell. Finn found it very amusing of me, but I was too fascinated to care.

Next came the trunks of silver, gold, and pearls, which produced multiple shouts from the crew. Everyone was excited to get their share. I took a few pieces of jewelry for myself. I had every intention of keeping what I picked and wearing them everywhere

I went. There was a variety of gold bangles, necklaces, rings, and gold hoops. After the chests, there were mostly odds and ends like silks and oils. Finally came the most prized possession in my opinion. Books. When John saw my excitement for them, he chuckled and told me to take what I wanted.

Of course, I knew I'd be parting with them when I went back home, but there were still months of sailing left in the future. I flipped through what the merchants used as their main form of entertainment and found a brand-new edition of Robinson Crusoe. It was a simple leather bound, but to see it with so little wear was a unique experience. I had a moment of wanting to squeal but thought better of it, as I did not feel like John teasing me about it for what I suspected would be weeks.

To our surprise, when given the option of joining us, all of the merchants refused. That left quite a few people to maroon, and our captain knew as much. Leaving that many souls in one place together was a gamble. One John didn't want to take, and he had to make the difficult decision to leave them behind. As it was, they could probably survive for a couple of days without supplies. We had stripped the cargo vessel of everything.

The ship had taken a hard blow from the cannons, but they still had a chance of getting help within a day or two. I felt uneasy about the decision to leave them behind, but I had no say in the matter. While our ships were still connected, John walked over, handing the men two guns and a choice.

"Sorry state you've found yourselves in. Good luck lads," the captain told them.

Soon after we sailed away from the vessel, and amongst the shouting that could still be heard from the men stranded, a loud shot rang out. I looked back, seeing the smoke faintly rise. Why would they shoot? They all had a chance of survival. They just needed to wait it out. Was there an argument? Was someone punished?

We continued with little change, but I was struck with a feeling of guilt that was eating away at me. Even if I wasn't the one who pulled the trigger, I feared I had helped in the possibility of more deaths. The crew cheered and celebrated our victory, spirits being raised after finding more food and alcohol. This would hold us over until we got to Horta. The men who retrieved the goods had done well in John and Marco's book, which meant that from here on out they could slowly be trusted with more of the weightier responsibilities on board. They were elated with their performance, and I was happy for them.

I guessed that our next destination would take around two weeks, but that was a very loose estimate. I told the captain as much, and then our conversation moved to other things. He said I was continuing to make good progress. It filled me with a sense of belonging to know that I was now relied on and always had something to do with my hands. I tried to think if I had felt that back home but didn't really think so. I did miss my lighthouse and my little island. But I had everything I needed there, which wasn't what I thought at first.

I still longed for more... I wanted a companion. It felt like some guilty confession, being as independent as I was. They wouldn't add anything essential to life. But wasn't love essential? Isn't that what humans base their lives around? It was cliché to say, and maybe it didn't suit me, but it was within my nature to crave something more out of life. I felt like I didn't get a fair shot with the little relationships I had. There was something about the sea that was so romantic that you couldn't help but want to fall in love.

Everything that had happened so far felt too easy; both vessels we had encountered had surrendered quickly. I knew the kind of reputation that surrounded buccaneers, but I didn't think work would come so easily to them. It made me wonder if there were fights yet to be had for this crew and if there would be battles that wouldn't be so easy to come back from.

My mind was brought back to the present as the captain and I sat at opposite ends of his cabin. He had found a small golden mirror earlier that week and put it on his desk so that we would both have areas to get ready for the day. He was sifting through some of the clothes we had gathered from that day, tying various sashes to his person and securing one around his forehead. It was almost purple, a very deep faded red with a hue of blue. He seemed to be satisfied with his new appearance, which only added to his eclectic style.

I was busy looking through my jewelry and inspecting the detailed golden hoops from one of the trunks we had found. I found myself jealous of all of John's piercings, allowing him to wear multiple pieces of art.

"Where did you get all of your piercings?" I couldn't help but ask.

"Oh, throughout the years. Had most of 'em since I was a lad. Why? Are you envious?" He turned to face me, leaning on his armchair.

"Just this once I might be." A small smile graced his features.

"Well then. We can remedy that."

He went over to his dresser, and I heard rustling as he searched through the drawers. Eventually, he sauntered his way to me with a needle in hand and a small piece of cloth. He leaned very close to me, his breath tickling my skin.

"Now, where would you like them?" Everything with John felt so easy. Back home I would've had to think months and months before getting another piercing, worrying about who would judge me and who would openly complain about it. Here I knew he would view me as he did himself, and so would the crew.

"Here, next to the others."

It would be my third piercing, and I didn't worry about John being the one to do it. He proved himself to be capable, despite the way he carried himself and the approach he took. He very gently tilted my neck to the side and bunched up the cloth behind my ear. He looked at me for the go-ahead, and I nodded. He pierced my skin with the needle, quickly drawing back and securing the hoop. He dabbed the blood away with the same cloth and then repeated the process. Once it was done, he took a step back, looking over his work. He bowed dramatically and waited. I turned to look in the mirror and was impressed. He placed them just right, and I was quite pleased.

"Thank you, Captain."

I found that he was not done, as he came walking back over with a bottle of alcohol. He wordlessly came back into my space, grabbing ahold of my neck with one hand. I tried very hard not to go red and hoped that the dull throbbing in my ears would be enough distraction. With his thumb, he tilted my jaw to the side. Then he poured alcohol on my new piercing, for sterilization. As he went to put the bottle back he finally gave his reply.

"Anytime, darling."

There was still the issue of having a proper place to sleep. Earlier that day the captain and I had gone down to the common sleeping quarters to assess if there was room for one more hammock. There was not. Space was cramped as it was, with too much crew and not enough ship. It would be a little easier once we got rid of our prisoners perhaps, but that did not solve the problem at hand. We had set the task aside and then was the time to finish it. I could not in good conscience spend another night there with John. I knew the men talked, as all of us do, and would no doubt be confused as to the constant moving of my sleeping situation.

"John? What shall I do tonight?"

I could tell by his stature he was hoping I would just throw caution to the wind and stay in there for the night.

"Well dearie, I did just go through some effort to make room for you here."

"How kind of you. But you know exactly why that's not an option. It was fine for a night or two, but now I really must be getting a proper space."

He huffed and grumbled, most likely being lazy about needing to do anything other than drink that late in the day.

"Fine. If you insist."

He opened the door wide, striding out without waiting for me to follow. I walked briskly to keep up with him, and we found ourselves in front of the first mate's cabin.

"Really, John? This is your idea of finding me somewhere to sleep?"

He ignored me, barging in on Marco and Finn playing a deck of cards. They both looked up at the sudden interruption.

"Gentlemen! Adira needs a place to sleep and refuses a spot by her captain, so she seeks refuge with you lot."

I wished at that moment I wouldn't get an earful for slapping him. So instead I stood there, awkwardly hoping the men would show mercy on me.

"Erm, I'm not sure how much room we have for her, John," Marco tried to tell his captain.

Finn stayed silent as usual, watching the whole exchange with amusement.

John replied, "Well we'll just have to make room then!"

He exited the room, leaving just the three of us to stand there with anticipation and confusion. After several minutes went by, he came back in with his arms full of stuff. First, he went to the corner of the cabin, laying down spare planks of wood to resemble something of a bed frame, and then covered it with several layers of ratty quilts. After it looked somewhat like a bed, he topped it off with one pillow and a linen blanket. Finn and Marco watched him silently, sadly having no say in the matter.

He dragged a trunk into the room next, placing it at the end of the bed, and put the little mirror he found me on top. Once that was done, he took a curtain panel that looked older than the ship and placed it on one side of the ceiling, hammering it in to move onto the next side. A few moments later he seemed to be done and stepped back to view his work. Seemingly satisfied, he nodded to himself and turned around to me, beaming. At this point, there was no staying irritated with him.

"Thank you, John. It looks... nice...."

He nodded at me and walked out like he was never there in the first place. The three of us were left to talk about the implications of me now being a semi-permanent resident in Finn and Marco's cabin. They simply had two hammocks strung up, with hardly anything filling the rest of the space.

I decided to speak up first. "I was hoping this would fare better with the crew."

They both laughed in reply. "They'll find anything to gossip about."

I supposed it was true that there would be constant chatter surrounding me being the only woman on board.

"I don't doubt it! At least with you two, I won't be accused of the captain showing me favor."

They looked at each other, and then at me.

Finn asked me, "Would it be that horrid if he did?"

That made Marco try to hide a smirk, and we eventually all wound down for the night.

The time came when we made it to Horta. It was a town of little commerce and almost no industry. I was brimming with excitement to set foot on foreign land and saw buildings scattered all along the harbor through my telescope. Granted, most of them were churches. Finn explained it was an easy place to trade, with little law enforcement. But I was confused as to why we were leaving the officers here. There was plenty of life; it made no sense to have them marooned here.

"It helps no one to leave a bunch of folks stranded in the middle of nowhere, where they'll starve to death. Johnny just wanted to get them far enough from home to give us leeway," Finn explained to me, as I made my question known.

"But it seems like leniency to me. Pirates are nothing like I thought they'd be."

"Yes. Well, the ones you read about the most are the ones that get caught. Sure, there's plenty of sea dogs that'll murder and torture souls, but it tends to make the law angrier, don'tcha think?"

It did make sense. The world wasn't all black and white. Pillagers could live a life of questionable freedom while still upholding a set of morals. Not a perfect set of morals, mind you.

"But then why did the captain give the merchants guns? They had a chance of being rescued," I couldn't help but reply.

"Every man deserves the choice, even if they aren't very good options."

"It's just that in both situations, we're aiding in their possible deaths."

"We can't determine what they'll do, lass. Or what will become of them. We spare lives where we can, and the rest has to be laid in the grave."

It was a difficult truth to accept. The thievery was something I never truly despised, but the violence was a treachery I didn't want to involve myself in. Even with John being a laid-back captain, the hard decisions that had to be made could not be avoided. I was trying to wrap my head around this side of the job, that not every adventure would be a good one. Every thrill in life had its decline - this one was a scrape on the conscience. I tried my best to listen to Finn's advice. To put the thoughts to rest. Did every one of us have a hand in someone else's life?

Eventually, the subject went to the back of my mind, when Marco and Finn thought it best to steer the ship a little past the harbor to a more secluded beach. It was nestled closer to the right side of the island, on the same side as their lighthouse. As Finn brought us right onto the sandy shore, men started jumping down with ropes. Soon enough all of us were going down, and we brought out the officers tied up preemptively and secured to a palm tree a couple of feet away from the ship. Then as a group effort, we started pulling the ship in one direction and watched as it slowly tilted to its side, creaking in the process.

You could see clumped-up seaweed, barnacles, and who-knows-what-else leached onto the hull. We continued dragging the ship on land, and, by the time we were done, my arms were burning. We had managed at high tide, which worked to our advantage of pushing the ship along with us. Once the hull was fully accessible, we were all given an assortment of scraping tools, knives, and razors. Everyone worked in a line, scraping and picking at the barnacles. Our razors were dulled first, to prevent us from damaging the ship. I thought about how much easier this would be if we had a power washer.

As hours passed by and we scrubbed between scraping, John had Marco go into Horta to find us some fresh provisions. The captain wanted us to feast like kings, a prelude to what was to come in Spain. While Marco was still out, we picked some oranges that were local to the island, and John was cracking open coconuts for their juice and flesh. When involved in hard work and elbow grease, these light refreshing fruits were preferred to anything that would weigh one down. Even when involved with such a tedious task, most of us were smiling. The sun was shining, the sea breeze keeping us cool, and we were all singing together with the smell of citrus all around us.

Chapter Twenty-Five

Finally, at the end of the day, we had most of the barnacles and seaweed removed. We did not find any shipworm holes, just mold and tiny creatures making their home. About halfway through the afternoon, we flipped the ship to the other side, making sure we were thorough. The sun was well on its way of leaving us for the night, which was when Marco and some of the hands came back with arms full of baskets and cloth parcels of what had to be food. In preparation for our meal, we laid out any spare blankets that could be found on deck, along with barrels and small wooden crates turned upside down.

Some of the meat and fruit were to be stored for the rest of our venture, and the remaining goods were local cuisine that I had never heard of. The first small basket uncovered was Bacalhau, which was dried and salted codfish, soaked in milk before cooking. It had been the national dish of Portugal for some time, which Darien took time to explain to me. The next was a sweet pastel de nata, a custard tart. When I saw Boone opening a case of piri-piri chicken, I was delighted. I didn't care what seasonings it had, it was land food.

There were so many dishes it was almost overwhelming. They all appeared to be from a tavern, which made me wonder if Marco paid for all of it or acquired it by other means. There was a comforting soup in the mix called Caldo Verde, which was a mixture of kale, onions, potatoes, and garlic. It was a simple concoction, but it was warm and full of vegetables I hadn't had in what felt like forever. John was gnawing on meat that he informed me was called Leitao, which just seemed like a fancy word for roasted pig. There was also something that looked similar to a charcuterie board, with various pieces of bread and cheese, one of them being so soft you could scoop it out with a spoon. For drinks, we had fresh water, more coconut juice, and port wine, which was a Portuguese favorite.

Once everyone was stuffed beyond belief came the festivities. We got a fire going, large enough for the whole crew to surround. Stewart, the new cook, started playing the fiddle for us to dance around the fire and sing with. We sang Drunken Sailor, as it seemed most appropriate. The crew used different verses than what I had remembered listening to as a child, but the first recorded version had been in the early 1800s, so it still had a while to go until it would be what it was in my time. We all participated in jigs, and the men took turns swinging me around in the sand. Even Marco was letting loose and having fun.

The men continued to party, but I found myself growing tired. I was somewhat of a grandma in the sense that I liked an early bedtime. I got a hammock from the ship and tied it up around two slim trees far enough away to drown out some of the noise. I was feeling comfortably warm from the alcohol and being surrounded by the fire all night, but I brought a small linen blanket just in case. As I got comfortable, I took watch of my shipmates. There is something so humbling and profound about looking at other people enjoying themselves. It's such a simple act, but it reminds me of all of the reasons to keep going. Seeing them all smile and dance with one another, stumbling around drunkenly, and laughing like fools made me feel connected to them on a level I had not previously felt. It's one thing to work together. To be in close quarters together. But to relish in the rewards of life - that's what binds people.

My eyelids started to droop when I made out a figure staggering its way toward me. Once I saw it was John, I knew I probably wouldn't be sleeping soon.

"Dira! I'm disappointed, darling. This is your first party and you're here sleeping the night away! Have s'more wine, perhaps that'll get you feeling more alive." I rolled my eyes at him.

"Some of us value the hours at night to recharge, Captain." He was incredibly bored.

"'M sure, but these are the finest hours! You can get up to so much mischief at night."

"And what exactly do you have in mind, John?" He stretched his hand out rather dramatically, waiting.

"Come and find out," he said.

Sleep was a thing of the past as I slid out of my hammock, taking John's hand. I let him guide us aimlessly, as we went into the lush greenery of the island. We were walking past the crew and onwards.

After what felt like forever he led us back to the shore. This was probably on the other side of the lighthouse, putting us at a distance from everyone else. The moon was shining bright, cascading the ocean in shimmering light. It was just the two of us, the sounds of nature all around us. The waves crashing in on themselves, birds speaking their own language, and the trees swaying back and forth.

This sort of serenity was worth staying up for. But it caught me by surprise that John decided to bring me here.

"This wasn't at all what I was expecting." He looked at me, incredulous.

"What were you expecting?" Every statement that came out of that man's mouth felt like he was suggesting something else.

"I don't know, going into Horta to steal some more drink, or more dancing by the fire." He gave me another shining grin.

"Well we may not be by a fire, but we do have moonlight."

With that he picked me up around my torso, hauling the both of us to the sea. I yelped with surprise, squirming. But the captain had a steady grip on me, and as soon as my feet reached the water a calm came over me. The protesting quickly switched to laughing at how ridiculous this all felt. But it also felt so very right somehow. He hummed something I didn't recognize, and I found that I quite liked it. The tune relaxed me, and in doing so I let him guide us through the water. He still held onto me, and I allowed myself to grasp onto his arms for stability.

He twirled me around, making me smile like a fool. I didn't think this was something that John was capable of. The dancing was lighthearted, both of us beaming and goofing around. We were moving with no clear direction, just letting the feeling come to us. As the night wore on the stars made themselves known, almost winking at us with their twinkling.

I could almost forget that John had killed people, and that only days from now we would be stealing from others. It was easy to push it all away and only focus on the way the captain's jewelry shone in the moonlight, his eyes dark and endless, and his grip on me making me dizzy.

The morning after was bustling with activity as we all made efforts to leave Horta. As we were hauling things back up the sloop, I saw Boone running towards us through the bushes with a chicken in both arms. It was quite the sight, but didn't surprise me considering who it was carrying the animal. I had to laugh at the thought of Boone trying to stealthily steal someone's chicken. John slapped him on the back for his efforts, as the whole crew could benefit from fresh eggs in our diet. After an hour or two of preparation, we were nearly ready to head out. Marco had kept our captives tied to the same tree as the day before, and they looked at us with annoyance. They probably thought we were stupid for letting them off easily, and I couldn't help but agree. I wished I had the time to explore such a beautiful town but knew the longer we were there, the more attention we would draw to ourselves.

That morning we passed many other Portuguese islands. Our course was chartered for the Bay of Biscay, and we briefly saw the mountain of Ponta do Pico from our telescopes. As we started to sail at an angle, we swooped by Velas. There were a couple more formations we breezed by in the coming hours that had many of us leaning on the railing to watch them fade out of distance. Leaving our enemies out for anyone to find had me wondering how John was not being chased at every moment for past wrongs. What kept these men from seeking their revenge? How did this captain manage to carry on his ways with no consequence? I had these questions mulling about in my brain throughout the day as I organized loot and sewed clothing.

Despite the two and a half months I had spent with this crew, there was one man who did not seem any more comfortable with me than the day I had arrived there, and that was Marco Teale. I had picked up on his kindness but knew that he possessed a serious spirit. No doubt taking up the worries John did not feel burdened with. Marco thought of the men at all times and was fiercely loyal to his captain. I was curious about his past with John and Finn, but would not be privy to it unless Marco felt the need or want to tell me himself. I kept reminding myself I should not care so much for these souls as the days ticked away and we made it closer and closer to Spain. As I went down to the cargo hold to find some spices to pair with the meat for lunch, I spotted Marco. He was rummaging through the leather goods we had acquired, and I silently watched. Eventually, he caught me staring.

"One of my holsters has seen better days. Thought it might be time to replace it," he said.

"Do you want me to take a look? I've become something of a tinkerer."

He looked at me wearily, before handing the accessory to me. I inspected it, turning it around and finding all the weak points. I started to nod as I formulated the remedy needed.

"This'll be an easy fix. I can stitch the thinning sections together and add some clasps," I told him, watching his expression.

"Thank you, Adira. You've become quite helpful around here, not sure what we'll do without you once we make it back to the colonies."

It clicked for me as to where his thoughts were. He didn't want to become too attached or too reliant on me, knowing I'd be gone soon. Perhaps we were more alike in personality than I had cared to notice. In personality, Marco was my equal. In spirit, it was John. Could kindred spirits be found on a pirate ship? It seemed too soft of a term for these men, but it made all the sense in the world to me.

I replied, "You'll go on as you did before me. But I hope that you'll always see me as a friend, Marco."

I was given a rare smile by the man, and I viewed it as a victory. Perhaps I'd tell Finn about it later. I hoped this was the beginning of an understanding between the two of us.

"I think you'll always be welcome here, if you ask me."

Chapter Twenty-Six

The day went on much more pleasantly after my confrontation with Marco, and I felt like I finally had a positive conversation with him. It was almost time for dinner, and Stewart was busy preparing for everyone's meal. There was kohl still smudged around my eyes from several nights before, which made a pair of John and I. I smiled at the thought, wondering if I'd come back to my time hearing new stories of a pair of pirates. How would I even occupy my time when not worrying about the crew and following star courses?

I was brought back to the present when Stewart came out, asking for my help. I was somewhat of a Renaissance woman around here when navigation was not needed. I probably wouldn't get to work on Marco's holster until later that night. I jumped up from where I sat, following the cook to the galley. He had me get to work peeling potatoes to boil them while he prepared some beef we had managed to steal from one of the local markets. Because of the duration of the trip, I felt fairly spoiled with replenishments of fresh provisions.

During our work, Stewart and I chatted about his past in the Navy. Once the meat was salted, he worked on a plum duff and I started a batch of grog. The officers may have treated him well, but he explained to me all the hardships and struggles most ships faced fighting for their country. It was no wonder why most men turned to piracy rather than remaining a dignified member of the Navy. Why would you want to serve in a place with such harsh conditions, with little to no benefit? And war was such a stupid fickle thing. A bunch of old men who didn't care about other people's lives, just their own status and benefit.

Eventually, dinner was done and we called the men to come take their portions. Once everyone nearly had their share, I took my wooden tray to go eat with the trio I'd grown so fond of. It may not have looked well to show as much favoritism as I did, and to stick with those who held the highest ranks, but on a pirate ship, no one seemed to care. Everyone sat with whomever they pleased, social cues be damned. I loved it.

I spoke up, "Do you think the men back in Horta will cause us issues down the road?"

I could tell they all thought the way I spoke sounded strange to them, probably using phrases and words that weren't in their vocabulary yet. It was an ongoing attempt to understand each other, and I was surprised we had managed fairly well.

"More than likely. Everyone here knows it's a somewhat risky business to head back to Boston when this is all said and done," Marco replied.

Finn nodded. "We'll be going into tha lion's den, that's for sure."

I felt guilty then, knowing their enemies would be alert as soon as we were back in America. I would not know what would become of them once I was to leave. I'd look for historical records, but I knew there would only be so much recollection.

"We have plenty of time to make it into safe waters. We'll be gone before they can bat an eye," John said, trying to reassure everyone at the table.

Boone walked by with his grog then. "Shoulda killed 'em when we had the chance!"

I wanted to disagree with Boone, but, at the end of the day, both decisions would leave the crew in a tight spot. If we had killed them, that would've had the Navy sending out a rescue mission, only to be enraged when realizing what we did. There was no right course of action; the captain was left to choose from the lesser of two evils.

"As long as we don't get caught, we'll be just fine. And Captain Sterling has never gotten caught," John replied.

Finn laughed then. "Ya know that's a straight lie, Johnny."

The conversation took another turn as the men bickered about how often their captain had been in scrapes. But they were all alive, and free. That's all that mattered to them. As long as they had those two things, they didn't care what the world threw their way.

Dinner ended with my worries long forgotten, and I was left standing out on the deck again under the moonlight. I had begun to know the moon in all its phases, and, in turn, saw why the poets worshiped it. I thought of the mermaids then and how throughout our escapade in Horta I could tell they were our silent followers. On a night like this, or as the fog in the morning would clear, I would see something move and take form in the water. I wished I knew what the mermaids' interest was, and, even more than that, I wished I had an opportunity to talk to them.

As if knowing they were being thought about, I saw something under the water move and glitter. She emerged from the surface, and, after my heart raced for a minute, I wondered where the others were. The creature looked at me in curiosity, similar to the first interaction I had with her kind. I had a desire to be closer to her level - to see her up close. I grabbed hold of the nearest rope, climbing over the railing. I slid down as much as I could, keeping one leg bent and grounded onto the grooves of the ship and the other dangling above the water. I held onto the rope with both hands, while being amazed that she was not perturbed in the slightest.

I wondered if she would speak to me, as I saw her swimming closer to me. In the back of my mind, I knew that I should be scared. But I was filled with so much fascination and intrigue. We looked at each other with the same wonder. Everything about her seemed to be shifting constantly.

I was the first to speak. "What's your name?"

She continued to look at me, seeming to debate whether she wanted to disclose that information.

"Aerwyna," she told me in a soft, melodic voice.

It was such a unique and strange name, and I wondered if all mermaids were named with such majesticity.

She pointed to herself. "Friend of the sea."

I had to assume she meant the meaning behind her name. I was trying not to overwhelm her with questions.

"I'm Adira."

"Adira... you are not like the others."

"I don't understand, what do you mean? Why have you been following us?"

She considered this for a moment, trying to formulate a response.

"I was... sent. To watch over you."

I was no closer to feeling a sense of understanding than I was when I had first met the mermaids. I was confused and felt a weird feeling in my gut. One that made me want to reach my hand out a little closer. Aerwyna followed my movements, drawing her hand out of the water. Her long nails and slender fingers hovered closely next to my own, and I felt a pull toward her. I wondered what it would be like to swim with a mermaid.

We were drawn out of the moment when movement could be heard from the deck above, but I didn't want the conversation to end. Aerwyna was startled by the noise, lowering herself in the water just slightly.

"I think I'll address you as Wyna if it's all the same to you!"

Before I could say anything else, a head peered over the railing. When I looked back towards the water, Wyna was gone.

Upon climbing back up the railing and onto the deck, I saw that it was John who decided to interrupt me. Figures as much.

"What were you doing down there?"

"Well, I was trying to have a conversation, before you so rudely interrupted me."

He feigned offense, placing a hand on his chest.

"And who, exactly, did you grace with your presence?"

"A mermaid. Seems to me that we have a stalker, Captain."

He scoffed. "You can't trust mermaids, darling. They all have ulterior motives, if you ask me."

"Well, good thing I didn't ask you."

He gave me a look, silently saying touché. But then, even in the darkness, I could see worry etched in his features. It couldn't be seen easily, but it was there.

"I'm serious, Dira. They have an interest in you. That's never led to good things in the past."

I shook my head. I didn't need him to treat me like a child. I didn't want to think of why else he could be warning me.

"You said yourself they're just big gossips. Nothing wrong with that."

"Yes, to most of us, that's what they are. But they don't usually get close to us mere humans unless they want something," he said in a hush as if they were listening to our conversation. And maybe they were.

"But what could they possibly want from me?"

"Not sure. P'raps it's one of those things we best not know."

"I don't like not knowing things."

He laughed then and seemed to have exhausted his efforts of trying to get me to drop the subject of mermaids. For the time being at least.

He started to make his way to his quarters before throwing his head back towards me.

"Any chance you'd like to come in?"

He said it with a level of cheekiness. But there was no doubt in my mind that he was partially serious.

"No can do. I don't think you could handle it."

"I think you'll find that I can handle quite a few things, love."

I turned to him then, feigning annoyance.

"Let me ask you one question. Have you ever slept in the same bed with a woman you weren't romantically involved with?"

"Don't be daft, darling, every woman who's met me has had romantic feelings for me."

I rolled my eyes. "I'll take that as a no then."

He strode over to me, swerving as he did so.

"Y'know, I'm starting to see why that lad of yours left you."

I was not expecting him to bring Jason up in jest, and I felt my cheeks burn just a little.

"Don't forget, Captain, *I* left *him*."

Chapter Twenty-Seven

I could smell the oranges from here. We had brought
two crates full of oranges onto the ship when leaving
Horta, and they had been filling the ship up with
their lovely fragrance. I had been thinking of
everything yet to happen and wondering if things
would go in my favor. When my head felt buzzing
with too many thoughts and too much unrest, I
stayed on deck all day. Right up against the railing,
watching the water move. The ocean has always been
grounding me. It's the soothing gauze to my old
wounds, caressing me and urging me to serenity.
Lately, I'd been transfixed more than usual,
imagining the whole cities that must live under the
surface. I never thought in my lifetime I would see
what I knew to be a myth, but here I was being
proven wrong every day. The knowledge I had come
to have of the world felt like something few were
acquainted with, and I wanted to guard it with
jealousy.

I looked for my new secret admirer but did not see
her. She must be more careful during the day, not
wanting to deal with the crew. Once the morning
chores had been taken care of, I stood close to Finn as
the ship was told what we'd be getting up to in Spain.
It was creeping up on us. There had been more
research gone into our activities than I had thought.

We would be put into pairs of two or three at most, all with different cover stories.

Marco had connections throughout Spain, in all brackets of society. His sources told him that there would be an elite ball held towards Granada, in the castle of Alhambra. I wish I had known this information earlier, despite it being fairly close to the bay I had charted for. As Finn and I discussed docking, we figured the closest we could get would be Málaga, which meant a day's journey would still be ahead of us once we found a safe space in the harbor. It would be an elaborate heist, one that required lots of coin. We had enough to put on a good show as upstanding members of a higher class, but it would be our acting and discretion that would be key. Marco was in charge of this operation, as he was most familiar with the territory.

The local governor had current possession of the palace, but that's not what we were going for. Marco had heard in passing that King Philip would be visiting the governor and his wife after coming back from another war involving Italy. Not only would the king be traveling with valuables, but no doubt the castle would be full of precious artifacts on display. They would want to leave an impression on their majesties. We were to take as much as we could and then make our way back to Málaga.

Our task as of right then was to give the sloop a complete makeover. We wanted the Spanish to believe we were made of money. This meant extensive paintwork, updated wardrobes, and finer speech. The Spanish and Americans were currently allies, so John would be posing as an American governor, with Marco being his lieutenant, and Finn being his treasurer. The rest of us would be the remaining cabinet members and servants. It was a lot to prepare for and everyone had their fair share of work, but it was also challenging and exciting. In my mind, it felt like an elaborate prank. Marco had finished telling me that I would be coordinating with him for everyone's outfits on the occasion. The first challenge of the day was the captain.

I was in the captain's quarters every day I'd been here, but this situation added a whole new level of fun. I secretly adored the way John dressed, despite the dirt under his fingernails and the salty grime that built up on us all. My job was to make him look like he belonged in the upper class. We stared each other down, like two animals stalking the same prey. He gave me a self-indulgent grin, as full of himself as he was. I sighed, knowing I had my work cut out for me.

"Your braids and hair trinkets need to go," were my first words.

He scoffed as if the mere thought pained him.

"But you adore my hair." It was my turn to scoff.

"What makes you think that?"

He batted his eyelashes. "It's all in your eyes, darling."

"Yes, well, it does have character, doesn't it? But it'll have to go."

He got to work unbraiding strands of hair and meticulously picking the bits of gold and gems out. He turned back at me, expectantly.

"You're doing great, Captain."

I picked up a brush and wet it down with the basin of water in the room. I strode over to him, and he almost looked eager for whatever was next.

I said a little impatiently, "Sit down, will you?"

"As you wish, m'lady."

Everything he did had to be played up. I let him show off and then got to work. I kept one hand gingerly around his cheekbone to steady him as the other hand brushed through his hair. He insisted on looking at me, which had me fidgeting like I drank eight cups of coffee. As I got all of his hair brushed back, I brought a ribbon out of a drawer. I ordered him to stand back up and tilt his head up. I went behind him to tie the ribbon in his hair, giving him a low ponytail. If I enjoyed running my fingers through his hair, no one needed to know.

I turned him back around to face me, surveying the change. It didn't suit him nearly as much as the messy mane of braids and jewels, but he looked good. Another thing he didn't need to know.

"You'll have to clean your face of course. It's an absolute disaster."

"Is it? I hadn't noticed."

I walked to his wardrobe and opened his armoire. There was quite a variety of fabric colors and styles. I knew raiding an array of ships would give us plenty of options, but this felt like dressing a Ken doll. Spanish fashion was heavily influenced by the French, which meant bright colors that caught your eye. I found a fashionable long velvet coat, set in a deep almost burgundy red. I immediately thought of Captain Hook, which brought a smile to my face. I decided to pair it with a cream vest and baggy breeches.

A few moments later I turned around to see John in the outfit I chose. It's funny that something as simple as clothes can completely change a person. He fit the part.

"You look like a governor, Captain. I think this just might work."

He took the coat off, already annoyed with wearing it.

"Let's not prolong suffering, love."

I laughed despite myself and left him to his own devices. I had to find something for myself to wear. I went down to the hull where the rest of the trunks full of clothing were, opening all of them. I laid the matching sets out, organizing everything into groups and by what would have likely been the most expensive. I eventually found a long heavy gown, which was cream-colored and had jewels on the bodice. It was elaborate in every way and had a deep royal blue trim with lace around the neckline.

Blue was the most popular color of the time, which left me surprised I hadn't seen more of it in John's collection. The next of my findings was the corsets. I had worn a couple back home but found them more stressful to get on than they were worth. The corsets of this century were steel boned and gave a woman that desired V shape. It was hard to tell if any of them were going to fit me, and I had no way to measure them. I had to hope that when we reached Spain someone would be able to help me get into one.

On a brighter note, there was still plenty of jewelry to choose from. I wanted to keep wearing the necklace from my family and the rings I had gotten. But I decided a couple of blue pieces would incorporate nicely with the gown. Once I found ones of a similar shade to my dress, I set the pieces aside and put everything for my ensemble into a bamboo box.

Marco was working on his own look, so I went to Finn. From the hull, I had found a gorgeous olive green satin vest with embroidery, which would pair beautifully with Finn's fiery hair and pale eyes. The other popular fabrics in the 18th century were cotton and linen, and I found a coat in the first material set in a dark gray, similar to deep slate. They had matching breeches, and I chose a couple of rings for the Scotsman as well. As Marco and I surveyed the outcome, we were very pleased, and, to my surprise, so was Finn. He was quite happy and refreshed to be in a new outfit and colors. One man's glee was all I needed.

The rest of the crew was fairly simple. They did not need as much oversight, as they would be placed under lower ranks than John's longtime friends. The only one that gave me a hard time was Darien, insisting on having feathered sleeves and looking for a teal getup. It was ridiculous, but it would work. Then Boone of course chose an outrageous powdery pink and white set that oddly suited him. But I kept in mind that loud colors were fashionable, and, as long as they were fancy and in style, I had no room to fuss.

Chapter Twenty-Eight

A couple of nights later, everything was ready for our arrival in Spain. The ship looked brand new in its fresh layers of paint and oil, and the crew had gone through painstaking efforts to polish their acting skills. I was the one who had the most trouble with it, but Marco and Finn were quite patient with me as they taught me everything they knew. At night John spoke of all the places he'd been and the places he wanted to show me. I had to remind him that I was going home after this hurrah, but he seemed certain it wouldn't be my last.

I found myself wishing he was right. It was becoming increasingly difficult to imagine myself back in my own time. I felt like I'd be leaving behind all of my friends there. What friends were there back home? There used to be Jason, and maybe we'd be friends again. But who besides my family? Everyone I had connected with was there on that ship. As far as Aerwyna went, I was hoping to encounter her again that night. I purposefully volunteered to be on watch so that hopefully no one would interrupt any conversations I might get into.

It was probably close to midnight, as everyone was either down below or in the cabins, and I could see the soft golden light emitting from each of the rooms. I had found it easier to sleep since arriving there, with the noises of the vessel at night. The wind on the water and the creaks in the wood were soothing to me. John was a light snorer, and, despite my initial annoyance, it had eventually become a part of the ambient sounds that lulled me to sleep before I had to take my leave. I watched the moon high in the sky and peered into the water.

The moonlight made everything look like it was shifting and glowing, so when Aerwyna popped her head up out of the water, it caught me by surprise. She was a beautiful creature, with hair that took on a purple hue at night and soft features. On her ears lay little starfish, moving their arms about. I couldn't help but give her a little wave as I made a loop in one of the ropes for me to sit in and lowered myself down the side of the sloop. I left my boots up on deck so that I could submerge myself in the water to truly be eye-to-eye with my new friend.

She swam right up to me, glistening as she did so. She held something in her hands, a little clam pill box encased in gold trimming. I reached out to take it, examining the trinket. I opened its clasps, and inside was a golden-like substance. I looked at the mermaid, unsure what she wanted me to do with it.

"A gift," she said. "For your smell."

I was about to laugh at her boldness before I realized she probably meant it was perfume. I brought it to my nose and found it did smell quite nice. It was a mixture of fragrances - lilies, saltwater, and vetiver. And a hint of cypress? I smeared some behind my ears and around my collarbone, already smelling the refreshing scent. Then I felt a little guilty. I had not thought to bring her something and thought about what was on my person. I had on a golden bangle with carvings and freshwater pearls embedded into the metal. I took it off my wrist, handing it to her. She took it eagerly, and I saw curiosity fill her features.

She slipped it on her much more slender wrist, and her eyes got wider by the second, holding out her hand to look at it. Then a smile graced her, seemingly happy with the exchange. The blissful look didn't last long, however. She came closer to me, in all seriousness.

"Why haven't you joined us?"

"I can't. Don't you know that? I can't breathe underwater."

This statement confused her, and I wondered if mermaids were just dense. Her eyes went to my legs submerged in the water, as if she was just now processing that I was human.

"I don't understand...."

"You and me both, sister. What are you protecting me from?"

I must've been leading the conversation in uncomfortable territory, as she looked uneasy after hearing my question.

"What tribe are you?"

"I'm American if that's what you mean."

She tilted her head in one direction, so I took it as that was not what she meant. It would be an ongoing process of trying to understand one another. As silence ensued, Wyna's whole body started to tense up, and I could see the fear slip into her eyes.

"What? What is it?"

"I'll be close by, stay on guard. He's close."

Before I could ask her who he was, she dove back into the ocean, her fin being the last thing I saw. I don't know what sort of creature could make a mermaid afraid, but I decided then and there I would not like to encounter them. I quickly pulled myself back up to the ship, and, as I stepped back on deck, I took great care in being as silent as possible. I did not need to wake up any of the crew and have them worried over something that could be nothing.

My boots slipped back on and I treaded carefully around the ship. Everything outside of the sloop was eerily quiet, and I did not want to be the one to break the calm. I watched and waited for several more moments. A few minutes later, I swore I could make out movement in the deep. We were anchored at the moment, as we had been ahead of our schedule for several days. The dark mass in the ocean seemed to multiply in size every few seconds, and I froze where I stood. I could not make out what it was down there, and the fear of the unknown was paralyzing me.

The darkness had spread out past each end of the sloop, and I found myself praying to God that nobody would come up and start making a fool of themselves. My hands reached out to the rigging of their own accord, gripping the ropes so tight that I was sure my knuckles were white. A moment passed by and the ship started to move. But not as if it were sailing. It started to sway from side to side, and I realized with terror that whatever was down there was pulling on our anchor. The ship started to groan in protest, and if I continued holding onto the rigging I worried I may fall into the sea with that thing.

The creature was tugging with great strength, and, after a couple more sways, the ship started to lean to the side. I couldn't breathe as I raced to the mast to hold on. I heard a door bolt open, and immediately I knew it was John. He came rushing out, eyes blown wide with alertness. He staggered on, trying to lean on the doorway for support. Our eyes locked, several feet away from each other as he silently questioned me. I was too afraid to say anything out loud, but John seemed to know what he was doing as he started to army crawl his way up to the side of the ship that was high from the water. He peered down, trying to take a look.

This didn't last long, as another pull on the anchor had him double backward on the other side of the railing. I couldn't help the yell that escaped my throat, calling his name. He held on like a monkey and swung himself back around to the right side. After another sharp tug, the side of the vessel almost reached the water, and John went flying from the right end of the ship to the left. I heard a loud "OOF" and looked down to see a pile of limbs. He took a minute to recompose and then flung himself over to me. If this was any other moment, I would compare him to a leaping cat.

"'Ave you manned a cannon yet?"

I shook my head, still refusing to let go of the mast as the ship continued to grumble.

"I've always believed in learning under fire," he proclaimed.

Despite my death grip on the mast, he pulled me by my wrist, leading me down below as a couple of men started to stir.

"Why aren't we waking the men up?!"

He continued running to the guns as he replied, "This particular beast is testing the waters if you will. Seeing how many of us there are to devour. Would rather it not be worth the fight, hm?"

There was no time for any other questions, as I was handing him gunpowder while he opened the porthole. I hoped the water wouldn't come rushing in with how close we kept ending up to the surface. It all happened in a rush, and before I knew fully what was going on, John was yelling fire and grabbing me.

Then a bang was ringing in my ears, and I wished I'd had the time to fill them with wax. Everything trembled and shook as I tried to hone in on my hearing. By the time the ringing faded, so did the shaking. John and I peered out the porthole and saw the dark substance slowly subside as it retreated deeper into the sea.

Behind us came a voice. "What in God's name are the two of you doing?"

We both turn around to see Finn, looking exasperated. Boone was following close behind, as more of the crew started to wake.

John started talking. "You think we could've made all this noise ourselves? What do you think we were doing?"

Finn went over to the porthole, but the beast was probably gone. He looked back at John and I. In that moment Finn's age showed through, as his exhaustion was easily displayed.

"We had another run-in, didn't we?"

"He's taunting us," John replied.

It was my turn to speak up, annoyed that no one was telling me what we were dealing with.

"Is anyone going to tell me what that just was?"

John leans on the gun, nonchalantly. "That, my dear, was our lovely little friend the Kraken. Ol' Kraki. We've mentioned him before, haven't we?"

Mermaids were one thing to run into, but the Kraken? A deep-seated fear in me just became real, and my lungs were trying to catch up with the rest of me. I was so sure it was a myth, completely blown out-of-proportion sightings of giant squids. Records of the colossal octopus had only started popping up at the beginning of this century. And, of course, there's the horrifying fact that the name's origin means sea monster.

How is one supposed to go forward with that information? In any given situation, there are usually two typical responses. Fight or flight. And then there were those that fawn. It's me, I'm one of those people.

"Wait a minute. You just said another run-in?"

John and Finn looked at one another, then back to me.

Finn said, "Back when we captured the galleon, some of the men thought they had seen a small island formation a couple of miles out. We didn't stop at the time, but later that night a few of the hands decided to row out after a couple of drinks. The rest of us didn't wake up until we heard screaming, and by then it was too late. We had to leave immediately. Ever since then, it seems like he's been following us. Almost like he wants to finish the job."

John looked uneasy after Finn finished his explanation. As for me, I felt like I wanted to vomit. The adrenaline was still running, which prevented me from doing so, but I was well and truly terrified. Thankfully, the captain always seemed to know what I was thinking and tried to reassure me with his normal laid-back demeanor.

"Nothing to worry about, love. We've managed to avoid death up until now, our odds mustn't be that horrible."

Well, that wasn't quite as reassuring as I had hoped. Finn retreated from the room, to come back moments later with a bottle of wine. He handed it to me wordlessly. It was another bottle of the port wine from Horta, and I took several gulps before handing it back. At least this would help ease my nerves. Our conversation ended shortly, as most of the crew ended up surrounding us within a few minutes. Finn and John both tried to raise their spirits, telling them that the captain and I had injured the creature.

I wasn't entirely sure we had, and they weren't convinced either. They all looked anxious and were probably remembering their shipmates' deaths. But there was nothing that could be done, and it was a well-known truth that everyone there was at the mercy of the ocean. This would not be the first near-death experience, nor the last. I remembered Aerwyna and hoped she was okay. There was no way to communicate with her or warn her of danger. Maybe there would be a system we could establish in the future.

Once everyone calmed down and went back to their hammocks, John told Darien to take over watch. Darien was not thrilled, and I insisted the captain let me finish out my shift.

"Once that high leaves you, you'll be crashing like a ship running aground. I'd rather let Darien finish than have you sleeping on deck."

He made a fair point, despite Darien's scowl. I dragged my feet back to Marco's cabin, to bed. The wine had started to kick in by the time Finn and Marco entered the room. No one spoke a word, all of us favoring sleep too much and wishing her to visit us early that night.

Chapter Twenty-Nine

We had made it to Málaga. It was a mountainous region, with the castle of Gibralfaro nestled in the peaks. The architecture there was elaborate and grand and had already lasted for centuries. There was no problem docking our sloop in the harbor, as we had the appearance of wealth. Marco immediately left the ship to find us horses and carriages, as there would be about eight of us going to the ball. The rest of the crew would stay on board and keep watch.

The banquet was to be held at night, and we had high confidence that we would reach Alhambra before sunset. We wasted no time getting ready, some of the men getting dressed openly on deck. I went inside John's cabin to see him buttoning up the vest I picked out. I unlocked the sea chest with my outfit inside, sorting through the undergarments. I pulled up the cotton shorts after the tights were on. Next was the corset. I got it onto my frame, but it needed to be laced.

"John? Can you help with this?" I called.

He looked over from his position by the mirror, his eyes roaming over me. He hadn't even come close yet and I could feel the heat rising to my face.

"'Course, darling."

I walked to him, standing in front of the mirror so I could make sure he was doing a good job. He came to stand behind me, and I felt nervous to be looking at myself in the mirror. Worried that I would see my scarlet blush and the tips of John's red ears. The hairs on the back of my neck stood up as his hands ghosted over the ribbons at the top of the corset. Currently, the only support I had was holding my hands to the front of the corset tightly until I was held in. He finally started to get to work, and I could feel the calluses on his fingers as he tightened each side, brushing against my bare skin.

Moments later he was tying the ends together in a neat little bow. It was just the right amount of snugness to feel secure and comfortable. I turned around to thank him. He was still standing so close, he had yet to look down at my face, and for that I was grateful. His eyes seemed blown wide, pupils almost twice the size they normally were. The same as they had been many nights before. I could feel those knots in my stomach again, and he seemed to be waiting for a signal to move in and kiss me right then and there. His lips were parted ever so slightly, his breath heavy and hot.

"Thank you, Captain."

In just three little words I could see those eyes deflate just a smidge as he resigned himself to the fate of not getting any closer to me.

"Is there anything else, love?"

Hopeful. He was still hoping I'd change my mind and grab him. I believed I might've if I had not been plagued with my overactive thinking since birth. There were too many downsides to this. I didn't want to be attached. I didn't want him to break my heart. I didn't want to leave and have a piece of my soul left behind here (even though I was already doing just that).

"Just a moment," I said.

I stepped into the heavy gown of silk and pearls and diamonds and swished my way back to him. He buttoned me up, looking at me the entire time through the mirror. He wanted me second-guessing. Once he was finished with my dress he took the necklace out of the chest, before coming back to me and putting his arms over my head to drape the jewels around my neck. He took his time brushing my neck with his knuckles as he clasped the two ends together. I hated him. Did I mention that?

"That'll be all, John."

He went to put his coat on as I slipped into my pumps.

"Right."

There were only the finishing touches left to our ensembles, and we could hear Marco's voice outside of the cabin. Once all of the jewelry was adorned, I swatched some of the perfume Wyna gave me onto my person.

As we climbed into the carriages Marco had fetched, I thought of Cyra. This would be her moment. She would've loved to dress to the nines, ready to impress a king. Boone and Darien insisted on manning the horses, which left Finn with John and me in one carriage. In the other was our boatswain William, Paul, and Marco. All of us kept weapons on our person, concealed under the elaborate layers of clothing. I kept a small dagger with a mother-of-pearl handle strapped to my thigh, while John had a flintlock pistol near the back of his belt and a throwing knife on his side. Darien insisted on bringing powder flasks, which were basically grenades with style. Marco had somehow managed to strap a cutlass to his back, which had Finn and John bickering that one wrong move would result in a unique self-inflicted injury.

As we rode through the mountains, we talked of our arrival, fifty bad scenarios, and all the in-betweens. It was going to be a long day. The sun beat down on us mercilessly. Frequent stops were made to make sure the horses were properly hydrated, along with getting sufficient rest. These breaks were met with more drinks and meals in small villages filled with too many dishes to count. The change of pace from constant work sailing the sea to being able to rest and sleep during a journey was welcomed by everyone.

Well within the day, we reached Alhama de Granada, a small town located on the outskirts of the city of Granada. The town got its Arabic name from the thermal baths outside of town. Since Roman times the hot springs had been in use for their healing properties, Marco explained to us. Boone overheard, pronouncing that we should take a quick stop.

"Jolly idea! What do you say, Dira?" John asked me.

"But we're already in our nice clothes!"

John scoffed, which had a smile creeping on Finn's face. "We bloody well know how to take them off and on again, dearie."

"Loosen up, lass. Ya know you want to," Finn said to me.

I beamed in response. John in return let another gold glimmering grin out and proceeded to bang on the roof of the carriage.

I could hear Darien yelling next. "Hoy! Can you not speak out like a normal captain?"

Finn and Marco started laughing, as Finn said, "Johnny lives to annoy, lad!"

The bickering continued as we slowed down to the outskirts of town. Marco poked his head out, telling us we were close. We followed the town's river, and in minutes we all got out and started to walk. Boone was running ahead of us, undressing as he did so. There was no time to advise him to watch where he was throwing his clothes. Darien dragged his feet behind us as we quickened our pace. Soon we reached the bubbling waters, and it looked glorious. The men started undressing in front of me, with no shame.

I shimmied out of my gown, hanging it over a tree branch to keep away from the dirt. I threw my dagger into the pile of weapons. I left the jewelry on and padded over to John. He quickly untied my corset, eager to get in the water.

"I've un-tied quite a number of these in my life. It's coming naturally to me now."

"In my time, we'd call you a manwhore, John."

He threw his head back, laughing.

"Yes, well, not much time for all that nonsense out at sea is there?"

With that, he walked away, and I flung the corset off, stretching as I did so. I did something like crawl into the water, not wanting to show off any skin. Although it shouldn't matter. These men didn't think that way out here after so many years together. They simply swam about, chuckling to themselves and splashing each other. I soon joined the fun and felt my muscles go lax after months of hard work on a ship.

Knots seemed to ease themselves, and everything felt a little like jelly in the best way possible. My skin took on a sheen, which I attributed to a healthy glow. I kept my head above water, not wanting to mess up my hair, and had to try to chastise the men to stop splashing so much. This seemed to motivate them further in their efforts. It was then that I was reminded that males never really grow up. They just have fleeting moments of maturity and responsibility. But they were all still children at heart. I swam a little distance from them, to observe and relax. I watched as they made fools of themselves, carefree for however brief a time. I thought of Wyna again, wondering if she was all right. Was she patiently watching over the ship back in Málaga? I hoped I could see her again later that night after our rendezvous. I was then brought back to my surroundings. The water was a milky aquamarine, with steam rising all around. Surrounding the pools was lush greenery. It was a small oasis, and I wished that we could stay longer.

Alas, we had a schedule to keep. I was the last to leave the water, feeling rejuvenated. The men had gotten dressed quickly, and John held out his hand, averting his eyes. I grasped it, and he hoisted me out. I put back on my underthings and then clasped my corset, coming back over to the captain. He started to lace me back up in a swift fashion. His hands lingered on my waist, and, despite the dizzy feeling flooding over me, I smacked his hands away with a patronizing look. He threw them up in surrender, following a devilish grin. We both made our way back to the carriage, where the others were waiting.

Not long after our moment of spontaneity, we were in a drawn-out line of horses and buggies waiting to be let into the grand palace. I was going through that day with other lenses, hardly my own. It felt as though I wasn't in reality, but some altered place where I would forget the events that were happening the following day. The harder I would try to recall them, the more faded the memories would become. Things there felt so surreal. Is this what living was supposed to feel like? Marco had us stay quiet while we waited; he wanted to be the one to introduce us to the party.

Eventually, we got through the main gates, and I started to hear the mingling around us. I could hardly understand what anyone was saying and suddenly regretted not taking Spanish in high school. There was a live band playing, and the violin stood out to me the most. As we passed through grand archways, in the courtyard sat a wondrous fountain. The sheer intricacies of every corner were a sight to behold, especially for someone who'd lived in America for her whole life. With Marco still taking the lead, I walked beside John as he picked up a glass of wine from one of the waiters, sniffing it first.

We were paid little attention, as there were much more politically important people than the ones we were playing. I watched everyone interact, noting their clothing and airs. The choices in dress were colorful and bright, purposefully drawing attention to themselves. There were feathers and flowers, velvet and satin, diamonds and emeralds. Reluctantly I had to admit that John was more striking than anyone here. I could tell he was having quite a lot of fun seeing things through fresh eyes based on how he was looking at me. Finn, on the other hand, looked quite uncomfortable. You wouldn't think he would be the one with social anxiety, but it was clear that standing in a palace among the elite was not his scene.

John patted him on the shoulder, while Boone and Darien gossiped behind us. Despite our protests, they had made the other crew members wait outside with the carriages. Marco then pulled us aside, a little distance from inquiring eyes.

"Now's our time to split up. Mingle a little, act like you're enjoying yourselves. I will be keeping an eye on the king at all times. Darien and Boone, I want you two going on opposite ends of the palace and spying out the guards. Once you find them, keep them occupied if we come close. I want the three of you to blend in as much as possible. I say in an hour or two we can get this moving," Marco whispered.

We all nodded, waiting for him to go off and start worming his way in with the crowd.

Boone and Darien went their separate ways, and I caught Darien saying under his breath, "Always the bottom jobs."

That left the three of us, standing in a corner.

Chapter Thirty

We started the night with the governor. John, Finn and I all introduced ourselves to him and his wife, taking note of all of the expensive little trinkets he had on his person. He seemed elated to have American representatives at his banquet and thanked us repeatedly for coming. The governor struck me as a schmoozer. He told us that the meaning of the name of his home quite literally translated to red fortress. In great detail, he relayed how much the site was worth. I could practically see the greed in my friend's eyes.

Lucky for us, his bragging gave us vital information on what areas we should be bringing to our attention. We praised him for his accomplishments, and he soaked it in like a dog getting a pet. However, he practically flew away from us as soon as the king entered the room. We looked around, seeing Marco in close vicinity. Finn took this moment to break apart from John and me, hoping to get familiar with the next room - the Courtyard of Lindaraja. We were situated in the Palace of the Lions for the time being, as we still had some people to talk to. Or at least, pretend to talk to them. As we walked about, I noticed with amusement that John's walk had completely changed. Normally he went on with a sort of stagger masked as a strut, but he now held his head high, with an air of grace in his movements. His shoulders were squared back, and he had the slightest twinkle in his eyes, something that he probably couldn't hide even if he tried. They held mischief in them, and an insatiable curiosity for life and adventure. If what they say about eyes being a portal to the soul is true, there was no secret what kind of person John was.

After eyeing a couple of small groups of individuals, we came into contact with two wealthy retired merchants. They were stout men with fancy mustaches turned gray and full heads of hair. They held onto their glasses of wine with a type of lax spirit. Thankfully both of them spoke in broken English, no doubt picked up from their travels.

"Who might this lovely lady be?" one of them asked.

The other chipped in, "Your wife, sir?"

I started to shake my head before John wrapped one arm around mine, pulling me close to him. He gave them a smug smile if I ever saw one.

"Yes, gentlemen. My darling wife, Adira. Keeps me in check, this one."

I wanted nothing more than to glare at him and pinch his side. Instead, I smiled a little too sweetly, feigning the role of a doting partner.

"John is quite useless by himself, I assure you!" I told them, and I could see him grit his teeth ever so slightly, while the two men laughed politely.

We conversed for a little while longer, talking of foreign places and the beauty of where we stood. As they walked away I finally shot John the look I was holding back.

"Married now, are we?" I couldn't help but say.

"If you'd like, darling."

Those big brown eyes of his were looking directly at me, challenging me.

"You and I both know you're not the marrying type."

He raised an eyebrow, in fake offense.

"I could be, you know! 'Cept I'd never be home for dinner...."

I wondered if marriage was in John's future. If there'd be a wife one day, waiting at home for him to return from the sea. Would she make him meal after meal gone cold? Would they be faithful to each other? Would he have children one day? I shook myself from these thoughts, of the life he would lead in my absence.

Thankfully Finn approached us once again, a well-timed distraction. He whispered to us in hushed tones.

"Checked in with Darien. There are more guards than we thought. They're bringing out the rest of the men from outside; all eight of us should be watching our backs."

John nodded as Finn walked back into the sea of people around us.

"Perhaps we should explore a little more," John suggested.

I agreed, so we headed into the room adjacent to Finn's stakeout. Inside the Comares Palace lay another courtyard, and, instead of a fountain, we found two fountains flowing their water into a pool. It was reflective and drew everyone's attention, the centerpiece of the room. Myrtle bushes were aligning the pool, and only later did I realize the courtyard was named after the greenery. We were surprised to see this section of the fortress nearly empty and wondered where the rest of the crowd had gone. Deciding to worry about it later, we used the vacancy to our advantage. Searching high and low, we evaluated what treasures could be pillaged there. The architecture screamed late 14th century, and John laughed at my oohing. They were built to impress, as Comares translates to "open your eyes and see."

The two halls lining the pool were filled with galleries, and I was thankful I secured a satchel to my waist under my gown. The galleries reminded me of one of the rooms from the Metropolitan Museum of Art, encased with small sculptures and ancient jewels. I reached for one of the statues, stuffing it in my bag while hoisting my skirts up. I could see John pouring gems into the interior pockets of his overcoat. We suddenly heard footsteps and froze, coming up to each other and opting for a fake stroll. Once the footsteps became louder and the person came into view, we collectively took a sigh of relief. It was only Paul, and he was looking at the halls with the same sort of wonder. Once he saw us, he rushed to the captain for an update.

"We've already extracted several antiquities without notice, but not sure how long it'll last. Finn had me come search for you and see if you needed any extra hands," Paul told us.

John replied, "Music to my ears! Get William to go with you and take as much as you can from these halls. Dira and I will go see about that tower."

Paul nodded and started jogging to go find his shipmate. The Comares Towers sat on the north side of the courtyard, and we headed towards it with haste. To get there we passed through the Sala de la Barca, a wide rectangular hall behind the northern porch of the court. What we saw in the tower elicited a gasp from me.

The tower held The Hall of the Ambassadors, a square chamber that was the largest room in the Alhambra. The domed ceiling was lined with tile work, creating designs that reminded me of a starry night. John told me it was meant to represent the seven heavens. This was where the majority of the people were, and I could see why. The original purpose of the room was to hold the sultan's throne or serve as an audience chamber. As I took in more of the artwork, the music started to change into more of a ballad. I watched as the crowd started to pair off in twos, assembling to dance. I had never seen ballroom dancing in my life; the only dancing I had ever become accustomed to was square dancing, the most podunk country dancing of them all, held in a high school in my hometown. The events were typically held just to meet men your age, and they were dreadfully awful. Nothing was pleasing about them at all. What I saw before me could not even be compared. The movements they followed were filled with grace, creating live art. I watched with awe as they continued in a fluid-like manner and with serene emotion.

"Care to dance, m'lady?" John asked me, coming to stand in front of me.

"I'd be most obliged, Captain," I whispered in his ear.

He grinned and held out an arm for me to hold onto as he guided us to the middle of the room. As a new ballad started, one of John's hands swept around my waist, as the other entwined with my own. My left hand placed itself on his bicep, and, as I chanced a look at his face, I saw him staring at me with a voracious intensity. I felt as if at any moment I might start melting from the heat in my face, as my heart beat at twice the speed. I tried my hardest to maintain eye contact. We started slowly, each foot going in front of the other, or side to side, in long strides.

I could hardly make sense of the movements at first, getting confused and having John do all the work. After a few moments, though, we got into a sort of rhythm. All of a sudden it was like walking on water. It was like we were on Horta's shore again dancing in the moonlight, but this time there was no mistaking it for a dream or a whim. It was an entrancement, and, despite us dancing in between couple after couple, he was the only one I was focused on. I could feel his hand pull me closer to him, and I was aware of his touch every second. There was no telling how much time was passing and whether or not we were being noticed. I blamed it on the music. The dancing. Anything but my own wishes.

Every so often he glanced down at my lips, and not for the first time I wondered what his own would feel like on mine. There was no bickering between us now. No fighting for who was the more capable, or digging for information. It was as though all of the insecurities and doubts vanished as soon as we started to move to the music. It was lovely. Did it have to end? The ballad started to finish, and, for the first time, I noticed those around me. Only then did I notice we'd been dancing right next to the governor and the king. John noticed too, and we looked around for Marco. He could be seen from one of the three windows, watching through the courtyard. The dance ended as John and I came to a halt. My hand slipped away from his arm, and the other let go of his grasp, but he still had one arm around me, reluctant to pull apart.

It was then that I caught the king's attention. His eyes had been wandering around from woman to woman throughout the night, and it seemed he'd finally noticed me. I gave him a small sweet smile, and John noticed who I was looking at. The king smiled back, letting his eyes linger for a little too long. He started to head over to us, perhaps to ask me to dance. As his gaze wandered, he seemed to hold emphasis on my hands. I looked at them too, with new curiosity, wondering what could be capturing his interest. Then, in silent dread, I remembered the ring I was wearing.

Chapter Thirty-One

The best way to describe the king's features at that moment is hatred. Pure, unadulterated hatred. He grabbed the arm of the governor, jerking his hand in our direction, speaking quickly. The governor's face filled with horror, and he was soon off scrambling to find guards. King Philip's attention was back on us, and he was looking straight at the captain.

"You," the king spat out like venom.

John and I looked at each other, wide-eyed.

"I think it's time to go!" John exclaimed.

He took hold of my wrist and we bolted. We wove in between the stunned couples as the king continued to yell out. Sounds of scuffling and shouting could be heard, and, once we reached the Comares Palace, it took one look at Marco to know our raid was done. He leaped into action, running to go find the other men. As if it wasn't already bad, we heard pistols firing behind us, and suddenly we were looking back and ducking every couple of seconds. There was barely time to react, and I cursed my slow-processing brain. John was tugging at me every now and then to prevent me from getting shot while we made our way to one of the many gates. The fortress seemed never-ending, and we caught a glimpse of Paul helping Darien carry out crates almost as big as them. Once we finally reached the northern gate we heard a cry come from behind us and saw William falling to the ground. There were no second thoughts as we backtracked, making our way to him.

William took a hit to the leg, and he could barely stand without shooting pain. John and I did the only thing we could think to do, which involved each of us holding him up as he held onto our necks and continued running. We slowed down significantly, and I could hear the guards catching up to us. I couldn't go to jail. I couldn't get shot. I didn't have time! I couldn't get stuck here! I pushed my body more than I'd ever done, continuing to help carry William and get us out of there. Suddenly shooting came from another direction, and I was relieved beyond words to see Finn enter my field of vision. He started firing at our opposing forces, giving us more time. We started our way toward him, and he quickly took my place to help William. Finn handed me his pistol, and I shook my head at him. I couldn't do what he was asking.

He shouted, "Don't fight me on this, Adira! It's either them or us! Remember that!"

They immediately picked up the pace and couldn't duck at all while carrying William. It was when a bullet grazed Finn's side and a strangled scream escaped him that I realized I couldn't continue to do nothing. I immediately gave them cover, came behind them, and started jogging backward. I took my best aim and started to fire out. Several shots transpired, and I managed to hit one of the guards in the shoulder. It gave us enough time to leave the room and head into the Court of Lions.

We shoved guests out of the way as they elicited screams and gasps at our dramatic departure. Boone came into view, running with filled sackcloths in both arms. We were all trying to just get out alive with as much loot as possible; there was no thought of the damage we left. Leaving the court, we were back towards the entrance, and we saw Paul beckoning us back to the carriages.

John and Finn raced to Paul as they struggled to get William in with as little pain as possible. My attention was drawn to Marco as I saw him engaged in a sword fight with several men in the entryway. I reached for my dagger, hoping to provide some backup. Racing towards them, I made no sudden sounds before jabbing the steel into one of the guard's thighs. My goal was not to kill, it was to escape. They yelped out, and I yanked my dagger away. The man fell to the ground, which left Marco with only two men to defeat. By then John, Finn, and Paul had come to join in the fun. They easily tackled the rest of the guardsmen, and, before anything else could be done, we heard an explosion to our right. The best guess was Darien got out his powder flasks. Which meant they went back for another round of goods. Marco was cursing and racing his hand through his cropped curly hair. We needed to leave, and there were still two of our men in there. I briefly wondered if John would leave the men there to rot or die, but that train of thought went out the window when all four of them started fighting their way back in. They seemed to have a handle on things, so I took it into my own hands to go find the two idiots.

I reached the Lindaraja Courtyard, and that was where I found the fools. They were still trying to pick stuff up, their arms full of who knows what. Crates, bags, boxes, all of it was in their hold. Meanwhile, there were about ten men against us. The odds were not looking great.

I shouted at them, "You fools! We should've left already! We have to go!"

"That's lookin' quite obvious now, miss," Boone told me.

Darien had two powder flasks left, and they couldn't be wasted. As we got cornered by the guardsmen, I saw a glimpse of John flailing his arms with his gun out and Marco close behind him with his cutlass. The sight made me want to laugh just a bit, and I was sure I would later. Finn came staggering out with them, and both he and John used their pistols to start firing. A commotion ensued, both parties shouting and scrambling about. Darien decided to cut the misery short and threw one of his flasks directly at the men, and, as it impacted, smoke swooped in and it sounded like thunder in my ears. We made a run for it, and it was almost a competition to see who could reach the gates first. Finn was now gripping his side, and Boone was dropping things with every corner we turned. Once we were nearly out, Darien threw his last flask backward as a precaution.

We piled into the two carriages with all of the stolen goods strapped to the roof, to the floor, anywhere with a smidge of spare space. The horses nearly tripped on themselves with how fast and jerky we were moving, and multiple crashes could be heard as we ran into several other people. Everyone was holding their breath through Granada as we heard bells sound off, alerting the whole city to our presence. We wouldn't be able to stop unless we were at least an hour out, and I prayed that someone thought to bring gauze for William's leg. I hoped John wouldn't try to come back here anytime soon, as the whole country would no doubt be making his capture reward sound very tempting. The captain poked his head out, and gunshots were immediately heard. He jumped in his seat and shut the windows, realizing we were going to be followed for a while. We swerved around, trying to avoid having the horses shot at as best we could.

Reaching Casabermeja we decided it necessary to stop, for the horses' sake and William's. It was a poor town, and we stayed on the outskirts for our break and started laying out any spare materials we had on the ground. There was a pond close by, and Finn ran out with buckets. Marco and John gingerly lay William down on the ground and took one of the cushions out of the carriage for his neck. None of us were surgeons, so we shouldn't have been messing with his wound, but if we did nothing he could've bled out. It'd been left alone too long as it was. Paul lit an oil lamp, holding it near William's leg. Once Finn came back, Marco poured water on the wound, and William started to yell out. Darien gave him a rag to bite on, trying to stay as quiet as possible to avoid any curious townsfolk. After his leg had been cleansed with the little we had available, John took out his knife.

William passed out as soon as the incision was made, and Finn had to stick his hand in and fish for the bullet. There was no cringing or fainting at the sight of blood in this line of work; you had to have a steel-like resolve. Once Finn found the bullet, we got to the hard part. None of us had sewing needles or any medical equipment, so we had to improvise. Boone gave us one of his studded earrings, and I ripped out a small ribbon from my dress. Marco secured it to the small needle and got to work. It was messy and god-awful looking, but it was better than William dying or losing his leg. After the job was done everyone sighed out of relief, and we threw ourselves onto the ground. This would be the only stop for the night, as staying anywhere for a bite to eat was too risky. After we took five minutes to catch our breath, we got back on the road.

Two hours later we were back in Málaga, and I saw the sloop waiting for us in the harbor. John yelled at the men on deck to throw down the plank, and we got busy loading everything on board. Marco and Paul carried William into one of the cabins, and the surgeon Terrence took over from there. Finn told us we were lucky to have one at all. I could see the pain and exhaustion in his eyes, as he knew he'd have to wait his turn to get any stitches until William was taken care of. The crew rejoiced over our surplus, and we found that they'd been busy supplying the ship with fresh provisions and expensive foods. They were not surprised to hear of our close call, as supposedly they'd witnessed closer. We should be grateful no one died. That's just the life of a buccaneer, I was told. I found to my dismay that I sort of enjoyed the chase. I didn't like seeing my friends hurt, or the idea of getting killed or imprisoned, but the rush of it all was exciting.

We sailed immediately into the night, getting as far away from the coast of Spain as possible. Everyone was given a portion of the treasures, and we went on as if nothing happened. Simply another victory, another excursion. A few men stayed on watch, but the rest of us partied. Our fine clothes were removed immediately, settling back into loose outfits made to move around comfortably. We drank and ate and sang and told the crew of our day. John may have left out our dancing, but the men loved to hear every detail of our transpires. The captain was proud. He was proud of everyone, but I felt a warm feeling knowing part of that was directed at me. Every moment there was taken in stride; we had all acted with recklessness on many occasions, but it was a fault of us all, and it was accepted. It was something I had become comfortable with, but isn't freedom always a little bit frightening? I was allowed space there, and choices. I could be whoever I wanted. But deep down I think freedom scares me. I have never known it. Not truly. Life can be a sort of cage that cannot be broken, and I have been under constraints for most of my years. I wanted no strings anywhere, yet the future had its reins on me. And I was doing nothing about it.

Eventually, the night was almost over, and Spain was almost completely out of view. I couldn't really see

Wyna again until the ship slowed down, which upset me. I would only have three months left there before I would have to go back, if that. I wish I could understand what the mermaid saw in me and why she felt drawn to me so deeply. I hoped we could sort it out. I hoped I would see mermaids in my time, now that I knew they existed. Did they no longer swim around the New England coast? Or maybe they were going extinct a couple hundred years from now. There was still so much I didn't know and may never find out. The sea would never run out of things to tell me. As I thought about heading back to the captain's quarters, I took one last glance toward the ocean. I squinted as I saw a couple of small formations out in the distance, which confused me. We shouldn't be reaching any islands for quite some time.

One of the hands, Charlie, was covering for Finn at the helm and seemed to have a one-track mind, as he hadn't noticed the land yet. Not wanting to bother him just yet, I brought out some of the maps and charts, rolling them out on deck. As I suspected, our course wouldn't be taking us along anything until we glided by Horta again, which would take roughly a month. I took my telescope out, zooming in on the masses. It was hard to see any sort of detail in the darkness as we continued to move through the water.

Then I remembered what Finn had told me right before we reached Spain. How those sailors died, thinking they had seen small islands to explore. I had not seen the creature out of the water, and, although I could not see much that stood out to me now, just knowing it was on the surface petrified me.

"Charlie? Did you notice the-"

"The land that isn't land? Yes, miss. Been waiting for us all day a ways out from the harbor."

I realized none of us had a choice that night in sailing away, reluctantly leading us closer to the Kraken. I gathered all the maps together, jogging to the captain's quarters. I opened the door and saw John in bed already as he looked up at me.

"You all right, love?"

I shook my head violently, making my way over to him.

"It's following us, John. It's out there."

He started to sit up, trying to fight off sleep.

"Course it is. What would you have me do about it?"

I couldn't believe he was being so nonchalant about a sea monster stalking us.

"You're not at all concerned that a monster is out there, just waiting to kill more of your crew?"

Even standing here, knowing it was around, put me on edge.

"I don't like it, Dira. But what can I do to make the beast stay away? I say let's not worry about it until it decides to eat one of us. And by then, it won't really matter, will it?"

He was unfathomable. Right of course, but it didn't help ease my nerves one bit.

"Hasn't anyone tried to kill it?"

It was probably a dumb question, but I needed to ask something until I could calm myself down.

"All any of us can do about it is continue to run away. When it's bigger than the ship that holds us, there's not much man can do to ward it off."

"But it can be injured. We know that. There's a chance of survival, if we have another encounter."

"Em, sure."

I wondered if it went for John directly if he would finally feel some of the anxiety the rest of us did. Or if he already felt the fear but just masked it with charisma and carelessness. Whatever the case, clearly nothing could be done. I just had to be okay with falling asleep knowing that at any moment I could get killed by a giant octopus. It was a task that proved difficult as I lay down for what felt like an eternity. I felt a little invincible, just a little, after that day. The Kraken may be their constant companion, looming death over their shoulders. But that did not stop them from continuing, and so it was my job to show some trust.

Chapter Thirty-Two

I was sitting with Aerwyna a week later as we talked of our two worlds. She seemed to finally accept I was not like her, but that didn't stop the mermaid from asking me to swim with her. She spoke of the Kraken and how ancient the creature was. A few mermaids had been known to befriend it, but it was a rare occurrence. They must know the beast from a young age, so I was told. Mermaids are fast and agile and can outswim most things, so they use it to their advantage. She proceeded to tell me that they could manipulate water, and she demonstrated.

In her concentration, she moved her hand out of the sea, making small movements. Close to her, droplets formed out of the water, creating a separate body of water. She dropped her hand, and the water fell back into the ocean. I watched her in awe, completely immersed.

"We can control the weather at times, too," she went on to say. "When we get in disputes or need to defeat our enemies."

They work together with other sea creatures to keep the ocean safe, usually deriving power from underwater currents. It made me sad for my kind and the way we only ever further destroy the land we walk on. Mermaids seem to live in constant danger, but they handle it with grace. It was another warm starry night, and neither one of us wanted our time together to end just yet.

"Why won't you swim with me, Adira?"

I smiled. "I couldn't keep up with you, Wyna!"

I hated the sadness that filled her features every time I turned down her offer. But the girl was persistent.

"Trust me."

She grabbed hold of my ankle, pulling me down into the sea before I could react. My lungs filled with water as I became disoriented, and I quickly raised my head above the surface, coughing violently. Wyna held me up, and I felt inferior at that moment. It didn't matter, and I found that despite almost drowning, the water felt nice.

I asked her, "What about the Kraken?"

"Our kind can sense him. We stay away from him when he's in a mood."

"Yes, but-"

She was done with the conversation, and she pulled me back down. I didn't know where she was going to take me, but as my hand slipped into hers, I did not stop her. We plunged into the deep blue, and I felt the coolness of the water continue to wash over me, making me new again. I hardly had to move, as Wyna did most of the swimming for the both of us. I saw the bottom of the sloop with moss already latching onto the wood. My eyes didn't hurt from keeping them open, which left me surprised. Wyna continued to go deeper, and I feared I would run out of breath. But as we kept swimming, I did not feel the loss of oxygen or hyperventilating kick in.

I looked towards my friend, amazed at this discovery. Was it her presence that kept me from drowning? Was she protecting me in some way? There was no need for a light source in the endless darkness, as her skin shone and her hair continued to glow. Then a couple of tendrils of my hair came into view, and I saw that I was also glowing. I tugged at her, pointing at my hair. She simply smiled at me, as if she knew this would happen all along. We continued to swim, and I saw all sorts of life around me. There were schools of fish paying no mind to us and sharks moving out of our way. They seemed to have a sort of understanding with the mermaid next to me. It was amazing, and I had to try my best not to open my mouth with a smile. I nearly had to stifle a scream when we started to swim with a group of whales. Wyna swam up right next to them as they sang in a different language together. The peace on her face was what calmed me down, as we were really at no harm amongst these creatures. They seemed to be in a conversation for some time before we parted ways. We reached a brood of jellyfish, and Wyna swooped lower, trying to avoid their sting. They too seemed to try and swim upwards, out of respect for her.

We had been swimming for a while, and I started to get nervous as to where Wyna was taking me. I should've been feeling the water pressure weigh in on me by now, slowly crushing me with each increment we declined. But there was nothing, and it made me wonder just how much power Wyna was capable of. The sea seemed to be at her mercy. Or perhaps they were connected. We went on for what felt like forever until I started to see other glowing entities. I couldn't tell what they were, and it wasn't until we got closer that I realized I was around other mermaids. They were everywhere. To my right was a little grove, filled with coral and glittering gold, and in the middle were two mermaids, sorting through chests that looked like the ones held on the ship above their heads. To the left lay what remained of a shipwreck that sat on the bottom of the ocean floor for who knows how long. All of the mermaids started to notice Wyna and me and began swimming towards us. Soon I was enveloped by several of them, and they twirled me around in a giant hug and combed their fingers through my hair. It felt like I was with a bunch of my best friends at a sleepover.

Wyna talked to them in some ancient tongue from what I was seeing, and I could only float next to her in confusion.

"Can you understand us now?"

She just spoke to me, but her lips had not moved. Had I heard that in my mind?

"In a way," she replied.

Oh my god, she was reading my thoughts. And I was somehow reading hers. My mouth flew open, and my hands flew to my throat, too late to stop what I had just done. And then, nothing happened. I simply started to breathe the water in and out.

"What's happening?!" I demanded.

Wyna looked at me with almost pity as the other mermaids observed us. Wyna went over to me, touching the side of my neck. That's when I felt it. There were grooves in my neck. I started to freak out with this new transformation. I was going into a panic attack, and Wyna must've sensed my fear, as she held onto both of my shoulders.

"You're alright, Adira! This is natural!"

I brought my own hands to my neck, feeling the gills do all the breathing for me. I tried thinking in my mind, to formulate a sentence.

"I don't understand. How is this happening?!"

The other mermaids chose that moment to enter the conversation, seemingly also telepathically linked to my mind.

"You are a child of the sea," they told me.

"I... I'm not even from this time, I am no one here."

Some looked confused, others sympathetic. It was what I had told Aerwyna when we first met, and I had gotten the same reaction from her. Wyna took my hand into both of hers again, and I could sense how desperately she wanted us to understand one another. I was glad she was not intruding in on my thoughts, appreciative of her self control.

She said, "We have sensed you since you arrived."

"So, you can telepathically feel every species?"

She tilted her head to the side, a slight shrug on her shoulders.

"It is similar to how whales communicate. Through frequencies. But rarely do we feel a strong pull to one as we do towards you."

I didn't know what that meant.

"Perhaps from the time disturbances. Maybe you can feel when someone doesn't belong here," I offered.

One of the mermaids, who had ginger hair and a tail that was more aquamarine in color, spoke up.

"We know when one of our sisters is close by. We can feel the tug in our souls, letting us know we are not alone. This feels similar."

I replied, "Yes, but I am not one of you. I wouldn't even be talking to you if it weren't for Aerwyna."

"Over the centuries of humans and merfolk living together, we have tried to bring humans down here before. We can help them breathe and direct them, but you should've died a long time ago down here," Wyna told me.

I touched my gills again, looking at her.

"You didn't do this?"

She shook her head. "No human can transform themselves as we see before us."

"What does this mean?"

The mermaids looked at each other, no doubt having a private conversation. Wyna looked back at me.

"Who is your family, Adira?"

"I don't see how that matters. They are people in your future, hundreds of years from now. None of us are of real importance!"

The ginger spoke up again. "And you know that they are human?"

These questions were getting a bit stupid.

"Of course they are! We're just a bunch of rednecks. Nothing more."

They clearly didn't know what that term meant. It was getting late, and I was starting to worry someone on the ship would notice I was nowhere to be seen.

"You need to realize that your world is not what it seems. Do not just accept what you've been told," the ginger told me.

I was getting tired and on the verge of lashing out with how mystifying this whole encounter was. Wyna could sense my irritability.

"Why don't we show you around, Adira?"

I sent them my affirmation and they motioned for me to follow them. I struggled to keep up with them and saw only the ends of their tails glittering in front of me for quite some time. Wyna found my hand again and brought me to the front of the group to see where we were going. We headed for the shipwreck and found that the ship had not decayed as much as I originally thought. It seemed to be slightly split in the middle, all jagged and torn.

I asked them, "What's the story here?"

Aerwyna told me that the mermaid with ginger hair was named Alorna. I felt drawn to her, which was just one more thing that was hard to explain even to myself.

"One of the Kraken's more recent victims. Poor souls. We tried to give them a more respectful burial the best we could," Alorna told me.

So this was what could become of our ship. Sinking and being pulled down with the sloop was a very real possibility. We reached the exterior to what I could tell was a frigate, and whatever colors it originally had had been torn away during the struggle. It felt sad in a way, and the mermaids seemed to sympathize. As we reached what would've been the captain's quarters, the mermaids had maps and charts pinned all about on every flat surface, and I realized they probably didn't get as many chances as we did to see any advancements in navigation. They had knowledge as to where everything was, clearly well acquainted with the layout of the ship.

Aerwyna had started to giggle with the other mermaids, trying to figure out what purpose an item they had found had. Alorna stayed with me, and I decided to explore this pull I had felt.

"Alorna, have you always swam in these waters?"

She gave me a quick glance, her silky fiery locks flowing like a separate living creature all around her. She was a true beauty.

"Yes. We are all part of the North Atlantic tribe. Our queen is my sister."

It made sense for the merfolk to have a sort of government or kingdom of their own. Every intellectual species needed some form of order.

"What makes one in your kind royal? Do you have a pure bloodline?"

I knew technically she did not have to answer any of my questions, but she seemed comfortable with me and knowing in her nature.

"Precisely. Our family has special advantages that the rest of our people do not. We are allowed a lot more freedom, in certain aspects."

This made me ever more curious, wondering what made royalty so special.

"We are direct descendants of the first mermaid to ever swim the seven seas. Your people like to come up with wild strange stories of what they see in our home. But listen to me when I say that most of what they say has very little truth."

Her explanation reminded me of one of my first conversations with John, and I wondered if he gained some of his knowledge from these mermaids.

"I have so many questions; do you have whole cities like we do?"

I could tell she was amused by my excitement.

"Of course we do. There's kingdoms all over the place. Dynasties, boroughs, and empires. The Queen sent us here; she and I were the first to feel when you arrived."

"Do you always sense things before the rest of your kind?"

She nodded. "Usually. We felt a sort of connection to you that is hard to describe in your language."

Alorna's eyes wandered, and I saw that Wyna had been listening to part of our conversation. They looked at each other, maybe having another secret conversation.

"I think it's time we head back," Wyna finally told me.

I nodded, taking one last look at the royal mermaid.

"It was a pleasure to meet you," I told her.

"Perhaps we'll meet again," Alorna said.

Wyna took my hand and propelled us upward. Even my fingers had not pruned. Every normal physical sign that should've presented itself had never shown. It is an eerie feeling to realize you no longer know what to expect from your own self. I felt as though the mermaids were holding something back from me. Wyna sped us through the deep blue, and soon I could see the moon high above the sky again. Once we reached the surface, I could feel the gills on my neck retreat back into my skin, as if they were never there. Wyna looked at me, trying to gauge if I was okay.

"Don't fret, Adira. This will become more clear over time."

"What is your interest in me, Wyna? Is all this trouble really for one alerting sense?"

There was that uneasy look in her eyes.

"You fascinate us. We wish to understand you."

Right. There were things she wasn't saying, and maybe because she thought I wouldn't accept what she had to say. I had to just relent that it was a talk for another night and that goodbyes were what was in order right now. She hugged me, maybe sensing my anxiety, and I grabbed hold of the rope I had let down and climbed my way back up.

I stayed by the railing for a while longer, trying to make sense of what happened down there. There was so much to worry about aside from what the creatures in the sea thought of me. It seemed like a low priority at the moment, but it was gnawing at me. I felt like I didn't have enough time. Not for the first time I thought about prolonging my stay there, but I knew it would be a hindrance to everyone there. I had to cut ties even if just for a while, to make sense of my time.

I made it back to the captain's quarters, knocking and entering before the person inside could really say anything, and found that John was not asleep yet. He was at his desk and appeared to be sketching. I couldn't make out what the subject matter was from where I stood but realized that was probably why his hands were so often smudged black.

"I didn't take you as someone who contributed to the arts, Captain."

He continued in his work, not looking up.

"I dabble in many things, you'll come to find."

It was true that almost every day of knowing John I learned something new about him that I had not expected. He seemed a little melancholic that night. I sat on his bed, which faced his back.

"What troubles you, John?"

He closed his sketchbook, keeping it in his hands.

"I just wonder how you'll fare back in your lighthouse. Back in constraints. I know I couldn't do it."

He said it as though we were the same and he was speaking as if he'd tried a slow life on land. Perhaps we were, perhaps he had.

"Truthfully I don't know. Maybe I'll grow tired of it all."

He put the sketchbook on his desk, rising from his chair.

"And by then it'll be too late."

"I don't know that. It could very well be that I just travel between our two worlds, for years to come."

He came to the bed, leaning on one side.

"You can't exist in two worlds, Dira. One way or another, you'll need to choose."

I did not wish to think that way. I wanted one foot in every door, refusing to let go. This discovery was still fresh, and I wanted to bask in it for a while.

I asked him suddenly, "Where will you go after I head home?"

He contemplated it, because the captain was the sort of person who did everything on a whim. He was spontaneous and relied on others for any type of order to happen.

"I received a letter back in Boston before we hoisted you up the galleon. From the Brethren. They want me to restore the code."

"Well, that's rather vague."

"They want me back in the Caribbean. To restore the pirate republic."

There was one place in the West Indies that would've recently been a pirate downfall, and that place was Nassau.

"You mean Charles Towne, don't you?"

He nodded.

"The governor in chief has tried restoring order to the town for a few years, but several Brethren members have been trying to oppose his efforts. They think I can push the chief over the edge and bring back our homeland."

It would be an impossible effort. By 1732 the Golden Age would have been history. Not to mention King George I issued his Proclamation for Suppressing of Pirates only three years before, and the majority of the pirates I had read about signed off on it, with the exception of Blackbeard and Charles Vane. If I had not read about John Sterling in any history books, I doubted he would have made himself known by signing off on the pardon. But going to Charles Towne also meant a high chance of getting caught. And that seemed like a place the captain would steer clear from.

"And you're going to help them?"

"It seems a hopeless cause. The chance of freedom or entrapment is a nasty gamble."

I wondered if I had a role in convincing John not to go to Nassau. Would it be his rejection that kept him safe from being hung?

"Perhaps you should decline their offer then."

I could see he was worried about whatever outcome would befall the town, as it would be a stepping stone in the destruction of his way of life.

"I've got time to think about it... and what troubles you, my dear?"

So he saw right through me. I wanted to tell someone about that night, what I had seen and learned. I wanted to let someone in on the weird things that were happening to me.

"Nothing substantial, Captain. I worry about sea monsters and half-women, things that are vacant in my world. That's all."

He searched my eyes for a moment, trying to catch me in a lie. He gave up, though, and I stood up to leave. A glare in the window caught my eye, and I thought I may have caught a glimpse of Wyna out in the water, watching the two of us.

Chapter Thirty-Three

We reached the series of islands in Portugal as time crept up on us all. Instead of porting in Horta, we opted for Ponta Delgada on Sao Miguel Island. It came to us before Horta did, and we were all wanting to see something a little different. This place was known for its citrus exports, and the division was nestled in multiple volcanic structures. Stewart told us he'd been there before and that inside one of the ancient craters lay lakes in the richest shades of blues and greens. Despite the lush atmosphere that begged for exploring, he warned the crew that Delgada was home to well-known cults that snaked through the city looking for new members every hour of the day.

The town started off as a humble fishing abode, where fishermen took comfort in the safe coves. This was good news for us too, as we took to one of the coves away from the wharf, hiding in nature's security. The majority of us took off to go find simple pleasures to fill our day with. Upon entering the city center, the city gates, or Portas da Cidade, greeted us before anything else. This was the first line of defense for the harbor, and they towered over us. The path had classic Portuguese black and white cobblestone floors. During our explorations, we noted the hot spring pools available and the geysers near the Furnas village. They were a sight to behold, so very different from anything I'd ever seen before. What surprised us more was that the people in the village relied on the volcanoes to cook their food. We were awe-struck, and John insisted we must try.

Several of us sat outside of a villager's humble abode as they cooked us meat stew. They placed it in a metal pot and proceeded to bury it in volcanic soil. Once the stew was done, the people brought it to our table for our inspection. Finn poked at it and we came to know it consisted of cabbage, carrots, potatoes, blood sausage, pork, and beef. Trying not to offend our hosts, I stealthily picked out the bits of sausage. Its slow-cooked method made the whole meal tender in texture, and there was nothing left in our bowls by the time we were done. Afterward we perused the markets, where we were met with a variety of wicker creations, lace, embroideries, and scrimshaw. There were children running about and shouting in every direction. Woven jewelry caught my eye, and John and I found ourselves in a conversation with the old woman who made them about the appreciation we had for craftsmanship. She was so moved by our enthusiasm she ended up gifting us woven bracelets and hair pieces, which we accepted graciously.

Marco came up to us, telling us that some of the locals were harvesting pineapple, handing us a couple. Still standing, we all took out our knives, cutting off the spikes and carving out pieces of the flesh to eat during our roaming. My time with the crew had taught me that something we all had in common was the universal motivator that is food. When we learned how cheap the wine and cheese was there, we reached somewhat of a stupor, buying as

257

many bottles and wrapped cheeses as our hands could carry. Boone became a mule of sorts, with bags strapped to his back full of our findings. We lost Marco again, and we split up more and more as there was too much to see and do before the night was over. All around us, we were surrounded by volcanoes and mountains, and a sliver of the sea could be seen at all times. There were flowers there so richly colored in magenta and pink that it made me wonder if you could grind it up and use it as lipstick.

Several of us made it to the springs that had water that resembled citrine and oranges, until we got sick from overeating. But then there was contentment in sitting on moss-covered mountains, losing yourself in nature, and devoting your time to a new culture that is someone else's whole world and livelihood. Just in a day's time I had learned and seen things in that place that seemed to only exist in movies and travel brochures. The type of enlightenment I had experienced was what I had come to know, the only high worth riding. It was a humbling thing to realize how very small we are in this world. Knowing that there is endless beauty yet to be seen. It's the type of feeling that led me to believe that nothing in life is truly worth worrying about. That everything must work out because the earth will keep turning and the rest of my brothers and sisters will keep living. It is our job to make the most of it.

That was what I thought of when I found myself going back to the ship by myself. It'd been a short trip, almost a fever dream in the grand scheme of things. Just a chance to run around and let ourselves breathe before making it back to Boston. There wasn't a ship to careen this time, or prisoners to let loose. I was covered in new pieces, from my jewelry to a wicker satchel, and linen rags a little girl insisted she tie my hair up in. But it suited me in some odd way, and it made my heart ache that I would not be able to take any of these treasures home with me. They would gather dust in one of John's old chests, until one day he eventually threw them out.

I was brought out of my thoughts by a voice calling my name. I turned around to see Stewart running towards me in distress. I met him halfway, and he nearly stumbled into me. I gave him a moment to catch his breath before asking what in the world was going on. He was nearly heaving, and I tried my best to hold onto him for support as his knees were buckling every couple of seconds. This man had clearly not gone out of the galley enough.

"They've got 'im,'" was all he told me.

"Who's got who, Stew?"

He went wide-eyed. "The cult! The cult of the Holy Spirit! They've got Leo!"

Leo was one of the young boys on our ship that had outgrown his role as a powder monkey and was being trained to take on a bigger task. Despite Stewart's warnings, the boy was still young and oblivious.

"Well, what do we do?!"

The both of us started running back into the city mid-conversation to save time. I didn't know if Stewart's knees could take it, in between ragged breaths and his sandy hair flying behind him.

"We've got to get him back before it's too late! I can't find the captain!"

Of course. He was probably stuck in some tavern rambling and drinking.

"What exactly will they do to him?"

"The cult of the Holy Spirit believes in promises being made to God throughout the year. It just so happens to involve sacrificing the living."

I looked over to him, my turn to go wide-eyed.

"You can't be serious!"

"'Fraid so, miss."

We picked up our pace, as a celebration had broken out all over the streets with flamboyantly dressed individuals singing praises to the Almighty while holding something up. Of course, that something was Leo, strapped down and pleading for his life. We had yet to find any other shipmates and were running out of time. An intervention needed to be made, and for that to happen we needed more bodies. Stewart and I split up, and I started looking in all the taverns. The first two were where I found Finn and Boone, and they immediately got up from their tables upon hearing of Leo. They went off to gather more of the crew, and I made my way down the strip of businesses. Every minute I wasted searching for the captain was a minute closer to Leo's demise. I continued on frantically, determined to save this boy I barely knew. Eventually, in the fifth tavern, I found John. He was sitting on the counter in the front with women on each side of him. I felt a tad angry at him but didn't want to unpack that at this moment. I grabbed him by the arm, yanking him outside.

"I was having quite a nice time there, you know."

"Well while you've been busy chatting it up with the whores, Leo is going to die by a bunch of deluded Christians if we don't do something!"

This seemed to have piqued his interest, and thankfully he knew exactly what I was referring to. We started running back to the square where the sacrifice seemed to be taking place, where we saw Leo crying for mercy. I caught sight of Stewart and the others, and we formed together, hoping to create enough of a group to intercept those psychos. Without much thought, we charged them and headed for Leo, swords and knives raised high in the air. We let out our battle cries, fighting through the crowd. Once we started reaching the group of men holding Leo down, they brought their weapons out, and we were frustrated to realize they wouldn't be giving our boy back without a struggle.

Well, so be it. We became two intersecting forces. Something that looked like confetti was getting thrown around as the celebration continued, as we had seemed to excite the cult followers rather than dissuade them. It seemed to me that we were just potential sacrificial add-ons. I started to wish Darien had more of his powder flasks as the struggle for dominance made itself known between the two groups. They'd started to chant to themselves, which just confused us more. Maybe that was the goal, as some of the men had slowed down to stare at them in disgust. Finn and Marco's voices could be heard to keep fighting, and more of the crew had found us by then to join in on the rescue mission.

Some of the bulkier men had resorted to tackling their enemies, and onlookers started to cheer us on. This gave them a renewed energy, soaking in the attention and knocking people out of the way. Finn eventually made his way up to Leo, and one of the cult leaders jumped at the two of them, trying to stab Leo and get it over with. Leo was screaming then, and Boone grabbed the cult leader and held him down as Finn took Leo over his shoulder and made a run for it. The rest of us followed suit, hoping that we'd averted the crisis. This didn't really work, as the crowd started to chase us like they were the monkeys in Temple Run. I could practically hear my heartbeat through my chest as we pushed onward. Marco was trying to tell us to stop because at this rate they'd try to take over our ship if we didn't end things then.

I was quickly running out of stamina and started getting desperate with my movements. Finn was still holding onto Leo for dear life as the rest of us acted as a barrier around the two of them. The cult members were starting to slow down then, and I was praying that they decide we were not worth the hassle. Marco had a sword in each hand as he tag teamed multiple individuals at once, and gunshots were fired from John and Stewart. Knowing I wouldn't be able to last much longer, I ran to Finn, hoping I could still help in some small way.

"Let me take Leo back to the ship!" I proclaimed.

Finn nodded to me, too occupied to give any other response. I cut the rest of Leo's bonds loose and grabbed his hand. We ran and weaved through the sea of people, trying to stay undetected. For the most part it seemed to work, and we got into a jog once we were outside of the city gates. We both staggered onwards once we reached the rocky shoreline of our cove. After running up the plank, I decided against chewing Leo out for his gullible spirit. It could've easily happened to me. I felt a knot of guilt knowing I'd left the crew to fare for themselves, but I would've been no help to anyone if I lost all strength in the arms of one of the cult leaders. There were still ways I could participate even then, so I started to prepare the sloop for departure. Leo jumped into action, helping without a word. Everything was ready within minutes, and we were left waiting for our shipmates.

Soon enough we saw the outlines of our pirates and took a collective sigh of relief. They were still running towards us, no doubt in a hurry to leave the manic island. I was antsy to take off as numerous hands made their way back on board. Eventually Finn made his way back up, and I saw out in the distance some of the locals coming into view. So they were not that successful then. Finn knew what to do, racing to the helm as we got the sails up. John came up with the last group of misfits and hoisted up the plank just in time for the cultists to come stumbling into our cove. Many of us were shouting at each other, trying to scramble out of this nook as quickly as possible. Some of the people outside of the ship resorted to climbing her, which set John in a frenzy as he started to fire his pistol again.

The action kept them away long enough for us to shimmy our way into deep water again, and Finn was nearly jumping at the wheel. The cultists finally gave up on the chase, and Leo was laughing at them mockingly. While some of the crew shared his upbeat attitude over escaping, Marco was looking at the boy with a parental type of disappointment. He went over to Leo, taking him by the shoulder, to have a little chat. It was true that for serious conversations, Marco was the one to rely on instead of John. The crew knew very well that it was hard to take the captain seriously at times. I'm not sure they'd fare quite so well without John's first mate. Many of us had resorted to sitting on deck for a while, trying to unwind from the unexpected fight.

No one was hungry, having stuffed ourselves to oblivion. Instead we craved rest and knew exactly how to destress. The sea brought every one of us comfort, so we let the ocean breeze ruffle our hair and listened to the comforting sounds while we sailed away from the Portuguese Islands. At some point in the night, while we all looked up at the stars and spoke in whispered tones, John was back by my side. We seemed to gravitate to each other, like two opposing forces.

He asked me, "Didn't think you'd get another adventure in, eh?"

I smiled, genuinely happy to have lived another.

"It was a pleasant surprise. Now I know what cults are truly like."

He laughed at that, and we spent several companionable moments in silence.

"You'll miss it, you know."

I hated that he kept bringing up what awaited me in Boston. This was the only time in history I had ever gotten the chance to truly live in the moment, and he was ruining it.

"I know. But mark my words, I'll be back."

We both knew it may not happen the way I said it would. This fickle thing was unpredictable, and I could still end up here again someday, but John could be on the other side of the world when I made my return.

"P'raps. But what's left back there?"

It was something I had asked myself way too often. I was getting deja vu with this conversation, and I wanted to avoid it altogether.

"My family's there. My livelihood."

"Is that all?"

I huffed at him. "What do you mean is that all? That's quite a bit."

"If you say so, darling. But you won't be tied to your family forever. And you're more free here at sea, you can't fool me."

I couldn't. He was right. Going back in my time would feel like a pit stop. Time to figure out what was going on, if my family was okay, and then I'd be trying to come back here again. Now that I had a taste of this life, normal 21st-century living wouldn't be enough for me.

"Let's just enjoy tonight, John."

I could see him looking at me a little too long out of the corner of my eye, and I wished he wouldn't.

"Starting to sound like me, love."

And I was, wasn't I?

Chapter Thirty-Four

Time continued to pass by quickly, taunting me that my time here was growing short. The feeling that things wouldn't be the same the next time I saw John and his crew was increasing every day. A month had gone by since Ponta Delgada, and Leo had picked up the slack all around the ship, trying to prove himself still useful. We already knew he was, but it was nice to see him so passionate about wanting to keep his progression in the ranks. The night was nigh, and everyone was below deck drinking to our good fortune. Nothing out of the ordinary for the life of a buccaneer, as many nights had passed exactly as this one. My tolerance for alcohol continued to increase, as drinking rum was almost completely necessary out at sea. Everything had to be watered down. I did not usually drink more than I had to, however.

That left me on the deck where I usually was, taking up John's hobby of sketching. I wasn't nearly as good as he was, but it kept me busy. It wasn't a good idea to keep a journal with me, knowing if it ever survived the test of time it would change history in possibly major ways. Not to mention the crew getting their hands on it would be an endless embarrassment. Distractions showed themselves; the way the colors were mixing in the sunset prevented me from looking away. The soft pastels were exploding into their vibrant counterparts. I wondered then if I could speak to Aerwyna that night, weary with where we left off our last encounter. I wanted to trust her, but the unknown never settled well with me. I liked the comfort of being able to control when I entered a state of uncertainty and wonder.

I thought that if I mentally called to her long enough, she would appear in front of me. Still unsure how their telepathy worked, I didn't know how effective this method was. I started to walk towards the railing, ready to test my theory. To my surprise, Wyna was not who I saw on the other side. I stilled, staying silent and watchful. Perched on the side of the sloop was Marco, talking softly to a mermaid with striking emerald hair and a tail to match. They seemed to be well-acquainted with one another, smiling and drawing closer. I felt like I was interrupting something I should've never seen in the first place. If Marco felt it necessary to tell us he was in contact with merfolk, he would've told one of us. Of course, I didn't either. There wasn't time to look into the reasons why, as the mermaid whipped her head around to look directly at me. Then I remembered that she probably knew the moment I had seen them, sensing my presence.

Marco turned to follow her eyes, and we made eye contact. He didn't look as surprised as I thought he would at the realization of being found out. I felt guilty then, despite doing nothing wrong. I wondered if the mermaid talked to Wyna, if she knew I had nothing to pit against Marco. There was no code saying that pirates couldn't befriend mermaids. I said nothing and backed away from the railing. While walking back to Marco's cabin, I heard the splash of water indicating a departure, and then running on deck.

"Adira."

I turned around, looking at the uneasiness settled on Marco's face.

"I won't tell anyone. I swear it."

He beckoned me away to the door of the cabin, and we went back to the railing.

"Perhaps I should explain."

"You don't have to tell me anything, Marco. There's no reason you should be pushed to do so."

"Yes. But you and I both know John's opinion on mermaids isn't exactly pleasant."

"He's not friends with them, but surely he doesn't hate them or anything."

He looked a little uncomfortable.

"I thought, I thought he may have told you. It was bold of me to assume...."

Those words should never be said to a curious person.

"Assume what?"

He shook his head like the mere mention of John should've been avoided.

"Nothing. He'll say something if he chooses."

"Is this... is whatever he feels endangering anyone?"

"I don't know. I don't think so."

"Well, that's reassuring."

We were straying from the conversation at hand, of what I saw. I did not care if Marco told me nothing of that night, but I wanted him to have peace of mind.

"I worry how John would react if he knew mermaids followed his ship like bloodhounds. Because of me."

So he didn't know about Wyna and I. Maybe this was an opportunity to release my own load while comforting him in some small way.

"Maybe not all because of you."

He looked at me now, waiting for me to continue.

"I have been in contact with one as well. She believes we are connected. Or something like that."

Marco took in this new piece of information, and I could see he was trying to make sense of it.

"Emma had said that more of her sisters were traveling with her. I had thought it unusual."

Emma was his lover. Or friend? Either way, they must've been comfortable with one another.

"Are you and her...."

"We love each other. I can't explain it. But we do."

"That's… that's wonderful Marco. I'm happy for you. Truly."

He looked at me with bewilderment, not expecting my answer. The way I looked at it, if you had the blessing of falling in love and finding happiness with someone, treasure it. Doesn't matter where it comes from, or if it's not how someone else would do it.

"Others call me crazy."

I definitely didn't understand the logistics of a human and a mermaid being together, but it had been talked about for centuries. Those stories had to have come from somewhere. Maybe some of them are about Marco and Emma.

"It may not be the most usual thing, but why does it matter? You're a pirate. You're all about going outside of what society expects."

"Humans and merfolk have never really coexisted peacefully. One or the other tries exploitation, and uses one for their own benefit."

This would make sense as to why mermaids could not be proved real in my time. Or any time, really. Apparently, only certain groups of people were given the gratification of knowing the truth.

"How did you two meet?"

There he was, shifting again.

"It's a story that can't be told without John's permission, sadly."

This was all I could be told of the tale then. I doubted I'd be able to get out the full story from the captain, especially with the little time I had left there.

"I see. Well, don't fret. There's nothing to worry about!"

At that moment, the door to the captain's quarters opened, and out walked John. I could practically see Marco tensing beside me as both of us turned to him. John seemed questioning, but not quite skeptical. But Marco walking back to his cabin did not help the situation. John took Marco's place beside me and looked out to the water similar to how I had only moments before. I wondered if he suspected what was going on.

"Marco alright?"

He asked me nonchalantly, but I could tell he was concerned.

"Just a little tired, Captain."

He looked me straight in the eyes again, and I could tell he was not buying it.

"I know when you're lying, love."

"Why don't you go ask him yourself then?"

John was no idiot, despite the way he acted, and he seemed to be piecing together at least his version of the truth without Marco needing to say anything.

"This wouldn't happen to be about our fishy friends, would it?"

Dang. So he did know. Maybe he'd been watching the both of us, all this time, without us knowing. I wouldn't put it past him to keep it to himself until confrontation was necessary.

"What's it matter to you? We can't have our own social life on this ship?"

There seemed to be a small fire burning in his eyes as we got into heated territory.

"All I care about is the wellbeing of my crew. I wouldn't want them to be put in danger over something so trivial. I may be very lenient, but I don't stand for that."

Something definitely had happened for John to be so fidgety over merfolk. Time travel did not bother him, the great sea monster himself didn't faze him, but this did?

"There's nothing to worry about here."

He was not willing to let it go quite yet.

"How often do you talk to them?"

I considered staying silent, but that would only move him to go talk to Marco directly. Perhaps that was best, but I was personally hoping he'd slip somewhere and let me in on whatever happened to him.

"Once a week or so."

His jaw had clenched, and I wondered if I touched him there if he would calm down.

"I don't like how they linger, Dira."

"I'm sorry, John, but you can't dictate our lives."

He started to shake his head, and I wondered if this was another matter where he just wanted to be right. Why did we have to get into disputes like this?

"You're putting us in more potential danger, the both of you."

"No more than you!"

This comment didn't seem to upset him as much as the fact that I wasn't immediately offering up my friendship with Wyna. Maybe I didn't have reason to trust her. But if this was the one happiness Marco had, like hell was I going to let John ruin that.

"You should be more careful with that tongue of yours."

That was the wrong thing to say.

"I have no interest in mutiny, Mr. Sterling. Just the strange disdain you have towards another race."

I was making him more uncomfortable by the second.

"Believe me, they aren't all they appear to be."

"How can you be so sure?"

He wasn't budging.

"This is not something I have to discuss with you. Perhaps you can hold off on any more nightly excursions."

With that, he stormed off in the other direction, back to his quarters. I didn't know how to unpack what just happened, so instead went into Marco's cabin to call it a night. I opened the door to see the two men already in their hammocks. I wondered if they had heard any of what just happened. Marco looked at me questioningly, and, not knowing what to do, I averted his gaze and went straight to my bed. It was too much to say without words. There was so much they would have to work out after I left. I doubted it would be solved with me here.

I knew John was an actor. He put on facades when he couldn't properly deal with what was going on around him. I could see through him. I wondered if his friends could too. I thought so, and I wished these men knew how to communicate better. I hoped I would leave an impression on them and that they would work whatever this was out in my absence. Turning to my side, I put the problem in the back of my mind to beckon sleep my way.

Chapter Thirty-Five

Eventually, we made it to Boston. We sat outside of her harbor, drifting to and fro. John had fulfilled his end of the deal. I had aided in their riches and had the trip of a lifetime. I wouldn't trade anything that had happened for the world. There would be a storm rolling in soon, Finn was sure of it. We stayed close to Little Brewster Island, where I could easily swim out. I felt nervous about what that day would hold for me, and the ship was silent. It was as though everyone here held their breath in solidarity. It was early in the afternoon, and soon I would have to say goodbye. The clouds were already starting to darken. John put up airs in front of the crew, but there was no lie in the way his mouth was turned downward in a melancholy state. Had we not revealed deep wants to each other, with brutal honesty we had perhaps been too afraid to use with others?

There was still so much that was up to the future to decide. I didn't know if I would see these people again. I couldn't guess if I'd stumble upon merfolk in my time. Would I ever see that series of pretend islands again, tempting me to drown around its shores? Would I ever feel quite as fulfilled as I had in those six months? The answer was not known, which scared me. I started to truly believe my shipmates would miss me. I thought I would miss the absolute buffoonery Darien and Boone got into. I'd miss the crazy stories Stewart told, not knowing if any of it was true or not. I'd miss Marco's aloofness because I knew deep down he had a burning compassion for everyone on that ship. I'd miss Finn's no-nonsense manner and the hour-long conversations we could get into. I'd miss them all. I thought about getting back into the dress I had come in until I realized I didn't think I ever took it with me off the galleon. The clothes on my back would be my little souvenir, a memento.

I thought about how it would be best to get within the lighthouse's range, without putting the ship in danger. Ultimately it was decided I'd swim out once the storm made itself known. It was a risky thing to do, but I insisted. I feared it would be any minute now, with the thunder already growling softly in the sky. Everyone had gathered on the deck, ready to see me off. I looked around at this makeshift family and the place that was my home for several months. There was a weird emptiness in my stomach, which I felt should've been in my heart, for it truly hurt to leave. I took my time with each pirate that I had gotten to know, saying my goodbyes.

I started with Finn. We looked at each other, unsure what to do. There was something like a smile on his face, and the man decided to bring me in for a hug. I couldn't help but smile, surprised at his show of affection. He had become a second brother to me. He ended the hug with a steady grip on my hand.

"You'll be missed, lass."

Boone and Darien merely exchanged salutes with me before they went back to fighting with each other. I shook hands with Charlie, Paul, and William. Stewart tipped his hat to me, and Leo hugged me out of gratitude. I made it to Marco, and, knowing he wouldn't be the one to initiate a hug, I took it upon myself. While in my grasp, I whispered to him.

"Tell Emma and her sisters I said goodbye."

He nodded, touching my arms lightly as I pulled away. He was a man of few words in these sorts of situations, but I could tell he'd miss me. Just a little bit.

Inevitably I had felt uneasy about seeking out Aerwyna after that night. There were a few times I thought about going to her, to tell her of the captain's feelings, but something told me it would not be wise. Marco had continued to meet with Emma, as I had told him little of John's reaction. I considered telling him that the captain knew, but it would give him added stress that seemed pointless. I kept it to myself, trying to lessen his load. Besides, he knew whatever it was that John went through. Desperately I tried to figure out what it was for the next almost two months of sailing to the New England coast. But with no luck. It was something in his troubled past that he had locked up, not to speak of again.

It wasn't all for naught though, as Marco had begun to confide in me about Emma. What they dreamed of, and she even greeted me a few times. I was a safe person for them, someone they did not have to hide from. It was nice to be that for someone. Emma could go on land if she chose, but Marco wouldn't be able to see her world unless a royal granted it. Being with a mermaid was a special privilege, one that wasn't taken lightly. If all humans were given the chance to live with them, it could mean the end of their race. So if a mer happened to fall in love with one of us, they would have to vouch for them. Although Emma trusted Marco, he was not ready to leave land. And she was not ready to leave the deep blue. Instead, they met up whenever they could, talking of their two worlds.

Thinking back to the present, there was only John left to talk to. The man who could've left me to the streets of Boston, but took a chance and taught me much in the process. We started with a staring match. I couldn't tell who was winning as the both of us started to smirk at each other. I didn't know how to say goodbye to the captain. I leaned in and kissed him on the cheek, right above the stubble around his jaw. He had taken the moment to grab hold of my arms, proceeding to look at me inquiringly. I made to move away, and as I did so he called out for me.

"Dira?"

I turned, looking at him again.

"You could stay."

He had said it softer, almost shy, like he couldn't believe he was asking. It started raining, and I knew it was time to go.

"Maybe someday."

I gave him one final glance, eyes wandering to the rest of the crew. Savoring the moment just a second longer. Then I jumped. Plunging into the water, I immediately started drifting away with the choppy waves. The wind was picking up, so I took one last look at the ship before swimming forward. Even with the waves fighting against me, being in the water served as a comfort. I kept propelling forward until my lighthouse was the main view. There wasn't much difference to it other than perhaps looking a little smaller. I stayed afloat where I was, not wanting to get too close to its rocky shores. The lightning was already picking up, and the ocean was threatening to drown me with its strength in movement.

What I was doing felt crazy. No person in their right mind would be doing what I was. The lighthouse shone brightly, and I could almost make out the current keeper getting to his small rowboat. Panic rose in me, and, wanting to stay unseen, I took a deep breath and let the waves push me down. Things would go awry fast if the keeper decided to come try and rescue me. I tried staying submerged as long as possible but could start to feel my lungs giving out. I peeked my head above water for a quick breath of air and saw the keeper hesitating towards the shore. I quickly ducked my head back under and the process repeated itself. I could hardly hold my breath when suddenly a tingling sensation started at the sides of my neck.

As my eyes peered above the surface, I could see a light brighter than the lens of the lighthouse flash all around me. It made a wave of its own, knocking me around, strong and powerful. I lost my sense of direction, getting jostled around in the water. The light became so bright I could see it with my eyes closed, and everything felt disorienting. I briefly wondered if any of the crew was worried seeing me get tossed around closer and closer to the small island. There was no time to react as I felt what I didn't feel the first time. It could best be described as a strong pull. I felt everything shift and move like I was getting propelled and pushed in different directions. There was no telling how long this lasted, only that when it was over I pushed myself towards the surface once again, as the light had completely subsided.

I looked back, where there was no sign of the ship I had come from. As I looked forward, there was no more sign of the keeper and his boat. I started swimming towards the lighthouse with the assumption that I had successfully traveled in time. Again. I stayed cautiously optimistic as I started climbing my way up the rocks on the shore of Little Brewster. I saw that the light was not on in my lighthouse. Could this be my time? As I finally got on solid land I coughed out the saltwater lodged in my throat, aware that I probably looked like a sewer rat. I ran to the lighthouse, throwing the door open. I staggered up the winding stairs, to the top, of the balcony, my boots squeaking with each step. And there it was. My teacup. Left here, shattered from falling over. I stood there for a moment, stuck in this state of utter shock of having succeeded. There was no getting stuck somewhere I did not know, in a time unbeknownst to me.

It was then that I laughed. Starting as almost a half snort, it turned into a full-on manic laughing fit. This worked! I was right. Looking around me, I saw some of my books scattered about and things left where they were exactly six months ago. I could hardly believe it! I rushed back to the little house beside the lighthouse, anxious to see it. The wind was still howling all around me as I opened my front door. I was greeted by the familiar sight of my kitchen and the living room. Everything was exactly the same. It was such a cathartic warm feeling seeing all of my things in one place again. Oh, how I wished I could've taken everything with me from our raids back to this place. My body seemed to finally take in that I was back home, as I nearly fell to the floor from the exhaustion of the trip. I lay on the floor for several minutes, content to rest and have a few moments of silence. Only then did I wonder about my family. Had they tried to reach me?

Anxiety filled me once again, and I reluctantly pulled myself up and off the floor. I headed for my bedroom, in search of my phone. Finding it on my nightstand, I snatched it. 53 messages. Then I looked at the date. A week. It'd been a week that had passed since I left. Then I briefly wondered, would time traveling mess with my external aging? I scrolled through the never-ending messages, as my family had been worried sick that I had not gotten ahold of them. There was even one from Jason. I should call my mother, and tell her something. Then I smiled to myself. What exactly would I tell her? That I had traveled to the year 1720 and lived amongst real, living, and breathing pirates? That I had become one myself and had seen places I'd only dreamed of seeing, and saw creatures that I had thought were out of the range of existence? I'd have to create a believable excuse. It shouldn't be too hard, surely. It'd only been a week.

Then I remembered I was still in my wet clothes and had sopping hair. I needed a shower first. The thought alone excited me. I had not been able to use scented soaps and shampoos for half a year. My hair had grown even longer and lighter. I took all of my ancient clothes off, hanging them on the back of a chair. Rushing to the bathroom, I started to get the water as hot as I could. There were a couple of things about living in the present that I had sorely missed. As the water beat down on my back, I thought of John's face when I left. How pleading his eyes looked when he called after me, hoping I'd forget about the present and stay in his world. I had wanted to and still did. I felt a little like I was floating between reality, not keeping a steady foot in either direction. The water was starting to cool, signifying how long I had been in the shower contemplating things. I got out and braided my hair quickly, wrapping a towel around me.

Heading back to my bedroom I lit several candles, watching the storm outside my window become a dull background noise. It calmed me now that I wasn't in the middle of it, reminding me that in reality, I had only left the ship two hours before. I searched through my closet for an old cashmere sweater and gray sweatpants. Once I felt like I was going back to some level of normalcy, I realized how hungry I was. Would any of my food even be good after a week? I went down to the kitchen, in search of anything with a high level of protein. Sure enough, all of my fresh produce had started to wilt, but it appeared the milk and some of the cheeses and meat were still edible. I took a couple of bites of random things until it was enough to probably count as a meal. Once that was taken care of, I finally called my family. It could be heard in their voices how frantic and worried they had been until I told them that I had lost my phone and could not find it until earlier today. They had no reason to question this and were just relieved I had not been murdered, drowned, or starved.

Cyra begged to visit, but I had not given her a definitive answer. Truthfully, there were things I had to get sorted before inviting someone else to the lighthouse. I felt as though I needed time with myself to situate the uneasiness I had immediately felt with returning. Ultimately, I needed to figure out what exactly it was that I wanted in my life.

Chapter Thirty-Six

The day coming back had come and passed like a puff of smoke. It was like waking up from a really intense dream, and you are left spending the rest of your day reeling from the memories. The next morning I slept in terribly late, as it took forever to fall asleep. There were no sounds of creaking planks, men coughing and laughing, or the swaying of a ship. My only consolation was the sound of the waves from my window being left open. I made a note to check my emails in case the Lighthouse Association had sent me anything. Sure enough, they had sent me something two days before. They were concerned that I had not been putting the light on recently, and, if I did not reply to them within a week with a valid explanation, they would be sending someone out to Little Brewster. The thought of someone inquiring and invading my space was enough to make my heart rate go up, and I immediately put together a reply. I explained to them that I had been feeling very sick this past week and could barely get out of bed, hence the lack of lighting up the tower. If this continued, I knew that I would have only so many chances before they kicked me out and sent in a new replacement.

While checking up on all forms of communication, I finally got to Jason's message. He was worried about me, wondering why I hadn't gotten a hold of my family and if I was okay. It was nice to know that he still cared about me, even with how I had left things. I sent him a reply, telling him the same thing I had told my family. We messaged back and forth for a while, and I realized that I had been smiling at our interchange. I had forgotten how safe and predictable Jason was. I didn't have to think when talking to him. It was something that was lacking in my life at the moment. I decided then I wouldn't mind if we stayed friends. Perhaps it would be good for me. After all, there were not many people to talk to here.

My next order of business would require a bit of digging. I had begun to grow concerned about the consequences of going back in time. What things in history would change? Would a paradox really happen, or would everything we had suspected about time travel be a myth? Surely nothing too crazy had happened, as I got here just fine and things seemed perfectly normal. But even if nothing major had changed, I needed to know what exactly happened. I went downstairs, pulling all of my Age of Sail history books off the shelf after brewing myself a cup of coffee. It was a foggy morning, which was pretty typical conditions for the day after a storm on the coast. I sat down, sprawling the books around me, ready to delve in. In each book, I flipped to the year 1720 and onward. The first thing I noticed was that some of my books seemed to be a little longer than I remembered, which was what I decided to focus on first.

What I knew about the Golden Age of Piracy was that it fizzled out after the 1730s. Most of the pirates I knew of would have either been happily retired or hung by then. But as I scanned the pages of my extensive collection of piracy books, I saw that this appeared not to be the case! Now records and history state that the Golden Age lasted up into the 50s of that century, and I was dumbfounded. How could it be that the little time I had spent there created such a drastic effect? What kind of repercussions would have taken place with twenty more years of raiding the seas? I sat there in shock, replaying the past six months. The most notable thing we had done was pull the heist on Alhambra, but wouldn't John have headed there whether I was with him or not? I continued skimming the passages, trying to find any other precursors. Right there, in the middle of a chapter, I saw his name.

In big bold black letters, they talked of John Sterling and how it was he and his crew who had inspired hundreds of other buccaneers to refuse to sign the petition of pardon for pirates. It was their act of defiance that had kept John's way of life burning still. My eyes could not stray from the page as I read about Captain Sterling's success in rebuilding the pirate republic in Nassau, altering the course of history in the Bahamas forever. It was progressing up until the very end of his time, and I felt a chill come over me reading that John's cause of death was unknown and that many were to assume he died in the ocean as no one had ever found his body. My coffee was nearly forgotten about as I took this in. I wasn't sure how to process the fact that the person whom I quickly considered one of my closest friends had been dead for hundreds of years. It's one thing to read about his accomplishments, but stumbling upon the mystery of his death left a twisting feeling in my gut.

I closed all the books, putting them back in their place. There was still more I wanted to know, but I needed a break. Coincidentally, I was getting a video call from my mother. I accepted, knowing if I didn't she would just become more paranoid.

"Hi, Mom."

There was little to say, seeing as how we had just talked the previous day.

"Good morning. I was thinking of your explanation yesterday as to why you didn't call us. It seems like an awfully long time for you to be without your phone. Are you telling the truth, Adira?"

My mother, always straight to the point.

"Why would I lie to you?"

"I just think it's suspicious that right after you break Jason's heart we don't hear from you for a week."

I should've known this would go back to Jason. I was stupid for thinking otherwise.

"A mere coincidence. Of course, I feel bad about that. I don't know what you want me to say."

"I'm just worried about you. You have no one up there, and I have yet to hear any valid reasons as to why you broke up with Jason."

"I still care about Jason, Mom. But he's just so... unstable. We barely know how to talk with each other. I don't think we want the same things."

"That's what relationships are for! Building one another up and compromising!"

Why did she make relationships sound so miserable? I hated the fact that I wanted to please her.

"Well, I'm not good at compromising."

"And isn't it a wonder the boy who's into you is more than willing to compromise for you? For both of you?"

I felt exasperated. Maybe she was right.

"Isn't that a discredit to him? Shouldn't he be with someone that wants the same thing as him?"

She shook her head like she knew all the facts.

"Not necessarily. Your dad and I are completely opposite, and we are right for each other."

I thought about that, about all the times I'd heard both of them fighting to make things work and to understand one another. It was like they spoke different languages. I wasn't sure yet if I wanted something like what they had.

"I'm not saying it'll never work with Jason and I. Just give it time. Okay?"

I was trying to aim for peace with her. My family thought I was something of a black sheep for not wanting the same things the majority of people wanted. Maybe I was. I hated to admit that it made me feel incredibly lonely. She finally sighed, growing tired.

"I don't want to see you be so picky you end up alone, Adira."

Those words had been said to me since I became a teenager. From that time onwards I was told that my standards were too high. It made me want to tell her about these past few months all over again. If only she could see there were bigger things out there. Alas, I always took the blame. I always accepted it was my fault that I was the way I was. I just wanted to see her happy, and she would only be happy if I did things her way.

"I know, Mom."

It was all I knew how to say. Just a meek agreement. Dad entered the frame of the camera, and I tried plastering a smile the best I could.

"Are you any closer to figuring out those strange disappearances?" he asked me.

I was glad for the change in conversation.

"I think so. I may have some leads."

He nodded, glad that I was being productive with the one task outside of the ordinary I was given. I had forgotten that I would have to tell the Association of my findings sooner or later. They would want to know what I'd seen. I wanted it to be my secret a little longer. Then Mom panned the camera back to her.

"I think you should let Cyra come visit you. It would be good for you to have company."

"I'll think about it, Mom."

Our conversation drifted to more menial things, while her words had started to seep in my mind and leave uncomfortable thoughts in the forefront. I eventually ended the call, unable to socialize any longer. Mom remained suspicious, but what was the worst she could do? I was out on my own then. In all reality, she didn't have any hold on me. Or she shouldn't. But I had told the truth about one thing. I did care for Jason, against my better judgment. It was never in my plans to hurt him, and I really did hope he considered me a friend. I went ahead and texted him, not wishing for bad blood.

'Hey stranger. You doin' okay?'

He replied quickly, as always.

'Better knowing you're alright. I actually decided to quit my job.'

This was no real surprise to me, but it did leave me curious.

'Why?? Do you have anything lined up?'

'It was time. My boss never respected me. I want to open up something of my own. I'm working on it!'

I did understand wanting to be your own boss. It was a gratifying feeling.

'Well keep me updated.'

'Planned on it! How are you??'

Truthfully, I didn't know. I was feeling a million things.

'Life up here is fulfilling in a way I never thought possible.'

'I'm happy for you! I knew you'd thrive there Dira.'

The nickname struck a nerve in me. I couldn't understand it. Only John had called me that, and it felt cheapened by Jason saying it.

'Thank you, Jason. Don't you have any other nicknames for me??'

'All right then. Addi will have to do ;)'

We texted on and off for the rest of the day as I got everything in cleaner shape after having been vacant for a week. I was quick about getting the light on in the evenings, wanting to make up for lost time. I was glad that Jason did not harbor resentment for how I left things and was happy just to pick up on being friends. It gave me something small to look forward to, and I did hope that things went better this time. I told myself it had nothing to do with pleasing my mother. As the days went on in my lighthouse, I thought of my time at sea almost constantly.

To my surprise, there were no severe storms for a month. Nothing more than drizzles of rain or gusts of wind. Summer was in full swing, and everyone in the city was looking forward to autumn. I was getting more restless every day. My dreams had been filled with more pretend adventures with John and his crew as I thought about the captain going to the Caribbean and Marco finally getting to be with Emma. I hoped that they all got what they wanted. As for me, I was dreadfully bored. All the research I had intended to do about the lighthouse had been slow going. Where was I to start? I had looked into all of the people I had met in 1720, reading up on them, but had no idea what to look for when it came to the science of the phenomenon. Logically, I knew it had something to do with the electric charge of the lightning mixing with the elements of the lighthouse, but what made this one so unique? Was there a fracture or vulnerability in time around this area? I had so many questions left unanswered, with nowhere to go for responses. Of course, there were things I had looked into, different universities that had classes or professors devoted to finding out more about time travel, but none of them were solid leads.

In the end, I concluded that I would have to experiment more and gather more information. Another trip would be inevitable if I wanted more answers. That suited me just fine. One person who was more scientifically minded than me was Jason. If there was anyone to tell about what was going on, I was reluctant to admit it would be him. But we had been growing closer. It was nice to have someone to talk to, someone to call when I was bored and didn't want to listen to my parents nagging me. Granted, he probably talked to them about everything we talked about. It was best when I didn't think about it. He could tell I was being secretive and that I had changed, but he knew our relationship was still too fragile to comment on it just yet. We were in a strange sort of limbo that exes are when they try to be friends. He still flirted with me, and I still let him. But I was content with it not meaning anything and letting our relationship remain undefined. I worked better that way, and I was aware enough to admit I had trouble committing to people. He was working hard on proving himself to me and busy setting up his own business so he could go wherever he chose.

I had finally remembered that Thomas had asked me to go see the Boston Museum of Fine Art and was honestly surprised that I hadn't been yet. That was my outing for today. I threw on an outfit I would've loved to have shown John and went to sail the Mermaid's Lagoon. I had to endure the heat of summer twice and cursed the universe for my misfortune. But when I reached Boston's harbor, I could not stay mad long. Exploring something new always filled me with excitement. I walked with a skip in my step, ready for the art I was about to see to lift my spirits. When I walked through the museum entrance, I felt immediate relief. Few places could do that for me. Museums, bookshops, cafés, and the ocean seemed to be what captivated my soul and kept it steady.

I was thankful then that there was free entry, as I had no idea how much was in my bank account. I had probably gotten paid but hadn't checked my finances since coming back to the present. There was a certain smell to museums that was hard to describe. You almost wouldn't know it's there unless you've been to countless of them. It was faint and clean and reminded me of the importance of preserving our culture and creations over history. I walked around a little aimlessly at first, letting the art guide me. It was best that way, getting lost in halls you perhaps wouldn't have thought of going in if you spent too long looking at a map. I took in the guests around me. There was a field trip here, all of the children in yellow shirts, and a couple of chaperones that looked paranoid. Then there were the influencers, carrying their tripods around and annoying the security guards. I saw couples with their arms around each other, whispering things to each other, standing as close to the paintings as possible. There were a couple of old folk here and there, seemingly in small groups and conversing amongst themselves, or staring at something with their hands behind their backs. It was all mesmerizing. The people were just as much the art as the items behind the glass.

I meandered around the American galleries, looking for pieces that may have caught Thomas' eyes. Then I wondered if art was considered American based on the location it was created or the nationality of the creator. I decided it must be the latter, surely. Eventually, I made it to the European galleries, which always seemed to be my favorite. There was so much more variety amongst these halls, most definitely because of the more extensive timeline. I kept to the sculptures first, always captivated by the realism of every subject. Soon I made it to the paintings and took my time with each one. They all varied in which era they belonged to, but I had fun trying to guess before looking at the plaques. I had gotten to William Turner, whom I had never gotten the pleasure of seeing in person before.

The detail of his pieces blew me away, and I could vividly imagine myself in each of his artworks.

Having stayed on John's ship had made everything I loved about the ocean so much more real. It was when I was skimming over other coastal paintings that I saw something that caught my eye. In a corner, under a glass display, were charcoal sketches, wrinkled and yellowed from the test of time. The date on the plaque read 1720, which made me smile. I could've been somewhere else in the world while these were sketched. But then I looked at the pages themselves. Though roughly done, I could make out who the muse was. And it made my breathing hitch. These were John's sketches. At first, all I could do was hang my mouth open, looking at pieces from his sketchbook. What touched me more was the fact that I was in most of them. Of course, right on the plaque, it stated that John Sterling was the artist, and I wanted to laugh at the notion of him being classified as such.

One was done the day we had gone to Alhambra, and there I stood, regal in my full-length gown and jewels. He had roughly detailed the background from memory, as we had stood in the palace. There were two more. The first was a side portrait of me after he had pierced my ears. He drew my hair long and flowy, drawing attention to the rings wrapped around the small braids in my hair. I had a slight smile on my lips and kohl around my eyes. Suddenly I felt a lump in my throat, seeing how he portrayed me. In his eyes, I looked quite breathtaking. It made my heart ache, missing him. Missing all of them. The second must've been called completely from memory, as I stood proudly at the helm during the hurricane we had faced early on in my journey. There were roughly sketched pirates in the background, and I tried to guess who each of them was. I was pretty confident that two of them had to have been Marco and Finn. Boone could almost be made out in the corner, with his bald head and burly beard. I wanted to break open the glass and take all of the sketches for myself. No one would know that it was me in the depictions. I don't know how long I stood there, hunched over those drawings.

Did another museum have more of his sketches somewhere? Had John painted pieces eventually? My mind was so invested in conjuring up these questions that I had missed the rest of the art in the room, including a full-length oil painting of the captain himself, looking smug as ever, standing next to me in clothing fit for pirate royalty. I would never know. After having seen the sketches I decided I couldn't stay in the museum any longer. I was too distracted and needed something to eat. Something to take my mind off of the buccaneers I had left behind for more than five minutes. I started walking the streets around Mission Hill, finding my way to a small gastropub called The Squealing Pig. Around the pub wafted the most amazing smells, and for a moment I forgot about the museum, my stomach taking the lead.

Chapter Thirty-Seven

Inside it was dark and smoky, with ambient lighting. I seated myself and took up a menu, and had a hard time choosing over the extensive options. There were wood-fired pizzas, toasties, soups, and of course every kind of pig meat you could think of. It was one of those places that had probably been around for over a hundred years. I ended up getting something simple which consisted of baked ham and sharp Vermont cheddar. After I ordered I realized I had mistakenly ordered alcohol and was lucky they did not ask for identification. Drinking had become ingrained in my everyday life in the past, and I forgot things were different here and that I had not officially turned 21 yet according to the law, despite having done so physically. As I people-watched while waiting for my food, my phone buzzed at my side. It was a text from Jason.

'You won't believe where my next client is located.'

He relied on friends and family to spread the word about the start of his business, which involved different renovation services. Although I had witnessed firsthand how much work was left to be desired after Jason finished a job, I was happy that he was finding something to suit him better. Hopefully, the skill will come in time.

'Barcelona?'

'Wouldn't that be great? Now the real answer doesn't feel as glamorous as I thought.'

'Are you going to tell me anyway?'

'Right. I'm heading your way Addi! This client is right outside of Boston!'

My heart rate was picking up at the thought of Jason being close to me again. Nervous energy was filling my stomach, and I wondered what this would mean for me.

'Wow! How in the world did someone in Boston find you?'

'Honestly, I had put out inquiries around the area. I was hoping I'd get an excuse to come up for a visit. Hopefully on better terms.'

So it was definitely about me. While the fact made me feel warm inside, I didn't want to feel pressured.

'Well, that's great Jason! Yes, you'll definitely have to come stop by.'

'I was actually kind of hoping you'd let me come to the lighthouse. It would be a huge help.'

If I told him no, that would be contradicting. I was talking to him again, and we were friends again.

Friends do tend to allow each other to stay at their places. It didn't have to be weird, right?

'Of course. You're sleeping on the couch though!'

'I wouldn't have assumed anything else! Thank you endlessly!'

I felt almost bummed he didn't take the opportunity to bicker with me, but I had to remind myself that is something John would've done, not Jason.

'That's what friends are for! When should I expect you?'

'Next week. I hope that's not too soon for you.'

'Not at all. I'll have things ready.'

The conversation fizzled, and I put my phone back down. I let out a long tedious sigh. This was a good thing. Or at least, I was trying to convince myself it was. Mom would be pleased. If anything, perhaps I could get his thoughts about some of the electric energy around the lighthouse. I had not decided yet if I should tell him anything specific, but I knew he was my best bet considering my scientific interest lay more in geology and marine biology. Even astronomy was something I had dabbled in, but this was out of my wheelhouse.

After the much-needed meal break at The Squealing Pig, I went to get groceries in the various markets, anticipating Jason's arrival. I was thankful that I had taken my bike, which had a hefty basket on the front and room to strap goods to in the back. Riding around Boston had me feeling as if Little Brewster and this city were in two different parts of the world. Sometimes I forgot how close my lighthouse was to civilization. It made me wonder how everyone here could be so ignorant of what was happening around them. Did anyone ever suspect the special abilities the Boston Light possessed? Or was everyone so wrapped up in their own lives that they never bothered to notice the strange things they saw in the sky? The majority of mankind I thought almost didn't want to make progress. They were afraid of the bigger picture. Of something extraordinary presenting itself. I had to conclude they liked it that way.

Eventually, I propped up my bike near the Long Wharf pier, waiting to load everything into the Mermaid's Lagoon. I wanted a moment of observation. The sailboats speckled around the harbor made me think of the Portuguese islands. Despite the crazy cult and the short-lived time we had there, I knew it would be one of those memories that I would always look back on with fondness. Both islands we had gone to held special places in my heart. Horta was where we had our long night spent with oranges and wine and singing around a fire. It was where John took my hand and led me to the water, and surprised me with a dance. There were times on that ship that I couldn't wait to get away from him, but then I looked at myself now. Barely any time had passed and I missed him already. What would he say if he knew as much? He'd tease me relentlessly. But that was part of the fun. I wondered what it said about myself that I longed for people more when they were gone. It was true that I liked being chased. I liked the game of cat and mouse, but had I ever been able to progress from that?

It wasn't exactly a new revelation. I almost chastised myself for thinking of such a trivial thing when there were more important matters at hand. But it was something I worried about constantly. Was I even capable of loving someone? I loved my family, but had I ever loved someone besides them? Watching the water always had a way of bringing out the philosophical questions in me. There was a desire somewhere in me to have a person to call my own. To know that if I fell, someone would be there to pick me back up. But I wondered if I would have to make myself stay with someone and get past all the unbearable layers to finally find what I was looking for. Was my mind trying to tell me to give Jason another chance? I suddenly felt tired of dwelling on it. There was only so much reflection I could take in one day. I picked myself back up from my spot on the pier and made my way back to my little boat.

Sailing back to Little Brewster calmed me down as being out on the ocean always had. I unloaded all the groceries into the small cottage, trying to busy myself. It was no surprise to me that I had bought too much. The case was always I either went overboard on groceries or spent like I was but a peasant. I sectioned off all of my dry foods that could stand to be stored somewhere dark and musty. After putting the rest of the goods away I took the remaining items and headed up to the attic. I had a spare shelf up there that did perfectly for overflowing pantry foods. While organizing to the best of my abilities, I realized how much junk up there had been left to be sorted.

Perhaps this was the perfect task to finish off my day with. Getting right to work, I pulled out all of the dingy boxes that were pushed to the side corner.

They were all full of stuff that Thomas must've decided wasn't important to him. The first box seemed to be full of pictures, which delighted me. I flipped through them, getting an idea of what Thomas must've been like as a young man. Every picture had a sort of melancholic feel to it, which matched him. He had this air about him that made you believe his life was a tough one. From what I knew, that was true. The shots had all been taken on one or two cameras it seemed, and were experimental. Thomas took shots around the lighthouse and the cottage. They were quiet moments, all lonely and sparse. What troubled me was that none of his family was there. It was just the sea and this island. Was he really that alone? It made my heart heavy, thinking he perhaps never had anyone.

I took out another box, which was full of clothes that reeked of mildew. Very typical for a man to leave tons of clothes they didn't want anymore all stuffed up and hidden somewhere. The third box seemed to have no order whatsoever. There was no rhyme or reason to the contents. There was an old fisherman's hat, a couple of pens, a few more pictures, and other miscellaneous items. I couldn't help but admire all the photographs. Finding one with Thomas standing next to the lighthouse, with a pipe in his hand, I decided it needed to be framed. What better homage to the history here than pay attention to the previous keeper? I got rid of most of the junk in the boxes, after having placed the pictures to the side. It was when I was measuring the dimensions of the photograph that I turned it over, revealing faded scribbles in the top left corner.

The chicken scratch read, 'If you need to find me, contact this number.' Below was a ten-digit phone number, and I had to wonder whom it was intended for. I had started to develop the same superstitious spirit Thomas had possessed after seeing everything that I had this year. There was the same question floating in my mind since I arrived here. What had the keeper seen in his time? What did he know? Was this number still his? I wondered if I could pick his brain after all if maybe our acquaintance with each other wasn't over. Maybe he wouldn't want to hear from me. Why would he? I wanted to believe we were cut from the same cloth, and that, despite meeting from an occupation, two souls who understood each other would always be connected. It was settled then. I would call the number. If this was an impulsive choice, I'd blame it on Sterling rubbing off on me. I took the photograph downstairs with trembling hands, throwing myself on the couch. Dialing the number with bated breath, I waited.

"Hello?"

It was him. There was no mistaking that thick accent.

"Thomas, it's Adira."

There was a gruff on the other end, and I really could never tell what it meant when he did that.

"Was wondering when you'd find that note."

He said it as if it was a post-it left on the fridge that should've been seen ages ago.

"Yes, well, it wasn't exactly obvious."

"True enough.... So what made you decide to reach out to an old man?"

Was he going to play dumb? I hated beating around the bush.

"I think there are things about this job that you kept from me. Am I right about that?"

Silence ensued for a couple of minutes, and I almost thought he was going to hang up.

"So you've figured it out. Why the ships disappear?"

"Or why they look like they've disappeared."

"That's right. All right, listen. Meet me at Murray's Tavern in Revere. How's next Wednesday at seven?"

"Wait, why Revere? I'll have to get an Uber. Do you know how much that'll cost?"

"I'd rather not be recognized if it's all the same to you."

Was he a paranoid Polly or was there a legitimate reason we should be staying unseen?

"Fine, fine. Yes, seven on Wednesday will work."

Instead of receiving a reply, Thomas hung up abruptly. Technology wasn't his strong suit. Still sitting on the couch with tense shoulders, it started to set in that he left that note for me. Waiting even just a few days was going to be torture, knowing that he was probably the only other person who had traveled in time. Or maybe not. Maybe this had been happening since the lighthouse was built. It was then that I remembered Jason would be here next week. How could I forget something that I just agreed to mere hours before? It'd all be fine, I told myself. Jason didn't need to know why I was meeting with the former keeper; it had nothing to do with him.

Chapter Thirty-Eight

The weekend had come and passed, albeit slowly and dreadfully. Jason would be docking his rental boat on the island any minute now. Meanwhile, I was inside trying not to waste my day with idle energy. There had been some light rain the day before, but nothing significant enough to spark up another electric storm. It was probably the only time I wasn't too disappointed about the lack thereof, considering that if I had disappeared again it would have been harder to explain my absence if Jason had come here before I got back. I was anxious to pick his brain about the strange occurrences. He was studying physics in college, and this business of his was nearly a way to help cover expenses and hopefully student debt. I knew he was taking many different scientific courses and would have more knowledge than me about figuring out the why and how of time travel. Making it up in my mind, I decided that if my conversation on Wednesday with Thomas was not fruitful, then I would enlist the help of Jason.

Speaking of the devil, I could hear him outside. I opened the door to greet Jason, seeing him getting off his boat. His eyes met mine, and a small shy smile crept up on his face. Carrying two bags, he came over to the cottage, and I grabbed one. In the process, he gave me a brief hug, and we dispersed his things in the living room.

"Nothing's changed since the first time I've been here." He told me.

"It hasn't been that long!"

Of course, it was for me. Things were still awkward between us, and I wondered if it was a mistake to let him come here again. He was someone who wasn't very fond of the ocean, so the fact he came here showed his cards more than I would've liked.

"So. What have you been up to since the last time I saw you?"

It was a question to fill the tense silence, but I appreciated it nonetheless.

"Nothing exciting. Got sick and explored some pubs. What about you?"

"Well, you know most of it. Started the business, constantly studying... and I met this girl."

Against my own accord, my heart did a backflip at the mention of a girl.

"Oh? Do I know her?"

"No, we met online. She's not too far from your family's house it turns out. But she likes all the same things as me. It could turn into something really great."

He sounded confident about the situation. Meanwhile, I was getting a sinking feeling in my gut that I could hardly make out.

"Wow! That's, that's great Jason. Are you two...."

"Together? No. Not yet anyway."

Yet was the operative word. I should've been happy for him. There should've been a smile gracing my face as we spoke. Instead, I felt something akin to disappointment. I couldn't seriously be upset that Jason found someone, right? Wasn't I the one gallivanting with a crew full of men who I continually claimed understood me better than most modern men?

"Do you think you'll make it official?"

He turned to me, studying my face.

"It depends; I'm still considering several factors."

Not wanting to get pushy and enter a conversation I may regret, I refrained from asking him what factors he was talking about. There was already a look in his eyes I couldn't place.

"Well whatever makes you happy," I replied.

We moved on to other subjects as I put together a summer salad for the two of us.

"So, how long do you think this job will take?"

"Somewhere from a week to a month. It's hard to tell, a lot depends on the condition of the house."

I nodded and thought to myself how I could afford to get away if another storm presented itself. I didn't think I could resist holding back from traveling again. There was still so much I needed to be sure of, aside from the fact that it was the most exhilarating thing I had ever done.

Little happened the rest of the day as Jason settled in and we talked. I asked about his family, my own, and our mutual friends. It was a much-needed catch-up, and I was happy to hear everyone was carrying on as normal. Eventually, nighttime came, and I lay in my bed in total darkness. I kept thinking of the piece of news I had been presented with. Part of me was annoyed that he would bring up meeting a girl until I remembered that I was the one insisting we were supposed to be friends. Friends tend to mention this when they meet someone.

Was I feeling jealous? How can you feel jealous if you aren't in love with the person getting the attention? I looked at the reality of my relationship with Jason. We had been getting close again, we were talking frequently, and, as far as I could tell, Jason was taking the breakup well. Or had at least moved past it. Had I judged him too harshly? Maybe my mother was right, maybe I hadn't given him enough of a chance. But what difference did it make? He already had his eyes on someone else. I thought bitterly that it wasn't much time at all that he had been able to move on from me. I was confused with my feelings and in a state of restlessness. Wednesday couldn't come soon enough.

It was the following morning when he asked me a question that I dreaded answering.

"All right, so I've told you all about my new friends, what about you? Have you found anyone that's caught your eye?"

In the present, there wasn't a single person who I had met and connected with. It was embarrassing, the fact that it took living with pirates to get me out of my shell and meet people. When I was here, there wasn't anyone to talk to. Jason was the only friend who I had stayed in contact with.

"There's been some folk that have kept my interest. I haven't been all alone, at least."

"Well, maybe I can meet them! Over lunch or something?"

I was trying to downplay what the situation was, but I realized too late that I should've told him I had been completely alone.

"Oh, well, they're probably too busy. They lead very engaging lives."

"What do they do?"

Why couldn't I keep my mouth shut? I struggled, thinking of what to say next.

"Ah, most of them are fishermen."

Jason didn't seem to notice any falter in my voice and took the words in earnest.

"I guess that makes sense. Well, that's a shame, it would've been nice to see who you hang out with."

"Yeah, for sure! Maybe another time."

Thinking he believed me might've been too quick of an assumption, because his eyes were searching, his face quizzical.

"I feel like there's something you're not telling me. Are you okay?"

And there it was. I had failed in my diversion.

"Of course I am! Why wouldn't I be?"

It wasn't the strongest reply, and I could tell he didn't believe me, but I wasn't willing to disclose anything today.

"Okay. Well, I better get going. I actually have to do some work."

I bid him goodbye and then let out a breath.

Chapter Thirty-Nine

Opting for an oversized button-up and palazzo pants, I stepped outside the Uber, where I was greeted with a sign that read Murray's Tavern. The sky was just starting to change in color, and the dinner rush was ongoing. Walking inside the tavern I was overwhelmed with the smell of tobacco and cheap perfume. After the intensity died down I was able to focus on the surroundings, to notice Thomas was already there. Sitting in a corner booth, he had his hands folded together next to a mug of frothy beer. Sliding into the seat opposite him, he looked up from his bushy eyebrows, and I swore I could see a hint of a smirk on his face.

"Nice to see ya again, lass." His speaking reminded me of Finn, and it made me smile.

"Likewise. What's a retired keeper getting up to these days?"

"Nothing nearly as exciting as you, rest assured."

His reply brought to mind the very reason we had met up. A waiter took my order and then my attention was back on the man in front of me.

"About that. This position is a little more interesting than I was expecting."

This time he almost let out a chuckle.

"I'd suspect so. Tell me, where did ya end up?"

I was somewhat fearful to be the first one to say it out loud.

"The force of it all knocked me out. When I awoke, I was on a ship. Full of pirates, in 1720."

There was no backing out of talking about it now. It was out in the open, and it would be hard to dismiss. I watched as his eyes lit up while I explained to him my experience.

"Much more interesting than my experience, no doubt."

My suspicions were confirmed. He had gone through the very same thing as me.

"What happened?"

"Much like you, I had been curious about the passing ships at night. People were sure it was a legend, a tale that sailors liked to yap about in the pubs after a couple of drinks. Purposely I went out one night, swimming right up to one of the devils. When they hoisted me up I hardly realized what happened until morning."

"Was it the same time? 1720?"

"Couple years later, I believe. A merchant had found me sloshing about in the waves, hauling me up on his ship. We were thick as thieves, and we made trips frequently during my time on the island."

"He came to our time?"

"Aye. Granted, I never let him past the harbor. We both agreed it was too dangerous for him to know much about his future."

"How much history was altered?"

"Nothing too drastic, as far as I'm aware. His crew knew how we did things. They kept the status quo during our visits. Why? Did you do something?"

My face paled, knowing I had messed things up.

"I can't tell to what extent... but I know the Golden Age of Piracy has extended some 20 years."

Thomas gave me a look of incredulity. It's hard for me to believe it even now.

"My god, lass. You're lucky that was the only thing that changed. This is... this isn't good."

He didn't have to tell me.

"My thoughts exactly. I'm worried what this will mean. The pirates I was with, they are very influential. And I don't think my time there is done."

The man started to shift in his seat, eyes averting.

"What, what is it?" I asked.

"I don't know what all I can tell you. I can hardly remember what I am supposed to tell you."

He winced then, and I could see that last part he wasn't supposed to tell me. My suspicions arose, and I could only guess what he meant. We looked down at our drinks as an awkward silence filled the air. I didn't know how to get him to open up.

"I'm not going to pretend I know everything that's going on here, Thomas. I just want information. I want advice. I'm tired of people withholding the first one from me."

There was an inner conflict behind his eyes, and I could only sit and wait.

"I think you and I, our lives are more intertwined than I can explain. There are things in your future that set a course of history for the rest of us. What you do from this point on is something I can't interfere in."

"Well, then why did you invite me here?"

"Because I had to be sure. A long time ago, I met someone who looked just like you. After that, I knew the only possibility there could've been for me to meet her was for me to choose my successor."

"What are you saying?"

"I'm saying that the next time you see me neither of us will look the same. Everything that is happening now is just how it should be."

He was telling me to trust the process. Was he crazy?

"But the repercussions...."

He stopped me. "May need to happen. Perhaps things will always shift. Let it come."

Then he ushered me out of my seat, and we walked to the front to pay our bills. Walking outside, he gripped my shoulder, looking me over.

"Till the next time, Adira."

Then he was gone. Got in a car and drove away. If I were to understand anything Thomas told me that night, it would come to me later. And I never was patient.

Riding home was unnerving. I was anxious for the future, for the certainty it would bring me. My meeting with Thomas reaped little benefit, and I wasn't sure how sound his advice was. Upon entering the cottage Jason was lounging on the couch, phone in hand. He looked up, acknowledging me.

"You okay?" He asked me.

"Yeah. Just met up with the keeper that trained me."

"Oh. Is that a common thing?"

"I just had some questions about this place I was hoping he could answer."

"How'd it go?"

I nodded. "I think he's losing his mind a little bit."

He laughed. "That does seem to be the consensus for light keepers."

Thankfully, Jason didn't press on and ask too much about what was said. However, I couldn't deny that the meeting had not gone as I hoped. Silence filled the room, as I started to overthink everything Thomas had told me. I wondered if the lighthouse itself was acting as a wormhole. It seemed the most likely option. Wormholes had the limitation of only existing as far back as the creation of the time machine. In this case, the lighthouse was built in 1716, which would support my theory. This was the research I had painstakingly been involved in the night before, where another part of the puzzle seemed to fit together. Wormhole space-time requires a substance of exotic energy, which would be the lightning attracted to the vessel. This revelation led me down another rabbit hole, as I put together that the lightning acted as a quantum field, essentially being the electrically charged particles that made traveling between the two mouths possible.

I was thankful that I could put words to the experience I had undergone and could almost explain it in technical terms. But at the same time, I wanted to give up on worrying about it at all after talking with Thomas. Perhaps he was right. It was my own need for control that urged me for more details, and there was a possibility sitting next to me.

"So, what kind of things have you learned in your classes this past semester?"

Jason looked at me with a hint of surprise at my question.

"Nothing that would interest you. It's exhausting, all of it." That wasn't the answer I was hoping for.

"Oh. I'm just curious."

"About physics? Well, hit me with a question and I'll try to answer."

"Have you covered time travel yet?"

He seemed to perk up at the mention of it, as we had both been sci-fi addicts as children.

"Certain aspects of it, yeah. Lots of quantum theories, let me tell ya."

"What about wormholes? That's a pretty popular one."

"That goes hand in hand with quantum physics. It's almost a whole separate genre, I could go on forever. It's not very sustainable, though."

This got my attention.

"What do you mean? It's possible if the conditions are right. There are news articles about the progress we've made with calculations all the time."

"Of course it's possible. I don't doubt it's already out there. But it doesn't last. The electric energy needed to sustain the machine would out-balance the negative field, the weak point in time that started the possibility in the first place would eventually collapse in almost every scenario."

I felt my heart drop as I fully processed what he meant. This would not last forever. There would be an end to the option of traveling between the eras.

"Don't scientists have any sort of timeline for a collapse in those conditions?"

"It depends on so many different variables, it's almost impossible to generalize it. Maybe if there was a wormhole we already knew about, they could take a few guesses."

"So if you knew of one, would you be able to work it out?"

He laughed. "Gosh, maybe? I don't know. It's hard to imagine that I would be the one to undertake something that important. What's got you so interested in wormholes? Are you in a new fandom or something?"

"Ah, just revisiting some old ones. You know how it goes. You binge-watch one time-traveling show and you have a million theories."

"Well I may just have to watch with you, now I'm invested!"

I chuckled right along with him, and I let him turn on the TV and search for the series mentioned. We put on Timeless, and, as the pilot started, I could almost forget about everything else. Jason put an arm around me, and I found myself subconsciously leaning into him. To be close to another human was something I underrated. It was a comfort I often dismissed. That was how the both of us unwound for several nights in a row, and I was grateful for it.

It was during these moments that I wondered again what I felt for Jason. There was a sort of affection growing in my heart for him, but I felt scared to put a name to it. After all, it would be silly to admit anything after I broke up with him. But he was still there and didn't seem to care that in technical terms we were exes. Around the third night of us binging our show, he slipped out the L word, maybe without realizing it, as he bid me goodnight. I stayed up that night, not able to let it go. Not wanting to bring it up, I tried dismissing it instead. I almost said it back. Was love supposed to be this? A simple companionship, made of two individuals who were lonely and wanted someone to fill their space? My mother would say so. Maybe this was just the next step of life for me. If I were to lose the one opportunity I had to feel alive, perhaps this was just what people do to fill their days. Surely it was better than being alone, dying with no one around. It was then that I started to suspect that I needed to convince myself that I did love Jason.

Chapter Forty

Jason had been here for two weeks. With each passing day, I felt more urgency to put a name to these feelings. I worried that I would be too late in this development, that maybe it was this other girl he was now more interested in. In the two weeks that he had stayed with me, there still was no storm significant enough to see if the lighthouse still served as a time machine vessel. A few days ago when I heard thunder, I got excited thinking I was about to get another chance. I went so far as to take the Mermaid's Lagoon out and wait in the middle of the rain. An hour later I came back inside the cottage, disappointed. Jason had looked at me with bewilderment, curious as to why I would purposely get myself soaking wet and go out in the waves for no reason. I tried telling him that I thought I had seen a ship out there.

"I don't understand what's going on with you sometimes. Didn't this happen last time I was here?"

It was hard to keep what was happening from him. There were simply too many weird things going on for him not to have suspicions, and I wasn't helping the matter.

"I don't know what else to say, Jason."

He wasn't exactly fuming, but curious about my behavior. Sighing, he took a moment to think, looking around the living room.

"Y'know, I'm almost done with my job here. Then I can be out of your hair."

I felt like we always misunderstood each other, and I hated it.

"You're not a nuisance here, you know. I've actually kind of liked having you here."

It was a small thing to say out loud, but I saw his eyes light up with hope.

"Really?"

I nodded. "Yeah. There's something else I've been meaning to tell you, and I just haven't figured out the right time to say it."

His face fell, and I knew he was assuming the worst.

"I just... there's been a lot of time to think about how rough of a start we had, those couple of months ago. The timing wasn't quite right, and I didn't know what I wanted at the time. But I think I do now, and I know I don't want you with that other girl. What I'm trying to say is, I think I love you...."

It was awkward, and jumbled, and definitely not how I was expecting to admit my feelings to him, but it was out there now. I wasn't even sure I was going to say it until today. My hands were clammy as I waited for his reaction. I couldn't quite make out his face as he leaned on the wall looking at the floor. The more time that went by, the more I felt my heart drop.

"I think maybe we need to think this through. We should give it some time, see if this is what we really want."

Jason was the last person I thought I'd have to deal with losing feelings, but the sinking sensation in my gut told me that was exactly what was happening. He truly had wanted to stay friends, and I just made things harder than they had to be.

"Right. You're right."

He looked like he was in pain, and I couldn't tell for the life of me what he was thinking.

"A few months ago that's all I ever wanted to hear."

I wanted to ask what changed, but something stopped me from inquiring. Deciding maybe I didn't want to know, I removed myself from the situation. I told him I had to go tend to the lighthouse. There were tears just waiting to happen as I tried to tell myself it wasn't a big deal. I couldn't tell at the time that my feelings were due to feeling unworthy of love, however far from the truth that was. If Jason, my longest friend, couldn't accept me as I was, then what hope was there for me? If he did not want me, it was no one's fault but my own. I would have to learn to be okay with it.

But as I said, this all transpired a few days before. This, however, was Jason's last day here. We didn't talk about what had been said, and things almost went back to normal. There was still a slight tense energy in the air, both of us unsure if the confession should be addressed. I carried on my day as usual, filling the keeper log and reading a classic novel. Scrubbing the baseboards, checking the weather radar, and watching ships roll in and out of the distant horizon. As Jason came back to the cottage that evening, packing up, I knew it may very well be the last time I saw him. I waited in the kitchen, arms crossed, as he gathered all of his bags up. We were at a standstill, and I knew it was my job to make sure this wasn't a sour goodbye of my own accord. He stood in the doorway, waiting to see what I'd do. I let my instinct lead me as I wrapped my arms around him after kissing him on the cheek.

To my surprise he held onto me, tightening his grip. We stood like that for who knows how long. It was when he let go and looked back at me that I heard in the faintest whisper, "Can I kiss you?"

I hardly knew what I agreed to when I nodded. He immediately pressed his lips onto mine, softly, and I found it to be nothing like the first time he had kissed me. I was somewhat aware of parting my lips in return. He took it as an invitation, and, without any interruption, had started something of a challenge, and backed me up back into the house and against a wall. Before I knew it he had picked me up, placing me on the kitchen table. My hands found their way around his neck.

We continued for a while, as he told me how beautiful I was, how long he'd wanted me, and all the things in between. He wanted to hear me say I loved him one more time, and I gave in to his request. Some kisses were rough, and teeth nearly clashed. Once the moment passed I asked him to stay a little longer. It took no convincing. I told him I would no longer be scared, it wouldn't be like the first time. He was glad to hear it and swore that we should be completely honest with where we stood. I couldn't agree more, but I knew what that meant. And I found that I no longer cared if he knew. Wouldn't it be a wild adventure to share this special thing with another person? I was brimming with excitement on his behalf, knowing a studying physicist would be elated with the opportunity.

But I had to remember Jason was not superstitious. He came from a place of logic, with the additional occasions of believing something to be fact as long as he felt it was so. But this was a situation few must've found themselves in, and, being a person of science in practice, he had to have a reason to suspect. He would find it before too long. I had to be patient in the meantime. However, I couldn't help but wonder if he would actually want to be in another time. Lately, it was all I could think about, as I missed my friends terribly and missed the danger and excitement. But that was not in Jason's nature. He was the type of person who wanted a white picket fence kind of life. There was a gnawing feeling in the back of my mind that the very subject would be a conflict later on. As with most other things in my life, I tried to ignore it.

Moving past my confession, Jason and I made dinner. As we sat at the kitchen table, he could not stop looking at me and smiling. Things were seemingly good between us, and I was happy that he was happy. It wasn't the type of thrill I'd get during a ship raid or palace heist or even the brimming curiosity of swimming with Aerwyna. And it was certainly nothing like being with John. Not that I could compare the two. Because one was my boyfriend and the boy my family wanted me to be with, and the other was a thief who knew a little too much about what I was thinking without having to say it. I thought of how even then, as Jason kissed me again, he was always cold to the touch. I shivered at the realization, knowing that every time I had been near John, he radiated warmth. Nothing about him could be categorized as cold. Even his gaze meant to make the enemy fear him could only be described as fire and fury.

The following days were spent with Jason putting out job queries in Boston, and with me catching my family up on recent developments. They could not be more thrilled that I made up with Jason, and I couldn't help the smile on my face. My mother could finally be happy with where my life was headed, and I wouldn't be grilled about how unrealistic my expectations were. It was true, part of my feelings for Jason was born from fear. Fear that he would be my only option and fear that he would be the only one willing to put up with me. I of course enjoyed his company, when we weren't at odds, and most of all enjoyed the comfort knowing that there were no surprises with him. Everything one had to worry about when getting to know someone, I already knew about Jason. This was the course of action that would keep everyone at peace, and I felt contentment with the fact.

But nothing was ever perfect. I had been tracking the weather like a hound, and, despite Jason's usual obliviousness, he had picked up on my habit. Each day that passed he became more troubled by my behavior, more distrusting. It finally bubbled out into something of an argument, which left me questioning what I wanted to tell him.

"I don't understand you, Adira. You tell me you're going to be more honest with me and open, but then you act weird all the time with no explanation."

"What am I doing wrong, Jason?"

"You're skittish about the weather, you won't tell me anything about these supposed friends of yours, and every time I kiss you your eyes are somewhere far away. Is there another man? Someone better than me?"

I shook my head. "No, of course not! Those things have nothing to do with anything!"

"Why aren't you being upfront with me then? I should've known I wasn't good enough for you."

Desperate to show him he was misunderstanding, I grasped his arms with both hands, trying to get him to look at me.

"I choose you, ok? It doesn't matter who else is out there. There is nothing going on here, and these weird things will be given reason in due time."

"I just don't believe you. Maybe this was all a mistake."

"What are you saying? Just give me time, okay? I can explain everything."

His words had only planted doubt in my head, hearing him be the one to say it was a mistake. As if I wasn't trying at all to make this work. I wanted to make him and my family proud. I knew that the next chance I got, I needed to show him what was going on.

There was, of course, another development that had been puzzling me. I had originally thought that the reason for my mysterious gills appearing was because of Wyna's presence. But after a few early morning swims with Jason, I had started to notice that I could hold my breath a lot longer than I used to. It could be chalked up to being in the water more often in my life and building endurance, but after Jason commented on it, I grew weary. I wished terribly that Wyna was here so that I could ask her what this meant. But since coming back I had not seen a single mermaid. It was a worry that I tried not to dwell on, knowing that there should still be a city of some sort down there, near the coast of New England.

If Thomas had seen one, it wasn't out of the realm of possibility that they still surfaced so close to the harbor. It must've been human aggression growing throughout the years that limited their contact even more so for the past three centuries. Still, not knowing what it meant that my body was changing struck worry in me. What was more, I was drawn to the ocean more than ever. Being there had only increased my love for the sea and its inhabitants. I found that John was right in what he had said to me.

There was a growing discomfort the longer I stuck to land. Being on that ship of his was more freeing than tying myself here, to the lighthouse. For every worry I had that I would miss people and miss the comforts of staying still, he had proved otherwise. I was stuck between the conflict of what I wanted to do and what was expected of me.

Chapter Forty-One

It was time. I could almost feel it. The day had started out with thick fog wrapping itself around the island, where I could hardly see what lay beyond the distance. Forecasts showed we were to expect a thunderstorm, and I thought with unbridled glee that today could be the day I go back. Jason was still with me, but he would be gone in the middle of August, and we had just started the month. In preparation, I changed into my pirate attire and had Jason get into something he didn't care about getting wet. He was laughing at me and shaking his head. As we progressed into the afternoon, the weather had taken a turn for the worst. The thunderstorm was in full swing, and the wind was beating against the cottage. I was buzzing with anticipation, eager to see if my intuition was right.

"So what exactly are we doing?" Jason asked me, all quizzical.

"You're just going to have to trust me. Can you come to the lighthouse with me?"

He was suspicious, but nodded and followed. The rain poured down on us as soon as we opened the cottage door, and I could already feel the rush of adrenaline kicking in knowing what may be happening in a matter of minutes. I was nearly running to the lighthouse, with Jason close behind. The whole tower rumbled from the water pounding down, and I jogged up the spiraling stairs with wet boots. One level below the light, I got ready to go to the balcony. This was the risky part. As I moved to open the door, Jason grabbed my hand.

"What are you doing??"

"I can already see lightning out there. We need to be out on the balcony."

He shook his head. "For what exactly?"

"You're not going to believe me, but there's a reason I asked you about wormholes. This place, it's a vessel! The theory is true!"

"You aren't making sense! This is crazy!"

"Let me prove it to you! This is the reason for your mistrust, let me show you!"

I yanked his hand forward, taking him out on the balcony with me. He was shivering and huddled close to the door, but my eyes were on the sky. Every minute the lightning came closer, and all I knew was that I didn't want to be caught off guard this time.

"Jason, we're going to have to jump off this balcony. Can you do that?"

If it was even possible his face went paler.

"What!? Adira...."

Not waiting for him, I began slowly climbing the fencing. The railing was very thin, and it took every ounce of focus not to slip. Once I felt stable enough, I turned back to Jason. The waves were picking up as the storm intensified.

"Come on! It's now or never!"

He slowly came over to where I stood, his hands shaking as they gripped the rails. I stayed low as he took his time climbing on top. Once we were on the same level I took his hand.

"When I tell you to jump, jump."

His breathing was raspy, and I wondered if he would pass out before he had the chance. It was any minute now. The light was going round and round, and the lightning was nearly right next to us. I started to brace my knees for what was about to happen.

"NOW!" I yelled, and we both leaped.

Nothing was in our control now. The wind nearly carried us completely as we started diving downwards into the crashing waves. We plunged into the water, close to the rocks. Jason struggled to keep his head up, gasping for air. I made my way close to him, knowing what was about to happen next. As the waves carried us farther out, the lightning strikes seemed to almost form together around the lighthouse. I could only make out glimpses with blurry eyes, adjusting to the salt water. As my head went under once more, I could hear a loud rumble fill my ears. I tried looking for Jason, reaching my hands out in front of me. Before I could manage to get close enough, that big wave of light and energy burst forth and reached us. I immediately felt myself being flown back, with a ringing in my ears and nothing but the feeling of disorientation.

Not making out what direction I was in after being tumbled down below the surface, I made my way back up for fresh air. Everything was gray with rain still pouring down, and, as I looked around, I noticed with panic that Jason was not to be seen. Diving back under, I scanned the water frantically for any sign of him. Several feet down, I caught a glimpse of him unconscious. I propelled myself towards him, pushing and kicking until I could grab him with one arm. Bringing the both of us back to the top was a little harder than I thought, but I managed. We bobbed to and fro as I tried to see anything that would tell me which way to swim. I noticed with a small ray of excitement that we must've traveled in time at least a little, as between the fog and rain I could see glimpses of night. Finally I could see the light from Little Brewster, but it was miles out. We had been kicked back farther than I realized. There would be no ships attempting to sail out in this weather unless they had to. Resigning my fate to swimming to the lighthouse, I tried waking Jason up.

Smacking him several times on the face did nothing, and the same went for shaking him. I cursed at the sky, for Jason having the same reaction as I did when traveling back for the first time. Letting out something like a growl, I tried my best to keep him up. But despite his small frame, he was still heavy. There was no great way to hold onto him and swim efficiently. Nevertheless I kept an arm around him, swimming closer to the island at a slug-like pace. The wind and waves kept pushing me in the opposite direction I wanted to go in, almost in spite of me. Already my arms felt like they were about to fall off. The wind was doing funny things to my hearing, because I swore I could hear men shouting somewhere close by. But then a few more glances to my right proved my hearing was just fine. Out in the distance came a sloop racing through the water. Seeing a chance at less miles to swim, I started paddling and yelling at the top of my lungs. I couldn't make out anyone on the vessel, or any of its details, only the slight glow of the lanterns and the continuous shouting.

We were nearly next to the freeboard as a rope was cast down into the water. I tied it around Jason and me and signaled them to hoist us up. There was no time to think whether the people up there were friendly or not. It was either this or possibly drowning. Within seconds we were being lifted out of the water, and I could let out a sigh of relief. Soon after we were brought onto the main deck with a crew full of men staring at us while the rain continued on. Then with a closer look I saw familiar faces, and it was then that I grinned. Marco Teale was standing right there with wide eyes.

"Adira?"

"Marco!"

Before being able to help myself, I leaped towards him, closing the distance in a crushing hug. After a second he returned the gesture, and I heard Boone say, "It's Miss Fellows!"

The crew cheered, and I felt a sense of belonging wash over me. Marco let me go and glanced to the deck where Jason was hunched over coughing up water.

"Oh, my bad. Everyone, this is Jason. Jason, this is John Sterling's crew. These people are who I stayed with last time I was here."

Jason, bewildered, blurted out, "Last time?!"

I watched him carefully, but before he could do much of anything, he was throwing up over the railing. The crew laughed and joked at the boy, and I felt a little embarrassed. Finn made his way through the crowd of men, beaming at me. Within seconds he had his arms around me and was lifting me in the air.

"Well if it isn't our very own navigator. We weren't sure if ya were goin' ta show up again."

Before I could reply, my attention was drawn back to Marco as he spoke up again.

"What are you doing back here?"

Always the one to get straight to business.

"I told you I couldn't stay away for long. How much time has passed for you?"

He and Finn looked at each other before Marco gave his reply.

"Just two days. The only reason you caught us was because we chose tonight to leave Boston."

"That's incredible. It's been almost two months for me. Where's John?"

There were more nervous glances until Finn spoke up.

"He's back in Boston."

"What? As much as he trusts you two I don't think he'd let you sail away with his ship."

Darien chimed in, "Well it wasn't exactly his choice."

I waited for someone to give an explanation while being aware that Jason was still behind me not saying a word.

"Ah he... he got caught ya see. Was drinkin' up a storm after ya left and got sloppy. The Navy had followed us as ya know, back to Boston, and had him in shambles before the evening. The few of us on land made a run for it and here we are," explained Finn.

Immediately I was livid. Never had I thought John's mates could be so disloyal. Marco must've seen the look in my eyes as he grabbed my arm.

"It's not like we didn't try, Adira. There were too many officers. We were outnumbered. It was either have all of us hang at once, or leave and try to regroup."

I shook my head, furious at the lot of them.

"No. You're a bunch of cowards, all of you. Leaving your captain for the gallows.... What's wrong with you?! Here I am to see all of you again and start off on another adventure, and you've all left John back there to die!"

Marco looked at me, both stricken with guilt and pity.

"Our way of life isn't always about freedom. You know that. This is the risk we all take."

I shook my head, not willing to accept the fact that the one person I wanted to see more than anyone wasn't there.

"I'm sorry, I just don't accept that it's too late for him. He's not supposed to die yet."

The rain had slowed down, and the moon came out to light the gloomy weather. I motioned to Jason.

"Come on. We're leaving."

Before Jason could say anything, Marco interrupted.

"And where exactly are you going?"

"I'm going to get John."

Jason finally grabbed my wrist, saying, "Um, I'm still trying to wrap my head around whatever just happened, but they just told you he's in jail. Where he should be. If this is all real, then that's where he belongs."

I knew Jason might've had a little more self-righteousness with regard to pirates, but I was hoping that he would put up with it for me. It was my problem to assume such.

"I'm sorry, but he's my friend, and he doesn't deserve to hang."

"You don't know this man!"

Marco butted in, "No one's leaving this ship! Got that?"

Somewhere in my mind, I knew Marco was acting captain in John's absence, but I didn't have to follow his rules.

"I never agreed to take orders from you. So I'm going. And my boyfriend is coming with me."

Jason made a coughing sound, probably wanting to protest, when Finn came right up next to me.

He whispered closely, "Please tell me that isn't who I think it is."

I had forgotten that we had talked about Jason in depth and could only shrug with a wince. Finn shook his head, disappointed. I felt embarrassed again, wondering if everyone there would think I shouldn't have brought him along. Another assumption on my part, thinking they would take him in the way they had with me.

The deck was silent, everyone waiting to see what Marco would say next. He looked distraught, and I knew it couldn't be easy to have a say in what hundreds of people did.

"Finn! Take us back to the harbor."

Finn hesitated. "Aye."

As Finn moved to the helm, I was left questioning Marco.

"What are you doing?"

"We're going with you. I'm not going to lose two friends."

Gripping his shoulder, I smiled at him. This was the right decision. I know they were all scared, and for good reason, but we had the disguise of darkness. It would have to be enough, and I tried my best to help Marco with our plan of rescue. Jason would be with me, which the crew disagreed about, as I was going to be part of the group to be inside the prison to fetch John. They argued that he had zero experience and was no better than driftwood (when Jason heard that I thought he was going to have a meltdown). But until he felt more comfortable, he was going to have to stick with me. I brought him into this, so he was my responsibility. William, Paul, and Charlie were in charge of providing distractions for the exterior of the prison.

Once inside, Darien and Boone would be our second level of deflection. If they could maintain the guards near the threshold, Finn, Jason and I could break John out. The rest was based on a lot of luck. Marco had me follow him back to John's quarters, where he laid out all of the weapons I had used when I was here. It almost made my heart swell that they had kept them aside. I kept having to remind myself that next to no time had passed for them. Stuffing the dagger into my sash, I pulled a belt from John's wardrobe to sling around my shoulder. Jason watched me wordlessly, still shaking every now and then. I walked over to him, handing him a knife and pistol.

"Can you use these?"

He gaped at me. "Do you realize what you just asked me?"

There wasn't a whole lot of time to coddle him, which I might've done if we were back in the present. But we weren't. I stood close to him, searching his eyes and hoping he would just go with it.

"Hey, we made it. This is my world, and I want you in it. I want to explore all of this with you. We just need to do this little thing first."

"No, Addi, this is what seems to be the eighteenth century. You belong with me, back in the twenty-first century. And you're asking me to possibly hurt someone else over a criminal."

"There's so much to tell you, there's just not the time right now. I need you, Jason. Please."

I knew telling him that would do the trick; he liked to feel needed and admired. That feeling won out every time. Sure enough he sighed, his shoulders sagging.

"I'll just be following you, nothing more. Okay?"

"That's good enough for me."

He stopped me from leaving, not satisfied with the conversation.

"What just happened? Are you telling me that we just traveled through time?"

"I wanted to tell you sooner, but I knew it was a difficult thing to grasp. I'm still reeling from it myself."

"What you said back there, you're saying you've already been here? With pirates no less?"

I nodded. "For six months. These people took me in when I was scared and confused. Don't judge them too harshly."

"Six months?! Adira...."

"I know, it's a lot. I'll tell you everything I know later. I promise."

We went back out to meet the others, and we were almost back in the harbor. It was a comfort to know these British colonies were still new and developing, and there shouldn't be that many watchmen in theory. They could only spread out so far, being as new and sparse as they were. Marco decided to stay just beyond the docks, not wanting to deal with alerting the harbor master. The ship kept to the shadows, staying silent, with all the lanterns snuffed. We lowered a boat down with patience and gentility. Our success relied on our agility and silence, and everyone was tense. Jason's knee was bobbing up and down, and I laid my hand on top, trying to steady him. I thought again how foolish I was to think this was something Jason would want to be involved in. He was nothing like me. What I thought had been feelings of love were quickly beginning to look like a sense of duty and responsibility.

As we made it to land, everyone split up into their respective groups. Bidding them good luck, the three of us went off with Darien and Boone. Even then, I felt lighter than I had in the present. I had missed these men and their crazy escapades. We waited for our cue, seeing how long it would take William and the others to pull through. It did not take long, as we heard scuffling and loud arguing. They put on a good show. The guardsmen looked annoyed, but their attention was drawn nonetheless. But there was one lingering at the entrance, and he seemed intent on staying there.

Finn looked over at us whispering, "I'm going to deal with him, you two go ahead of me when you get the chance."

I nodded, watching him run over and cover the man's mouth with his arm. Dragging him away, it was our turn to move. I motioned for Jason to follow, and we slipped inside the front. Upon entering, there were two men at a table, playing cards. They hadn't noticed us yet, which was why I pulled Jason to the side.

I whispered, "I'll take the one with the keys if you can manage the heavier guy."

"No, no I can't. I've never gotten in a fight, not even in school."

"Just try to knock him out, Jason. Use the back of the knife I gave you."

Refusing to hear any more protests, I leaped in front of the two men. They immediately rose from their chairs, red in the face. Pouncing for my prey, I started to strangle my opponent. It seemed to work at first, before the man rammed me into a wall and knocked the air out of my lungs. Sliding to the ground, I caught a glimpse of Jason on the other side of the room, getting choked. Rolling my eyes, I picked myself back up and ducked a punch from the guard. Knowing I was no match for him both in height and weight, I pulled out my dagger and jabbed him in the stomach. He doubled over immediately, and thankfully at that moment Finn came running in. The guard was staggering towards me as I motioned for Finn to help Jason. He grumbled in frustration, and I started to prepare for what was next. The guard grabbed me, trying to squeeze the life out of me. My feet were off the ground, and I tried wiggling myself free, but to no avail.

Running out of options, I sank my teeth down into his arm. He immediately dropped me, howling and calling me a dirty wench. I took the end of my dagger and gave him a hard knock on the head. It seemed to do the trick as he tumbled down, and I reached for the keys on his belt. Finn finally managed to tear Jason away from the second guard, and he came scrambling over to me and leaching onto my waist. Once Finn was done knocking guard number two out, he looked over at me, irritation written out all over his face.

"I'm not sure why you had to bring your little pet, lass."

Jason only gripped me tighter, and I breathed out a sigh of my own annoyance.

"Doesn't matter now. He's not my pet, by the way."

Finn chuckled. "Well he's no man."

It was such a low blow that I almost felt sorry on Jason's behalf as he peeled himself off of me and puffed his chest out. We started making our way deeper into the complex, where we came across two hallways full of cells. Many were still empty, which must've amplified the Navy's desire to lock John up.

I spoke up. "Maybe you should go with Jason down one side, and I take the other. You can protect him better than I can."

He nodded, but I could see he was clearly not happy about the situation. Neither was Jason for that matter, but it'd have to be a discussion for later. Walking down the long narrow hall, I stayed on high alert and tread slowly. It was mostly quiet, with the occasional coughs and shuffles. Every time I passed an occupied cell, the ones who were awake sneered at me and called me names I never want to hear repeated. After a while it motivated me to quicken my pace. The hall started to wind in other directions, and I had to stop myself from slipping into feelings of despair. Further down, I started to hear a faint singing. It was a horrible song if I ever heard one, and there was no sense of rhythm at all.

Going completely still at the sound of footsteps behind me, I whirled around to see Boone and Darien running to meet me.

"How'd it go?" I asked them.

"Well enough, miss. We gave them some fine drugs to chew on; they'll be out for a few hours I s'pect," Boone told me, slightly out of breath.

I wasn't entirely invested in how they convinced the guards to do such a foolish thing, so I took Boone's words at face value and continued walking. The singing became more and more audible, and with a twitch of my lips I swore I recognized that voice.

Boone voiced my suspicions. "Ain't that the cap'n?"

We jogged to the very end of the hall, with a sight to behold. There was John, laying on his back on the nasty ground singing god-knows-what.

Darien knocked on the iron bars. "Wakey wakey."

Jason and Finn made their way over while John barely raised his head, unenthusiastic. As he caught sight of me, that seemed to rouse him from his stupor, as he scrambled to his feet.

"Dira?" He asked.

I beamed. "Who else?"

He grinned, that familiar twinkle in his eyes shining through. "Couldn't stay away, hm?"

My cheeks burned, aware that Jason was right behind me. "Well look how I found you. You're hopeless."

His head lolled to the side. "Just a bit o' drinkin' did me in."

Finn chimed in, "Was more than just a bit, this time Johnny. But enough lollygaggin', let's get a move on."

John tipped his head back in agreement. Finn got to work picking the captain's lock, and Jason whispered to me.

"So he can call you Dira and I can't?"

I felt a surge of what was either aggravation or embarrassment, and I couldn't determine which was which.

"Now is so not the time, Jason."

It wasn't the response he wanted, no doubt exasperated with me. At that moment I felt saved from an awkward conversation, as we started to hear bells going off.

"We're out of time!" Finn exclaimed.

John was nearly jumping in anticipation, and we were all set rigid for Finn to finish picking the lock.

After what felt like an eternity he set it free, and John came swaggering out. Every part of me wanted to rush in and hug him, but circumstances prevented me from doing so. Instead, I unsheathed a sword I kept in the belt slung around my shoulder, handing it to him wordlessly.

"Good on ya, love," he commended.

With no time to waste, we ran towards the entrance. Prisoners spat and howled at us, but we hadn't the time to get angry at them. As we reached the gates, the guardsmen on the ground were stirring, and outside there were people running in the streets. We saw officers running towards us, and before long they were blocking the entrance. Taking matters into my own hands, I snatched the pistol out of Jason's back pocket and pointed it toward the men. Finn and Darien followed my lead, and we all had our guns ready and loaded. The officers were scrambling to get their muskets out, and I decided to let out a shot above their heads for show.

Some of them jumped and some crouched, and John held out his sword, ready to strike. He reeked of old rum and who knows what else, but it was almost sour. I hoped he thought of having someone wash him down once we got out of there.

"Let us pass or my men will be forced to show their better aim."

The leading officer was nearly foaming at the mouth with rage as his own men begged him to let us go. Neither group could really afford to lose one of their own at the moment. But the officer was selfish and

347

had something to prove. He told his men to charge, and we showed no hesitation. The bells continued to go off in the city, alerting everyone of our breakout. We fought tooth and claw out of desperation. Jason started to show a little more gumption, being forced to do something. None of us really wanted to hurt anyone, but we planned to all leave whether our path was blocked or otherwise. John had taken it upon himself to engage the leading officer in a sword fight, as the rest of us tried to defend ourselves with a little less honor.

Our chances of escape seemed more promising once we saw William, Paul, and Charlie enter the mix. It has been said that one buccaneer has the same worth as three ordinary naval officers, and, in this instance, I believed it to be true. Not only were several of us more bulky than our counterparts, we had more skill in warfare and a higher sense of loyalty. We trusted our captain when it counted and upheld ourselves to the same code. It was a disgusting thing, knowing that there were rogue pirates who would go against their fellow men just for the sake of protection from the government. That part of history only made me realize that pirates were no worse than the men of politics. If anything, they had more sense. They were driven to their way of life, which I would never forget.

Eventually, our fight ceased, the remaining conscious officers scattering about and increasing their distance from us. We made haste in hurrying out to our small rowboat, and even more so upon seeing groups of men taking to the streets and running after us. When the Navy took John, they had probably counted their chances of interference as unlikely. The American colonies had started to frown upon piracy around 1713. This could've changed of course since the last time I read the history books. Nevertheless, the sea rogues knew that their spots of haven were drawing fewer and farther between. I was unsure of everything at this moment, knowing the smallest things I did could alter everything. The first time I had been here there was still the bliss of the unknown. But now the only thing that comforted me was that the only other time traveler in the world seemed to think what I was doing was within reason. The idea of letting go of the worries of the aftermath was most desirable.

Somewhere in the distance from the shore to the sloop, we were getting shot at. Darien and Boone continued to row, as Finn and I tried our best to cause a distraction. Our goal was nothing more than to make it to the ship alive. No real damage could be done without cannons from this distance, and we took comfort in that fact. Overall, the mission had gone better than I hoped. Finally, we made it to the ladder, and one after the other made their way up. Everyone on deck was rejoicing for the return of their captain, except for a few grumbling hands. The celebration only lasted for a moment, as the main goal was to get as far away from Boston as possible. I took action immediately to the tasks at hand to set sail. We hoisted the anchor, and the hustle and bustle of a crew working together ensued. Jason was somewhere in the middle of it all, completely helpless. He knew nothing of the sea, only ever being by a lake in the Midwest, and had no desire to partake in the work of her servants. This did not go unnoticed by John, who had yet to be told who this strange boy was on his ship.

Chapter Forty-Two

Once we reached a respectable distance from the harbor of Boston, everyone could relax. But not all was well. Each time John's crew came back to the colony, they made more enemies. It would become harder and harder for us to return. The Navy would only reinforce their men and protection of the city, and would be more than ready next time we ran interference. It meant that we had to bide our time until it was unsuspecting for us to return. Jason and I were a burden on this ship, and it was a wonder that I had come back at all. John made sure to remind me of the fact. The first thing he had done once it was safe to do so was grilling me in the privacy of his cabin. I could tell he was glad to see me, but I was a complication. And he needed to hear certain suspicions confirmed.

"So the little fool out there is who you had waiting home for you?"

"He's... we only just got together is what I've been trying to tell you."

John wasn't pleased in the slightest. He acted like the fact Jason was on his ship was going to send him to an early grave.

"Can he do anything useful? From what Finn tells me, he's no better than the mold growing on the belly of this ship."

"He's never been around the water, John! You're going to have to be patient, if you even have the capability."

He scoffed. "Oh I think I know a thing or two about patience, darling. Anyways, it seems you owe me now."

"How is that exactly? I just helped save your sorry arse!"

"Ah, but we wouldn't have been back here if it hadn't been for you. Seeing as how we cannot go back for a while yet, and you'll inevitably expect me to take you two lovebirds back there once more, you owe me."

"Alright then, how shall I repay you, Captain?"

As heated as he became, the question I posed seemed to invoke silence from him. He parted his lips as if he had something to say, but then shut his mouth and huffed.

"Oh I'll let you know when I think of it, love."

He said it with a toothy grin, and it brought out a smile of my own. We stood very close, and even that alone made me feel like I was being a hypocrite. John had this air about him that just demanded to be paid attention to. Every time I looked at him, I felt like lunging at him and crashing my lips on his. But I had to remind myself how horrible of an idea that was, especially since I was now committed to someone just on the other side of this vessel. It compelled me to change the conversation before anything else transpired, but he beat me to it.

"I can't have you keep doing this, Adira."

His saying my name like that had me just slightly concerned, being so used to the slur he had, withholding the A. "I-"

"I'm not done. You put this crew at risk by coming back here. They had the right to leave. They were keeping to the code."

"What, you were okay with becoming a rotting corpse for all to see? Pirates don't get the pleasure of living in prison, John."

"I'm no stranger to that fact, dearie. And frankly, we're a dying race anyways. What's one more rascal to the mix?"

I shook my head. "I can't believe you right now. The John I know would not accept defeat so easily."

He laughed. "Well, that was before I met you, and isn't every man allotted to having a crisis of faith now and then?"

"Not you. Had I known you'd be acting this way perhaps I wouldn't have left in such a hurry."

"Can you really say that?"

I felt like he was trying to get me to unknowingly admit something with the way this conversation was going. But I wasn't about to give him the satisfaction.

"Should I have not come back then? Truly?"

He had a hard time answering.

"What's done is done. And anyway, you're so pleasant to look at, have I ever told you that?"

The man was deflecting by means of flattery.

"You charm me, Captain. I'll let it go, just this once."

His intense eyes were set upon me once again, and I had to say something.

"So now that we have that settled, where are we setting course to?"

"Oh I see, so you think I just leave your position open for you to take back at any moment?"

It was said with an air of playfulness, which I had missed too much to get all worked up.

"Of course not, I'm just saying if you happen to need some assistance in navigation, I would be happy to point you in the right direction."

"Well in that case, I suppose you'll do. I was thinkin' about St Augustine, but the Spaniards are not too pleased with us at the moment. Even if I do have a few connections. We may have to go further down, perhaps somewhere in Jamaica."

"Weren't you considering going back to Charles Towne?"

He shifted. "Well, it's something that'll need to happen soon. That, or make my way to Tortuga. Which is another possibility. We need to go somewhere where we won't have to worry about shifting eyes."

I sighed. "A long journey, then. That'll be fun to tell Jason."

John was not sympathetic in the slightest. "Aw, does the poor wee man have things to get back to in his world? Or did you two not think of that before coming back our way?"

It was my turn to shift. "I didn't exactly give him much warning before we traveled."

"Even better! What made you decide to bring another person here I wonder?"

"Because I love him!" I blurted out.

That shut him up real quick, and I almost immediately regretted saying it. His demeanor turned sober, as his eyes searched mine for any signs of a jesting spirit. I tried very hard to stay composed and not look away from his gaze. Whatever he saw there had him look away suddenly, fixated on the wall behind me. There was an uncomfortable silence simmering before he spoke up again.

"And does he love you?"

I was surprised at the question and surprised even more at my hesitance.

"Of course he does."

He didn't look as though he believed me, and I had to let it go for now.

"Well then. Congratulations, I just adore young love."

In a flash, he was back to his usual self, as if that somber episode had not even occurred. I was on thin ice with him. However, I still wondered why he chose to stay in a town that had it out for him and got careless enough to drink himself into oblivion. Why would he do such a foolish thing?

He continued, "I do think we should head towards Tortuga for the time being, with how politics are at the moment."

I nodded, the both of us knowing there would be little to do for me as a navigator with such a voyage. Almost every pirate out there knew how to get to Tortuga. Although being French territory, the governor was most accepting of buccaneers, as it suited him greatly. Not to mention the Brethren of the Coast held their meetings there for the time being, with how unstable Nassau was at this time. Soon, I suspected, John would be the one to change that. I wondered if I'd get to be a witness in all of it. This was probably a good opportunity for him to check in with the other prominent members, although they most likely wouldn't enjoy hearing that he had been captured for something so careless. After the course was set, John dismissed me, and I knew things would be slightly tense between us for a short while. I took the blame completely, for it was my own fault for not thinking how it would truly affect the men if I returned so soon.

Of course, there was no way of knowing how long the time jump would be, but I did know how difficult I had made things for them in Boston. Despite being a useful asset to the crew, I was a liability, and now I thrust another person on them, another mouth to feed that, for the moment, could not hold their own. Finn and John were right in their accusations of Jason for the time being. The realization stung, but I had known it all along. I went back out on the deck, where I could see Marco talking to Jason. Curious, I went over to them to overhear them discussing sleeping arrangements. Jason was arguing with him that it wasn't fair that I got to sleep in the first mate's cabin when he had to sleep with the common crew. It was a stupid thing to fight over, considering it was a blessing in itself that no one had thrown Jason overboard yet. I cut in, hoping to alleviate some stress from Marco.

"It's fine, I can sleep next to Jason below deck and William can take my cot in your cabin, Marco."

Marco seemed irritated that I compromised on Jason's behalf, but above all, he was usually the first to resolve a conflict, and was relieved to have a solution. After walking away from the two of us, it was just Jason and I out under the stars, against the railing. He looked absolutely worn out, which I couldn't blame him for. It was probably the most eventful day he'd had in his life. I was somewhat nervous as to how to address everything that had happened today. Not knowing where to start, I let him be the one to bring something up. Silence held us for quite a time, and I watched the water, wondering briefly when I'd get to see my mermaid friends again. Eventually, Jason finally spoke up.

"What is wrong with you?"

It wasn't what he said, it was how he said it. His voice was small and belittling. It immediately set me on edge.

"Um, what are you referring to?"

He turned to me. "I mean I knew you were naive but this... can you honestly expect me to be okay with you considering these heathens to be your friends?"

I was stunned into silence at his sudden confession.

"Come on, Adira. Your mom warned me you had unrealistic outlooks on life, but I never expected this."

Wow, that struck a nerve. I stayed quiet still, trying to see where he was going with all this.

"I knew something weird was going on. I told your family I thought you were lying to me. I can almost accept that we time traveled, but I can't believe you'd be stupid enough to get involved with pirates."

Truthfully I couldn't quite understand why he was harping on the fact that I was with pirates for half a year. How did that affect him more than time travel itself?

"Why is that the factor you're focusing on? Are you not amazed at what you experienced today?"

He was lost in thought again, shaking his head.

"I can hardly process it. While you were talking to the captain I had time to think about it, and it would make sense looking at it as a weak point within time. But what caused that weak point? What makes the lighthouse an ideal vessel for a wormhole?"

The same thought has crossed my mind.

"It's the oldest lighthouse in America, I know that much. And I know the history here is rich. But beyond that I'm as lost as you. That's one of the main reasons I brought you here."

"Yeah, about that. I'm not sure what you thought you were doing bringing me here, but I would've liked some warning first. Because I guarantee I would not have agreed to it."

"Why? And you wouldn't have believed me anyway! Why would you pass up such an amazing opportunity to study something you've been learning about for years? We used to sit and talk about how cool it would be! What happened to that?"

"I like my life, Addi. In the present. I don't mind writing about or studying sciences from the sidelines. Have I ever been a person that struck you as a hands-on academic? This is just too much for me."

He was right. Jason had always been more reclusive in that way, and I had been too for most of my life. It was not until I broke away from my family and my familiar environment that I became more involved in everything that life had to offer.

"I... I'm sorry, Jase."

"And what about the captain? You seem awfully friendly with him, especially if he's allowed to call you something I can't."

"We're friends, Jason. That's it. And it would just be weird if both of you called me that, it's nothing personal."

"You seem very chummy with each other. I don't know how I can trust you at this point."

I kept my head down, unable to say much of anything. What could be said?

"How long do we have to be here?" he asked.

"Two months, give or take. Plus it all depends on weather conditions when it's safe to come back to Boston."

He let out a deep sigh, his head hanging low.

"How do you expect me to live in this disgusting place for two months?"

Jason's complaining was starting to really grate on me, and I didn't want to argue with him tonight.

"I hate to say it dear, but you're going to have to man up a bit and learn how to be useful around here."

He looked as though I just asked him to kill himself.

"I never would've thought you were capable of stabbing a man. Did you even feel anything when you did it?"

It was a change in subject, and it sent me reeling. Of course, I had, but then again, would I have stabbed someone so easily before my time here?

"It was out of defense! I didn't aim to kill!"

"No, the fact you did it at all is what's upsetting, Adira. How can you not see that?"

The truth was, I was a changed person. I still despised violence and would never hurt someone with ill intentions, but I was more willing to if it prolonged my life or the life of any one of my shipmates. What kind of person did that make me? I had not had a moment to think about it yet. Jason spoke up again.

"I think I need to be alone for a bit. Can you wait a while until you come below?"

"I guess so."

Then he was off with dragging feet, and I was left alone. Finn was at the helm, looking at me with a mixture of mirth and pity. He grabbed Leo, having him take over before coming to me. I tried avoiding his eyes, but Finn seemed to find humor in the situation. He was chuckling lightly to himself, and the circumstances made me feel like a little girl for some reason.

"So what was all that about?"

I sighed. "Just Jason telling me how horrible I am for bringing him here. Which, he's not wrong, it was foolish on my part. I should've kept this to myself."

"It's not wrong to want to share an amazing discovery with your beau. No one can fault you for that, lass."

"I just... it was all too rushed. You know, I told you how things were before. Maybe I've been trying to force something between us when it never belonged."

He chuckled again. "You think? Every time ya mention him yer at war with yerself."

"I always thought it was because I was in love with him and just in denial."

"Ye know what I think? I think there was never love of self, but love of familiarity. And we've seen where that's got ya."

How was the Scot always sound in his assumptions? It bothered me.

"I should be thanking you for helping him back there."

"Aye, ye should. Not sure where Johnny's gonna place 'im in the crew. He'll probably be swabbing decks if I know the man at all."

"You're probably right about that."

"He was acting so strange after ya left, never seen him so crabby before in me life."

I felt a twinge in my heart, knowing how I'd handled things lately. Could I ever do the right thing for once? Everything I'd done that year had affected everyone around me in the worst ways.

"Oh, I'm well aware that I left things badly. He's had no problem telling me that."

"I wouldn't take it to heart, he's all knotted up from you leaving at all. I have a feeling he thought he could convince ya to stay on buccaneering instead of returning to your world. Once that man has his heart set on something, it's very rare that he doesn't achieve it."

"But what's it matter to him? I could easily be replaced by any other crew member."

"Oh, I wouldn't go saying that, lass."

I chewed on the things he told me, thinking about hidden reasons John could have for staying upset. Finn sensed my frustration and continued

"Few people, if any, have found themselves in yer boat. Don't go moping about because ya haven't gotten it all right. Just keep going forward, to the horizon."

"Has anyone ever told you how scary it is that you're always right?"

"Ye should go tell that to the captain."

We laughed about it before Leo was calling him back over. He patted my shoulder and went on his way. It was a reassurance that I had desperately needed.

Hoping enough time passed by for Jason to calm down, I went below deck and fastened my hammock. Jason was lying in his, staring at the ceiling with a small oil lamp burning at his side. I blew the lamp out, bidding him goodnight. His reply was terse, but I brushed it off and reinforced in my mind that things were going to work themselves out.

Chapter Forty-Three

The following morning everyone was up bright and early, and Jason made everyone well aware how much he despised the fact. Upon hearing of it, Marco gave him a bit of a verbal lashing, as the whole crew was growing tired of his complaining and it had not even been a whole day we were with them. We were still in the clothes we wore the night before and would probably not have a fresh set for some time. As we all broke our fast, there were only a select few who were given the privilege of drinking coffee with the captain. John must've not been that mad at me, as he invited us to dine with him and I was given my usual mug. It was with great dismay that Jason realized he was not given coffee with the rest of the table. When he voiced what he felt must've been a grave mistake, the captain informed him it was not such. I felt only slightly guilty while sipping from my mug, and this was the one drink I refused to share with anyone else.

Jason blurted out, "Why am I even sitting with all of you then?"

My cheeks went hot at his sudden outburst, and everyone at the table went silent. John looked as if this was some game we were all playing, very amused at my boyfriend.

"You wouldn't be if it wasn't for the woman who's claimed you."

I was fairly certain Jason felt like his masculinity was being threatened, and I had to hold back from laughing. Finn had the same expression as I did, and that was the last thing Jason dared to say during breakfast. I had a smile on my face since waking up, feeling at home on the ship. The ocean breeze in my hair and the rushing waves passing us by was an experience I had sorely missed. My callouses had not even left my hands completely.

Finn was managing the helm without the need for any charts or navigation, as experienced as he was with our course. My job for the day was to help Marco in his efforts to make Jason useful. This was a harder task than we had initially thought, as every time we took him out on the main deck he got seasick. His sea legs were going to be a difficult thing to acquire, and no one was motivated to help seeing how short this voyage was. Jason was normally very good with heights and climbing, and the rigging should've been an easy task for him to start with. He was anxious to prove himself, so he had started before looking at the ocean and hurling. Marco was losing his patience, which in itself was a hard thing to do, and Jason was losing his will to live. The few times the captain had been around, he looked on with disapproving eyes.

Jason did eventually climb the rigging without the fear of the water, and once he did so he was a real natural. Unfortunately, that was the end of the seafaring tasks he was good at. The assessment we conducted throughout the day proved so. Truthfully there was no real need for him, as there barely was for me. We were essentially added hands on this journey, no more and no less. He was hopeless in combat, but with our conversation last night, I expected that to be the case. I was still having a hard time coming to terms with the fact that I was more exposed to it now. It was a good reality check, having him bring it up. Reminding me that I still had morals that needed upholding. In my opinion, the good still outweighed the bad here. We rarely had to threaten with the name John was making for himself. I would not be surprised if the pirates made him royalty, somewhere down the line.

Around that afternoon, Marco and I got a chance to talk. He was antsy about something, and I had a feeling I knew what it was. The first mate was worried he had not gotten the chance to talk to his mermaid yet. I knew the feeling, although there was bound to be more urgency coming from him. We made a mutual plan to talk to the creatures tonight, once everyone was asleep. Neither one of us were prepared to deal with John again, and at this point I had stopped pressing Marco to tell me why John was so particular about this situation. He would tell me if he wanted to. But as we sat and gushed about our merfolk, I came to the realization that Marco had not had any experience like mine. Emma had not taken him below to any burrow, and I was surprised at the fact.

"It's not something I'd get to experience unless I made a full conversion and completely sacrificed this world," he told me.

"Well why would it work for me and not for you?"

"I'm not sure. Emma tells me Alorna has been with you, and that could potentially be why. Alorna is royalty, so she could easily gift you the act of aquatic breathing."

"But I had not met Alorna until we reached the ocean floor. Aerwyna told me that had it been any other human, I would've died after five minutes."

He was puzzled, and I explained the gills I had miraculously grown during my escapade.

"Perhaps you aren't fully human. Have you considered that?"

"Well it just isn't the case. My family is all human, there's no weird uncles or anything like that."

"I wouldn't be so quick to dismiss it, it hasn't been out of the realm of possibilities that merfolk and humans mix bloodlines. Sometimes they do it on purpose."

"Are you saying that somewhere back in my family history, I could have a great-great-great-grandmother who is a mermaid?"

He shrugged. "It's very possible. Most humans that have mer heritage can go their whole life without realizing. Most just feel a pull to the ocean that they can't explain, but fewer actually do anything about it."

It actually would solve a lot of questions if I had mermaid genes somewhere in my family.

"But then why would I be the only one who feels a special connection to the sea? What about my parents, or siblings?"

"I don't have all the answers, Adira. We can discuss it tonight with the ladies. If you really want to know."

I nodded, and, admittedly, it was all I could think about the rest of the day. These were the conversations that I was most eager to have coming back, and it was to my wonder that since arriving here again I had not thought of the present once. As soon as Marco and I were done with our conversation, the captain emerged from his cabin. Jason found his way next to me in an instant, almost always seeking me out anytime John was close by. John noticed after a while and began sauntering over to the both of us.

"Ah, Mr. Becker. Would you be a dear and swab the entire deck for me?"

As soon as the words left John's mouth Finn's eyes were on me, holding back laughter. He had called it. Jason was seething, only giving him a grumble as a reply. After he left, John stayed where he was, watching me. He stumbled closer, eyeing me over.

"And what shall we do with you?"

"Whatever you wish, Captain."

"Is that so?"

"Within reason."

"Ah, there it is. Must you add that impertinent detail?"

"What is it you want?"

"There's a lot of things I want, darling. But few that I have the power to obtain. So I suppose for the time being, unless you permit me to throw your pigeon of burden into the sea, I'll have Paul show you how to coop."

The cooper was in charge of assembling and maintaining barrels, which one would think would be a side task of the carpenter, but cooping was a lucrative business. They were essential in any crew that needed to restock for food, water, really any form of supplies.

"It seems like a waste when I won't be here for more than two months."

He rolled his eyes. "Can we stop pretending that you actually like where you come from? You must start trusting your gut, like any pirate."

"Maybe I don't want to assume you'll be here once I take Jason back."

He narrowed his eyes, inquisitive.

"So you think I will just continue on waiting for you every time you need to pop back for tea? I have a crew to run, love. To be frank, I don't plan on coming back to this side of the coast. Like I told you before, you're going to have to decide which world you want to belong to. And I can tell you right now, your lover isn't cut out for this one."

Not giving me a chance to reply, he started walking away to talk to Finn. I was hoping that in time, Jason would start to adapt to being on ship. It was an unlikely hope, and I had to start thinking if I was willing to give up everything I wanted to stay with him.

Chapter Forty-Four

That night, Marco and I finally had the main deck to ourselves. Jason was exhausted after swabbing the decks all day and went below as soon as dinner was done. The alcohol had made him sick as soon as he drank it, and it only added to his seasickness. Every now and then we could unfortunately all hear him throwing up in the bucket beside his hammock. The sky was clear and the moon was held high, so the both of us had gotten wooden planks to tie to the end of ropes. We lowered ourselves down with the makeshift benches and waited. I thought at first maybe we wouldn't hear from our scaly friends onight, until I saw a faint glow beneath the surface. The two of us watched the light for a while as it drew closer and closer. Finally, two heads emerged from the inky blue, and Marco and I beamed.

Abandoning our benches, we splashed into the sea and embraced the merfolk. Aerwyna spun me around, giggling and gleaming. I realized just how much I missed her then, watching her purple hair shine and eyes glimmer. And there, right in front of her, my own skin started to have a natural sheen. I'd never seen Marco smile as much as he did when he was with Emma.

"Did you travel home?" Wyna asked me.

"Yes, how did you know?"

"We couldn't feel you anymore. I told the others you had likely gone back. But here you are again!"

"I had a hard time staying away."

Wyna beamed. "I am glad of the fact. Emma of course has had her own reasons for wanting to stick close to your pirate friends."

The two lovers blushed at the mention of their attachment.

"Where's Alorna? And the others?"

Emma and Wyna exchanged glances, as Marco avoided everyone's looks altogether.

"She has found it best to keep a distance from this ship," Emma told me.

This raised only more questions in my mind and admittedly distracted me from the previous matter I had hoped to discuss with the mermaids. Why would Wyna and Emma feel comfortable gliding right next to the sloop, but Alorna, who's no doubt more powerful than the two of them, feel cautious?

"And why is that?" I couldn't help but ask.

Wyna, hesitating for a moment, responded, "She knows she is not welcome. It would be foolish for her to tread here. She stays below, where she can be reached should we need her."

Had her and John had a run-in at some point? That could be the only conclusion, as I did not think any of the men would be stupid enough to mess with the mermaids.

"Because of the captain?"

They nodded collectively, but were unwilling to indulge anything further. As was the case with anything involving John's strange dislike of mer. I tried my best to let it lie, but my curiosity is ferocious and would only become increasingly difficult to ignore.

I told Wyna of the recent developments I'd noticed anytime I was in water for an extended amount of time. She was as puzzled as I was, and, whatever her suspicions were, she kept them to herself. There would come a time where neither one of us would be able to continue to observe and do nothing, and if I could push it forth I would. But I was at her mercy and knew that no matter how much I asked, she would not share her thoughts with me until she was ready. It was my job to learn to be content in her company and glean as much as I could from her.

Our conversation was cut short, however, as above on deck stood the captain, bellowing out, "Teale! Fellows! Up here now!"

Where Wyna seemed concerned, Emma looked annoyed at the interruption. Marco didn't quite wince but was caught between a grimace and a glare. We started swimming back to our roped benches and hauling ourselves up with contempt. Upon reaching the railing of the sloop, we climbed over reluctantly.

We stood there, waiting for whatever John had to say. There was no guessing that he was not pleased with us going against his wishes.

"Did I not tell the both of you to relinquish these nightly meetings?"

As frustrated as the captain was, Marco looked even more so.

"I don't remember anywhere in the code stating that the captain has the right to govern what his men do in their recreational time, John."

I was once again impressed with the eloquence Marco presented in speaking to John, where I would've drastically failed.

"No, no it doesn't my friend. But this is my ship. And if you wish to continue sailing under my authority, I suggest you follow my lead."

The more words that left John's mouth, the more agitated Marco became. The captain seemed to forget that despite his friendship and loyalty with his first mate, love is too powerful a thing to be ignored.

"Now you know I would follow you to the ends of the earth if you asked, Johnny. We're mates, and I will always remember that. But I can't continue to say nothing about this grudge you are holding against an entire race. It is not you. One bad experience does not mean they are all the same!"

I kept my mouth shut, watching the scene unfold. I felt pride on Marco's behalf, for him finally speaking up, but also anticipation at the potential answers that this conversation could provide. John's jaw clenched, and his eyes darkened. Perhaps this prejudice was deeper rooted than I realized. He looked highly uncomfortable and was shifting on his feet.

"I don't see how you can trust them. Not after... you weren't there, mate. Not until you had to come drag me out, half exhausted from the fight. Or do you choose to forget, because you happen to fancy one of them?"

They seemed to have forgotten me, as they continued in their spiff, as I became more confused.

"It's true, you are the one who had to live that, and I'm sorry for it. But that's like asking every she-pirate we know of to not employ a single man on their ships."

John averted his gaze from Marco then, looking towards the sea. Pondering, most likely.

I finally spoke up. "I don't know what happened to you, John, but I know Marco and I would never purposefully do anything to endanger the crew."

I was rewarded with a glance from John, as he looked doubtful still.

Marco replied, "You should tell her."

The captain let out a sigh. I felt as though I was slowly piecing together an idea of what happened with Marco's comments and only anxious to help.

"Just... forget I said anything. It doesn't matter," John uttered as he started walking towards his cabin.

I followed him, saying, "I don't think we can do that if this continues to be an issue. Do you realize how much this means to Marco?"

I doubted Marco liked being spoken for, but I wanted to drill it into John's thick skull that it was time we stopped avoiding whatever happened. The mere idea of me continuing the conversation seemed to have struck a nerve in John, as I could picture the steam blowing out his ears.

"You want to know my little pity story? Fine."

His words were gruff, and when he took my hand, it was the roughest he'd ever been with me. He dragged me to his cabin, slamming the door shut. Once we were inside, it was eerily silent aside from the steady breathing coming from him. He was pacing around and opened his mouth several times before shutting it again. It was clear he was trying to piece together what he wanted to tell me, and I almost felt guilty for prying. After a while of staring at him, I took a seat on his bed. The small act seemed to calm him slightly, enough for him to stand in one place for longer than a second.

"I want to make clear that I do not wish for pity or any other form of sympathy you may feel concerned with. This is me telling you the reason for my caution, that is all."

With my nodding, he continued with pleading eyes. It was an unspoken rule that nothing said there left that room, and I could only hope he knew me well enough to trust that it wouldn't.

"When I was a lad, barely twenty-five, I was just becoming what I am today. It was only Marco and me; we did not even meet Finn until a year later. Having in possession only a small sloop, I was looking for ways to prove myself amongst my fellows. I had always been around pirates and knew that mermaids existed. It wasn't until that year that I saw one for myself. While in the Caribbean, I was trying to make connections that would aid my rise to riches and had been kept in many tucked away small deserted islands on errands for scum of various kinds. I and my pitiful excuse of a crew were scouring various lagoons based on this map we had been given."

His eyes were far away, lost in a memory, as he told me of his recollections.

"There was one particular lagoon, which at first glance was nothing but darkness and gloom. But we were determined and continued searching the pool for what we thought would contain a treasure worth more than any of us had ever laid eyes upon. The further we searched, the stranger things had become. Everywhere around us was a thick, opalescent fog, keeping us all in wonder. We could hardly see anything, and we hadn't realized the complexity of what we had stumbled on. At that point, we were all split up to cover more ground. None of us realized the treasure we were seeking was essentially a breeding ground for mermaids."

There was suddenly something lodged in my throat at the realization of where this memory of his was heading. I watched his face carefully, as he looked as though he saw ghosts. His expression could only be described as haunting.

"When she arose from the water, I was entranced. Her beauty was like nothing I had seen before, and more than anything I was curious. She smiled, her eyes beckoning me. I relented, crouching down to her level. It was to my surprise that she could talk to me, and we could understand one another. At the time, that's all it was. We simply talked. I asked her her name, how she got there, and if she had heard of the map. Every question was answered with grace and honesty. Upon checking in with my men, they had come to find similar meetings. That's how Marco and Emma came to meet. He was in love the moment he laid eyes on her. She had told him their duty there was to accompany their younger sisters to the lagoon, to show them their rich history and heritage in those waters. When we realized our commissioners had sent us there to capture them and sell them to the wealthy, I was appalled. Slavery and the likes never appealed to me, and I would've never agreed to taking on the journey had I known that was the price. We burnt the map within the hour, and the mermaids rejoiced with gratitude. They let us spend the night there, where we would figure out what to do in the morning."

I started to wonder if there was a bad side to the story, if John was simply weary of merfolk because of the greed men had revealed to them. It wasn't until he took a deep breath, continuing on, that I realized the worst was yet to come.

"Alorna and I conversed into the late hours of the evening, and I was almost sorry to think of having to leave so soon. She was royalty, which intrigued me more so. And yet, that morning, I had awoken in the sand with horror. In my sleep, she had started to advance upon me. I remember scrambling away, only for her to profusely apologize. Claiming it was her curiosity of humans that compelled her to come so close. It was my own stupidity to believe her. I had foolishly let my guard down, letting her lead me into the water. Once I was back in and I thought we had put it behind us, she kissed me. I had enjoyed it at first, as you know I am rarely known to turn a lovely woman down. But she proved to be otherwise. She had become almost violent, and I tried to tear her away. The more I resisted, the more wretched she was. Her long nails tore through my skin, and she used her own nature against me. Every inch closer to solid ground I got was twice that getting pulled back under. She was going to drown me."

John's hands shook, and my own body was rigid with anger. To think I could feel drawn to her, to want to befriend her. I wanted nothing more than to forget it all, to scold myself for putting John into a situation where he must relive such a terrible experience.

"John, you don't have to continue...."

"I think I must."

He was still standing at the edge of his bed, looking everywhere but at me.

"It was Marco who eventually heard the struggle. In those moments I was fighting for my life, close to drowning and being nothing more than used goods. What an awful end to my story that would be, eh? All it took was Marco taking his sword out for Alorna to give up. I was exhausted; the poor lad had to drag me back to the ship. He was the only one I trusted to tend to the wounds, and bless him, he kept silent when the crew begged him for any details. I owe him my life."

At that moment I watched as he raised his shirt, and I realized where all the scars had come from. He would never really be rid of the awful memory. On each side of the curves of his hips were deep angry gashes, pink and white from the time gone by. There were several other punctures around his abdomen, and more on his arms that I had never equated to being from something like this. I was lost for words, as his eyes searched mine.

"These are what I have to remember her by.... I very well know they won't all be so monstrous as she. But they are capable of the very same. Of her murderous spirit, worse than most pirates I've ever known. Try as I might, I can never forget it."

I understood so much about him at that moment. I wanted so badly to make it all better, but it was so long ago in his life, and for better or worse this was one of those things that had shaped him. I had never expected this to be the reason for his prejudice. In the midst of my thoughts, he let out a chuckle.

"You'd think I wouldn't go near a woman ever again. But what kind of pirate would I be? To hold one bad occasion against all you lot. I've tried my best, I have tried to forget. I'm sure though you'll have reason enough to believe it to be a lie. Especially if you've been talking with the likes of her."

Did he really think that little of me? I dared not tell him how I had been with Alorna, not now. I wasn't sure if I could even look at her again, knowing what I knew now.

"I... I am sorry for my hesitation to believe you in the past. I would take it back if I could. Truly I had no idea, John."

His head was turned downwards, looking at the scuffed floor. He almost looked ashamed.

"I would never wish that upon anyone. And for what it's worth, you couldn't have known. It wasn't your fault."

I watched as he gripped the end of the bed frame with one hand, and I could almost see him trying to reign in his emotions.

"Oh but it was, love. I had been a fool, being as gullible as I was. I do not hate them, but I hate her. And every time I see them, they remind me of the one instance where I wasn't in control."

Rising from the bed, I stood face to face with him. I was too dense not to see it before. He truly believed he could have prevented it.

"You more than anyone know there is little we have control over in life. The tides take us where they want to. You never deserved what happened that day, but you also don't have to let it hold power over you."

"I don't discuss philosophical thinking, Dira. Don't make this into something bigger than it is."

Putting up his mask yet again. It was in his nature. I knew it was to protect himself, but I could only hope my words reached him underneath it all. I rolled my eyes in response, resigning myself to playing into his game.

"All I was trying to say was that I think nothing less of you, Captain. You are still a force larger than life, in my book. And, I'm sorry. I'm sorry that I had pushed you into saying things you weren't willing to share."

He gave me a halfhearted smirk. "We won't speak of it, love."

I smiled in return, and there was a vulnerable air about him that I couldn't ignore. Silence fell over the room once again, as it usually does after someone confesses a part of them they rarely show to others. Even with as much as he had told me, I knew he still left out much. I didn't need to know all of it, as what was shared was bad enough. There was nothing left to do in his cabin, as I could not comfort him. As much as the thought crossed my mind, it would not be received well.

"I think I'll just see myself out, then."

Right as I had my hand on the door, he called out my name.

"Dira? I'd appreciate it if you didn't relay all of this to what's-his-name, if it's all the same to you."

"You mean my boyfriend? The boy I keep telling you about? Don't worry, Jason won't hear a word."

He flashed a grin. "Ah yes, my swabber. Goodnight then, darling."

"Goodnight Captain."

It was awkward to leave in such a way, but I didn't see a better alternative. Upon closing his door, Marco was set on me at once. I nearly jumped at the intrusion, when I should've expected as much.

"Really? Were you here this whole time?" I asked.

"Well? What's the verdict?"

Right. I had completely overlooked getting a different response from John after his reveal. How could I? My eyes glanced at Marco uncomfortably.

"Perhaps we should just give it a rest."

He looked baffled, and I couldn't blame him.

"Give it a rest? You're telling me you're okay with not talking to Aerwyna?"

"And you're okay with associating with the likes of her?"

That shut him up for the time being, as he gaped at me.

"What do you want them to do? Alorna's royalty, they can't overthrow her."

"And why not, exactly? Look, I don't care if you want to keep seeing Emma, but I need to seriously think whether or not it's worth it to me to keep seeking out Aerwyna. I'm shocked that being John's closest friend you wouldn't be the least bit concerned with Alorna still lurking around."

I left him standing on deck chewing on those words and went down below to seek solace.

Chapter Forty-Five

Thankfully, by the time I made it to the common sleeping quarters, everyone was asleep. I was in no mood to answer questions or talk civilly with my shipmates. Making it over to my own hammock, I opened my sea chest, rummaging through for a clean shirt. After a quick change, I saw Jason get up from his hammock, a sultry smile playing on his lips. Although I was tired, I wanted just a few moments of being held, hoping it would calm my nerves. I let him come over to me silently and melted into his embrace. It was no more than a minute later I felt his lips on my neck, and I was too exhausted to do much of anything in return. I wished to talk to him, to say anything about how he was faring, but perhaps he needed this more than words. Allowing him to do as he pleased, I leaned against the wall, the shadows of darkness being the only concealment from the rest of the crew. In between kisses he finally spoke up in a whisper.

"I was wondering when you'd be done up there."

"I kept Marco company during his watch."

"I would've preferred it if you were down here with me."

Jason's neediness was a comfort at times, especially knowing it was a push in the right direction with hoping he would enjoy it here soon enough.

"Distance makes the heart grow fonder, as you know."

He was still kissing me, and I threw him a bone by playing with his curly hair.

"I needed this," he told me.

It was true we had not really been close in this way since arriving here. Guiltily I realized I had not had the time to really desire it, and it wasn't until now I remembered how lovely the simple pleasure was. But my mind was elsewhere. I was still taking in the information John had supplied me with. It had me thinking of his character, of how bare he seemed to me now. He was a more complex creature than I could've ever known, and every time I learnt something of him it was a new piece to the puzzle. John made up an entirely unique map that I found myself drawn to study. In my musings I could hardly hear Jason saying my name. I searched for his eyes, enquiring.

"Adira... what would you do if I had a ring tomorrow?"

I was thrown off by the question, unexpected as it was.

"I... I don't know."

Jason's whole body language could be described as high-strung, and I could only watch him carefully.

"I'm asking if I proposed to you tomorrow would you say yes?"

What was he thinking? Here we were, in a place he had made it very clear he despised, asking if I would accept his hand. Each second that passed by with my silence added to his mania.

"I'm not saying no, Jason, I just... we have all the time in the world for that."

I was trying to avoid another argument while being as truthful as I could. Jason was not ready for marriage. I couldn't even understand why he was bringing it up, now of all times. It was very recently that I tried to delve into what could be feelings of love, and this was only confusing me. I wanted to ask him why he would even ask such questions, but he looked like he would have a full-blown panic attack at any moment. I was treading into tricky territory. There was such a thing as too many deep conversations in one day, and I had an overflowing amount of them. My comprehension of picking apart all of these men had tired me out, and I wanted nothing more than to turn over and let sleep take me.

"Let's just... call it a night," Jason said after a prolonged pause.

As simple as that, he went back to his hammock, refusing to look at me. Did he seriously expect me to jump up and down, screaming yes? I got in my hammock, baffled as ever with how the day had gone.

It felt like a series of unfortunate turns, and I was ready to be done with it altogether. I stared at the ceiling until my eyelids felt too heavy to remain open.

The next day there was but one person who felt keen to talk to me. Jason had made it clear that he was still upset with my answer the night before and reminded me how much he hated it here. One of the first things everyone heard in the morning was the shouts of John and Marco in the captain's cabin, having it out. Most likely Marco pressed the right to see Emma. I did not find him in the wrong after the day before but could not in good conscience continue to see them for myself. It was his business if he wanted to still chance it. John would not let Marco see Emma unless someone talked to Alorna, telling her to stay behind. Even if she would not go near the ship, she still followed us and lurked in the depths. I had never considered it frightening until now. Had Marco even known the full story of Alorna's deception? Did he simply think she was oblivious to John running out of air?

Once John had come out of his quarters we carried on as before. I was happy to put the day before behind us, as his past had not changed my opinion of him in the slightest. He was still the same person, and I could only feel a strong protective spirit over my captain despite him being as capable as ever. My attention was moved elsewhere, as Paul was taking our first lesson in cooping. We were down below, in one of the storage rooms. The captain had suspected that we would run into other merchant vessels on the way to Tortuga and wanted to be prepared to hold the extra cargo. This trip was more than a means of running away, it was a chance to secure success for the whole crew. None of them were too pleased with the negatives that came with holding us here, and I was willing to make it up to them in any way possible. On ships of this size shipmates often juggled different jobs and tasks, and being Paul's assistant would be a week or two endeavor.

Provisions were thankfully restocked before John managed to get himself arrested. There was still plenty in the hold from our Spanish escapade, but I knew its intention was pure pleasure on the shore leave everyone would have once arriving in Haiti. Marco would be in charge of divvying it out and trading, but I had given up my share with my departure. The hands found that to be the number one positive of having Jason and me on board, considering we couldn't very well take any treasure home with us. It was in the first hour of working with Paul that I realized his previous job was working for a brewery. He had been in charge of making the large wooden vats in which the beer was brewed. Along with the kegs, he had been taught from an early age how to make barrels of any kind. Never had I realized that even the barrel-shaped containers were not actually barrels, but also tuns, pipes, puncheons, and hogsheads.

During the enlightenment of classifying, I was told there was a difference between wet and dry coopering. Wet coopering was often used for liquids and dry coopering for tobacco and gunpowder. It was clear Paul was proud of his craft as he went into the history and how it'd been used since the 1200s. I listened with fascination, excited to learn more about him and his trade. I thought again how much I enjoyed most of John's crew and could easily befriend them all with just a little time and gab. The wood we had to work with was oak, because of its breathability to let the contents of whiskey and wine mature with age. Once Paul brought out the tools and let me inspect them, I quickly realized they were heavier than tools of other trades. Paul started with the mallet first, to rive the tree trunk. The hardest part of the trunk between the core and outer layers is what should be used. I recognized them to be traded from Horta, which then seemed like a lifetime ago.

The hardest part of the profession came next, as he used a heading knife to shape the outside angles of the staves. He informed me it took a careful eye and attention to detail.

Eventually, we got to the trussing, which involved a metal dresser filled with pieces of wood. We moved the malleable cask to the heat with the bottom head out and lit it on fire. Paul had me push a heavy iron truss hoop over the cask. Once it dried and set it was called a gun. The hoops that fit over the cask were also made of hickory or chestnut and would be notched near both ends to be interlocked. This process was tedious, taking around five hours to complete. We both had worked up a sweat and sheen, and soon enough we were in our very basic layers of clothing. The work was satisfying though, and I was glad to be a part of something again. Paul and I had found our worn rhythm of working in the same space, and he was glad to see that I was catching on. This stuff was easier to me than it had been to learn navigating, ship terms and flag language, and all of the other intricacies of being a sailor. It was truly a different world out here.

The two of us soon agreed on a well-deserved break and traveled upstairs for some fresh air and good spirits. But as soon as I saw the sight before me, there was shame and empathy to follow. There Jason was, mop in hand, being booed by various hands on deck. They mocked him and spit at him, and he had not the heart to stand up to them. He nearly withered up like a wilted flower, averting his eyes from the attention he had gathered. Paul and I exchanged a look before I walked closer to Jason, in view of all the hands. Some of them at least had the decency to stop in my presence, but there were still several continuing to give the boy a verbal lashing.

"Alright folks, that's enough! I'm sure you wouldn't want me to go knock on the captain's door and tell him you've been slacking in your work to spit on the swabber."

It had to be said, for no one else wanted to stick up for him. After the words left my mouth they grumbled about, eventually returning to their posts. I was left with a very embarrassed Jason. He refused to look me in the eye, and I found I had little to say to him.

He eventually uttered, "They've been saying things every time you turn your head, Addi. I can't take this kind of mistreatment."

"What would you rather do? Go back to Boston where you are known for helping a criminal escape death?"

His jaw was ticking, and the wind was doing nothing to help his mess of curls. I knew he had nothing to counter with, and I could feel pity for his situation. If only he wouldn't have questioned me so much back home. Perhaps I wouldn't have felt so compelled to prove that this was real. That I wasn't crazy. But it didn't matter now, none of my foolish decisions did. We were here, for better or worse. He was less cut out for this era than I could've possibly imagined. Never had I known a man to quiver in a challenge quite like Jason. Everything that happened to him he found to be a significant component to his deep-seated trauma. At first, I had felt compelled to soothe him and to understand his tragic feelings. Now I realized how menial it truly must've been. To be put simply, trying to understand Jason was exhausting. For the rest of the day, I kept him at arm's length. There was that question lurking in the back of my mind. Was he worth letting go of all this? I had made a promise to him, but now it all felt so meager and pitiful.

Those thoughts plagued me well into the night, as the familiar sounds of the crew settling down hummed all around. It was my turn for the nightly watch, and I regretted my late night previously. Finn and I talked for a while until the men finally got a late start on dropping the anchor. I wouldn't be surprised if they took so long from wasting daylight hours over bickering about Jason. Once nearly everyone was down below or in their respective cabins, I could finally let out a breath. There was nothing like being on a ship at night, completely alone, as the moon painted the water with light and shimmer. All felt right with the world in these moments, and I wouldn't trade it for any other experience. My peace did not last long, however, as I recognized a shadow making its way to the left railing of the sloop. It was none other than Marco, and he wasted no time pretending I didn't see him. He was being stubborn about the captain's wishes, and I hastily kept in the middle, being able to see both sides to the argument.

It had been in many records of mermaid and siren sightings for sailors to be lured by the beauty and then sent drowning to their deaths. Never had I thought they could've had any merit, or mermaids filled with such dreadful psycho tendencies. I wanted to stay in my bubble of naivety and believe they were all friends of the sea, with not a drop of evil. But every race out there was capable of wrong, and none more than humans and their resemblances. I knew John knew the very same, but no doubt it was his own experience he was trying to put to bed. He faced not only assault but a very close brush with death, which is not so easily forgotten even in his career. I was willing to give him grace and time, but it was no wonder that Marco did not agree. It was still foreign in this time for men to express any heartfelt feelings or let on that they faced something so traumatic, and I could not blame John for withholding what happened from his first mate in fear he would become a laughingstock.

I knew Marco would never laugh at something so grave; it was not in his nature. But it was the situation surrounding it that would cause uncomfortable conversations which the both of them seemed to want to avoid. And so it was that I was at a standstill, in more ways than one. I felt an unsettling notion take hold in my stomach, and I wasn't sure where it was stemming from. It took siege of me and filled me with dread that I could not place, sending my whole body rigid and practically glued to the main mast. Was it not the very same place I had kept to when the Kraken taunted us all that night? I had almost forgotten about the creature that seemed to be holding a grudge, chasing us across the ocean. There was so much to ponder over, and I wondered if it was already scheming another attempt at our demise. I had a small hope that the mermaids would at least warn Marco, as they had me, to prepare us all.

Speaking of, the first mate came back over the railing around an hour later. His soaking pants left fresh droplets all over the deck as he made his way to me. I tried to push down my feelings of indignation as he spoke.

"They wondered where you were tonight. Aerwyna was saddened to hear you were willing to give her up so easily."

I replied a little stiffly, "And she hasn't been completely forthcoming with me. I think my caution is well placed."

"What exactly did John tell you?"

How much did I really want to relay? John had spoken to me out of confidentiality, even if it was prompted out of hostility.

"I don't know if he ever told you everything that happened that night, but Alorna would've killed him had you not arrived when you did. Does that not alarm you at all?"

"John shouldn't have put himself in that situation. I'm not saying I trust her, but I put up with her for Emma's sake."

"What does Emma say?"

"She has recently been thinking that the royal family will be changing, but I'm not sure why. Supposedly that hasn't happened for centuries."

"Why now?"

"I asked the same. She said they desperately want peace, and Alorna and her sister are not peacemakers. They want someone to lead them to harmony."

"Well as lovely as that would be, it hasn't happened, and they still let Alorna follow them."

Marco threw his hands in the air. "What are they supposed to do? She is still their superior, and that cannot be helped. I have not seen Emma nearly as much as I have since you came here. They think you have something to do with all of this."

This was a new piece of information and something I could not see why Wyna hadn't told me herself. Maybe that was why Alorna had been with them, to make sure I was not a threat. It would explain much.

"As much as I have reason to hate Alorna, I don't see what I have to do with any of it."

He nodded. "Yes, I told them as much. But they think what they think; I have no control over that as you well know. I can only hope answers will come in time.

And Adira, you know as well as I that Emma and Aerwyna are no threat to John. They mean no harm, and they would protect us if it came down to it."

I did know. That's why I hadn't made a beeline for John when I saw Marco tonight. There was a compromise to be made.

"What if you convinced the girls to talk to Alorna? Tell her if she goes back to their kingdom and lets Wyna and Emma handle things, that we can resume as usual. I have a feeling the captain would be more open to that."

Marco's hand went to the back of his neck, mulling it over. He slowly nodded.

"That could work. I'll discuss it with them tomorrow. Oh, and one more thing. They've seen the Kraken lurking around the sea floor tonight right below the sloop. They had to set up camp somewhere else."

Every mention of the monster seemed to set my heart lurching, as I thought about the Kraken waiting for everyone to fall asleep and then taking us all.

"You didn't think to lead with that?"

Marco gave a half-shrug. I worried that at any moment the ship would be rocking uncontrollably. Or pulled right under.

"You need to tell John. We may need to have more hands-on watch."

He nodded. "Not like we'd be able to do much. But I will let him know."

Marco hesitated before going to John's cabin. After all, he would have to explain to him how he got the information.

Chapter Forty-Six

The following night proved to show the mermaids were reasonable creatures. After talking to Marco, and with John's approval, they agreed to ask Alorna to take her leave. Alorna should trust them enough to allow both of them to hold things over without her. We were merely waiting on confirmation. John had, like I thought he would, dismissed the Kraken lurking as just another day sailing the seas. Whether he thought we could outrun the beast or avoid it until it went away, he treated the subject with an aloofness. In other news, Finn was managing the helm so well that we were a few days ahead of schedule. We were somewhere around Cape Hatteras, and the wind seemed to continually find favor with us.

Jason and I, however, were still at odds. He had barely looked at me since our last conversation and seemed intent on having a miserable existence. John's words were ringing true every passing moment here. I kept fighting, thinking the longer I stayed with Jason the more we'd become compatible.

But the boy was insistent on arguing about every aspect of my life. Where was that side of him I had grown to love so much? That supported my goals and was willing to pass life by my side? It seemed his true colors were finally starting to show through, and I was hoping I could keep up with the changes. On the other hand, John seemed to be slightly more tolerant of him, which was more than I could've asked for. He was trying for my sake.

But the day was dragging on, as, truth be told, I did not like being stuck below deck in a hot stuffy room to make barrels and caskets. As Paul and I sat in silence carving more wood, I knew he could tell.

Paul spoke up. "Perhaps I could talk to the captain and see if you could be used elsewhere. I've been managing just fine on my own, as wonderful as your work has been."

I nodded. "As long as you're sure."

"Plenty, miss. You weren't cut out for this work. I'd much rather think of you up there, with the salty air catching in your hair."

The thought made me smile, and there was no doubt that I agreed. Two hours later we left our project to go on deck. Paul immediately went in search of the captain, as my own feet moved me to the front of the ship near the bowsprit. Before I could help it, I was making my way across the spar and gripping the wood with everything I had. Only once had I been on this part of the ship before, during my training period. But this was a whole new experience. There was no fear this time, just the feeling of gliding through the sea. The water was a beautiful sapphire blue, reminding me of the dress I had worn in Alhambra. Every sound coming from the sloop was almost blurred out by the tune of rippling water. Never before had I felt so free, so full of life. It was like being suspended from nothing, just moving closer to the horizon.

Seagulls were flying above, and I could almost hear them bickering with one another. I could not say how long I had been dangling my legs above the ocean, but as I studied the scene around me, there was a disturbance a good mile out with bubbling water coming up the surface. It was causing waves of its own, and the hairs on the back of my neck stood up. The wind was beating around me, and I could make out the faint sound of someone calling my name. I whipped my head around to see it had been Finn, waving for me to come back. But my curiosity was transfixed on the anomaly we were getting closer to. Within seconds it had become half a mile, and that's when the panic set in. I started scrambling up, clumsy with my movements, trying to get back on solid ground. Finn met me halfway, yanking me backward and into the safety of the main deck. Nearly everyone had come up, and Marco and John had their telescopes out and pointed toward the water world.

Jason found me, already clinging to my waist, clammy and shaking. I was still fairly unaware of what was going on when I saw something rise from the sea. Slowly, like something out of a nightmare, came long arms with rows and rows of suckers and claws. They were a sickly purple, with a thick sheen of grime, even bits of seaweed clinging to the skin of the creature. They started reaching for the ship, and, almost immediately, adrenaline was flowing. I turned towards John, although direction was not truly needed. The only thing to do now was fight.

The captain bellowed out, "All hands on deck!"

Chaos ensued. Everyone was scurrying about, looking for any weapons we could get our hands on. William was directing the powder monkeys to load the top cannons, and I was running for my sword. On my way to the artillery, I saw Jason running past me.

Stopping him, I yelled out, "Jase! Where are you going??"

He halted, looking like a crazed animal. "I'm going below deck! I'm going to have a heart attack if I stay up here!"

Not even waiting for a reply, he went racing downstairs. Coward. There was not even time to strap anything down to the bones of the ship, as it was only a matter of minutes at most until it reached us. I kept running towards the top, and a jerk to the ship nearly sent me flying. The Kraken had us in its hold. The wood was screaming as it got crushed ever so slightly, the creature still taunting us. I finally grabbed my sword and a pistol and then bolted to join the others. Back above, things had gone from bad to worse. There were hands in the air, being held like trophies in the grasp of the arms.

Fear was gripping me like a vice as gunshots and screams were ringing all around. One of the monstrous arms came snatching Stewart up, and I immediately took my pistol out. Trying to avoid shooting the cook, I aimed and fired several rounds. It merely fidgeted, Stewart still firm in its grip. My eyes briefly locked with John's, and a silent agreement could be seen through the both of us. Nodding, swords held tightly, we started charging towards Stewart. We were nearly right next to the one arm, and it towered over us. Following John's lead, I leaped off the planks that were already tipping to the side, aiming for the railing. We were still climbing, as if the current obstacle was nothing more than a rock wall.

The arms seemed to be moving with a mind of their own, and John and I seemed to have the same thoughts about what happened next. As the Kraken's arm came down to crush us, we raised our swords high in the air. They ripped through the flesh, enough for the creature to flinch, even as my arms quivered. But it was merciless and remained firm to the ground. I dragged my sword further down, creating an incision. Becoming desperate, I was cutting through the arm like a loaf of bread. It was getting hard to breathe, and I could feel my heart beating wildly trying to avoid the urge to hyperventilate. John eventually found my hand, firmly grasping onto it just for a moment. With the added strength of another blade, we were able to climb and tear our way through the arm to the other side. We were twisting and stretching and clawing our way out, with our eyes shut tightly. It was all tough, likely snapping tendons and nerves as we went on.

I was sick to my stomach and wanted nothing more than to hurl, covered in the innards of the beast that stank to high heaven. But it seemed to hardly do anything, as the arm was back in the air looking for its next prey. It appeared to be weaker, so there was some small measure of hope. I swore I could almost hear it grumbling and growling, and I got a strong sense that this was a game for the creature. With relief, I saw that Stewart was no longer in its grasp, but not a moment later I heard my name being screamed out coming from the other side of the ship. Turning my head, I saw the victim of the screams. To my disappointment, it was Jason. The Kraken was slowly crushing the life out of him, wrapping its arm around him and suffocating him. He was crying frantic tears and continuing to scream for me. Finn came running over, offering to give me a boost to set Jason free.

We both started scrambling towards him, and then Finn was bracing his knees with his hands stretched out. Time was of the essence as I placed one foot in his hand, leaping up as he pushed me forward. I was up in the air for a fraction of a second before I reached my arms out and grabbed onto a claw. I gasped, feeling the tearing in my hands. Looking up, I saw Jason only a few feet away from me. Making the most of the distance, with my dagger out, I started climbing my way up, grabbing onto claws with one hand and pushing my dagger in with the other. The nausea from swinging back and forth was enough to deter me, but I was nearly there. Once I was level with Jason, I started thrashing the monster wildly. The arm was jittering, and it was enough to loosen its grip on Jason.

I yelled towards him, "Grab my hand!"

He grasped onto me with surprising strength, and I tore him from the last few suckers. Immediately he was falling and dangling from my arm. I was straining with shaky breaths, trying to hold onto him. But the Kraken merely traded one prisoner for another. Twisting itself, I felt a claw start to poke itself into my back. There was no way I could move while still holding onto Jason.

"I have to let you go!" I screamed, eyes drifting downwards.

Jason was shaking his head violently, urging me to hold on. I tried motioning for him to climb down, but he continued to refuse me. He then tried gripping my wrist with both hands, which only put more pressure on my already overworked muscles. My arm was starting to feel like jelly, and everything was in between tingling and stinging, and I knew that at any moment I was going to lose my grip. In just a few seconds the arm had wrapped around me, and the suckers were pulling at me. Before even realizing it from the pain, I caught a glimpse of Jason falling to the deck. Trying to look past the searing sensations, I saw him hit the floor. He must not have been too hurt, as he was soon scrambling to a corner near the main deck to hide. Somewhere in the back of my brain, I was a little miffed that my boyfriend didn't even try and see if I was okay. I realized while setting Jason free I had let go of my dagger, and there was no way I could reach my pistol or even see what I was doing. Things started to feel like a roller coaster, as I was being thrown back from the explosion of a cannonball. It seemed the crew had successfully blown a hole in one of the other arms, and there was cheering coming from below. The injured arm fell into the water with a ginormous splash, and screeching could be heard. Everything was rocking, and it was then that I felt a tugging in my mind.

It was Aerwyna, I could feel it. She was trying to tell me something, but my mind was still racing and I couldn't quite hone in on what it was. They were there though, somewhere beneath the ship. And then there was a force of some kind pulling on the creature. It was resisting and refusing to let go of me, but there was a tug-and-pull effect happening. Could it be the mermaids trying to interfere? I remembered bits and pieces of them telling me they had certain aquatic abilities. They could be trying to pull the Kraken away from us. I prayed they would do something, as the arm around me tightened, and I could feel the suckers starting to stretch my skin. It was agony, and everyone else was continuing to fight. I kicked my legs frantically, trying to get just a smidge of more space. The only thought in my mind was wishing this monster would leave us alone.

I could see the men reloading their cannons, and several others slicing whatever they could. The next thing I felt was what must be a shock wave, as all of the Kraken's arms quivered and shook, falling back into the sea. I tried to scream, but nothing came out as I was being dropped several feet, still in the Kraken's grasp. Another dramatic splash enveloped me as I hit the surface of the water, rendering me disoriented for several minutes, sputtering and coughing. I watched as the ship started bobbing back and forth, trying to balance itself after the creature had let it go. Somehow, the crew was still firing cannons, and I could still feel hits and tugs from what must have been the mermaids below. My attention was quickly drawn to the arm still around me, and I started jerking around violently to get loose. To my horror, the Kraken was retreating and taking me with it. I tried to scream before being pulled under, and one of the last things I saw was John diving into the water after me.

Chapter Forty-Seven

I was in a frenzy trying to unleash myself, twisting and banging my head against the arm of the beast. It was a whole other obstacle trying to remember to breathe, knowing the mermaids were following close behind. I caught a glimpse of the Kraken's dark soulless eyes, with flecks of deep red and glowing gold mixing around its pupils of pitch black. That sight alone was frightening in its own right, and I averted my gaze. Seeing the monster in its own territory, dragging me down, painted such a vicious picture it sent me squirming faster than before. The creature was larger than I had assumed, and it was a wonder we hadn't died yet. I was terrified to the core. My eyes traveled upwards, seeing John fight to swim as fast as the Kraken was retreating. I tried using my legs to swim overhead, but the tactic was useless. Every muscle was against me, sore from nearly being sucked to death. I briefly wondered if the monster had managed to take any other victims, but if it had they were already long gone. The only thing keeping me alive was probably the sword latched to my side poking into the arm. It was a panicking balance to keep the unsheathed weapon from puncturing my thigh instead of the arm encircling me.

After what seemed like forever, John reached me, grasping onto the arm. The first thing he managed to do was get my arms free, which was an immediate relief. No sooner had we made progress than the arm, almost out of reflex, tightened around my waist once more. The pain in my abdomen had multiplied, and as I cried out there were whirls of bubbles obscuring my sight. Some of the claws were starting to puncture my sides and legs, and I could already feel the throbbing set in. Next, I saw Wyna and Emma gliding forward, tearing at the Kraken and tugging at the claws. John had his knife out, trying to slice me free. I could see him struggling, losing momentum as seconds ticked by, and fighting to hold his breath. His face was contorted, trying to focus, but I could see he wouldn't last much longer. Before I even realized what I was doing, I was tugging him forward and crushing his mouth against mine. At first, he was stunned, losing the last remaining breath he had to the sea. Completely frozen. But then he was responding with vigor. His hands went up to cup my face, as he took oxygen from me. I could feel his stubble prickle my skin, and his fingers rough around my jaw.

It was the last thing I seemed able to accomplish as the fight left my body. I'd been constrained and clawed at for too long, my limbs screaming in protest. Even with my arms free, I felt like a corpse floating around. The Kraken had tried to encircle my rescue party with its other arms, but with a sweeping motion of Emma's arms, she was able to keep them back. It took all of her strength to do so, leaving Wyna and John to tear at my captor mercilessly. The monster clicked its humongous beak at us several times in a taunting manner. It had every intention of eating us alive, determined as we were to avoid it. The mouth was shiny and charcoal in color, surprisingly untainted from the ocean and other creatures. Wyna had momentarily lost interest in her powers once she saw my sword. She'd always been attracted to shiny things and then was no different. Taking the sword from my belt, a malicious grin spread across her face.

They each took a side of the arm and ran their swords through the thick rubbery skin. John's hair was floating around him and glimmering here and there with all of the golden rings and trinkets catching the little light there was with the moon then shining into the sea. Wyna was her own light source, and I watched in awe as she twirled around the creature. She held the sword like a child might, but she was eager and excited to use it. It gave her a new momentum. Together they finally tore me away from the creature. As I started drifting, John immediately hooked onto my waist with one arm. Wyna moved to help Emma continue to push the monster downwards. I watched as they held their hands out, successfully thwarting the Kraken towards the sea floor. John was propelling us to the surface, as I was practically dead weight in his hold. At last, we'd reached the top, and we were both taking lungfuls of delicious air.

With his other hand, John was brushing the wet strands of hair out of my face. A rope was cast down from the sloop, and he dutifully tied it around the both of us. Finn was the one who lifted us up, and I felt no better than a ragdoll. As soon as my feet touched the planks my knees buckled. John and Finn were at my side again, holding me up. It seemed that now that the immediate danger was gone, I was practically useless. We'd attracted a crowd of shipmates, as voices talked over each other asking if I was alright. A string of reassuring words left my mouth, and then I took in the appearance of the ship. I was fairly certain we had holes in the lower decks from how low the sloop sat in the water. Most of the railing was gone, and by some miracle, the masts were at least intact. Bits of the deck looked like they had gotten pried apart, and there were several caskets already floating out to sea. The amount of work that would need doing... did we even have the supplies needed?

John let go of me, as I still had an arm slung around Finn. He looked me in the eyes briefly, silently asking if I was okay. I gave him a small nod, and then he turned back to the crew. Marco was pacing around the little sections of decking that hadn't been ruined. There were groans all about as Terrence tried to help the injured men we'd acquired in a matter of an hour or two. I didn't even want to know what I looked like. I was aware that I was probably still bleeding, but there were too many others who needed attention before me to help the matter. I watched Paul bring out loads of wood, and Darien and Boone were already sawing away. Stewart was having a heart attack with the loss of supplies, and Leo was trying to help the injured make their way to the surgeon.

I finally saw Jason, seemingly coming out of nowhere. He found me, and he had nothing more to do than to widen his eyes at my appearance. Finn was trying to lower me to the ground, sitting me upright with a barrel that had gotten thrown to the side. I felt like passing out, and I wanted nothing more than to sleep. Apparently, it was vital that I didn't close my eyes yet, because Finn was pushing me to stay awake. Jason stayed standing a few feet away from me, in a state of shock. I had a craving for comfort and reassurance just then. Holding my hand out, I urged him forward. He came reluctantly, almost ashamed. There was a weird feeling I had that something was wrong. He took my hand, looking down at me.

"I don't deserve you," he told me.

I was too exhausted trying to figure out what he meant. There was a part of me that was frustrated he did nothing during the attack. He wasn't even there when I was being dragged under, it was John. It was John who was looking at us even now, keeping an eye on me. I hoped it was my turn to patch up soon. Between the intervals of hammering I heard and screaming of amputated limbs, I gave up on trying to stay awake.

Chapter Forty-Eight

When I started to stir, I realized I'd been put somewhere else. Looking at the surroundings once more I noticed the bed was John's. John. We kissed the night before. Well, maybe not a proper one. It was more of a survival tactic than a kiss. But my lips were on his, and he had kissed me back. There was the chance he was desperate for air too much to think about what he was doing. My head was swimming, and I had a feeling there was opium in my system. Which was a tad frustrating, considering we had a very little supply. I would've rather saved it if I'd been given the chance. It was already light outside, meaning I had at least slept through the remainder of the night. Terrence was putting on new bandages, and I looked down. There was quite a bit of me black and blue already.

"How long have I been out?" I asked him.

"Only a few hours. Most of the crew is working on repairs. Captain's brought you in here, saying you had passed out. You may have a concussion."

There was still a bit of ringing in my ears, and I tried wrapping my head around what Terrence just said. The cabin was empty aside from the two of us, and once again I was missing Jason's presence. What could he possibly be doing?

Terrence spoke up again. "The pain will start coming back soon. I gave you a rather small dose of opium for the wounds. You have several tears in your hands and scattered punctures in your back and legs."

The bandages he had taken off were soaked with blood, and the new ones he was putting on had a small layer of honey. I had a feeling John told him to take such precautions, but I was not happy being afforded this level of luxury. With so much we had lost, this was too much. But Terrence was right, I was already feeling the dull ache in my limbs again. There was little I could do to protest at this point.

"The bruising set in is quite severe, you're going to have to take it easy for a few days at least. With proper rest, mind."

I stayed silent, trying to accept my current condition. It sounded like I'd practically be on bed rest, with maybe small tasks assigned to me for a week. I didn't handle downtime well and despised the idea of it when so much had yet to be done.

"Is there any chance I can be up and moving today?"

He gave me a pointed look. "With enough rum, perhaps. I'd advise against it, but I've heard from enough mouths you're not a very good listener."

Had I had any more energy, I might've had the decency to act surprised. Instead, I simply raised an eyebrow. He went ahead and handed me a bottle, already knowing I'd ask eventually. Popping the cork off, I started downing the hot liquid. After a few minutes, he was finished reapplying the bandages and told me I shouldn't be dealing with much more bleeding from here. With his help, he brought me to my feet to help me get into a new set of clothes. I didn't bother tucking anything in with as much pain as I was in. Sitting back on the bed for a moment, I tied a bandana around my head to keep my hair out of my face. The pressure also helped with my splitting headache. Terrence stepped out of the cabin, and before too long Finn came to see me.

"How ya holdin' up, lass?"

"Like I got squeezed by a giant sea monster."

He came bearing food, two biscuits, and a small mug of coffee. It was more than I expected, and I hoped they had been able to retrieve some of the caskets last night after all. While I finished up with breakfast, I asked him the question I'd been wondering since waking up.

"Where's Jason?"

Finn shook his head. "Hopefully fixing the rigging with the others, if he knows what's good for him. Johnny keeps giving him tasks, but the lad ends up looking out to sea within minutes after the order."

He had looked much the same the night before I had checked out.

"Could you help me up? I think I need some fresh air."

"Certainly."

He held out his arm, and I used it as a bar to steady myself. There were shooting afflictions in my thighs and abdomen, but I pushed through. Eventually, I was back on my feet, leaning heavily on Finn. He guided us to the door, and I was greeted with the sight of the captain arguing with Jason. The crew was trying desperately not to be invested, but it was a hard act when John was raising his voice and gesturing wildly. Finn helped walk me closer, and I heard the tail end of their spat.

I heard Jason say, "I don't understand why you're heckling me about this."

John, exasperated, responded, "Because you're doing nothing! And don't think I didn't notice your disappearance last night. Hiding like a rat. Meanwhile, your better half was defending enough for the both of you!"

There was a twitch in Jason's eyes, and I knew whatever he said next was not going to be good.

"I didn't ask to be here! You all disgust me! And don't act like you weren't chomping at the bit to be her savior. If I had been the one to get her loose, it would just give you one more reason to hate me, knowing I would have been the hero instead of her infallible captain."

"You don't know what you're talking about."

"You think I don't see how she looks at you? How you look at her? You've probably gone further with her than I have. She's probably betrayed me worse than I...."

"Than you what?" John said, looking severe.

I couldn't believe what I had just heard. It was like a kick in the gut, a sinking horrible revelation. My hands shook, and I could feel Finn's grip on me tighten. Tears were stinging my eyes already, and a fiery shame on my cheeks.

"Don't look at me like you don't know what I'm talking about. I'm not the pirate here."

I chimed in, "What are you saying, Jason?"

He couldn't even look at me, shaking his head.

"This... this isn't working. It's all harder than I thought," he told me.

"What-" I started, but he interrupted me before I could finish.

"*She* would've never been this careless. I wouldn't even be here right now if I had just stayed with her."

There was so much I wasn't getting.

"But, what about the ring? Did you not mean what you said that night?"

He shifted, while everyone looked at us.

"I don't know anymore...."

"So what, you're just going to make the same kind of promises to this other girl? Maybe to multiple girls? On the verge of proposing to them all?"

He laughed in my face. "You're the one acting like a little slut. You've probably banged every person on this ship."

My mouth dropped at his reply, but it was John's expression I couldn't look away from. His head was turned downwards slightly, and his eyes were almost black.

"*What* did you just say?" He said it in almost a whisper, and everyone around us was dead silent.

He started to turn away, and I almost heard a cold chuckle leave his throat. Jason's eyes briefly turned to me, and I saw no emotion there. Somehow, that hurt worse. But before anything else was said, John was facing Jason again with his fist raised as high as his head.

He hit him square in the cheek right below his eye, and Jason's head flew back. Before he got a chance to recover, the whole crew heard a loud thud as John tackled him to the ground. We were all too shocked to move and watched as the scene unfolded. The captain was pinning him down, using him as a punching bag. Jason was grunting, trying to get words of resistance out. I was still frozen in place, as John continued to bang his face in.

Several seconds ticked by before I gained a bit of sense back and belted out, "Stop! John, stop!"

It was like he didn't even hear me. He was still sitting on Jason, pounding the mess out of him. I was staggering forward, my hands tugging at John's shoulders trying to pry him away. No one else was doing anything, probably out of fear and respect for their captain.

I doubted he'd processed my request, but in time he halted. He'd barely broken a sweat, as he looked down at Jason wheezing and crying. I stepped back, and John slowly got up, leaving Jason on the ground, nothing more than a pile of limbs.

In a low tone, he said, "Put him in the brig."

Then as Marco and Finn lifted the boy, as an afterthought he added, "And he gets a dozen lashes at dawn."

At this point, it was useless for me to say anything. Jason yelled the whole way down to the little cell. There was no mistaking it then. John had made a public show of his indignation for me. I wasn't sure if he had it in him to be so bold. And then there was, of course, the other thing. Who had he even been talking about? It must've been the girl he mentioned those few months before that he had so much in common with. Why hadn't he told me they were already together? Why lie about it? I was so confused, and so hurt. There was that shame, too. Somewhere in the scheme of things Jason's opinion of me had dwindled into something so pitiful.

What must the crew think of me? Only just then had everyone started to go back to work, while the captain moved closer in my direction.

"You should get some rest, love."

"So we're not going to talk about how you just beat the life out of my boyfriend?"

"Oh, I'm sorry, did you not hear what he said? Don't tell me you're still thinking about that bag of dirt!"

I looked away. Was I? I didn't know what happened next.

"Perhaps he was right. I mean, it's true. Don't most pirates operate much in the same way?"

"No no, darling. Maybe some, as men are vile beings. But you don't make a promise to someone and go the other way. Not in my book."

Even after today's revelation, somehow I believed him. After all, despite my confusing feelings for the captain, I had remained with Jason. I had promised to stick by my decision.

He continued, "You just chose someone with no respect."

As much as it burned, he was right. There was no sense arguing about it.

"I need to know what you'd like to do with him," he told me.

"Well, he has to go back to our own time. I can't just leave him stranded. Who knows what the repercussions would be."

He sighed. "I figured you'd say that. Well, he's not leaving the brig. Not for the remainder of his time here."

"Do as you like. He's betrayed me. I don't know how we can be cordial after that."

"That's better. Was worried you were getting all domestic, thinking you'd put up with his sorry arse."

Whatever we had during my childhood, the man I thought he was was long gone. I still had the bottle of rum in my hand, and I took another swig to hopefully ease the ache in my muscles. Terrence was giving me looks near the helm, and I knew what he was thinking. The injured men were down below, taking their time to rest. The lower decks had been flooded from what I'd been told, and there was no sleep for the crew when having to patch holes and pitch buckets of water overboard.

I dreaded the thought of stuffing myself back in my hammock after having another night in a bed. There wasn't much of me that wasn't sore, and I had a feeling my bruises and cuts would only be aggravated from the angle I'd be putting myself in. My legs were already starting to wobble, a silent plea for me to lay back down. I watched as John looked down at his crew from the main deck, Finn and Marco joining him after securing Jason in the brig. He looked as though he wasn't really paying attention, his eyes somewhere distant. I hoped he didn't take any of Jason's words to heart.

Even if I knew how hard it was trying not to think about what just happened. Even worse, I had been wondering if there was some truth to what he had said. Obviously I wasn't whoring around, but was there reason for him to believe John and I were yearning for each other? It was such a silly idea, and it had crossed my mind before, from things I'd heard the crew say under their breaths.

There hadn't been much time to think about the night before, about everything that had happened. The captain and I had made quite the team. Maybe things hadn't gone our way completely, but we rarely needed words to know what the other was thinking. All it took was one look, and we were of the same mind. He had been the one to jump in after me, when everyone else would've considered me as good as dead. I thought for so long John wanted me around because I was the only woman available, the only thing tangible. Yet there were so many opportunities he had to find company elsewhere. There were those women in the Portuguese islands, and, from what I could tell, he hadn't taken them to bed. There were all of the rich and enchanting women at Alhambra, who he easily could've charmed. But for whatever reason, he had stuck close to me. Had I been a fool? Had I misjudged his character? I had known he was a better man than he let on, but I was beginning to wonder if there was more than that.

Chapter Forty-Nine

The time came when we made it to Tortuga, also known as Turtle Island. The north side of the island was completely uninhabited, and the south had but one harbor where ships could enter. The inhabited portion of Tortuga was divided into four parts, the harbor being located in Cayonne. The other three were miles from the port and mostly plantations. What the captain didn't think to mention was that Tortuga hadn't been labeled a safe space for a couple decades. I knew the Brethren were practically in shambles, on the brink of extinction, but I had not thought to put two and two together. Finn seemed not the least bit concerned as John directed him to sail into the north side. The ship creaked as we glided through the reefs and up into the shallow white sand. No one seemed surprised in this course except me. What exactly were we doing here?

Our sloop seemed concealed for the most part by a rocky inlet and half hidden in a cove. That was one blessing, I supposed. Granted, it was still worse for wear from the Kraken. Of course I could no longer assume that Tortuga had ridded itself of all pirates. According to my time, whatever I did here had the Golden Age lasting longer than expected. Perhaps it hadn't completely been outlawed yet. I was confused and unfamiliar with my surroundings, which was not a good matchup. No sooner had we stopped than everyone came up on deck, already jumping off ship. I climbed down the ladder with my boots off, feeling the soft sand between my toes. Boone was soon behind me, grasping Jason in irons. As soon as he saw me, Jason spat at me with eyes of burning contempt. It did not go unnoticed by Boone, as he slapped the back of Jason's head.

"You're lucky the captain didn't catch that, scum," he told Jason.

Truthfully, Jason was the least of my concerns at the moment. I was somewhat aware that I was suppressing the situation, but I couldn't find it within me to unpack it all just then. Marco came over soon enough, informing us that we would be careening the ship again due to the attack. It sounded like it'd not be the whole crew, however. I caught sight of Finn and John, talking a few feet away towards the lush greenery of the island. Walking over to them, I intended to find out what our plan was.

I started with, "Gentlemen, care to explain why you chose here of all places to hide out?"

John looked to Finn, amusement spread across his features.

"I find it hilarious that this woman thinks she deserves the right to know what the captain's plans are at all times," he said.

Finn responded with a smirk, a playful expression in his eyes. Despite John's words, the captain continued on.

"It was either this rock or Charles Towne, and I believe you know why we couldn't go there with the both of you."

The Brethren needed John. They were anxious to reinforce their authority over the seas, and John was a valuable asset to their survival. The pirates were something of a dying race at that time in history, or at least they were before I had interfered. If John had sailed us to Nassau, he would not be able to pick up and leave readily. There, however, was losing its appeal to pirates. They may have had their meetings there in the past, but it was then wherever was convenient.

"Well what shall we be doing here? It sounds like we cannot even make it into port without the risk of hanging," I asked.

Finn spoke up. "Not necessarily, lass. The governor has his favorites, always will. Johnny did him a favor, way back when, and still owes him. He'll look the other way for a while yet."

It would do for a week or two. The biggest inconvenience would probably be making the trek to civilization. A couple of us started to head out, while the majority stayed behind to finish repairs. Jason was strapped to a tree somewhere, sweating bullets. I felt antsy to get away from him properly. Our little group was led by John and Marco, the rest of us following close behind. I reluctantly washed my feet in the ocean and slipped my boots back on. It was sticky and blazing, and I was glad to still have a bandana wrapped around my head.

It took an hour before we started to hear sounds of the port. We had passed a tobacco plantation and got curious looks from the workers before finally making it to Cayonne. You could tell immediately that, despite the efforts to clean the town up, it had clearly been a pirate haven. There were brothels, taverns, and various markets strewn about. Many of them had been repurposed, but it appeared there were still a couple in business. I caught glances of a fort, still guarded and in use. Granted, by my time Tortuga would be one of the poorest places in Haiti with a small number of inhabitants.

John seemed to know where he was going, walking through the streets with his drunken-like strut. In reality he was rarely on land and therefore had to get used to his land legs rather than the other way round. Most of the civilians we were passing looked like plantation owners and merchants. The majority seemed to be French, but I couldn't tell for certain. Eventually we reached a tavern called The Snapping Turtle, with an inn attached on the second floor. It was somewhat run-down compared to the rest of the buildings on the street, but I could hear music coming from within. As we walked inside, the smell of vanilla rum and tobacco hit me in the face. It was a pleasant aroma and had a calming effect on my nerves. There were sounds of coins rattling, dice rolling, and plates clinking. The majority of the room had a wooden interior with simple iron sconces and chandeliers. The chatter was somewhat muffled against all of the other noise. We stood near the entrance as John walked straight up to the bar.

I heard him say, "Estella! How the devil are you?"

The stout woman behind the bar, with crow's feet and muddy hair, turned around. Her eyebrows raised before she squinted her eyes at the captain.

"Johnny, is that you, boy?"

"Aye."

I didn't have to see John's face to picture the toothy grin he had probably adorned at that moment. Estella wiped her hands on the cloth around her waist, shaking her head with a wry smile.

"Suppose you're no boy now. What're you doin' back 'ere?"

My curiosity was brimming, wondering how frequently John went here in his youth. What kind of past did he have? Did he grow up around pirates?

"Jus' countin' my ducks. Who's all here?"

She leaned her forearms on the bar, contemplative.

"Bartie might still be around, had been braggin' about four vessels he robbed a couple of months back. Jackie was askin' 'bout ya, has them two lasses with 'im."

She couldn't be talking about Jack Rackham, surely. Marco, Finn, and I started walking closer to the bar as John scratched at his stubble.

"Have anyone that can send word for me?" John asked the barmaid.

She nodded. "I'll send one of the lads. 'Ave you talked to-"

"No, and unless someone's dying, I won't be. Even then, it won't be me." John interrupted her, mid-sentence.

Estella rolled her eyes, shaking her head. "You're more stubborn than him. Ya know that?"

I barely caught the scoff that escaped John's mouth as he looked away. A couple of seconds ticked by before he replied again. He gestured over to me, and I reluctantly crossed the remaining distance between us.

"Speaking of stubborn, meet our navigator. Adira Fellows. Dira, this is Estella, practically me aunt."

Estella nodded at me, a small smirk on her lips.

"Nice to meet ya, lass. I can see why you replaced Finn with such a bonny face as hers, Johnny."

John chuckled. "We still have the old Scot with us. He's lurking in the back somewhere."

I spoke up. "It's nice to meet you. I didn't think I'd have the pleasure of meeting anyone from John's past."

She laughed. "Doesn't surprise me... first name basis with Johnny already, are we?"

I blushed, not having a very valid excuse for that one. It was very different for a woman to call a man by their Christian name than their equals. Never mind the fact he was my superior.

John saved me from having to reply, butting back in the conversation. "Lots changed around here, hasn't it?"

"Not as much as you think. The governor and France may 'ave their airs, but they have plenty of work ahead of them until it's free from these sea dogs."

The captain shook his head. "It'd help if all of these scoundrels stopped accepting these fancy letters of Marquess. Doesn't do none of us any good."

Estella hummed in agreement, and we listened to the humdrum of the tavern once more. Finn and Marco finally came to join us at the stools.

"Hello boys. I assume you're here for a reason, the lot of ya," she exclaimed.

"There any rooms available?" John asked.

Estella gave him a pointed look, followed by a reluctant nod. She got a pair of keys out, but held her other hand out for payment. John threw his hands up dramatically.

"Aw, come on, no favors for one of your favorite oldest guests?"

She huffed. "Don't make a fool of me, Johnny. Just a few of those shiny coins'll do."

The captain chuckled, fishing around in his pockets. He let a few shillings drop in her hand, wiggling his eyebrows. Estella stuffed them in a pocket in her skirts and gestured us forward. We followed the tavern keeper upstairs, going to the right. With a jingle of her keys we were led into a spacious room with a couple of beds lined against the four walls. Clearly its purpose was for groups like us - usually from a ship seeking refuge. There were candles in the corner, a small set of chairs, and a table. Not luxury by any means, but more space than most of us were used to on the sloop with clean linens and no foul smell.

"Tub is still in the same spot, you'll find," Estella told us before she started descending back downstairs.

There was a small window with bars, and I could see the hustle from the street. Cattle being herded, conmen beckoning women to their stands, and children racing each other. Finn plopped against one of the beds, stretching out like a starfish. Marco had his arms crossed, picking at his lips every few seconds. William was with us, and he shuffled his feet to the window. John had his thumbs looped through his belt, his eyes roaming. I sat on one of the beds, looking up at the men.

John finally spoke up. "Alright, here's how it is. We'll stay a week or two, give the Navy time to go a little bonkers lookin' for us. Estella already sent the message out, and we'll see who comes. I recommend we all lie low and don't cause a fuss. We should be safe here. Relatively anyway."

I chimed in, "Meet up for what exactly?"

"Johnny's gonna throw the Brethren a bone, I reckon," Finn responds.

Of course. John looked a little miffed at the idea, but he must have found it necessary to send a message out.

I asked, "And what'll that accomplish?"

William responded, and I think it was the first time I'd heard him say a full sentence all day. "We need a new ship, everyone knows that. Hopefully it'll disguise us when we go back to Boston. The Brethren can help us."

"Not only that, they'll have inside information about trading routes we can scavenge from. We'll need a course of action after we drop you off," Marco said.

"About that," I replied.

All heads turned to me. "I've had plenty of time to think about what I want. About where I belong. And I've decided my place is here. With all of you. I'd like to stay, if you'll have me."

There was an immediate grin plastered across Finn's face, where Marco looked like he expected it all along. John's face, though, was surprisingly neutral.

"And what about your lover?" he asked.

"Ex-lover, you mean. That is the tricky part. He still needs to go back to our time. I need to make sure he gets there and maybe say some form of goodbye to my family. But I'm not sure how long I'd be gone, or if I can even come back."

John's eyes drifted upwards as he mulled over my words. Everyone was silent, trying to think of a solution.

Marco spoke up. "What if we asked Emma and Aerwyna? Perhaps they'd be able to stay around the colonies, and once you can make it back, one can watch over you while the other informs us of your arrival."

John pursed his lips. "That could work. With a bit of tweaking."

"So, you don't mind if I stay then?" I couldn't help but ask.

The captain's face softened. "You belong with us. It's that simple."

"We've all grown quite fond of ya," William added.

Finn nodded. "You're part of the crew now, no goin' back, lassie."

It was settled. My place was with them. There were details to be worked out, and there were things to be arranged, but I knew this was the right decision. Nothing in the world made more sense. I was never so free as I was out on that ship, with souls similar to my own and nothing but the endless blue.

Chapter Fifty

The rest of the day the men told me stories of past pirates. They spoke of Henry Morgan, who was the founding member of the Brethren. It was March of 1721, and my head swam trying to figure out if I was a year older. I was still trying to weigh out how it came to be that Jack Rackham still lived, when in all of the history books he was supposed to have died in October of the year before. What had we done that was drastic enough to change someone's future? When I took Jason back to the present, would I even recognize it? History was beginning to change too much. If one man lives, how destructive can it be? I kept thinking of Thomas, and how he told me not to worry about the repercussions. But time was an ever-changing thing, and what he knew then could be a completely separate reality from today.

Was my happiness worth changing history? That was what it came down to. I didn't know the answer. Part of me reasoned that it didn't matter. I wouldn't be around to know how things differed, and perhaps it was all moot. Truth be told, I was ecstatic at the possibility of meeting Anne Bonny and Mary Read. Even if they were supposed to be dead. Was our success at Alhambra the thing that sent Jack looking for John? I was roused out of my thoughts by everyone heading back down to the tavern. Soon we were at a table in the center of it all, and Estella brought out a wooden platter of bread, mutton, and cheese. Our eyes were drawn to the door as Boone and Darien came in to join us. They told us of the progress back at the ship, and that after a few more days John should be able to sell the sloop for a reasonable price.

Our assortment of drinks came, and someone two tables down had gotten on top of it and started dancing. It looked like a jig of some sort, and his group was cheering him on. Finn and William started laughing at him, and soon enough we were all clapping. We downed brandy, ale, port, and spirits of various kinds. Estella brought out fried fish, and we ate till we couldn't stand to look at food. Finn caught the eyes of one of the barmaids, and he went off to follow her around. As we reached night, one of the patrons had swooped an arm around my waist. I could smell his stench from where I stood, and I slapped his hand. That seemed to motivate him further, and I felt his breath tickle my neck as he tightened his grip on me. Slowly, I reached for my dagger strapped to my thigh. Once in my grasp, I pointed it in his side, and he lurched.

John was at my side in an instant, grabbing the man and tearing him away from me. The stranger staggered, and John placed himself in front of me.

"Have you no manners?" was all the captain had to say to the man.

Everything went on as before, as John whirled around to face me. Maybe it was the brandy, or the candlelight, or what he just did, but I couldn't stop looking at his eyes. The corner of his lips was twitched upwards, and he was at complete ease. I raised my hand, reaching for him. But before I could grasp at him, his hand had caught my wrist.

"I'd rather you didn't, darling," he told me.

I didn't understand him. I was sure my face must've been displaying my confusion with how he regarded me.

"I... I don't want to be, what did you call it? Your rebound? I believe I'm worth more than that, love."

He looked uncomfortable like there was more he wanted to say. No one was paying us any mind, not with so much happening around us. I don't think he even wanted to admit the little he did. There was so much I wished I could tell him. But before I could, he backed away from me. It felt sour, and yet nothing happened. I realized then that I wanted him. I wanted him desperately, near me at all times. I was afraid to use stronger words, even in the solitude of my mind. But it was unmistakable then. How had I not known it before? I fought and fought, I resisted. There was no need for it. There was no other who understood me as he, and there never would be. I watched him even then, solemn, but a small smile playing on his lips. He had an arm slung around Marco, and they talked and laughed. It hit me like a ton of bricks, what I was feeling for him.

There was all the time in the world to tell him. To show him he was not my second choice. I don't believe he ever was. It's a sorry thing to be in denial, but I was tired of putting on airs. I made a vow then, in Estella's tavern, amongst the merry men, to be as authentic and true to myself as ever. I wouldn't waste any more time. I had to hope my past decisions wouldn't come back to bite me. I should've never gone back to the present as it was.

Five days later there were several more ships in the harbor and on the north side of the island, from what we'd been told. The streets weren't quite so loud, as everyone was in a state of disarray. One of the pirate ships that had come took one of the governor's children as ransom; an insurance plan. The deal was once they'd held a meeting there at Estella's tavern in peace, they would return the boy to his family. The Brethren members had been in Jamaica, which resulted in a speedy departure and arrival in Tortuga. It was already late in the afternoon, and Estella was busy at work getting ready for the meeting. I was helping her clear out one of the back rooms, away from the bar. We lit several sconces and chandeliers and brought in chairs from the main dining hall.

Estella brought in empty barrels, and when I asked her what they were for, she replied, "These boys like to point their swords around and wave their guns about. If they want to meet 'ere they'll leave their weapons in the barrel."

I chuckled at that and realized Estella was the very definition of a den mother. I wondered how many pirates she'd helped whip into shape. After we were finished with our task, she went off to start preparing the food. I wondered whether John would let me listen in on the meeting. It was supposed to be for the

Brethren members only, but I wanted to see things for myself. Would the crews of the members be allowed to stand by? Only a few members had received the invite, as the rest were scattered about the remainder of the seven seas. I heard the door jingle and looked up to see Marco striding in. If I knew him at all, he'd probably ran off to see Emma again. I was not sure why he stayed on land at that point.

"Emma and Aerwyna asked how you've been fairing with your injuries. You've seemed to be healing well."

I knew it. "A few scars and a limp is all that's left, it seems. How is Emma?"

He smiled. "She'd be happier if I never left her side."

"Well why do you? You two are obviously smitten."

The first mate fiddled with a loose string on his coin purse. "John needs me. He won't say as much, but I worry about him. He can be quite reckless, and I don't trust Finn to keep him in line."

A best friend is just as important as a lover. Maybe more so. I understood his hesitation. "John's an adult, Marco. And he has me now, even if he doesn't accept it yet. You worry too much. He's in good hands."

He looked at me with fondness, and I felt my chest tighten. It was a comfort to know we were now friends. "Ah, suppose he does. You're good for him, Adira. I'm glad you've decided to stay. Perhaps... Perhaps I can consider it. Once you're back for good."

It felt good to know Marco trusted me with John. We'd both made bad decisions, but, somehow, we'd been able to keep each other in check. Marco went upstairs to the room we'd rented, and I was left thinking of the future - and what it held.

Chapter Fifty-One

The time had come. I was about to see for myself all of the pirates I'd read about as a child. I watched as they filed into the tavern, and all of the patrons stopped and stared. The residents of Tortuga had not seen a Brethren meeting since 1688. At least that's what Finn told me. Marco was the one that stood outside of our private room, greeting them all. We had not seen John yet, but according to Finn he rarely showed up on time. Finn did his job narrating as each member came through the door. The first to arrive was Black Bart, or 'Bartie,' as Estella called him. He was the main contributor for what the pirate code was in this age. I remembered vaguely that he was the one to adopt the skull and crossbones flag. I'd have to go out to the harbor and spot his ship later, I decided. He was a stout man, lean in build and wearing a powdered wig. It took me by surprise, as none of the men on John's crew bothered with wigs. Least of all their captain.

The next to come in was Edward Low, who had been thus far raiding the Caribbean and eastern Atlantic. He had come in port with a fleet of three, which seemed like showing off to me. Finn said to keep my distance from him, as he was one of the more savage men of his kind. Marco addressed him as 'Ned' when being led in. Finn, being the gossip he was, told me how his wife had died, and ever since then had shown grace to women. Perhaps he wasn't so savage after all. Just a tortured soul who had a daughter somewhere in the world unaware of her father's existence.

In came the last three, perhaps the ones I was most excited about. Calico Jack and the pirate queens themselves. Anne Bonny donned a mane of flowing red hair as she came in laughing with Mary Read. Mary appeared to be in her late 30s, and she wore yellow linen pants that stood out amongst the crowd. She was almost taller than Rackham. The three of them looked fierce, and I was momentarily stunned. John was still missing, and the pirates were not known for being patient. It was up to Finn and me to go find him. But as soon as we got up, there he was, walking through the entrance. Not a care in the world on his face, as if he didn't have the Brethren waiting on him in the other room. I was too antsy to hear the contents of the meeting commenting on his tardiness. We followed him in and watched as the pirates wordlessly dropped their weapons in the barrels. They all took their seats with a couple of other buccaneers I didn't recognize. Probably from their respective crews. There were just enough people for the small room, and there were light chuckles and muffles of conversation floating in the air. John had not taken a move to sit down, which perhaps was appropriate, since they had all come to meet him here. There were drinks spread about the table, and my nerves eased a little at the casualness everyone had. I had not been sure what to expect. Bart briefly got up to set a book on the table, leather-bound and larger than a tablet. I assumed it was used as a reference, as Finn whispered to me that it was the pirate codex. Everyone was talking about our success at Alhambra. They looked to John, patting him on the back and raising their drinks.

John still held no real level of order as he started the meeting. It almost seemed to be a reunion between friends, rather than talk of business. There were a few common enemies I had come to find out. They talked of rogue pirates, men employed by kings to hunt down their own. It was a curious thing, to hear of the deaths caused by buccaneers they used to work side by side with. This was their main obstacle. There was of course the Royal Navy to consider. We were all living on borrowed time - they would find out our location soon enough. John asked if any of the ships had been followed. Rackham said yes. He had been followed since October. Which made perfect sense, seeing as how he was supposed to have died then.

John cursed, asking why Jack would still come if he had company.

"Maybe if our king actually did what he was supposed to do, we wouldn't be having this conversation," Jack replied.

King? He couldn't mean... could he? John looked at the wall, which only confirmed it. My captain was their king. Finn almost chuckled, watching me realize. But out of all of the pirate captains, why John? He wasn't much of a ruler; he barely had control over his own ship. I had never even heard of him before showing up on his galleon. Maybe he wasn't proper royalty, but these people clearly elected him. Was it as simple as John being effective? The questions distracted me from a good bit of the discussion. They had moved on to the subject of the Kraken. Every single one of them were fearful, as much as they tried to mask the emotion. It seemed that we were the only ship the beast had been harping on, and I only hoped our latest encounter would be the last.

"We need a more effective way of killing 'em. They are imposters to the ocean and everyone in its waters," Bonny said. Them?

John must've seen the lack of color in my face, saying, "Yes, Fellows. Every octopus isn't really just an octopus. They're all little Krakens. They take longer to age than most species, we've found."

Low shook his head. "The only way we've been rid of them in the past is by the mer. And it's not often they bother to mess with the creatures."

Bart pitched in, "I had a sailor on board that gouged their eyes out, once. That seemed to do the trick."

Mary shook her head. "This has been an issue for seafarers since the beginning of time. Why are we wasting time on this? Can we not just accept there will be losses?"

John grumbled. It seemed half of the meeting was just about recounting who was still alive. Finally, the captain got to the matter at hand.

"Well, since a Kraken nearly destroyed my ship, I may need some assistance." Anne raised her eyebrow.

"Don't tell me you brought us all the way out here, after years amiss, for us to give you a brand spankin' new ship!" It didn't take a genius to hear the irritation in Bart's tone. There were hums of agreement throughout the room, and John raised his hands in surrender.

"It's for a good cause, lads. My crew and I, we got a stop to make back in the colonies, and then we're all yours. I'm no more enthused with the changes in our world than you lot. But this needs to happen first. We need to slip by the Navy undetected."

They weren't happy about the idea. I could see their hesitance, and I couldn't blame them. John crouched away from responsibility and hated to display any form of helping others. Despite how capable he was. Eventually, Anne was the one who sighed, looking over to Rackham.

"Perhaps we should give the rat what he wants, Jackie."

John scoffed. "You speak very highly of your king."

"I'm seeing we should've given that title to Mary," she responded. I had to hold in the laughter. Oh yeah, we were gonna be friends.

Jack relented. "Ah, we could possibly work something out, Sterling. You've still got that galleon?"

"'Fraid not, Calico. It's in Davy Jones' hands now. I took a sloop from the Navy, months back."

"No wonder they hate you so, John," Low quipped.

There were a couple of small chuckles in reply. The request was left hanging in the air for a few more moments. Anne and Jack whispered to each other. Bart and Mary exchanged glances.

"Seeing as how your success will benefit us all, I am willing to do an exchange with you. Your sloop for one of my brigs." It was Bart who made the offer, and I saw the relief in John's eyes despite his neutral expression.

"That'll do nicely," John replied.

Not long after the settled trade, the meeting came to an end. It fizzled out, and it was Edward who announced the meeting was adjourned. We all raised out of our seats, and the mingling began. There was one person in particular I wanted to meet, and my feet were shuffling their way over before I fully registered what I was doing. Anne's attention was immediately directed at me as she looked me over.

"I confess it's nice to see another woman in the trade," she said in regards to me.

I felt all giddy inside, knowing who was talking to me. "Likewise. I'm a big fan of your work, yours and Mary's."

Her eyebrows raised slightly. "Heard that much, have ya?"

I had to be careful with what I said next. "Captain Sterling has told me a few stories. All good accounts, I assure you."

A small smirk played on her lips, delighted. "It wasn't always in my plans, this life of mine. But I wouldn't trade it for the world, now. Jackie and Mary, they're everything to me."

I suddenly felt overwhelmingly glad that they hadn't been hung. It may be catastrophic to history, but I couldn't feel sad knowing women so full of life and vigor got to live. Hearing her name, Mary came over to join our conversation. She leaned an elbow on Anne's shoulder, both of them completely at ease with one another.

"You must be Adira," she said.

"Yes, how did you-"

She cut me off. "John wouldn't shut up about ye. From what I've seen today I'm surprised he hasn't bedded ya yet."

I'm sure my eyes probably looked like saucers, not expecting to hear that. There was a blush already spreading about my face, and I had to think of something to say. I opened my mouth, but Anne broke me off this time with a distinct mirth in her voice.

"Don't bother trying to deny it, lass. It's not often we see a pirate in love. Johnny least of all."

In love. Love was something I didn't understand. I wasn't sure I even really knew what it meant. These women, they thought John loved me. I saw that he cared for me, that he wanted me, but I didn't really know to what extent.

Mary spoke up again. "In any case, sounds like we'll be seeing a lot more of each other. We women have to stick together."

I nodded. "I couldn't agree more. Perhaps I'll see you both in Charles Towne."

Anne laughed. "If Sterling keeps to his word."

"I don't think he wants to see the end of his way of life as much as either of you. He'll be there, even if begrudgingly."

The three of us parted ways, and Finn grabbed me to go meet part of Low's crew. Soon enough we were all acquainted, and the real festivities could begin. We exited the private room, ready to join the patrons of Estella's tavern and have some fun.

Chapter Fifty-Two

The night was spent well, most of us dancing and laughing till we dropped. After midnight we talked about the books we had read, the ones that captured our fancy. Bart was partial to Daniel Defoe's work, as he had snagged an early published copy of 'Captain Singleton' that had been onboard a publishing agent's vessel. Anne enjoyed Johnathan Swift, an Irish satirist who had a couple of works out at the beginning of the century. Mary raved about 'Love in Excess,' a portrayal of a fallen woman. Low talked of Alexander Smith, a biographer who had published two years ago. Jack informed us he wasn't much of a reader, and we looked at him as though he were crazy. John and I couldn't talk fast enough about the books we had ravaged as of late.

The next morning was the day we knew it was time to leave Tortuga. I could've stood to explore for a while more, but I was anxious to get back to Boston and dispose of Jason. I could barely stand to look at him. There was also the governor, who was desperate to get his children back. I felt a little bad we had to resort to such drastic measures as kidnapping. All of these things combined had us in a rush to finalize the switch of the two ships. Edward had left early in the morning before most of us were up to set sail. He was no doubt ready to add some distance between the rest of the buccaneers. The remainder of us would head out at the same time, safety in numbers until we got further out at sea.

The hands repainted the brig, in case anyone in the colonies recognized Bart's ship. We loaded everything on board, including Jason. He tried desperately to talk to me, but I had nothing to say to him. It was clear to me it wasn't just that he wasn't good for me. I was not good for him either. I just hoped when it was all said and done that my family would not so willingly believe everything he said. The thought was a reminder that once I came back for good, I would never see them again. What do you say when you know it's the last time you'll ever see someone? I wouldn't change my mind. I would tell them everything they needed to hear. That I loved them, that I'd always love them.

In just a few hours we were ready. Everyone was antsy to leave, antsy to get this necessary thing over with. I was grateful they did not fault me, even though I was entirely to blame. Soon enough Rackham and Bart were bidding us farewell, waving from their ships. The next time we would see them would be with the promise of a new future. Perhaps Thomas knew this would happen all along. I looked over at John, standing tall and proud on the forecastle talking with Marco. He was happy to have a new vessel under his command. I suspected he was just as ready to be done with Boston as I was. The crew had wasted a lot of time in the past few months, despite the successes. Both with rescuing him and making trips for me. We were all so close to freedom, and it worried me. Being close to a goal means you have a lot to lose.

Boone came over to me a few minutes later, a mixture of annoyance and hesitance on his face.

"Sorry to bother you, but that boy won't stop yappin' for ya. Says he'll kill himself if you don't come down there. I told him I encourage it, but I know you want him alive for some reason."

No avoiding it now. I sighed, taking a minute to resolve myself to a couple of moments of frustration.

"Thanks, Boone. I'll go take care of it."

Descending downwards, I could already point out differences between the brig and the sloop. Sleeping quarters were more confined, smaller, and bunched together. Instead of having multiple cells, there was one. There was Jason, sitting cross-legged in the middle of the cell trying not to touch anything. The brig was one place that was not a high priority when it came to cleaning and sanitizing. When he finally looked at me, I saw no real emotion. It was like watching a puppet trying to contort their face. Had he really seemed so different now, after one act of betrayal? Or had I ignored all of the red flags?

"What do you want, Jason?"

He tilted his head at me, like even asking was pointless. "Don't you think this is all a bit much?"

I shrugged. "This was the captain's decision. Maybe if you hadn't insulted him, you wouldn't be in there."

A short laugh came out, an empty sound. "He just didn't like that I was calling you both out."

Not even five minutes had passed and I was already irritated. "I'm not the one who commits to a relationship with more than one person."

He at least had the decency to look ashamed. We stood in silence, and I wanted him to just come out and say whatever it was he needed to say.

Finally, he spoke up. "I don't want this to ruin what we had. Can't we just be friends?"

I looked at him, incredulously. "So you lied to me, made a complete fool out of me in front of a ship full of men, calling me a whore, and now you expect us to be friends? Jason... I can't ever be friends with you again."

The little emotion on his face was clouded over, something more deep and sinister coming over his eyes. "You don't want to make an enemy out of me, Adira."

I narrowed my eyes, barely believing what I was hearing. "Is that a threat?"

He raised an eyebrow, not saying a word. Letting his previous statement hang in the air. How was this the same boy I grew up with? What had changed?

"I can't believe you right now. What are you saying?"

There was a muscle ticking in his jaw, and I couldn't recognize the look on his face. I didn't have any desire to stand there and make guesses as to his inner dialogue. Shaking my head, I started to turn.

"Don't call for me again. You'll see me when we get to Boston. And don't go telling Boone threats unless you're willing to carry through with them."

Coming back up, I tried to shake off the interaction. It did me no good to ponder on the matter. I saw John looking in my direction, feigning curiosity. Did he think I had gone down there out of my own accord? I went over to him, feeling a need to offer some kind of explanation. He looked everywhere but at me.

"No trouble with that bilge rat, was there?"

I shook my head. "He's all talk, as I'm sure you know."

There was a flutter of his lashes under all of that kohl, a ghost of a smile.

"So... you're still coming back?" He was uncertain.

I nodded. "To hell with the rest. Being here, it's better than anything I've ever experienced in my world."

There was much to be desired as far as cleanliness, and I wouldn't mind some of the food from my time. But the work, the satisfaction, the people - it was so very right.

There was understanding in the captain's eyes. We may come from different times, but we both chose this life. We'd seen how the other half lived and knew there was more to be had. It shouldn't be about solely

struggling until you drop dead. If I could help create
a way of life for others that was about freedom, and
having choices, then was there even a question of
what direction I'd take? There was still another thing
that needed to be said.

"John, about what you said earlier...."

He tried waving it away. "No love, 'tis fine. Let's
forget about it."

"No, no, let me say this. You were right. And, as hard
as it is to say, I'm sorry. You should know, you're not
my second choice. I was... I've been in denial. I won't
go on about it, but I was wrong."

There was relief coming through his eyes and a small
sliver of what I perceived as hope. "Finally listening
now, are we? That's progress, darling."

I couldn't help but smile. This was something.

Chapter Fifty-Three

We were almost in range of the colonies. With the new ship came sacrifices, mostly in space. Brigs held even fewer people than sloops, and we were significantly weighed down. When passing Cuba the captain considered taking on a smaller second vessel but decided to wait. If the Navy were to attack us in Boston, realistically we would need as many men as we could get. This was our best option until Massachusetts was no longer a pit stop. Marco and I had gone over the plan with Wyna and Emma, and they were happy to help, albeit a little nervous to be so close to the harbor. Jason had let me be after that little talk the first day back on board. Part of me knew his silence was not a good thing. He was brewing and ruminating about how mistreated he no doubt felt. I knew he wanted someone to blame. He couldn't hurt the crew. I was more worried about what he'd do when we got back to our present.

Every mile that passed brought on more nervous energy. It was that anxious feeling when you were about to approach the end of a journey, not knowing what came next. Despite having a plan, there was a lot left to the unknown. Not everything could be predicted. I wanted to see everyone get their happy ending, but life never worked out that way. Someone would have to pay the price. I kept looking over at

John, and he seemed more sure in his actions than he had been the first time I arrived here. It was a small comfort, to see his confidence. If one of us were to have it, I was glad it was him. Jason had been brought out from the cell, left handcuffed near the mizzenmast. He was being constantly watched, not to be trusted out of sight. The captain wouldn't have let him stay on board had I not given other reasons to come back to Boston. Once I said goodbye to my family, I could have closure. No more ties to the present.

I just hoped the wormhole would last long enough. Jason had long abandoned voicing any information he knew about the method of travel, but I had enough knowledge of my own to go by. Still, it was based on theories. There was no solid way of knowing how much longer the loop would last. I could get back to the present and have no way of jumping back again. The realization brought chills to my skin. I don't think John really understood that, he only knew of the sporadic patterns the storms come in. It could be years before we would see each other again. Or not at all. As for our disguise, we had every look of being a wealthy merchant ship. The crew was told to change their outfits about an hour ago, as soon as we were in view of America's coastline. We all looked the part, many shipmates even wearing wigs and stockings.

We had finally arrived. The harbor was not even a mile away, and Marco was posing as captain for the time being. There was a chance someone would still recognize John as a prisoner, so we took extra precautions. He was still up on deck, but acting as the common crew. No one would be the wiser. Boone smothered Jason's mouth with a rag for the time being, until we knew it was time to leave. We couldn't risk him yapping something to the first person to look our way. To onlookers, he would just appear to be a crew member who had disobeyed, made to stay up on deck in humiliation. It was evening, and the clouds were only just starting to roll in. With it being the beginning of winter, there was a fair chance of at least a rainstorm tonight. But I couldn't rely on it. Marco left the ship to go speak to the port master and let the man know our business here. We were under the guise of waiting to meet our clients, who were suspected of docking within the week.

It would have to be good enough to believe. Meanwhile we sent a couple of men out into the town to do as they please. More suspicion would rise if we did not allow any of the crew shore leave, as there was no reason for it. Most people itch for the very second of getting off a boat after a long time out at sea. Shore leave was the highlight of any seafarer's journey, and when the majority of their booty got spent. So it seemed everything was where it needed to be. As long as we got a storm in a few days, there needn't be reason to worry. Darien was pacing the deck, muttering his own doubts. Before too long Finn sent him down below, telling him to shut his trap. Those who were not sent off the ship were antsy. Being near the colonies meant a raised possibility of getting hung, swinging from the gallows.

Eventually Marco came back up, nodding to John. The port master must've bought it. We could almost all relax, the main threat being dealt with. Stewart came out with Leo to have the boy help him in town to restock the ship with cured meats and sea biscuit. Paul followed loosely behind, to fetch fresh water. It was agreed upon that they would start traveling towards Nassau and wait for me in open waters. Once I could make it back, the mermaids would act as a go-between. A lot could go wrong. That's what kept running through my head. So much could go sideways, and I wanted so badly for something to go my way. This could work. But more than likely, adapting would be required. Things would go wrong, they always do. I had to be ready for whatever happened. Even then, I could sense the captain looking at me every now and then.

Ever since I apologized things had been different. It was a small, minuscule change. Almost like an electric charge every time we were remotely close. We were headed somewhere, in a new place that I did not know the outcome of yet. I didn't know what would happen, and that was part of the thrill. There were moments I found myself acting like a loose cannon; maybe too much time around him. And I could see he liked it. He reveled in whatever it was I was turning into, and for once I didn't think too much about it. I liked to imagine it was me letting go. Letting go of what was expected and acting solely on what I wanted. On what felt right. There would be times for that small voice to come back, reigning me in. But it felt good to loosen up. Truthfully I was even excited to get back in the water, to dive in and feel the rush of energy from the lighthouse. It was riveting, something I may never fully understand. I wondered if it would feel any different this time. That's what had me looking out at the little waves, beating against the wood of the vessel.

It was three days before nasty weather hit. Three days of the act, having hustle and bustle on the ship and chatting with the port master. He was complacent, if he suspected anything. The sky was just as gray and dark as the previous times, looming over our heads and thundering. It was within the hour, I was sure of it. We were outside of the harbor, the lighthouse in view. There were no real goodbyes to be had this time. I had every intention of coming back, if it was within my power to. And yet... I felt like I couldn't leave, not right away. There was that buzzing hum in my stomach, urging me to do something. Boone had taken the rag away from Jason's mouth and untied his hands. There was nowhere he could go, not when this was his best option. John was walking over to me, a finality in his steps. The end of this stop of the journey.

"Well, this is it, love."

"Yes," I muttered.

My eyes were flicking up to his lips. I'd thought about it for so long, and I found I couldn't wait anymore. I closed the space. He responded almost instantly, and my hands snaked up to his neck and face. I was in complete control; he was letting me do what I wanted. He tasted like rum and vanilla, and I felt like I couldn't get enough of him. Before long I was backing him up against the main mast, trying to hold him in place. I could tell he wanted to touch me. His hands were going up, almost reaching my face before they floated idly by his sides. Rain started to fall down on us, but it was not stopping me yet. He had to crane his neck downwards significantly while I was on my toes. He was being more gentle than I imagined, and it was driving me crazy. I eventually let go, needing to come up for air. He had a dazed expression, never looking away. His lips were parted, and a smile was already creeping in. The look on his face was somewhere between pride and amazement.

"Scoundrel," he called me.

There was warmth pooling in my chest and in my stomach, and I didn't have it in me to care that the whole crew was watching what just happened. I could only feel the strong urge to do it again and feel his soft lips on mine for a while more. But the rain was pouring now, and lightning started to pop up across the little horizon I could make out.

"I will come back," was the last thing I said to him.

Jason scowled at me as he stepped up on the railing of the brig. I was still a little further to the left of him, and I couldn't even make myself feel shame for him watching what unfolded. There was certainly no hand-holding this time. As we saw the lightning get closer to the lighthouse, I knew we had to jump. Jason leaped before I had to tell him to. I hesitated, looking back at the crew. It was only natural for me to want to prolong the inevitable. John was looking at me, eyes wide blown and black like the eyes of a shark. He moved away from the mast, walking towards me. His hands went to my waist, holding me in place.

Our lips were crashing, and there was an urgency in his movements. His hands went to my hips. There was no space between us, and I wondered how we'd stayed away from one another so long. As one hand stayed around my hips, the other went to my back, bunching up the fabric of my top. What I ended up missing was the sight of Marco handing Finn a bag of pieces of eight, clearly over a bet. I'd be none the wiser. But as I pulled away, he brought both hands to my shoulders and pushed me off. I was hitting the water before I knew it, and, looking up towards the ship, I couldn't help but wonder what the rest of the crew thought of the little act. Scoundrel, I thought to myself.

After the dizzy feeling left, I kicked and paddled away from the brig, trying to create more distance. I felt that tingling sensation on my neck again, and a touch there confirmed my suspicions. The gills were trying to come back in place, and I wished there was time to wonder what that meant. Right then I could only take note of the racing in my heart it set forth. I at least almost had a rhythm at this point, a science of how to do this efficiently. It was all a series of swimming with the current, taking your time, knowing you'll get where you're supposed to be. I just had to trust the sea.

Within minutes I was feeling that familiar burst of light and energy reach me, a buzzing going off in my ears. I couldn't see anything, but I assumed Jason was going through the same. It was a whirl of bubbles and my hair whipping in front of my face. Once the tumbling stopped I could start to go back towards the surface of the water. Then I realized it was hailing. It was hitting me like little pellets, and it stung. I wondered if the impact would leave marks. I swished around, looking for Jason. He was a few feet away, coughing up water but otherwise coherent. I swam towards him, and he wordlessly started to paddle towards the lighthouse. We wouldn't know the date until we got to Little Brewster. It was amazing how quick the process was. In a series of confusing minutes you're out one era, into the other.

Setting foot on my little island, nothing different stood out to me. I took this as a good sign and continued. Reaching the lighthouse, I quickly opened the door and raced upwards. Switching the light on, I took a moment to breathe and look around. Everything appeared normal. My things were scattered about, the balcony door still strung open. I headed back to the cottage, where Jason had gone to soak the kitchen floor with salt water and mud. He was heaving and sulking. The two acts didn't look right together. I didn't bother speaking to him, knowing he'd just have an argument waiting to be voiced. Jogging upstairs, I reached for my phone. There were even more messages than last time, but it was the date that stood out to me. A month. A whole month had passed since we were there. It was not the kind of time I could really have afforded to miss.

There was an issue even bigger than getting back to my family. Grabbing my laptop, I sat down at my study desk by the window. Opening my emails, there was a lump forming in my throat. Between the missed calls and urgent emails, I was in trouble. It was the Lighthouse Association. Two weeks before they had sent out another warning email for failing to perform my lighthouse duties, and they had only gotten more frequent since then. Not only them, but the city council themselves had reached out to me. I apparently was terminated from this position a few days before, and they would be coming by the next day to remove me from the premises if I did not respond. My hands were shaking at that point as my fingers typed away a response. I just hoped there was time to change their minds. I knew I wouldn't keep the position, but I needed to stay on the property long enough to make it back to John and the others.

Even aside from that, if I disappeared prematurely, it could risk more people finding out about the wormhole. I couldn't see my family in person. It was the type of devastating news that made me want to drop to my knees. The Association already knew I'd been absent, and I couldn't do anything but wait. If they found out what really went on here, if they tried to interfere - it couldn't happen. I wasn't even sure what this most recent trip had done to history. Up until then, I had tried not to think about it, and I hoped I could make it there long enough to avoid the answer. Alas, there was little I could do about the situation. I had to focus on what I could control. And if there was any chance the Association or council was showing up the next day, Jason needed to be long gone. I could only imagine all of the things he'd have to say if given the chance.

With the reply written and sent out, I shuffled back downstairs to see Jason staring out the window. In the same place he was when I first came in. I watched him for a while, debating what it was he was thinking about. Maybe he just wanted me to notice his distress. I called out his name. He didn't move.

"You should go...." The statement at least earned me a head turn. He didn't really look at me, it was more of an acknowledgment that he heard me.

"I hoped so much...." I didn't really know what to say. What did he mean? Hoped that we could've carried on?

"You should've never come. Why? Why did you?" It was the question I had been wondering since John punched him square in the face.

"Because I was hoping you'd change my mind. I was testing the waters, as it were." I couldn't believe what I was hearing, which was becoming a running theme when talking to Jason.

"What, you mean to tell me if I had behaved a certain way, you were going to break up with your first girlfriend and claim me the winner?" He didn't even look guilty.

"You can love more than one person at a time, Adira. Even so, you didn't pass. I realized early on that you weren't right for me." I was starting to get worked up.

"I can't keep running in circles with you. I don't even know why I asked. But seriously, you need to leave." In the reflection of the glass I could see a smirk on his lips, and it made me nervous.

"Why? Worried I'll tell someone what's going on?" I didn't like where this was going.

"Something like that."

"Well, you can save yourself the trouble. I already talked to your superiors."

"You what?" He finally turned around to look at me, smug as ever.

"While you were wasting time, I was busy getting the number of the Lighthouse Association. I gave them a little anonymous phone call and told them I'd have some interesting information regarding their keeper. Figured it was the least I could do, after the treatment I had to endure. I'll be back in Boston before too long, they've already agreed to meet with me."

I hadn't even heard anything. Sneaky devil. I wanted to choke him. Properly choke him, see the life leave his pitiful body for a few seconds. I couldn't get my heart to slow down with all of this bad news.

"Get out. I don't want to see you again. Don't make me ask twice." He had the audacity to smile at me.

After he found his bags, I heard the front door open and shut. I was left with only the sound of the hail hitting the roof and the wind howling. This was... I couldn't even comprehend how bad this was. I wasn't sure how much Jason revealed or would soon, but I had to hope it was too crazy for them to believe. He was just a crazy ex to them. Hopefully. Then again, it matched up with my disappearances. They may believe a portion of the story, solely for that fact. I was trying not to feel a sort of impending doom and look at the situation rationally. Going back to my computer, I checked to see if by luck I got a response from the council. It was after hours, so it was no real surprise that there was nothing new in my inbox. I decided to get out of my wet clothes and throw them in the dryer. Throwing my hair up in a bun with a fresh set of clothes on, I could figure out my next move. I was desperate to talk to my parents.

Chapter Fifty-Four

A quick look at my phone confirmed they had been just as desperate to reach me. I wondered if I could convince them to come up for a trip. Seeing them in person one last time felt like a luxury I may not get to have. I felt bad then, knowing I wouldn't have a good enough excuse to give them for being silent for a whole month. Clicking on the video icon, I waited for my mom to pick up. I didn't even have to wait for a second ring for her to answer. As soon as the video feed connected, I could see the hope wash into relief on her face. It brought a lump to my throat, seeing her so emotional before words could be said. Her first sentence to me was no real surprise.

"Where the hell have you been?" She looked like she was going to cry.

"Mom, I'm so sorry." Was that the best I could do?

"I asked you a question, Adira. Do you realize how worried your father and I have been? We called the police!" This was nothing I didn't suspect.

"Can you just listen to me for a second? Without interrupting?" She looked skeptical, but I knew her curiosity would keep her silent. I got that much at least from her. She nodded eventually.

"Jason was here, as you know. He's on his way home now. We had...." How did I want to put this? "We had a falling out. He's been seeing another girl. Despite us deciding to try dating again. He was lying to me, and things got a little out of control. He didn't like that I called him out, and I think he's going to cost me my job." Mom's brows were furrowed together, and I could see the gears in her head trying to turn and make sense of things.

"What?! But Jason loves you. I don't understand...."

She still had that distant look in her eyes, lost in thought. This whole conversation was a whirlwind, trying to get everything out that needed to be said.

"It doesn't matter. You can't trust a single thing that comes out of his mouth." There was some remorse on her face.

"I'm sorry, Adira. I didn't think he was like that, I thought he worshiped you.... This is going to be really weird for your brother."

Right. Hunter was best friends with Jason. I hoped Jason didn't wrap him in any of his lies or drama, but that was too much to hope for. There was a burrowing realization that I could never explain the full extent of the last year to my mother.

"I know. I wish I could tell you more. There's so much I want to say…."

"Why? Why can't you tell me? Are you in trouble?"

"Please, just, can you come to the lighthouse? Would the family be able to come visit? Even just for a day."

She was looking at me like I'd lost it. Like I was not making any sense. And maybe I wasn't. All I kept thinking about was John's lips on mine and the insatiable need to be near him once more. He was the ruin of me, the thing decaying every bit of good and decency I once had. Or maybe I was never good. Maybe he had only brought out what was buried deep in myself already. Or perhaps the world had never been as black and white as I had previously believed. Whatever it was, I didn't care. I loved the power that came with knowing him.

"I don't know, honey. That's kind of a decision that needs more thought behind it than a whim." I knew that. I just couldn't stand the thought of not hugging the people that raised me one more time.

"I know it is. I just, I don't think I'm coming back home after this. If I get fired, truly, I'll be going far away." She started shaking her head again.

"But your family is here! I was hoping you'd work in your lighthouse for a year and come back to us! Where in the world do you plan to go?"

"Overseas, somewhere in England."

"Somewhere in England? Adira, you're not being realistic. What do you think you're going to be doing?" This was going nowhere. We were walking in circles from one unrealistic situation to the next. I was starting to feel despair.

"Mom, there's nothing I can say. I can't go back. I don't belong in cornfields anymore. If you and the family can't come to see me, I'm not sure we'll see each other again. For a very long time." I knew she was going to be dumbfounded. I knew this was all crazy, and yet I couldn't stop spewing out the half-truths.

"Well, I'm going to have to talk to your father. This is all very last minute." There was little else to discuss with one another. Without me sounding demented. So I wrapped up the call and hung up after two minutes. In the meantime, I was to wait for the city council.

The next day around noon, a member of both the Lighthouse Association and the city council showed up on Little Brewster. They took the ferry, and I had a feeling I would be the one dropping them back off in the harbor. The pair of them had accusatory eyes. The council member was thin, tall, and blonde. She looked a tad out of her environment in her business suit and acrylic nails. The LA member was no more than ten years younger than Thomas. He was bald, with a beer gut and a short beard gone gray. If it were different circumstances, I would be laughing to myself at how strange the two of them looked standing next to each other. But they were here on official terms, and the matter was next to dire.

Truthfully, I had not figured out what to say to them. I tossed and turned all night, thinking of what excuses I could conjure. But there was none. My one job was to keep that light running, and I had failed. They looked at me expectantly, after introducing themselves. The woman was named Claire, and the stout man was named Morris. But it didn't matter. We wouldn't be long acquainted. I brought them inside the cottage and made coffee for the three of us. As it took its time brewing, Claire and Morris laid their folders and notes across the dining table. It was a blustery fall day, and the sun was fading in and out between the clouds. For a while, no one talked. We simply avoided eye contact, waiting for the hot drinks. But once we all had a steaming mug in our hands, the subject could no longer be prolonged. It was Claire who looked up from her papers first.

She started, "Now that we're all settled, we have a couple of questions for you. It shouldn't take too long." I give her a simple nod, trying to keep my knee from bouncing.

"Morris, would you like to start?" she asked.

"All right then." He opened his folder. "Ms. Fellows, what do you have to say to the claims the Association and council have made in regards to you failing to do your duties?"

"What you claim is true. But not without reason."

His right brow raised as he intercepted, "What reason could be present for not doing your job for one month? Need I remind you that we had given you a written warning not long before this period?"

"I remember, and I am truly sorry for not heeding your warning. The reason for my neglect has something to do with your so-called anonymous phone call, which will be feeding you stories about my absence from work." I continued, "Mr. Becker had come to Little Brewster to visit me, as we were in a relationship at the time. He kept me from tending to the lighthouse, and it took me longer than expected to force him off the island."

Claire was writing in her notes vigorously before looking up, "Are you telling us Mr. Becker withheld you here?"

My mouth twitched downwards, as I thought to myself - two can play at this game. "Yes." Claire and Morris shared a look.

Morris' face had softened somewhat, as he looked at me again. "I don't mean to upset you or pry, Ms. Fellows. But for the sake of your position, we must ask. Did this man abuse you in any way?"

I looked down, for fear of breaking character. "Yes, he did."

Again, they both start writing down in their notebooks. They asked me a few more follow-up questions, although they had a tad more sympathy in their tones now. I realized my response to this

465

meeting was very piratical, and I found I couldn't wait to tell Finn about it.

Once they were done asking the necessary questions, we all rose from the table and headed to the lighthouse. They needed to verify that everything was working properly and in good condition. I guided them up the winding steps, and clinks against the metal were all I heard for a minute or two. Morris broke away from Claire, well acquainted with where to go and what to check for. Claire looked, once again, a little lost. I imagined this was not something she'd ever had to trouble herself with. After all, Thomas was quite the dutiful keeper. I was nothing in contrast. Morris checked the light, the fresnel lens, the foghorn, the structural integrity of the building, and all of the other things that make up a lighthouse. Some would say it's a boring and drab task, but there's a fascination to it that I cannot deny.

Once he was finished up, it seemed everything was to his satisfaction. It was my fault alone that kept the light from turning on. Which both of them knew from the start. We all stood outside as they whispered to each other and I remained mere feet away. They looked at me every so often in their conversation, and I was entirely at their mercy. I felt my muscles tense as they came back over to me, clearly reaching a decision. It was Morris who spoke.

"After gathering more information today, we've decided to suspend your termination. It is likely both parties will still wish to speak to Mr. Becker, but afterward, we will come together and make an informed choice."

It was perhaps the first moment that day when I could relax. I didn't hesitate to let it show on my face, and I thanked them for their consideration and time. I didn't need this forever, I just needed more time.

At midnight the storms had started. The sky was violent, beating against my bedroom window and pounding on the roof. I didn't remember a storm happening so closely after traveling the last two times. It was a guessing game trying to determine what was and wasn't normal here. I had a feeling in my gut though that this was a bad sign. Maybe I was beginning to pick up on superstitions, as I couldn't help but wonder if this was a precursor to the stability of the wormhole. As my eyes drifted to the window, watching the night light up and the rain belt down, it was the type of storm fit for travel. So close together, and the very clouds seemed to be under protest. Was this what Jason had meant when he said the loop would eventually end?

My mind was racing, knowing my chances to get back to the Golden Age were dwindling. Should I hop out of bed now, and forget a proper goodbye with my family? It was ever so tempting. What a fitting way to go. I could take the boat out and stage my unfortunate death. Everyone would assume my last breaths were spent trying to save some ship out in the storm. And yet there was a terrible nagging in the back of my mind. I knew that Jason would attract attention to this place. He would demand an audience, and I didn't want to think about the possibility of more people discovering time travel. I had to handle this delicately. Could I time my jump back to the wormhole's last breaths? I gauged I would not have to wait very long, as the signs of deterioration were already evident. This was unfortunately the best plan I had to secure my future and keep the rest of my kind far away.

The next two days were dreary and dark. There had been another show of light the night of the storm, indicating a means to travel. I had stayed awake, looking out my window for any stray ships. If I could just prevent others from stumbling on this life-changing knowledge, I'd be okay. It was a very selfish thing to plan for, but less and less was I caring about the implications of what that meant. I had not seen any mermaid tails or felt tugging at my mind telepathically, which meant thankfully Wyna and Emma must've kept enough distance from the lighthouse to stay safe from the angry waves. What I encountered was a message from Jason. I wanted to smash my phone against the wall when I received it. The traitorous imp was mocking me, telling me all the things he planned to say to the council. They had their meeting the day before, and I had not heard from Morris or Claire yet. It was a worrisome situation, and Jason was only adding to my distress.

He was going to be just elusive enough to raise suspicion and intrigue among the suspecting members. Telling them that I was withholding information about the missing ships, that I would be missing during storms at night, sailing the boat out to come back with nothing in stow. I was perhaps too confident in my initial impression of Morris and Claire, hoping that calling Jason an abuser would add doubt to anything he uttered. But I could also look like a liar and a thief. Which, I suppose, those days was true enough. The only good thing I had going for me was Mom's agreement to come up and visit the lighthouse. I stressed the urgency of the situation, letting her know any day here could be my last. She didn't understand and would most likely scold me when she got here. They were currently on the road, probably still at least six hours from Boston.

They would be confused still when I'd inevitably send them back home the day after they arrived. It was the only time I could afford to give them, and I would just have to make it count. Perhaps by some miracle, they wouldn't fuss about it. I watched the forecast from my couch, the weatherman on the TV expressing the conundrum that the last few weeks had been. Absent-mindedly I twisted the ring on my pointer finger, which happened to be a king's. A little ode to what waited for me in another century. I was full of little mementos then, another one being the droplets of gold dangling from my ears when John had pierced them there in his cabin. Mom had never gotten a proper look at me on our video chats, and I wondered what they would all have to say once they saw me. I felt like a new person, did I look it too?

Chapter Fifty-Five

It was nighttime, around 9 PM, when I had taken Mermaid's Lagoon out to pick up my family. I docked in the harbor, hopping out and looking around. It was relatively quiet, and lamp posts along the dock made the black water shimmer. My boat bobbed up and down as I leaned on one of the wooden posts. I told my family to look for my boat and have their car parked near the harbor. A few minutes later I heard my name being called, and my eyes drifted forward to my mom and sister waving at me. A smile broke out across my face, and we were all running towards each other. I hardly knew who to hug first. Gus, our sweet golden retriever, reached me first. Getting down on the ground, I let him trample me and lick my face. There was laughter in the air and my, how I'd missed the sounds of their voices.

As I stood, I found I didn't have to choose who to embrace first. They came at me in a group hug, and I was being squished like a plushie. I was nearly lifted off the ground, and a minute later I was finally able to breathe. Even in the dim light, I could make out every feature on each of their faces. They looked tired but just as happy to see me as I was to see them. I asked if they needed anything from Boston before we all huddled ourselves into my little boat. It was a pleasure to show them what I'd called my home for what felt like forever, to show them the tug that the lighthouse placed on its visitors. They were oohing and ahhing at the island, and I couldn't help but beam with pride. Even if this place wouldn't be mine for much longer.

My sister tugged on my hair. "It's so much longer. Lighter too." It was a small observation, and yet I was glad she noticed.

"The sun will do that, Cy." She rolled her eyes.

"Smart mouth." I laughed.

When we reached the inside of the cottage, they all dropped their bags on the dining room floor. I promised them a proper tour in the morning, despite what the next day would also bring. The lights were on, and they seemed to all be noticing me for the first time then.

"Have you been working out?" Hunter asked me. The comment made me laugh again, as I never could stick to a workout regime. I supposed I did look more toned, having worked on a ship and run around for several months. Then Mom squinted her eyes, and I got a thrill out of wondering what she'd noticed next.

"Your ears! Adira, they look wretched!" The third piercing. My hand instinctively went to my ear, touching the gold there. I swished around, letting the ornaments in my hair clink.

"She's a gypsy, alright," my dad pointed out. They continued critiquing me, and I was pleased to note I no longer felt shame at their comments. Instead,

471

some sort of sick pride was there at the reminder of being changed and different. I was entirely made of my own course, and I felt alight with the knowledge.

We all moved to the living room and watched as Gus trotted around the rooms sniffing and wagging his tail. There was that chatter in the air that I had so desperately been missing, and I let myself be washed in it for a while. There was a feeling of warmth in my insides, and I knew it to be contentment. Seeing them, and laughing with them, was a closure that I had been seeking. Now that I had it, I hated what I would have to do next. We scoped the subject of Jason. The awkwardness of him returning, of not knowing what to believe. I knew I had not helped enough to ease their doubts. They were still troubled. My parents and Cyra were leaning toward seeing him as a liar, but Hunter was the neutral party in all of this. He did not seem to particularly care what had or hadn't happened. Such is the common sentiment of those who hide from conflict. Rather, he simply seemed irritated that I had caused a wedge in his friendship with Jason.

I thought back to our childhood; at every instance, Hunter and I were with Jason. The longer I reminisced, the more I wondered if Jason was ever a good friend. Was he ever capable of being true and authentic? It was those qualities I was beginning to realize were rare, no matter the time period. Whatever the case, the situation had caused exhaustion on all sides. It was breaching midnight, and everyone was drooping. We laid out blankets everywhere, and I let Mom and Dad take my bed. I fell asleep to the steady breathing of my siblings huddled around me and the dog nuzzled close by.

My family was motivated by one thing, and one thing only. Food. As the sun rose my mom was up with it, somehow knowing where everything was in my kitchen and cooking breakfast. I didn't even think I had anything in there to cook with, which meant she came prepared. I smelled eggs and bacon, and a peek in the kitchen also showed Cyra beside her flipping pancakes. They had music playing, some mix of early 2000s songs that should've stayed buried in its time. Leave it to my sister to bring it back out of the grave. My dad was presumably still upstairs, while my brother taunted the dog in the living room. It was incredibly domestic and the most wholesome scene I'd witnessed in probably a year. That fact messed my eyes a little with tears, but it was only an added sign to get coffee started. Mom wrapped an arm around me as I started the espresso machine. Everything was making my heartstrings pull that morning.

Not even an hour later we were at the dining table, as Gus circled the premises for scraps. Hunter was eating at rapid speed, as the rest of us were talking like time and distance had never separated us. I felt incredibly relieved that Mom let my weird behavior go, placating me and my desire for family time. But even moments like this, as sweet as they were, must be fleeting. As breakfast passed, I showed them everything that sat on the island. They had seen most of the cottage, but the lighthouse was the real treasure. Gus refused to go in, instead standing guard

473

near the door. Dad guessed on the history of the building, while Mom decided against climbing the seemingly never-ending stairs. Hunter and Dad were bored out of their minds and panting as we reached the top, but they were at least pretending to care. The tour was mostly just for airs, and once it was done everyone headed back into the living room.

As Cyra washed the dishes, the rest of the family had their attention on me. They wanted some type of concrete answer. It was too bad I would have to disappoint them again. My fingers fiddled with the hem of my shirt, and I ended up catching one of my rings on the fabric. Tears were already springing back to my eyes, thinking that this was it. The last time we'd all be together.

"I needed to see you guys. I wanted us all together, one last time." The dog came to rest by my feet, looking up at me for head pats. I obliged.

Mom responded, "We are here, honey. What's going on? What can't you tell us?" Would it be easier to tell her I met someone? That I met a lot of people, who made me feel alive? I wanted to ease her mind, whether it was true or not.

"You wouldn't understand. This job, it's been amazing. The best I ever had. But there's a sliver of Jason's tales that are true. I've withheld things from the government, in a way. Things about the fading ships. If they knew, if they find out, I can't ever come here again. I need to fix this mess, and then I need to go somewhere safe, where they won't find me."

Dad looked at me with an indignant stare. "You're talking like you broke the law. Tell me that isn't the case. Is this just another Fellows' misfortune of some kind?" Fellows' misfortunes were what we called our family's bad luck. Wherever we went, people betrayed us and promises were broken. That was human nature, but our family somehow left a sour taste in people's mouths. We ended up with the short stick and usually got blamed for things that never happened.

"That's exactly what I'm saying. So you should know it's hard to explain a situation that has little meaning even to the victim." I told him. I witnessed a shooting glance between Mom and Dad. For some reason, it reminded me of the looks Wyna used to give me. Like there was something she couldn't quite tell me yet. Mom was continuing to give him daggers, but I heard Dad continue anyway.

"Maybe this is more our doing than yours." I wanted to laugh at the absurdity, because if they knew what this really was there would be no need for replacing blame. There seemed to be a silent conversation between my parents before Mom let out a long-suffering sigh. Which usually means I'm in for a long talk. In this instance, I truly had no clue where it was headed.

Mom began, "There's something we probably should've told you...." Her speech was cut off short by the ringing of my phone. Her surprise turned into relief as I looked at the caller ID. It was the council. I apologized to Mom before getting up and walking to the kitchen.

"Hello?"

"Ms. Fellows. It's Claire Hufton. I'm sorry to inform you that with no solid evidence, we cannot move forward with your claims against Mr. Becker. He spoke with us recently, and we have reason to believe you've been holding information regarding the missing ships' incidents. You know how serious that is...." Why they chose to believe him over me, I couldn't say. He had a way of making people feel sorry for him. But it was making my blood boil. My breath was catching in my lungs, and I reminded myself to respond.

"I... of course I do. What do you and the Association plan to do moving forward?" There was no point in commenting on the lack of evidence. It would be barking up the wrong tree.

"We may be forced to escalate the situation to a separate jurisdiction. A court case may have to be made if you deny your involvement with concealing useful information from the council." Good. Let them prolong it. Even so, they would no doubt be snooping around to gather more solid evidence. Even the public knew that the fading ships were a product of the roguish storms. They would be waiting in the fog and rain to see what I did. This was turning into something out of my control. Nothing was worse than being helpless. I could no longer wait for the right moment, I would have to go as soon as the next storm hit. It was not a good plan by any means, but it was the only one that I could see holding any real level of success.

The call ended and I was left standing by the kitchen window, similar to Jason when we had gotten back from the past. Which really wasn't that long ago. How things were progressing. Walking back into the living room, the family had gone quiet. No doubt listening to the conversation.

"What were you going to say, Mom?" She dismissed me.

"It was nothing. Your father and I just wish we knew what to do, or how to help you." I knew she was lying, but so was I. We were left at a stalemate.

"Who was that on the phone?" Cyra asked.

"The city council. Things aren't looking good for me."

Dad chimed in, "You need us to leave?" Dad reminded me of Marco, in the way he left no room for nonsense. He cut right to the chase.

"I wish you didn't have to," I mumbled. Mom got up, and suddenly I was in her arms again. I fought the urge to cry; tears did nothing for me. I felt the rumble in her chest as she spoke. It was a small comfort.

"The worst thing as a mother is to think you'll never see your child again. I want you to promise that when you can, you'll come back." How could I promise her that?

"I'll try." It was noncommittal. But it was the best I could give her. The rest of the family joined the hug, and Gus jumped at us, trying to get in on the show of affection. Cyra started to laugh as his nose nuzzled any opening he could find, and I tried to take note of every detail at this moment. Soon enough I was helping them pack up their things. It was a shame, how little time we had. But I got to see them, and that's what mattered. Outside as we prepared for departure, it was chalky and humid.

Another thunderstorm warning was sent out, which was becoming the norm from day to day. People in Boston were both tired of the gloom and beginning to recognize it as the new norm. I breezed right into the harbor, where their car was parked not too far away. Everyone stumbled out of the boat and onto the docks as rain threatened to spill over us. We said our goodbyes, reluctant and choking on our words. As sad as I was, there was so much on my plate to worry about that one thing ticked off the list felt like a relief off my shoulders. I walked with them to their car, soaking up as much time with them as I could. Watching as they loaded everything and drove away with hands waving goodbye. It was fine. Things were fine.

Chapter Fifty-Six

The next few days were an exhausting mix of phone calls, letting people on the island gather evidence and check facts, and hearing what crap Jason was spreading. He had already made his relationship with his dream girl public, and they were as good as engaged. It gave me a strange discomfort as if I wasn't good enough. Irrational thoughts and fears controlled me sometimes.

The ache of my family leaving was subdued by the reminder that I was running out of time. Every day that a storm brewed above me, I considered leaving. The eerie energy that came with them was stranger too, the fractures in the loop more erratic. I knew the phenomenon was reaching its end. If I didn't act now, I may never see my world again. The council and Association never seemed far away, and unfortunately worrying about what they would and wouldn't see was becoming irrelevant. The skies were under a near-constant state of darkness. Naturally, I was preparing for my exit. I couldn't take much, but I wanted a few reminders of this age, one of them being a locket that had a chain that reached past my chest, to tuck under clothes if need be. The locket extended into four panels when opened. In the slots were my mother, father, Cyra, Gus, and Hunter. I did not want to risk forgetting their features.

On my belt, I secured pouches of chocolate, and on the other hip, I stuffed as many toiletries as I could. The essentials. There was not much else I found I would miss too terribly. I sent one last message to the family, telling them I loved them. Now came the fun part. Walking outside, the wind had already picked up in the last hour, blowing my hair around. Even though the rain wasn't pouring yet, I'd felt a couple of droplets graze my skin while moving towards the rocky shore. I took a last glance towards my lighthouse, thankful it'd served me well. Thinking back to the now, I would've liked to take my boat out and make things easier for myself, but I didn't want to explain its nature should it end up in the past. Instead, I resigned myself to swimming out to the vantage point. I eased in, like backtracking on a rock climbing wall. As soon as my legs hit the water, I felt significantly more calm. Like I could breathe freely for the first time that day.

I was buzzing all over, feeling the energy I only did during the jumps. The rain had already progressed, and I could hear the thunder. I could hardly see in front of me with the thick fog and clouds turning almost charcoal. Paddling slowly, I was almost where I needed to be. There were sounds somewhere to the left of me that didn't sound quite like thunder. I kept my head low, but there was nothing to see. As the sound came closer, it almost sounded like a bell. And creaking. A sinking feeling in my gut told me that it was definitely a ship. I could almost guarantee who was out there. I saw shadows of light around me, and I knew lightning was starting to touch down. The clouds were practically touching the water, which couldn't be a good thing.

As I bobbed in and out of the lighthouse's radius, my suspicions were confirmed. There was a little U.S. Coast Guard boat swaying back and forth on the choppy waves. It was a sight that sent chills up and down my spine, especially as it went in and out of being merely a shadow amongst the storm. I felt at least grateful I put the light on in the tower before coming down to the sea. As the lightning became more frantic, hitting the lighthouse in the distance, I thought to myself that I should've already traveled by now. Had the wormhole already closed? I was feeling something like tremors in the water and hearing more phantom sounds. Before I could think, I felt an icy hand grasp my ankle and pull me down. A yelp escaped my throat, but it was only a series of bubbles under the ocean. A minute later I was face to face with Aerwyna. There was air filling my lungs and relief in my chest as I grasped onto her.

I let myself sag in her arms, tired already. This told me the wormhole was still there, but it was becoming more unstable. There might've been multiple energy blasts scattered between a window of time. Emma was there too, and she was rubbing my back.

"I'm so glad to see the two of you!" I told them. Emma had a look on her face.

"We're relieved too, believe me. But we have some news for you," she told me. I let go of Wyna, an arm still slung over her shoulder.

Wyna chimed in, "Your boys are here. Emma told them that you weren't here during the last emission, and the captain was insistent he come." This was not

481

good. More than not good, this was the start of a catastrophe.

I shook my head. "He can't be here. There's another boat out there. If they see John's ship...." Emma put a hand on my shoulder.

"Perhaps I can help with that. I may be able to push them back, some. But Wyna should stay with you." I nodded, happy enough with that plan.

The three of us swam back up, and I was anxious to see the brig. But as we made sight of the surface, there were people falling in the water and a rumbling. Above us were two hulls; one was the Coast Guard, and the other was the pirate ship I was so fond of. Which was currently sending cannonballs at the Coast Guard. For a moment I was too shocked to move, but the girls were grabbing me and swimming us over to the other side of the brig, where the Coast Guard boat wasn't visible. While we made the distance, I caught a familiar face I did not expect to see. Jason. And a girl, holding his hand. I wouldn't have even seen them had they not been leaning on the railing, right next to the water. It made me sick, and I recognized that familiar urge to choke him.

We emerged from the water, and I was gasping from the change in density. Our previous plan was irrelevant, and then the only move was to get out alive. I didn't even know if the wormhole was sustainable enough to allow us to jump long enough to start sailing with our tails between our legs. Wyna pushed me up towards the ship, and as I was flailing out of the water I caught one of the beams on the ladder. I held on for dear life, despite feeling like my arm socket just got ripped out. The ship was rocking from the momentum of the cannons and freak waves. But all of that faded into the back of my mind when I saw him. He was mad, and stupid, and had something black smudged across his face.

"John!" I couldn't help but call out for him. He looked at me, and there was relief and a crazy grin spread across his features. I continued to climb the ladder as he ran to the side of the ship. He'd called for someone to fetch some rope to haul me the rest of the way up.

But the men were shouting at him, and a glance around showed me the boat had switched sides. Modern ones could do that in a blink, and the pirates were fools who didn't know any better. The energy bursts were becoming more erratic by the minute, and I quickened my pace. It was then or never. As someone finally tossed me the rope, I heard Marco yelling. It caught me off guard, and then I saw him swinging towards me on his own rope tied to the rigging. I was confused, and then the worst happened. A shot fired out, and then he was falling. He was falling, reaching for me. I cried out for him, for my friend. I could see the flashes of red from his shoulder, almost his chest before he plummeted into the sea. There were screams, some from me, even more from Emma, and many from men on the brig. Then I stared into the face of the person who pulled the trigger.

Jason was still standing there, as shocked as I was at what he'd done. Others on the boat were yelling at him and grabbing for his arms, telling him to stand down. He gave in, in a sort of daze. I found I couldn't look away. But then there was the girl next to him, with cherry wine hair slicked back, grabbing the gun from his hands. Emma was crying below, and Wyna was yelling for me to move. The boat was so close to our own that I could hear her cocking the pistol as I was staggering upwards. Then another shot rang out. John was shouting my name as my whole body flinched, feeling the bullet graze my ribs. The next thing I knew I was the one falling, having lost my grip. I made a splash, and the pain was making the edges of my vision blur. My head hit something, and then everything went black.

Acknowledgments

I've spent my whole life reading stories, putting myself in the main character's shoes. But never had I imagined that one day I would write a story of my own. This book is a love letter to my past self. It's been a form of therapy, getting to write down parts of experiences I've gone through in my short life, along with what I wish in my wildest dreams would happen to me. The research I've put into this, the long nights, and the cups of coffee have all been worth it. This is my first work, but certainly not my last. It's been a wild ride, and it feels like baring my soul to the world to have it published and read by others. I can only hope it's worth it. Here's your sign to go ahead and write the book. Do the thing you've been thinking of doing, but haven't because you're afraid. And may we all find a John Sterling in our lives.

To my best friend, Jasmine Stanway, for all the late calls we've had where I asked for help and advice more times than I can count. To my cover artist, Addison Horsell, who took my concepts and ideas and turned them into a true piece of art. To Jackie Dowell, for sketching my scenes to life and inspiring me like no other. To my dad, who sat and theorized with me at the dining room table about time travel. To my mom, who reassured me when I felt like I couldn't go through with finishing it. To my grandma, for coming up with theories and plot twists crazier than I could've ever come up with. I may not have used them, but just the fact she thought of them showed me how much she cared for this story. To

Kate Aryanata, the owner of The Mount Vernon Inn, who always encouraged me to go forward and accomplish my dreams. To my beta readers, who showered me with artwork, opinions, and valuable time. There are truly a dozen more people I could mention, but let me just finish this off by saying every author needs a support system. And I feel incredibly lucky with mine.

About the Author

Kathryn Houghton lives in central Ohio with her family, originally from Florida. She loves her day job as an innkeeper, where most of her writing takes place. Specializing in nautical stories, she believes there's always an inspiration to be found in old sea tales. Her favorite places are museums, bookstores, and charming coffee shops. She runs a content creation profile on Instagram and YouTube @fieldsofliterature. In her other life, she's a mysterious soul living in a lighthouse by a charming coastal town.